# Our New Home

## Book One

by

Richard Norman Sheppard

OUR NEW HOME

**ISBN**: 978-1-9996794-0-8

# Contents

Thank you Lisa

*Dedication*

To the two most inspirational people in my life – my parents who, with all their love and guidance, afforded me a wonderful life, right up to and including the present day.

Special thanks go to Cathy who saw me through thick and thin, especially when on two different occasions I suffered a killer disease which, however, failed to do just that. To thee most wonderful child a parent could ever hope to have, Keri-Lyn, whom I love and adore dearly. To my brother and two sisters whose love and support over the years I shall always treasure. Then to my best friend, and ex-work and ex-band member, Lisa Hogarth who, without her love, help and support during my latest convalescence, this novel would surely have never been written and she would not have spent sleepless nights doing the editorial on the work. My grateful thanks, therefore, go to Roger for his understanding. Thank you Fabian.

# Warning

Authors suggested age restriction – 15

This trilogy contains some:-

blue language,
sexual connotations,
and religious references throughout,

which some people may find offensive.

*THE TREE OF LIFE*

I am sitting in our garden on a beautiful spring day and looking over the road to our neighbour's house. They have a magnificent tree. Its branches spread wide as if it is embracing the whole house. It is dome shaped, so from here it looks like a giant umbrella. I don't know what kind of tree it is, it might be a Wild Olive. It is an evergreen, and in summer it provides shade, in winter a protection from the wind. It is home to many birds, mossies, doves, etc. A lot of chatter goes on morning and evening, and I should think ants and all kinds of goggas like living there.

This made me think of my own life.

Our Lord has blessed me with many happy years, a happy childhood, a loving husband, four beautiful children and twelve grandchildren, and very soon now I will be blessed with the title of 'Great Granny', which I am very proud of. So think you can liken me to that grand old tree and hope that I, in my small way, have given shelter, protection and love, not only to my family but to many that I have come in contact with.

Thank you my Lord for "My Tree of Life".

Thelma Phyllis Sheppard (Née Wilson)  1921 – 2000

Prologue:

Why Me?

CHLOE WALKED INTO the living room and saw Dick sitting in the recliner chair looking forlorn and feeling sorry for himself.

"What the hell's the matter with you?" she asked, although perturbed at what she saw.

"I've got this almighty pain in my chest and no, it's not heart-related."

"How do you know?" she asked as he moved around uncomfortable in the chair.

"Well, the pain appears to be around the chest cavity but it moves from one side to the other. Then it moves around the back and then to the front again. I also have discomfort in the lower part of the abdomen on the left-hand side and besides, I'm finding it difficult to breathe."

Chloe thought for a moment. "I'm sure it's another Pulmonary Embolism. You're showing similar symptoms to the one you suffered seventeen years ago. Didn't Dr Dingley instruct you to stop taking the Aspirin-a-day?"

"Yes, and I never understood why. Although if I don't have to pop pills, there's no way I will take them."

"Right, let's trouble-shoot. Seventeen years ago in hospital, they gave you Heparin, and while there, weaned onto Warfarin before leaving. You took them, as far as I remember, for six months?"

"That's right."

"So, at the end of the six-month period, you came off the Warfarin and put on to a half-a-Dispirin a day for the rest of your life?"

"Yes,.... correct" Dick replied still moving around uncomfortably in his chair.

"So, when did you take the seventy-five milligram Aspirin?"

"I can't remember but it was when Dispirin became no longer available."

"And did you inform Dr Dingley?" Chloe asked, frowning.

"Yes I did. When I registered at Westdene Surgery back in 2003, I gave him my full medical history." By now his breathing become more laboured.

"Well, I'm still sure you are suffering another Pulmonary Embolism. Do you want me to take you to A&E or call the paramedics?"

"Let me take painkillers first and see how long they last," he replied, grimacing.

He swallowed two painkillers and tried his best to relax while watching a rugby match on the television. Just before the final whistle of the match, a severe pain gripped him around his chest, including the back and the lower part of the left side of his abdomen. The intense pain struck without warning and he doubled up and groaned.

A proud and independent person, and not wanting to show pain, Dick did not enjoy having to depend on anyone else's help. He far prefer giving his help to others in need than suffer embarrassment having others help him. Well, that's the way he saw it for he's much the same as his mother. When there was no public transport available, she walked to the shops in the village before asking someone to drive her the three miles from where she lived.

"I'm calling the paramedics," Chloe said in a way that brooked no argument, and whether he agreed or not made no argument for the pain seemed to have taken over his life.

The paramedics arrived and carried out the checks. They placed a mask over his nose and mouth allowing him to inhale a gas which helped to soothe the pain. They said it helps to pacify the anxiety taking hold of him.

With the paramedics now ready to take him to A&E, they found a problem. They must now lift someone who weighed one hundred and twenty-eight kilograms. Not content with just this problem, Dick stood one metre ninety-eight centimetres tall. How to carry him to the ambulance? is what they asked themselves.

"Dick, you are too big and heavy for us to carry you. Do you think you can walk to the ambulance?" asked the Chief Paramedic.

Setting pride, independence and stubbornness aside for once in his life, Dick agreed. It did not go as he hoped but he gritted his teeth and, with one of them on either side helping him, he made it.

On the way to Darwood Glen Hospital, Dick recalled various things being said and done, and further questions being asked, but he kept little memory of it. Once in the A&E, they examined him. Chloe informed the hospital staff of the pulmonary embolism he suffered those years ago but, this appeared to fall on deaf ears. After five hours of excruciating pain lying on the gurney, the Registrar, in his wisdom, decided there was nothing much wrong with him, so they gave him strong painkillers and sent him on his way.

Chloe became indignant, and although she objected to it, the hospital personnel were not interested in listening to her. This left her no choice but to take him home and they arrived after 3:00 a.m. on Sunday morning March 23, 2014. Although they gave Dick a host of various pain killers the pain itself did not subside and he remained terribly uncomfortable.

"What the hell am I going to do? I'm supposed to go back to work on Monday as I've been off for four weeks with this bloody Achilles tendinitis crap."

"In your state, there's no way you are going anywhere, so forget it."

"That's okay for you to say but, I'm being made redundant at the end of the month."

Not being one to mince words Chloe said "So what. To hell with them. What the hell are they going to do if you can't be there,... fire you? No, no, no,... you are not going anywhere. The only place you should be is the hospital."

"Those bloody idiots, who call themselves doctors and who are over-paid have no clue, and this bloody pussycat of a Government we've got still insists on bringing these damn idiots in from other countries. It makes me sick."

Dick spent the rest of the night in the recliner chair, but although he tried, he could not sleep. He never slept on a chair before, and the pain just did not allow him to sleep. The horrendous number of painkillers ingested seemed to him the more he took, the less effective they became.

Chloe retired for the night but, knowing the condition, found it difficult to sleep. They did not have a good morning, and by the afternoon, Dick grew more uncomfortable. Beads of sweat formed on his forehead and his tee-shirt was on the clammy side.

"I realise..... I can't....... but I should...... have a shower...... as I stink of...... a racing camel's crutch...... in mating season," he said to Chloe in a laboured voice.

"How the hell do you know what a racing camel's crutch in mating season smells of?" Chloe asked with a wry smile.

Dick tried to laugh through the pain. "I had..... the wonderful opportunity...... to sit on a camel not long after...... he finished his mating ritual,...... thereafter...... he urinated inside of his legs...... and I can assure you...... the stench is something else...... it pongs."

"And where did this take place?"

"Oh.... on honeymoon........ in the Namibian dessert..... back in 1985."

"You took your wife on a honeymoon to a desert?"

"Yes........ Rachel's idea....... and I tell you..... what,........ fantastic..... bloody fantastic..... and I'd...... do it.......... again any..... day but not........ with Rachel," he replied, while the gap between his words got bigger and his breathing became difficult.

"And why not?"

"Because........ I'm with......... you now.... you...... silly girl..... and besides you..... understand.......... the other reasons...... why."

This light-hearted banter ended as his breathing took a turn for the worse and he gasped for air like a fish out of water. He sat there gulping, trying to take in as much air as possible. Chloe said he should stop talking as it only made it worse. Later, his breathing returned to an acceptable level and he once again tried to settle and watch the television to take his mind off his physical problems.

He convinced himself it worked, but it didn't. At 8: p.m., the intensity of the pain increased to a level he never before experienced and the immense pain caused uncontrollable tears to run down his cheeks. He wrapped his arms around his chest trying to squeeze the pain out and rocked backwards and forwards hoping this helped. But the intensity of the pain, instead of reducing, just became worse and worse.

Chloe was beside herself and pondered what she should do next. After watching him reel around in pain, she decided she'd had enough. "Stuff this,... I can't just sit here and watch you suffer and I'm not prepared to put up with it any longer. I'm phoning the paramedics again."

Once more the paramedics arrived and tried everything to ease the problem. Chloe told them what happened over the last couple of days so, once again, off to A&E they drove.

At the hospital they examined the X-rays from earlier, so the doctors held a discussion about Dick's condition. Chloe repeated to them what she said about his history of pulmonary embolisms, but again it fell on deaf ears. They discharged him and Chloe fumed against "these useless people".

Back home again, Dick tried to chill out into what had become his new bed, the recliner chair, the only place he found comforting, and so he spent another night in agony and wondered of his future. Would he be alive? Would he be dead? If he survived, what would the rest of his life be like, as he was no longer a Spring chicken? Can he secure employment? His mind in turmoil with the thoughts going through his head, while fighting with his might to overcome the pain, did not stop. Instead, it drove him crazy just thinking of it.

Monday 7:00 a.m., by rights, Chloe should have been at work but she took time off to keep an eye on him. Due to his health issues, she understood anything may well happen. He took painkiller after painkiller throughout the day and, by 9:00 p.m., Chloe, once more, had enough and called the paramedics. Déjà vu, once more, set in as the whole saga just repeated itself again. They arrived back home from the hospital at 3:00 a.m. the following morning, still none the wiser.

As preventative measures declined, Dick's condition changed for the worse so, he put on a brave face to grin and bear it again. That Tuesday evening the entire episode re-played itself and

Chloe called the paramedics who arrived in good time. When they carried out their examination and listened to what Chloe said to them, they telephoned the on-duty doctor at the hospital and put him in the picture.

Chloe told the on-duty doctor of Dicks appointment with his GP at 11:00 a.m. the next day. As Dick suffered from huge and painful varicose veins, they conducted a sonic scan on the upper inside of his left leg, the results of which were at the doctors surgery, hence the appointment being made two weeks earlier. On hearing this, the on-duty doctor decided not send Dick to the hospital but prescribe strong painkillers and phoned the local chemist. So Chloe, at 10:00 p.m., drove to the pharmacy to get the new painkillers.

Later in the evening, and because the appointment was for the next day, the on-duty doctor thought this to be satisfactory. Chloe exploded and said to Dick the doctor's a total bonehead and another useless immigrant bleeding the 'system' dry at the expense of the patients.

So what could they do? Well, nothing. If the doctors did not do their diagnostics, the staffs ability to nurse the patient became void. So he and Chloe had to wait it out until the appointment when, the doctor could explain the results of the diagnostic report.

In what seemed an eternity, they at last sat in the waiting room of the GPs surgery. The moment the doctor saw Dick, his entire face dropped for no explanation necessary as he identified the problem. So he sat at his desk, wrote a letter, handed it to Chloe and told her to take it to the hospital straight away. Before they left, the doctor asked if he should phone for an ambulance. Chloe thanked him but said it would be far quicker if she took Dick to A&E herself.

At the hospital, Chloe dropped Dick off while she parked the car and somehow he walked to the A&E desk unaided. While handing over the letter, he noticed many people occupying the seating waiting their turn. The on-duty nurse read Dick's letter and, because of its severity, interview him without delay.

After the interview, they whisked him away to the A&E ward. There they attached various relevant paraphernalia to him and afterwards, they transferred him to another ward for assessment of the horrendous pain.

Chloe telephoned Dick's sister Cassie to update her. While Dick remained in this ward, she arrived having travelled six hundred and forty kilometres to get there and Dick asked Chloe to give his daughter strict instructions not to travel alone the four-hundred-odd kilometres by bus. The worry for him would be too much to handle.

The diagnosis report took another two days and found he suffered a Bilateral Pulmonary Emboli, which affected every lobe of his lungs. They too found him suffering from Diverticulosis, not a pleasant disease, and can cause pain and discomfort, and this they discovered by a cat-scan they finally decided to do.

Because the doctors understood the full extent of his ailments, they transferred him to the main ICU recovery ward. There, they had the unenviable task of informing him of his condition.

"People have died of something far less," said one doctor. This profound statement became outstripped by another doctor who said: "We cannot explain how or why you survived."

Dick thought both doctors inferred he should by rights be dead. But, being aware of the fact the danger period was far from over, this uncomforting news dampened his spirits. His lack of treatment over the past few days, including time being wasted in A&E, placed his health in a precarious state. He may well have died.

"Why me? This is the second time. So why me.... again?"

When the doctors left, at last the nurses administered the correct medication and Dick tried to sleep. But, the medication still not taken full effect, the pain prevented him from carrying out this natural body routine, so he just lay there with his mind in a whirl while sleep evaded him.

On one of these nights in the ICU, Dick recalled the weird experience when in the hospital back in 2001. He remembered lying there on his bed, drifting in and out of sleep and experiencing a floating sensation while he kept wondering why his parents had not yet visited him, which annoyed him.

"Don't be a bloody fool," he berated himself "If they arrive, you're a dead man," remembering he lost his parents, his father back in 1990 and in 2000, his mother. So if they did arrived, as he so wanted them to, he would be somewhere other than on planet Earth. As soon as he said this to himself it seemed he recovered from the illness and the following morning they considered him to be out of danger. Because of this good news, they moved him from the ICU and placed him in a general recovery ward for five days.

Dick wondered if the same thing would happen again so, on one of the nights he drifted into the unknown and once again wondered if his parents would come and visit him but, this time when he opened his eyes, he laughed it off as a bad joke. He, therefore, settled himself and decided he should try to sleep.

Because the pain had now subsided, he lay down on his left side, with his legs slightly bent and slightly drawn up towards his torso, and in that position, he fell asleep. But this time it was a deep sleep his entire ailing, and pain relieved, body so desperately needed.

A deep sleep that was also an undisturbed one, or so he thought for a strange unnerving feeling came over him. Someone or something stood next to him staring into his closed eyes.

Chapter One

The Alien introduction

THE THOUGHT OF someone staring at his closed eyes Dick found unnerving. A sensation something he had never experienced, and he became perturbed, so he tried to open his eyes but found himself unable to do so. This led him to get hold of the call button and ring for help, however, he was unable to move his arms or any other part of his body. To his utter amazement, he discovered any kind of movement impossible and felt something strange developing. He knew he wasn't dead so why no movement? What was happening?

About to go into panic mode, a high-pitched voice, yet also rough and raspy, spoke to him, the like of which he had never in his life heard before and it spoke in a constant monotone the whole time. Dick decided this might just be a great time to shit himself, however, before he could do anything, the voice spoke to him again.

"Do not worry about your illness; we will take care of you?" it said.

"Okay, fine," Dick replied, not understanding why.

The voice said, "Yes, everything will be okay and fine," and Dick felt a cold shiver go down his spine.

Dick answered the voice although his lips weren't moving. "Am I dreaming? Am I dead? Or is there someone there talking?"

The voice reassured him he was neither dead nor dreaming. It also said everything is real and happening right there and then.

"Okay, but why can't I see you? Why can't I have a proper conversation with you, one-to-one, eyeball-to-eyeball?"

"I'm afraid it is not possible right now. Once you have recovered from your illness, I'll be in touch as I have an important task for you,... should you wish to take it on?"

"What task?" Dick asked and waited for a reply.

"Hello," Dick called out, only this time he said it out loud.

"Hello," he again called out.

To his surprise, the bloke in the next bed spoke to him. "Do you want me to call the nurse for you?"

"No, it doesn't matter, thank you."

He lay there, not moving an inch and trying his utmost to understand what had just happened. Was he going mad? "No, I'm not mad. I'm sick, lying on my bed in the hospital. I might be loony but not mad" he said, trying to convince himself.

"So if you're not mad, what the hell occurred?" He considered the situation while he lay there for a moment looking up at the ceiling. "Buggered if I know" he answered his own question.

Dick stayed in a worried frame of mind for the rest of the night, waiting for his 6:00 a.m. wake-up call to see if it would happen. To find out if a genuine nurse would be standing there taking the readings of his vitals and hoping he would feel the skin of her fingers touching the pulse on his left wrist. He hardly slept a wink and sure enough, at the regular time, the usual nurse stood at his bedside. While recording his vitals, she asked if he had a good night's rest.

"Considering the circumstances, yes, I had a good one, thanks," he lied. "Tell me, how much longer will I be in here for?"

"Well it's only the doctor who can advise you. But if I had to guess, I'd say at least another eight days, given your current condition."

When she left, Dick rolled over to reflect on what happened the night before, but sheer exhaustion took over and he fell into a deep sleep.

The nurse's assumption proved to be correct for eight days later, Chloe received the good news he would be given his discharge papers on that day, and when they receive the printed out and signed discharge papers, they would wend their way home. By this time his sister, Cassie, had already gone back to her own home as she had her own household to run.

Recovery for Dick this time would be long, hard and tedious. It took over a year before the doctor said he could start with even the lightest of exercises.

Half way through the first twelve month period, Chloe remembered a specific conversation they had before Dick being admitted to the hospital. "Can you recall how worried you were about what would happen because you hadn't been to work for over a month and how I asked what could they do,... fire you, although they would make you redundant anyway,... remember?"

"Yes, I recall you saying that."

"Well, if you don't mind my saying but it turned out you were employed by a wonderful bunch of fuckers,... don't you think?" she said as only she could.

"I'm not sure what you getting at."

"When you were TUPE'd over to the new company, how many of the managers, or better still,... directors did you ever meet?"

"None."

"Exactly," Chloe exclaimed "and when you were in ICU, how many of your wonderful colleagues bothered finding out about how you were doing?"

"Once again,... none."

"Correct," Chloe said in agreement "and what about that wonderful bloody so called manager of yours? The one who was also TUPE'd over with you? The same one I gave advice about buying a new home? Did that bloody thing have the decency to even phone me to find out how you were doing?" Chloe asked, although fuming by now. "No," she exclaimed again and continued before Dick could reply "and there you were worried about your job and yet nobody in your office gave a fuck about you. As I say, a wonderful bunch of fuckers you worked with. Hopefully one day you'll have your revenge," she now said calmly and being well pleased with herself.

"Mmmm,... Yeah,... Point taken," he said unperturbed.

During all this time, Dick hadn't given the crazy conversation he had with the voice any consideration while still in the hospital. He wrote it off as a mad, mind-blowing experience caused by all the drugs they had been pumping into him. But, out of the blue one night, he once again heard the voice while lying in bed. He and Chloe slept in separate bedrooms for at their time of life, they felt it a better choice as each could therefore carry out their own business without disturbing the other.

This time when the voice spoke, Dick found the ability to move his entire body, so he sat up to observe the goings-on. To his astonishment, at the foot of the bed stood this small creature who, in height, stood no taller than ninety-seven centimetres.

His head, in proportion to his body, was enormous. His eyes were black and almond-shaped and huge—taking up about fifteen to twenty percent of his face. There wasn't much nose to speak of and a mouth so small one couldn't get a straw into it. Ears were also not recognisable.

While they looked at each other, the creature said "Hello" and Dick said "Hello" in response but in a shaky voice.

The creature introduced himself to Dick as Joel.

"Thank you," replied Dick once again in a shaky voice.

"Well then and, as you humans would say, let's get down to business," said Joel.

"Mmmm... before we do," Dick said unnerved "will we not disturb Chloe by our conversation, or would you prefer her to know you are here?"

"Chloe will not hear a thing as she is asleep, so we can continue our discussion."

Knowing this, Dick found himself at ease but, although bemused, on edge.

Joel, while looking at Dick with his big black almond-shaped eyes, explained why he was there. "Can you remember at age fifteen playing in a park with your friends, for no rhyme nor reason, you looked up into the sky? You observed what you would call a flying saucer,... correct?"

Dick was astonished as it was something he had never forgotten. "I remember. We were in Plumstead Park kicking a rugby ball around and something told me I should look up. I did and, as you say, I saw a flying saucer. It was high up as I recall, and after watching it in amazement for at least a full minute, although it seemed like five, it shot away in a Northerly direction. I've wondered to this day if it happened."

"Well, wonder no more for it happened, and I told you to look up and, although in your teams we've been watching you for a long-time, it's not been for us aliens, as you call us."

"Also," he continued "do you remember the alien mother ship you and a few family members and friends saw on your sister's farm on...,"

"Ah no, never," Dick interrupted "You mean September 05, 1996? How could any of us forget something like that? It was the largest object we had ever seen in the sky and the biggest event to have ever happened in our lives. I recall saying it was a flying city."

"Good, I was on that mother ship, and do you remember you saw three flying saucers come out of the mother ship and fly off in various directions? Well, I was the captain onboard the second one which, later, you and your brother-in-law notice fly back over the farmhouse."

Dick looked at him, dumbfounded.

"So, we have been watching you for some time and have decided you are the person to offer the opportunity of taking on a certain task."

"Perhaps if I knew what the task was, it would help me decide whether I think I can take it on."

"Dick, we have every confidence in you and that's why we have chosen you to do it."

"That's flattering, but what is it?"

"Not so fast," Joel said holding up his left hand. "Let me first explain, and when I tell you what the task is, it will be easier for you to understand and, I hope, make it easier for you to accept. Okay?"

"Yes, okay."

"Now we know how you feel about the various religion existing in your world. We also know you are sceptical in believing in God and what you were taught in school about the universe and its creation."

"All right," Dick said looking mystified.

"We know you are self-taught about the New Testament—why it was written and how it compares to the Old Testament and yes, we know you think it's all a lie because the New Testament does not depict what happened thousands of years ago and right up to the last word,... Amen."

Dick looked at him and could feel his eyes opening wider and wider.

"Now I will not go into too much detail because we also know how you feel about this planet called Earth and about most of the people living on it. There is, however, one thing I must mention is in the Bible, and it's the story of Noah." Dick frowned, but he remained silent.

"Yes, the story is true, however, it's not recorded that we, the so called aliens, caused the floods and now, this is where you come in. We will cause yet more devastation, but this time we will wipe out all of humanity except for a few select people and we want you to be the second Noah."

"Me?" Dick said confused "What the hell do I know about playing the part of Noah, for flips sake? You want me to build another ark, collect how many animals and choose people as well? How would I know what people, from what backgrounds and from what race, creed or colour?"

"Will you stop panicking? If ever we thought for one moment you were not the right man for the job, I would not be here at the foot of your bed asking you to take on this task, and just to put your mind at ease, there wasn't a single animal or organism, besides Noah and his family and a few friends on the Ark, as you were led to believe. That's right," Joel said seeing Dick with a puzzled look "the entire Ark was a databank full of the various

DNA from the different species on your planet. I thought you might like to know that. So, I won't go any further as you have enough to think about for now. I will wait for you to decide then you can let me have your answer tomorrow."

Dick looked at him, bemused by what he had just heard, and battling within himself to absorb it all. He now felt he should say something, but before he could say anything, Joel disappeared as if into thin air.

"What the hell is going on?" he asked himself. So he walked through the whole issue in his head and, once again, wondered about the possibility he was going mad. Whatever it was, the thing-in-itself was not normal.

He got out of bed and, in his birthday suit, made his way downstairs. There he poured himself a stiff whisky and water in the hope this might calm him down. That night was a disturbed and restless one for him, for he could not settle down and sleep just came and went.

The next morning Chloe looked at him and said "You look dreadful. Did you have a bad night?"

"Yes,... bad. I haven't had a night like that for some time now."

"What brought it on?"

"Don't know. Maybe it's because I have a lot on my mind, like am I ever going to get another job now at my age? You know...

silly ideas like that."

"Well don't worry about it too much. You are not fit enough yet and the Council are still paying you benefits, although only a few pounds a week which is better than nothing at all," Chloe pointed out to which he half-agreed.

After breakfast, and catching up on some early morning news and the weather forecast, Chloe grabbed her bag and coat and set off on her way to work.

"What time will you be home today?" he asked as she neared the back door.

"I've only got two-afternoon calls so should be home around three o'clock." Chloe was a carer, and on a zero hours contract, and her daytime working slots always fluctuated.

Both Dick and Chloe were proud of being tidy people, so he set about doing the dishes, vacuum the carpets and doing a general clean-up—but nothing too strenuous. Once finished, he went upstairs to check his e-mails and to see if he had won the lottery but, as usual, no luck. He now logged onto Facebook where the world and its mother published their pictures and their personal information, where all and sundry exchanged the biggest load of crap for all to share.

He did this to give him something to do, while convalescing, as it helped to while away the time. When he found something interesting, he could reply with his own negative or positive thoughts, opposite to which way the conversations were going. He loved putting peoples' backs up and took a fiendish joy in doing this. The often pitiful replies gave him a buzz and, extra ammo to throw straight back at them. The fun and laughter he got out of it were what made his day. What he couldn't understand was just how gullible people were and what idiots there are in the world.

Because of its general make-up and purpose, he hated Facebook, because various Government agencies around the world, and Facebook itself, use it as a *spying* tool which, in recent months, had been proven beyond doubt.

After having made a few peoples' day miserable, he closed the site and shut down the laptop. As it was still in the early hours of the morning, he jumped back into bed to see if he might be lucky enough to get some shut-eye.

In what seemed like no time at all, Dick awoke by the sensation of the duvet being pulled off the bed. He knew there was no-one in the house but he also knew there was some ghostly entity in the house and it disturbed him from time-to-time. He didn't, though, allow it to bother him too much, so he tugged back to pull the duvet back over his head as he had done on so on many other occasions.

However, this did not work for an almighty yank pulled the duvet off the bed and there he was, as usual, in his birthday suit. About to yell out, Dick opened his eyes and looked into Joel's big black almond-shaped eyes and he jumped right out of bed.

"What the bloody hell? I thought you were a figment of my imagination and the conversation we had last night was all a bad dream. But here you are again, so I suppose it wasn't a dream after all?"

Joel stood there for a moment looking at him. "Please put something on. You look ridiculous."

"Oh, thank you very bloody much," Dick muttered.

"You know, we could do something about that terrible body of yours," Joel said to soothe Dick's feelings.

"What the hell do you mean you can do something about this body of mine? What's wrong with it, anyway?"

Joel beckoned him over to look into the full-length mirror he had in his bedroom. "Are you proud of what you and I can see in the mirror?"

"No I'm not, but don't forget I've been ill this past year. Besides, I've not been allowed to do anything. I've not even been able to look at my drum kit for goodness' sake, let alone play the damn thing. So, with no exercise at all, what kind of shape do you expect my body to be in?"

"I don't expect you to be in any good shape at all. All your muscles have lost their shape, and it looks like your chest has fallen down to your stomach. This pushes it out which gives you the appearance of looking like a question mark or a beer barrel."

Forgetting Joel communicated telepathically, Dick said under his breath "Oh bugger me. I can't believe I'm having this bloody conversation—and with an ET type of person. Aaaarrrgh shit, get me out of this bloody dream."

"It's not a dream," Joel said to him in a soothing manner "This, I'm afraid, is real. I urge you to take it seriously now, so please put clothes on and, because we have a few hours available to us, let's go downstairs and sit at the dining room table. There we can continue where we left off last night."

"Oh for flip's sake," Dick said, pulling on his track-suit "Okay, why the hell not—what are you waiting for? Let's sit at the bloody table and see if my marbles are still intact. Come on."

Once seated at the table, the atmosphere became more relaxed and Joel knew he needed to put Dick at ease. He needed to get him to understand he was not dreaming and was time to wake up. This would not only be for now but also for the future.

Joel opened the conversation by saying "Upstairs I said we could do something with your body. So, would you like us to do something?"

His curiosity piqued, Dick asked "Something like what?"

"Well, your lung disease has now healed so much we can change your body."

"You can do what? How the hell can you change my body?" Dick snorted.

"How do you think humans got here? Who do you think put humanity on this planet and where do you think you came from?"

"Just like the rest of the entire human population, both past and present, I have no idea."

"Of course you don't and, as you say, neither the people in your world either. Well, the vast majority anyway."

"Wait, a minute—you said the vast majority. What do you mean by that?"

"What I mean is, there's a small group of people who have a good idea where you lot come from. Unfortunately for them, however, they cannot prove it. If only they realized how close to the truth they are."

"Oh yes," Dick said, not convinced "and who are these people?"

"It's your scientists, non-religious Bible study people, astrologers, people like that and to some extent, you."

"Me?"

"Yes, you Dick. I told you we've been watching you and we know how you think and what you study so yes, you fall into that category. You mustn't underestimate yourself. You know more than most other people around you, and those scattered around the world. It's also your composure, self-esteem and your whole attitude towards life that has led us to you. Yes, even when you were a young boy," Joel said while Dick sat there staring into Joel's big black almond-shaped eyes in amazement.

"So enough now. We have a lot to do, but first, you need to answer questions about your body. It may be hard for you to believe but you, humanity, are us, but only somewhat. We developed the so called Homo Sapiens a few hundred million of your years ago. We started this on a planet in a different Solar System and we took many of those years to get to where you are today. There're many of us walking around among you, so you could refer to us as your far distant cousins, in a manner of speaking. We created you and therefore we can alter you as well and, to a wide degree, still let you keep your overall self."

"So what do you intend doing?" Dick asked feeling more than confused.

"Well, that all depends on what you think you want?"

Not believing all he had heard, Dick said with a mocking sense of humour "Mmmm... I'd say health. I mean I would like to be one hundred percent fit again as I used to be back in my air force days. I'd also like to be as strong as I was in my rugby playing days. Oh, and to do powerlifting again. Although I say strong, I don't mean I want to look like a bodybuilder — they look bloody ugly, but that's just my view. Athletic shape, perhaps, but strong and powerful. But I mean,... strong and powerful."

Dick was enjoying himself now, so he continued "While you're about it, could you do something about my hair? That is the hair that's all over my body as I don't like having so much of it. But I need a lot more on my head as so much has fallen out with illness and age, and while you're about it, could you remove all these sebaceous cysts as well? They are a terrible eyesore," Dick said looking at Joel and assuming he would be told to stop play-acting and be serious.

Instead, Joel replied "We can. All those are easy for us. Why don't you give us a more challenging one to perform?"

"Okay, what about extra brainpower?" he asked, this time certain he would get a negative reply.

But no,... Joel told him "That's also part of the programme. But more of that later once you have accepted your new body, okay?"

Dick was amazed and thought he might as well go the whole hog and said "Okay,... now you know I always wanted to fly, to be a pilot, but I stuffed up along the way and became a bloody rock drummer instead. So,... it would be wonderful if you could give me the knowledge and the ability to fly any aircraft. But anywhere around the world, day or night, without having to have any more training and also,... to have the know-how of how to use the world's flight paths. You know, the whole bang-shoot, that would be brilliant."

By this time, Dick was sitting on the edge of his chair, believing all this could happen and this strange little 'man' could work miracles.

"It's funny you should ask because those abilities would come in handy later on. When we get to the point, not only will things fall into place, but I'll also explain further."

"So you can give me those abilities?"

"Oh yes. Everything you mentioned must be carried out."

"If you could do this, you'd make a little boy's dreams come true and this old man thrilled," Dick said, terrified of believing yet, trying to hide his excitement.

"That shouldn't be a problem. Now what about your left foot? We know you had a motorbike accident on April 4, 1974, when you crushed your foot so much nothing could be done about it. Would you like us to repair it for you?"

Dick, within his limited capacity, leapt up into the air and yelled "Eureka! at last someone thinks they can repair my funny foot. Oh yes please," he replied with great emotion. He was so overwhelmed he felt he had to have a drink and headed for the sideboard to pour himself a whisky and water.

"I wouldn't do that if I were you."

"Why ever not?" asked Dick frowning.

"If Chloe walked through the door and saw you drinking at this hour of the morning, the proverbial would hit the fan, as you would put it. Therefore, I don't think you need extra irritations in your life right now."

"Mmmm... good thinking there, Batman."

"You mean Joel."

"What?"

"You called me Batman."

"Oh, that," Dick grinned "Never mind about that. So when do you propose doing all of this and giving me this amazing body I've always only ever dreamed about?"

"Now."

"Now?" Dick asked in amazement.

"Yes, right now."

"What, right here on the dining room table?"

"No, don't be a damned fool. Not here at all. It will have to be done on the mother ship you saw all those years ago."

Dick looked at him aghast and was lost for words.

"Please, before we go any further, let me give you more information about the mother ship which I'm sure you'll find interesting."

"Yes, I would like that."

"Now we also know you were keen on watching all the space travels the Americans and Russians made in the '60s and '70s and you also found out about a certain Gemini program. In fact, it was the Gemini Eleven which launched on the September 12, 1966—remember?" asked Joel.

"Mmmm... yes, I think I do."

"Well, the astronauts noticed something but couldn't identify a bright object which seemed to change its shape every now and again right before their eyes."

"Oh yeah, now I know what you're talking about. I saw a program on the TV about that."

"Well, the officials in ground control said the nearest man-made object to them was a Russian satellite. It was the Proton Three and was only four hundred and fifty kilometres away."

"Yes, I remember that."

"Perhaps then you may also recall an optical physicist who was investigating the sighting and confirmed the object was not the Russian satellite? He was correct because he had worked out the object was thousands of metres in size. He had also worked out it was, in fact, four thousand eight hundred kilometres away from the Gemini craft."

"That's right, I recall it," Dick said feeling pleased with himself.

"As I mentioned earlier, this chap was correct in his findings."

"Joel, I've forgotten how he found this out. How did he do it?"

"The Gemini craft was off the South African coastline, above the thirty degrees South latitude and the object they sighted was above the sixty degrees South latitude. The orbit they were in, when they saw the object in relation to the Earth, it was situated over the Falkland Islands. I hope you can recall that."

"Now you mention it yes, I do."

"What this physicist said was, although the astronauts did not see the Russian satellite, what they saw was up for grabs. By this he meant anyone was at liberty to draw their own conclusions."

"Okay, so what are you trying to tell me?" asked Dick.

"The object they saw was my mother-ships, mother ship. So, for obvious reasons, it should give you something more to think about with your believing in my sincerity but, most of all, I wanted you to know that."

"Well thanks, Joel, I appreciate it. It gives me something to think about although feeling more than befuddled."

"Good."

"Okay, so what happens when Chloe gets home? If I'm not here, what do I tell her when I get back?" Dick asked, hardly daring to believe.

"If it will make you feel any better, leave her a note to say you'll be home at four-thirty this afternoon."

Dick scribbled a note for Chloe which he left on the counter-top. Taking hold of Joel's outstretched four-digit hand, they disappeared. In an instant, the dining room section of the open-plan was void of both humans and aliens.

Chapter Two

(a) The Rejuvenation

THE NEXT DICK knew, he was being led into a huge room. It appeared to be an operating theatre, similar to which one would see in an ordinary hospital. There he met seven other aliens, who all looked like Joel, although their heights varied, with one being taller than Dick. The room was lit by a brilliant white light which was not harsh on the eyes. However, he could not see the source of the light, and whatever the lux measure was, he did not know, but what he did know, the light was soothing and made him relaxed.

Although they did not speak to him, he was almost positive Joel was talking to his family, friends or co-workers, whichever they were. While he stood there, from out of nowhere, an operating type table appeared. They motioned to him to take off all of his clothes and lie down on it. Once he had made himself comfortable, Joel spoke to him.

"Now just relax and let our doctors do their work. I have explained what it is you would like done, and they suggested extra ideas of their own I'm sure you will be more than pleased with. So just lie back and they will turn your body into the shape and size you want it to be, both inside and out. You will not experience any pain, however, you may encounter light-headedness once they have finished, shall I say, updating your brain? So please, have no fear. I'm looking forward to meeting my newfound friend again, in a few of your earth hours." He turned around and walked out of the operating room and the doctors began their work.

They gave Dick smelling salts, which relaxed him. This was not to put him to sleep but to keep him awake in euphoria throughout proceedings. Although he had the sensation of the odd prod or push somewhere on his body, he could not see or know what they were doing.

He found solace in closing his eyes and, in his mind, humming one of his favourite tunes, The Second Waltz by Shostakovich, to help the time go by. At one stage his body raised off the table, so he opened his eyes, and from what he could tell, no-one was touching him. His body rotated one hundred and eighty degrees and lowered back down on to the table so he was now lying on his stomach and the proceedings continued.

These continued on for some time until he realised he was being raised and rotated again and, once more, lying on his back. Although he had been on the operating table for four-and-a-half hours, to him it was as if it were only there for thirty minutes.

When finished, they led Dick into what he understood to be a recovery room and there, to his amazement, he found himself not to be groggy at all. They gave him different clothes and a new pair of shoes and was about to get dressed when Joel entered the room.

"So my friend, how you like your new body?"

"Well, standing here in front of you without a..." he was about to say the word mirror when one appeared from out of nowhere.

"Mirror?" asked Joel.

"Yes, and why am I not surprised?" Dick said and stood in front of it. He surveyed his reflection and was gob smacked. "What the hell have you done with my private parts?" he asked, although with a proud smile on his face.

Joel stood there showing no emotion at all. "Don't you like the alterations?"

"Are you crazy?" Dick replied in a raised tone with a hint of laughter and bemusement in it. "I bloody love it."

"Okay, calm down. Now what about the rest of your body?"

With a huge grin on his face, Dick carried on looking over his body. He studied everything and tried ever so hard to keep his mind off his private parts and took in the rest of the marvel he laid eyes on reflected in the mirror. Everything he had asked for, he received, including the athletic type look with the shape and form.

When Dick got down to looking at his new left foot, he gawked. No doubt about it, they gave him a whole new left foot. He moved it around in circles, up-and-down, together in an up-and-down motion while turning it around in circles. The horrible lumps he had all over his body were no more while the surplus body hair appeared to be transplanted to his head. Dick stared at the mirror in awe and amazement, and to say he was over the moon would be an understatement.

His irrepressible sense of humour had not left him and "Mmmm... I wonder what kind of porn star I'd make? Naaa... forget it... not your style mate," he said and discovered he had, what looked like, a lovely new set of gnashers. So he moved closer to the mirror, opened his mouth and scrutinised each tooth. "Damn," he exclaimed.

"What's wrong?"

"Nothing. Nothing at all. I've never had my teeth in such beautiful condition before."

"It's was one extra the doctors gave you. Speaking of which, it was they who also gave you the added extras downstairs as an experiment to observe how you cope."

"To observe how I cope?" Dick uttered "Are you going to be observing my every move from now on?" he asked in trepidation.

"Well, not every move, but you must remember it won't be any different to the way it has been in the past. You've not worked it out yet,... not so? We've been following you for your entire life now. Well, not all the time. We allow discretion to play a part in offering you some privacy."

"Thank you. Thank you so bloody much. How would you like it if I were to spy on you? Oh, I forgot, I can't. But hey, look at me now. What do you say?"

"What I say is irrelevant. As long as you are happy, I'm happy. But for me, you are another ugly specimen representing your human race. Happy now?"

"Oh yes, happy, thank you. But, on a more serious note, I thank you for all of this. I mean, it's awesome. No, it is for me, and I suppose I can understand for you I'm not a beautiful creature but I don't find you attractive either. Heigh-ho, at my age, I don't care and besides, why should I?"

"Mmmm..." Joel said, musing about something.

"What's mmmm supposed to mean?"

"Well, it's about your age."

"My age? What the hell now?"

"Well, this is another extra the doctors gave you. You won't comprehend this, but your ageing process will slow down and come to a stop. The process will reverse where around the age of forty to thirty-five it will stay on hold."

Dick listened in utter amazement. "So my ageing will become stagnant. How long will it last? Not that I'm complaining, you understand."

"At this stage, let's make it a surprise, shall we? Now please put your clothes on as I'm tired of looking at your naked form."

"I'm not but okay," Dick said while smiling as he stole a quick glance at his privates once more while getting dressed. "Oh, you've got me new clothing and shoes."

"Yes, we had to as your old clothing would not fit you any more, and because of your new foot, you needed new shoes."

"What about all my other clothing at home?"

"Don't worry about that for now. In good time you will replace them."

While Dick was dressing himself he manipulates his body in ways he hadn't been able to since he was a young boy. The suppleness of his muscles and the ease of moving his joints put yet another huge smile on his face.

"By the smile on your face you are delighted with the outcome or am I wrong?" Joel asked, and although it was more of a rhetorical question, Dick was ecstatic, never mind happy.

"I suppose now you want to move a mountain with your new body to find out how strong you are?"

"Now that's an excellent idea," Dick said while sporting a huge grin.

While he was still smiling, Joel grabbed hold of his hand and in a blink of an eye, they were back in the dining room at his home. Recognising a familiar sound from outside, Dick sensed Chloe had arrived back home.

"You've got explaining to do so, until tomorrow morning...," Joel said and, once again, vanished into thin air.

"Hello dear," Chloe and Dick both said at the same time as she came into the dining room of the open-plan.

"Had a good day?" he asked her.

"Well, considering the backsides I had to wipe today, yes," she said with a slight grimace.

Chloe told him stories about the old folk, whom she looked after daily, and as this conversation was the norm, he got pleasure out of it. He listened as she told him how the old people were getting on for he was older than a few of them.

Chloe looked at him. "You've been shopping," she accused him.

"Shopping?" he squealed.

"Yes, shopping,... you're wearing new clothes."

"Oh shit I'm dead," he reflected. "Yeah, I treated myself for a change. I've not bought new clothes in a long-time, and both my suits are two years older than my daughter and my dress suit is... mmmm... now let me... it must be thirty-five years old."

He said this to sidetrack her off the subject but, she realized his suits were two years older than Kerri, and she didn't tax him on it. Instead, she made her way upstairs and change before making something for supper. Afterwards, she relaxed in her recliner chair for the rest of the day not moving until it was time to go to bed.

Once upstairs, Dick changed out of his new clothes and put on an old tracksuit he should've thrown out years ago, but they were comfortable attire and could hide his new well-shaped body. As he walked out of his bedroom, he had the urge to go to the loo. Afterwards, he made his way downstairs to relax in his normal position on the couch and wondered if he should take the anticoagulation pill he had to take at the same time every night as he had forgotten to ask Joel.

Dick mulled over the events of the day and decided Chloe did not as yet need any information over what had happened. So he made the wise decision to take the medication as usual. As always, at 5:50 p.m. the laughing ringtone on his mobile phone sounded telling him it was time to swallow the pill.

The following morning brought grey skies and a cool slight breeze but, overall, it was a nice start to the day.

"When is it again you need the colonoscopy done?" Chloe asked while they were having their breakfast.

"Damn" Dick screamed in his mind as he heard the buzz going on inside his head. He had forgotten, and now there might no longer be any problem inside his gut and so no need for the examination.

"Ermmm... it's the eleventh of February and I'm to be there at eight o'clock in the morning, why?"

"Well, don't forget I'm to drop you off and fetch you when it's over because you may not drive."

"Blast," Dick said to himself. "Oh yes, that's right," he said to her "I'll be going with you to your first call before you drop me off. You mustn't forget to give me your work mobile number so the hospital can call you when it's done."

"Okay, I'll do that tonight as I must now go to work."

Once Chloe had left, Dick had a shower before the impending onslaught took place when Joel arrived. As he was blow-drying his hair, the now too-familiar figure of the little alien appeared, and while now dressing, Joel carried on with what Dick now accepted as being in a classroom lesson.

"Before we start, I must mention a few things. The muscle definition and your hair... yes, I was listening to you, sorry... don't worry about it for now. In no time, it will fall into place but you must do minor exercises. This is to help you in the beginning and there's no need to exert yourself either. Also, you need to exercise your brain, and as you are a musician, this will not be too hard and, you will only need to do this for fourteen of your earth days."

"First, you must stop viewing so much television and write something—anything—a new song or a poem. Use your brain again as you used to do. I realise it's been difficult for you while you were recovering from your illness but there is no excuse now. So, I suggest you start right after I leave today—the sooner the better."

"Joel, you mentioned yet again the illness I suffered. This made me wonder, if you and your kind can do so many amazing things to our bodies, why did you allow this to happen... again?"

"It was most unfortunate for at the time we were setting up another project, as did a similar thing occur the first time but, we had no cause for concern because of your determination and the fight that's within yourself. So there was never any real danger from our point of view, and we were right. If, however, you're looking for an apology... well I'm sorry. Now stop whining. You're alive, aren't you? And with a new body, so be grateful."

"I wasn't whining, I was inquiring," Dick said, wondering if he had dodged a bullet. "So now,... we've gone through this body routine—and I am not only grateful—I'm over the moon, and for me, no more needs to be said or done. But what happens now, Yogi?"

"First Batman and now Yogi," said Joel, irritated, "what's wrong with Joel? It is my name."

"Never mind. It's only another silly saying," Dick said with a slight giggle "no offence meant."

"Mmmm," Joel said mollified "I don't understand it but okay. Now it's time to get onto the task I set you and I'm sure you want me to tell you of the hows, whys, whats and wherefores involved."

"I do," Dick said, able to conceal his excitement and curiosity.

So Joel started the next session.

(b) a New Style of Banking

"Now there will be many large purchases to make, and you will ask me what purchases, where is the money coming from, etcetera? Right?"

"Right," said Dick.

From out of nowhere, Joel produced a small wallet from which he took out four credit cards and handed them to Dick."You need to put Chloe in the picture which I suggest you do tonight. I am giving you two sets of credit and debit cards—you get one set and Chloe gets the other. You can use these cards and you need not worry how much you spend, or where or how you spend, or even how often you use them as there is no limit."

While Joel was talking, Dick studied the cards and wondered what the letters P.U.B. stood for, other than pub. So he asked Joel what it meant.

"Birds are the creatures you love most, and Phoenix is a bird. Pubs are the places where you spent many a happy hour in, in the past, with the bands you played in. With this in mind, we came up with the name 'Phoenix United Bank'. Do you like it?"

"I do," Dick said "it's something I may have chosen myself."

"This means nothing, because there is no such bank."

"Well, if there is no such bank, how can we use these cards to make the purchases? I mean, wont the banking industry, and even the Government, investigate this?"

"They will not," Joel refuted "They may imagine they are the clever ones but they are far from it. What they don't realize is who their actual creators are, and because of that we can, let's say, manipulate them. The same way they did manipulating you and the rest of the world, only they will never find out it's happening to them until it's too late. It's their turn to undergo the whip now if you understand what I mean?"

Impressed, Dick said "Oh I appreciate what you mean and I love the way your mind works and the way you do things. Okay, now what about pin numbers?"

"These will be the same as the ones you use on your existing bank cards and it will be the same for Chloe."

But Dick still had questions to ask. "So, if we are not paying for our purchases, who is? I mean, someone has to pay for them,?"

"Yes," Joel affirmed "but don't let it worry you. All you need to do is buy anything and everything you need to fulfil your task, and apart from that, we don't care how much you spend or on what you spend it. Go mad, as you say."

Overwhelmed by the whole notion, Dick said: "Right,... so if I wanted to, I can walk out the front door, go to a new car dealership and buy a brand new car of my choice with no questions asked?"

"That's it."

"Okay, but I still don't understand from where the money is coming? Are you providing these funds?" Dick asked, confused and concerned.

"No, we alien folk don't share our wealth using money. We use other means, but you must not worry about your funding. Remember what I said about manipulation as it should give you a good hint. I suggest we leave it there for now, please."

"Well, in that case, when do you want me to start?"

"You can start now, but I'm not finished, so sit back and give me your undivided attention as you need to understand what I'm about to explain to you," Joel said, concentrating his big black almond-shaped eyes on Dick.

"There is an airport South West of London, Maitland Airport, which was up for sale, closed, and re-opened again. Now it's up for sale once more and I want you to buy it. You know of this airport because you've been there. Tomorrow you are to telephone them to meet the owners to make them an offer, and if they refuse at first, up the offer, it's that simple."

"For what purpose?"

"All in good time. Next, you and Chloe are to hand in your notice letter to your Landlord, giving him a two month period. Once the airfield is in your name, you are to move into one of either the huge houses or big flats on the property. The choice is up to you."

Joel continued. "Chloe must resign from her place of employment and the sooner you speak to her, the sooner she can resign and the sooner the two of you can work together... understood?"

"Yes, I understand. I'll speak to her tonight and tell her about everything happening in my life in these past few weeks. She will say I'm mad."

"Oh, I hope so," Joel said which was the closest he came to make a joke. "If you wish me to come and visit you once you informed her, then ask."

"Ask? How the hell do I do that?" Dick asked looking confused.

"Oh, come on Dick,... use your brain. When I first made myself known to you it was telepathically, wasn't it? We can hear your process of considering or your reasoning about something. Yes, we too can hear your spoken word so, all you need do is ask, but important you warn Chloe first."

"Now before I go, and I'm sorry if I'm repeating myself, but you must do this straight away. Write out your notice letter to the Landlord giving him two months' warning. When you've done that, log into your search engine and look up Maitland Airport so you can phone the owner's first thing in the morning because I need you to land the Purchase Agreement as soon as possible," he said while Dick listened trying hard to absorb it all.

"Next, I want you to write a letter to the Council informing them you are once again liquid and they are to stop paying your benefits allowances. This is not a necessity but it will prevent the Neanderthals from knocking at your door. It's an aggravation we don't need, so please make sure you do it and post the two letters off tomorrow. Also, you must give your Service Providers a notice letter of two months'." By now, Dick was making notes on a piece of paper to make sure he forgot nothing.

"Yes, it's something you would do," Joel continued "but I want to make sure you get everything in order as soon as I leave tonight. Is that fair?"

"It is, and I understand."

"Good. There are several other items you need to do, but you have enough for now. I will stay in touch and we will face the next hurdle once you move South."

"Maitland Airport is the place where I once sat in the cockpit of a VC10 bowser aircraft?" Dick mused allowed.

"Correct."

"Mmmm... nice. That's a large airport which includes a museum, loads of hangars and if memory serves me, the longest runway in the country."

"I'm glad you're using your brain at last. So, until later..." Joel said and, as usual, in a flash, he disappeared.

"I wonder what my little friend is up to now? Still, I'd better get on with my tasks," Dick said to nobody in particular.

Chapter Three

The Explanation

AT THE DINING room table, Dick set about writing his two letters on his laptop. Once he had checked, printed, and signed them, he placed them in their respective envelopes which he had printed in advance. As he had no stamps, he would have to go to the Post Office the following morning to buy some.

Next, he got on to the Internet to find the relevant contact telephone numbers for Maitland Airport but he wondered if it would be as easy a task to find the owners. He looked at his watch and realised Chloe might be home. So, remembering what Joel had said, he left calling the telephone numbers for the Airport and try to contact the owners the next day.

He had the idea now would be a good-time for a whisky and water which Joel had made him put on hold. However, he decided to first wait until Chloe arrived home and instead, relaxed on the couch. He mulled over in his mind all which had happened in his life over the last year. For Dick, it was surprising how one's life can change in such a short time, but that was all done and dusted now and he couldn't wait for what promised to be in store for him.

So lying back he closed his eyes and smiled, absorbing the wonderful feeling of joy and excitement coursing through him. He even wondered what kind of Noah he would make—but decided he was being silly and the whole idea ridiculous. However, he also remembered Joel's words. He was the one they chose, and he vowed to do his utmost and everything possible, to fulfil the task Joel and his colleagues had set for him.

Chloe arrived home and they exchanged their usual greetings and Dick decided he would only talk to her after they had their supper.

"What would you like eat, dear?" he asked.

"A pizza, thanks, with my usual extra toppings."

"Would you like me to get this ready and put it in the oven while you go upstairs and change?"

"Yes, now would be lovely, thanks," Chloe said as she smiled, and frowned, as she made her way upstairs.

Dick prepared her pizza for the oven and decided he would have his usual boring ham and pineapple pizza. He left the fancy ones alone as he found they repeated on him. Besides which, they always have far too much cheese on them. Not for him.

In a little while, Chloe came downstairs and checked her mail. When the pizzas were ready, Dick sliced them and they sat down to their supper but before he took the first bite, he asked her if she would like a glass of wine. She never had alcohol during the week because of having to drive her car the next day to the patients she had to visit.

"Yes, stuff it. I'll I will have a glass of wine for a change."

"Good, and I'll have my usual whisky and water."

"Why don't you do just that?" Chloe teased him.

"Yes, I will do just that," he replied and got up to get their drinks. "Cheers," they said and continued eating their pizzas.

Although it's rude to speak with one's mouth full, he spoke about his time in hospital the first time around, the time when he had been so sure his Mum and Dad would come and visit him. Chloe remembered this and asked why he was bringing it up again now. He said he had experienced a similar incident, but cast it aside, which was why he hadn't mentioned it. She said it was okay and he shouldn't worry about it.

Dick cleared his throat, took another swig of his whisky and water and carried on.

"Well, the thing is, there is something else I didn't mention to you, and please, this will sound ever so crazy and you may consider I'm bullshitting you, but I'm not. Just listen to the explanation and everything will fall into place. While I was in the hospital this time around, I had a strange happening in that a weird person..."

Before he continues, Chloe butted in. "Weird?.... How weird?"

Dick shushed her with a wave "You always interrupt me when I'm trying to explain something to you, so stop it and don't put words into my mouth either. Just listen, okay."

"Sorry dear."

He carried on where he had left off telling Chloe all about what had occurred up to and including the present time.

Now Chloe was not the woman to show surprise at any stage of a happening or event. If it was something scary, she would rather just go into a corner and crap herself. This time, however, she did not. Instead, she got up and poured herself another glass of wine.

"You're driving your car tomorrow don't forget."

"After what I've just heard, I deserve another glass. Hell, maybe even a bottle or two."

"Don't be silly. Would it help if I showed you my new body and the shape it's now in? Not that it's developed yet either."

"Hell yes, why not," she exclaimed, "it's been a while since I saw you in all your glory."

Although Chloe was sarcastic, it had not been long ago when she had to help him get out of the bath as his ailing body was too weak for him to do it on his own and, from what she could remember, it was not a pretty sight either.

Although feeling a tad embarrassed, Dick stood up and stripped. In no time at all, he stood before her, buck naked. "When last have you seen a body like that? and, as I've said to you, it's not developed yet as the correct muscle definition still has to happen."

"Oh my goodness gracious me," Chloe said with a huge grin "I've never seen a body like that on any man before, not even in the movies. You look incredible. Mmmm... I see a certain appendage has got larger since I last saw it. Does it work?" she asked laughing.

"How the hell should I know? I've only just got the bloody thing. Okay, embarrassment time is over," and he pulled his clothes back on.

"You... embarrassed? No,... you don't get embarrassed," Chloe said, trying to contain herself. He looked at her and they both burst out laughing.

Before putting his shoes back on, Dick said "You ain't seen nothin' yet" and held his new foot out for inspection.

"Oh my gosh," Chloe squeaked "that's unbelievable. It's a bloody miracle."

"Tell me about it," he said as he put his shoes on then took another swig of his drink. "Anyway, let's get on with it, shall we?”

Dick put his right hand in his pocket and produced two of the bank cards. “Here, these are for you. You can use them and your spending amount is limitless. Now don't forget to sign the back of each card and you can use the same codes you use on the bank cards you already have.”

Chloe took them from him and said: “You're kidding me, right?”

“Nope. No kidding—they are for real.”

He continued “Tomorrow when you go into the office, you need to resign, and as you are on a zero hours contract, tell them your resignation will be with immediate effect. If you like, I'll draft a suitable letter for you.”

"Hey,” she cried out “just give me time to digest all this. It's overwhelming me."

“Yes, but now we've come to the part I've been looking forward to most of all, and that is for you to meet Joel. This will have to happen and I see no reason it should not be now... agreed?”

“Well yes, I suppose now is as good a time as ever. By the sounds of it, it will happen whether or not I like it.”

“Absolutely,” Dick said and asked Joel to please show himself.

Right on cue, Joel made himself visible. Astounded, Chloe watched as Joel remained cool, calm and collected and introduced himself. "Hello Chloe, I'm Joel."

Chloe extended a nervous hand which Joel took with two of his long digits to shake hands with her.

"There now, that wasn't too bad, was it?" said Dick.

Before Chloe could reply, Joel said "There's no need to be afraid. I'm Dick's friend and guide as well if you like, and any friend of Dick's is a friend of mine. So please Chloe, relax and if there are questions you wish to ask don't hesitate."

The following momentary silence could have been measured in nanoseconds as Chloe was trying hard to come to terms with having a real live alien standing there, right before her eyes. She turned to Dick and said "I must apologise to you dear. I didn't accept what you were telling me to be true and said it to be a load of bullshit, so I apologise."

"Not to worry about it. If your response was anything other than it was, I'd be concerned. Your reaction was what I expected and I'm sure Joel will agree."

"I do. I take it Dick has put you in the picture?"

"Yes, I have," Dick interrupted "but I still need to fill her in on more of the finer details, and because she has now met you, it will be easier for me and she will come to realize I'm not making any of this up."

"Well then," Joel said "You have enough on your plate to go on with for now, so I'll leave you two to it. But Chloe, take Dick's advice and resign tomorrow so you can enjoy the rest of your life. Although you and Dick will work side-by-side he, however, will do most of the work and organising. So until tomorrow, have a good evening and Chloe, sleep well."

"Joel wait before you go. The anticoagulation pill I take each evening to slow down the blood clotting, must I still take it?"

"That's a good question. I'll give you the answer tomorrow," and with that, he disappeared into thin air.

Chloe sat there looking at Dick as if he weren't there. She was a million miles away and trying to take in the mass of information he had presented to her. While looking at her, he noticed she wasn't seeing him at all.

"Chloe," he whispered, but there was no response, so he tried again. "Chloe" and again there was no response. The next time he tried, he grabbed hold of her left arm and shook it "Chloe—you okay?"

"Mmmm... oh yes, I suppose I am. Yes, I'm okay—just allow me a little time to come back down-to-earth again, will you?" she said with a sigh.

"Shall I pour you another glass of wine?"

"Yes please."

Dick poured her another glass of wine and another whisky and water for himself. "Great stuff, and with luck, I might just be able to get another one in tonight—whisky, that is," he said to himself.

The two of them sat there for a while, sipping at their drinks. Dick said nothing, giving Chloe time to contemplate the situation.

"What's the time?" she asked.

"Not your bedtime, if that's what you worried about. It's still early."

"That doesn't tell me what the time is," she retorted.

"Oops... the madam sounds irritable and not in the mood for friendly banter. I'd better check," he mused. "It's just gone six-fifteen in the evening," he proudly said.

"Oh," she replied unperturbed.

Silence fell once more and Dick felt uncomfortable. He decided not to push it and instead, wait for her to break the ice, so he sat, sipping away at his drink.

Chloe came back down to earth and asked "So what happens now?" in-the-manner of someone who didn't grasp what was happening or what to do.

"Tomorrow I have to go to the Post Office to buy stamps as I need to post two letters. Then I must get in touch with the owners of Maitland Airport to arrange a meeting," he replied. "As for you, I suggest you do as Joel said and go to the office and resign because I need your help on a lot of up-and-coming issues. Would you like me to type out a letter for you?"

"Yes please, if you wouldn't mind."

He made his way upstairs to type out the letter on his desktop computer. "Who should I address it to?" he called down from upstairs.

"To Marlene, please" she shouted back.

"Okay, but what's her surname?"

"It's Piper," Chloe shouted once more. "Marlene Piper."

"Thanks" he called back, typed and printed out the letter, and together with an envelope, made his way downstairs to hand it to her to read.

"Isn't it short? Shouldn't I give them two weeks' notice? I mean, that's what's in my contract," she said sounding concerned.

"Yes, but it is a zero hour contract and besides, your next employer is me. So why give a damn?"

"Yes... Yes, you're right, and after the way those bloody idiots in the so-called Planning Department treated me, why should I give a damn? As you say, you'll be my next employer," she exclaimed with a happy smile on her face. Satisfied, Dick smiled for it showed him she had now accepted the situation.

"You said you have to see the owner of Maitland Airfield?"

"Maitland Airport," Dick corrected. "Yes, Joel wants me to buy it."

"What, buy it in your name?," she exclaimed. "Where on earth are you going to get the money from and who will run the place? I mean, what do you or I understand about running an airport? You may well be knowledgeable in fixing or managing or even flying a plane, but you have no experience in how to go about running an airport."

"All good points, however, the current staff would have to stay on and if there isn't already a General Manager there, I must hire one."

"Yes, but what about the money?" Chloe asked getting agitated.

"Remember I have the credit and debit cards," he pointed out to her.

"Wow," she blurted out "This is to much for my tiny little mind," she said, taking a good mouthful of her wine and savouring the flavour as she swallowed it.

So she shrugged her shoulders and, taking up the resignation letter, signed it, placed it in the envelope and sealed it. With a black-ink pen, and in her own handwriting, she addressed the envelope. She now had an idea and telephoned the office to see if anyone was still there.

"Who are you phoning?"

"I going to inform the office what I'm doing so they can get a head start on organising carers for tomorrow morning to replace me."

"Oh stuff them..." Dick protested but, before he could say any more Chloe interrupted him. "I'm not doing this for the office, I'm doing it for the old folk I've been looking after. It's not fair to them if there's no one there to see to them at seven o'clock in the morning."

"Okay, point taken. Good idea. Right, I want to check these numbers I found online for the airport to see if they are correct then I'll phone in the morning. Um, listen. If you're going to the office tomorrow, would you mind buying stamps and posting these letters for me?"

"Yes, and shall I get something for a late breakfast or maybe an early lunch as well?"

"Good idea."

"Anything in particular?"

"No, I'll let you decide" he said, as he made his way upstairs to surf the net to find and check again the numbers he needed.

Chloe now moved herself to the recliner chair to relax in front of the TV while enjoying the rest of her wine.

The following morning she made sure she was at the office by 8:00 a.m. to hand in her resignation which involved a short meeting with her Manager. She handed over her office mobile phone, left and found her way to the Post Office where she bought stamps and posted Dick's two letters.

As she was keen to use her new cards, she drove to the shopping mall, and in case the new ones didn't work, she had her original cards as a back-up. However, she was awe-struck to find the new ones worked.

"Wonderful. I should have done more shopping, but I suppose there's always another day," she said, chuckling to herself about the newfound wealth "and all this time I took Dick to be mad in the head, gazing up at the night sky looking for flying saucers."

Back home Chloe put the shopping down in the kitchen before looking for Dick and heard him talking on the phone and assumed he must have got hold of someone at the airport. So she walked back to the kitchen, unpacked the shopping and put everything away except for the things she would use to make brunch. Fried bacon, scrambled eggs, fried tomatoes, fried mushrooms, toast and Red Bush tea was on the menu. Bad for the figure, she cogitated, but couldn't give a continental as it wasn't often they had that kind a meal.

When brunch was ready, she called to Dick to come downstairs.

While at the dining room table, he told her he had spoken to the owner of the airport and had planned to meet with him in two days' at 2:30 p.m. After brunch, as they were just about to clear the plates away, they noticed the now familiar soft sound and gentle light as Joel appeared.

"That was perfect timing," said Chloe.

"Well, I've been waiting for you to finish,"

"Why didn't you come and join us?"

"Thanks, Chloe, but we don't eat the same food as you, which you humans need to get the energy you need."

"May I ask how you go about it?"

"Yes you may. We only take in amino type acids in a liquid form which goes into the bloodstream, to explain it to you so you might understand."

"Oh, okay—I suppose it saves having to do the dishes each time?"

"Indeed. Let's carry on outlining what you must do, shall we? Chloe, would you mind bringing an A4 sheet of paper and a pen or pencil please?"

When she came back Joel said, "Now you have planned to see the owner....."

Before he could finish Chloe interjected, "How can you know?"

"As Dick knows, we can see and hear almost everything and while we are working together, we'll be watching proceedings. No, not spying on you, just keeping an eye on everything, that's all. I now need you to make notes, using bullet points, what you need to do next."

"Aargh..." Dick groaned.

"Sorry Dick. Yes, you hate Americanisms, but don't despair for it's not. However, it might help Chloe. First, your nephew Phil's invention, which is still in the drawing stage, we should discuss. Second, aeroplanes and next, La Rioja in Argentina," he said as Chloe made notes.

"Where?" Chloe asked and Joel spelt out the name for her.

"Regarding your nephew and his design. I need you to get in touch with him as soon as possible and tell him not to make any more changes to it. He has now reached the optimum level of its design which will work once built. I will inform who you should contact regarding the supply of the materials for the machine, including the best supplier of the magnetic materials or magnets. You will also need to approach a manufacturing company which you will need to build the machine's requirements. I'll give you those contact details. Then, once you have done this, you must buy a disused car factory up North as you will build, or be converting, cars using Phil's power unit and take my word, it will work."

While Dick listened, Chloe continued to make notes.

"Now I suppose you want advice as to the reason for a car factory? While you are doing all the work required, this will keep your Government happy as to your activities, and doing it this way, there won't be any nosy people prying around. We don't need them and besides, we realize how you feel about Governments. Also, I want you to buy passenger and freight transport aircraft. The freight aircraft should be the Airbus A400M, but you are to replace the engines with Phil's electric driven ones. You already understand how it works, so later you can explain it to Chloe."

"No, forget it. I won't understand what's going on. As long as it works that's what counts."

"For the commercial passenger planes," Joel continued as if Chloe hadn't spoken at all, "may I suggest the Airbus A320 or similar as you will need planes designed to handle short runways."

"Wait a moment, I've had a great idea," Dick said "I've always wanted to own a Super VC10, and those aircraft were designed for the shorter more rugged type airfield. So why don't I see if I can get these from the Air Force and, if not, have them built? The reason is, although I might pick up second-hand aircraft, I'll be unable deduce their condition and, besides, I must place an order for the A400M, anyway."

"What do you propose?" asked Joel.

"Well, I may be wrong but, I understand we will need these passenger planes to transport the people we will save. So, in doing basic calculations on how many people we will need to save, plus family and friends, I will need five aircraft. Now as I'm sure we'll be covering some distance, one of them must be a mid-air refuelling bowser."

"Okay, why the VC10?" Joel asked him.

"I've always wanted to own one, and it's the only sub-sonic airliner to hold the record for the fastest transatlantic crossing. Until the present time, nothing has beaten its record."

"That's not true," Chloe interrupted. "There was one of the big ones the other day—it was Jumbo jet which travelled at just under the speed of sound. I forget the actual speed, but it was fast."

"Correct," Dick replied "and although those aircraft can fly faster than the VC10 could reach, because of the cost of fuel, they never used its forwarding thrust power so, they haven't as yet broken the record. Also, the VC10s record was achieved without the help of the elements, whereas this one you are referring to had the help of the Gulf Stream, which was blowing at two hundred-odd miles per hour? Also, although it carries half as many passengers as the big Jumbo jets, it's far more comfortable and quieter because it's the only aircraft, besides the Russian built one, to use a rear-engine quad layout and besides,... I love them."

"Okay, you organise it," Joel instructed him "but just remember, you are to push whoever it is you have these planes built for you to do the work. We can't afford to waste any time."

"Why we are using aircraft? I mean, if I'm to be the new Noah, why aren't we building an ark or a ship like the biblical Noah did?"

"The original ark was okay for its time and served its purpose," Joel replied "It would, however, be impractical for today's requirements because of the populace and where they all live."

"Why's that then?" enquired Chloe.

"Well, the size of the ark was, as written in the Bible, huge by any stretch of your imagination and recorded as being in the shape of a ship, correct?"

"Yes, those were our teachings," replied Dick.

"Well, that's all wrong because its shape was round...,"

"Round," Dick expostulated.

"Yes,... its diameter was sixty-eight metres and stood thirty metres tall. We based the design on the Coracle—big, heavy and cumbersome."

"You said we. Did you design it?" asked Chloe.

"Yes, and that's because the idiot humans only used a small proportion of their brain," Joel informed her. "Now enough of that."

"No, no, wait a minute," Dick interjected, "I can recall you saying the ark was a databank or something, is that correct?"

"Yes, correct. We helped Noah, and as we had the DNA from every carbon living organism, including Homo Sapiens, we placed it on the ark. Imagine the size ship Noah would have to build if two of every single living animal and organism had to get onboard. No, if Noah had to do that, it would have been so big he'd still be building it today. When you are ready, we'll hand over the same databank of DNA samples and your scientists can do the necessary when needed," Joel said, while Dick and Chloe both stared at him dumbstruck.

"Does this mean some extinct animals will one day roam the earth once more?"

"Yes, Dick. Many of them, but not the dinosaurs."

"Well, thank heavens for that," Chloe said relieved "So, all of our teachers were giving us a load of rubbish for our entire school days... the bastards."

"Afraid so, but you can't blame them for their teachings too were incorrect."

"Okay, Joel, let's put that aside. Are the aircraft going to be the new ark?" Dick asked him.

"If you want to put it that way then yes. Now, regarding La Rioja in Argentina. There is a piece of land not too far from the town. We lived there for a few hundred thousand years inside a mountain, but nobody ever realized we were there. Some have suspected it but they had no proof. As we no longer occupy the space, you will have the use of all the inside, and in your terms, its vast. Larger than you could ever imagine, large enough to store all the aircraft inside, and more. But we cross that bridge when we get to it. Anyway, that is the property you must buy from the Argentine landowner because it is there, on the mountainside, you are to build a runway."

Dick listened to him with all ears while Chloe still scribbled away making comprehensive notes.

"However, before you build there, you will have to get permission from the Argentinian Government. First, you need to contact a person, whose details I'll furnish you with further down the line. He will help you with this and will also be able to give you all the information you need regarding which company you should use to construct the area. But first, we must prioritize."

"Now, the arrangement you have with the owner of Maitland Airport, keep it. In the meantime, contact Phil as his machine must be constructed as soon as possible. Also, find out about the plans for the VC10 and, get in touch with Airbus about the A400Ms."

"How many of those am I to order?" Dick asked, and Joel said, "Four should be enough."

"Should we get Phil involved in handling the ordering of the parts for his machine?" asked Chloe and Dick replied "Yes, a good idea," and Joel agreed.

"Once the purchase of Maitland airport has been finalizes, there will be enough housing there for all of you, including your daughter Kerri and her husband, and any other family members, friends and additional staff you will need to recruit. You must move them in there as soon as once you have taken over ownership of the place," Joel reiterated.

"I'll get hold of Phil today and Chloe can contact family and friends to arrange a meeting to explain everything," Dick said "I might even make a list of the people we will require to help us and perhaps arrange a separate meeting with them. Well, we see how it goes," said Dick, and Joel said "Good, I will leave you now to get on with it and I'll see you in a few days' time."

"For obvious reasons you don't want me to get in touch with you to inform how things are proceeding, correct?" Dick asked with a big smile on his face.

"Correct" Joel replied just as he disappeared.

## Chapter Four

## (a) The New Experience

"BUGGER ME! There's so much to do, so where do I begin? Oh, wait a minute. I'll get hold of Phil via Skype or Messenger and put him in the picture. He'll love this."

"Skype or Messenger? Besides the providers, you realize how many agencies there are around the world listening in on those conversations? Not forgetting emails and every other existing electronic device, especially the *smart* ones. Hell, you and Phil are always bitching and moaning about it. Do you suppose it's a good idea?"

"Mmmm... no... good point there, Chloe. It will be best if I see him in person."

"Yes, that's more like it. You can put your sister and your grandniece in the picture at the same time while I get onto the others. You should fly down there and hire a car at the airport."

"Yes, I'll do just that. In fact, I'll fly to Maitland Airport and go from there."

"Okay, why not do both on the same day when you see the owner of the airport? You know, kill two stones with one bird," she said and giggled realising what she said.

Dick too found it funny, and said "Mmmm... yes, makes sense. Aren't you the clever one?" he teased. "I'll just phone all of them for now and say I'll be coming to visit them. Are you coming too?"

"Oh ha ha ha," she giggled again "I suppose if I answer, you will say 'it's about time I came to', aren't you?"

"What?... don't be silly now," he replied, knowing full well he would have answered her so as it was a standing joke between them.

"Well, I suppose the answer must be... yes," she said smiling.

"Fine, I'll phone and book our tickets."

"When you're finished, you can get on to Airbus. Who are you going to commission to build those VM what's-it's that you want?"

"They are VC10s and the answer is I'm sure yet. I must research first. I would prefer a European company rather than North or South American, and definitely not Russian. It all depends on who has the best tooling to do the job because the planes exterior has to be exact. The inside, however, must have the latest aeronautical instruments and I will have to get Rolls Royce to supply their most up-to-date engines to fit the pods. I'll get in touch with BAE Systems to see if they would take this on. They are, after all, the only surviving subsidiary of the Vickers Corporation after they closed down."

All this went over Chloe's head, she tried to look intelligent even though she hadn't a clue what he was talking about.

Dick phoned their nearest airport and booked tickets for a round trip in two days' time and booking a car for the day. He phoned the local taxi services to arrange an early pickup time to take them to the airport. He also phoned his sister to tell her of their plans asking her to make sure Phil would be available and not going out fishing or working on his boat.

Once he had completed making all the arrangements, he surfed the net looking for potential car manufacturing buildings where the companies had closed years ago. Much to his surprise and excitement, he found three. He looked for a Real Estate Agent who could make all the enquiries on his behalf.

Dick found one without too much trouble and, once he had given him the names of the three buildings he had found, and all the specs for the building he required, the agent said he would get on to it straight away. Dick told the agent it was urgent and it would be a cash purchase and gave him a week in which to do his homework and get back to him.

Chloe asked why he had to get this building and why to build cars when they would go to South America. She said it made no sense. Dick reminded her Joel had suggested this as it would be a cover-up designed to keep nosy officials away. It would draw suspicion away from all the other transactions they would make, and the amounts of money they would spend using the new cards.

It would also be the main place for developing Phil's machine which he could get on with. Once Phil was up and running, they would be free to start the project of building the new runway which would take a good couple of years. They would also have to watch-over the proceedings of the required new aircraft. Dick gave Chloe an evil grin and said he would enjoy pissing off all A-holes in the world.

The new cars would not require petrol or diesel which would cause total chaos in the entire oil industry—from which Dick would also derive great pleasure. When the time came for all these people to go for the big swim, they would be pissed off, and most of them would find themselves bankrupt to boot. Dick rubbed his hands in glee as he mulled over it.

Chloe just shook her head and said: "I wonder if you'll ever grow up."

"Yes, but it is a new experience for us."

Chloe had found the telephone numbers for both aircraft companies, so Dick got on the phone and made appointments: the first with Airbus in France in three day's time, and the second with BAE on the day following. They were, therefore, going to be busy with the up-and-coming workload.

Later in the evening Joel appeared. He asked Chloe to make notes of manufacturing companies and suppliers of raw materials for Phil's invention. These businesses ranged between Japan, China, and the UK. He instructed Chloe to contact these suppliers and make appointments for the following week, Monday with the Japanese supplier, Wednesday the Chinese supplier and Friday, the UK supplier. So they spent the following day looking up telephone numbers, contacting the companies, and making appointments.

Joel had taken time to analyse each company and assessed their capabilities. The Japanese company would supply the automated components required to run the factory, and because they had smelting works, would manufacture and supply components needed for Phil's invention. A Chinese company, iconic supplier of world-renowned magnets, were to supply this main component for the invention. Then an English company would be asked to supply their cars, minus engines, to the factory in North England.

Dick's next plan was how he would go about hiring staff to operate the factory. He remembered there was a large work-force out there—people made redundant by various car manufacturers which had closed down. The Government were at fault for these closures due to their lack of ability to run the country. (In fact, the same could be said for today.) The factory owners were, therefore, forced to either move their businesses abroad or sell-out. He made notes about which people Phil might use and, therefore, would need to find good Factory Managers and Foremen whom he could use right from the beginning for he would need them to give their input as to the layout and workings of the factory floor.

Dick did some further plotting. He jotted down more notes of things he expected would play a vital part in the future of the factory. Also, he wrote a few names for the new company and came up with Phoenix intelligence (Pi). Motors For You. The Electric Horseless Carriage Company. The Electric Car Company. The Phoenix Car Company, and even something to remind him of his daughter,... Kerri's Electric Autos, or Kerri's Kar Kompany.

Dick quite liked the last one, and a few of the other ridiculous sounding names. An idea came to mind, so in the morning while on the aircraft, Dick would ask Chloe for suggestions. He finished his drink and made his way upstairs to pack one bag of toiletries, a change of shirt and extra smalls, just in case. When he had finished, he took himself off to bed as the taxi would be there at 6:00 a.m. the following morning to take them to the airport.

On arrival at Maitland Airport, Dick and Chloe picked up the hire car (a people carrier) and drove to his sisters' house. There, Cassie, her granddaughter Erica and her son Phil, were waiting for them. Once there, they would explain the situation and what they needed to do. After exchanging greetings, they sat down at the dining room table and Dick started things off.

"We only have a few hours as Chloe and I have a meeting at Maitland Airport. Right,... now my dear sister, remember how you always called me a bullshitter when I told you on countless occasions about the flying saucers I had seen?"

"Yes."

"So I'm sure you remember how your attitude changed when you saw the one on the farm all those years ago?"

"How could we forget?"

"Well, it's about... mmmm... how shall I put it? If you had ideas flying saucers were farcical, what I'm about to explain to you, you will seem even more so. Please don't laugh but listen as it will affect all of us and I mean... all of us. Let me put you in the picture what has transpired over these last few days and I'll explain why it's imperative for Phil to be here."

Without messing around, Dick shot straight to the point and told them everything that had happened. This including informing Phil what Joel had said about his drive unit.

Because meetings had already been arranged with the oversees suppliers, Dick proceeded. "Phil, as you understand your requirements, I suggest you be the one to see them. Once the raw materials are ready for shipment, I will give you an address in the North of England. That's where I'm in the process of purchasing an old disused car manufacturing company."

Cassie, Erica and Phil were listening open-mouthed, bemused by all he had said.

"Now, I will need the three of you to be ready to move at a moments notice within the next month. Cassie, you and Erica will move to Maitland Airport as soon as I give you the go-ahead and you, Phil, will move up North as I will need you to bring the factory up to speed as soon as possible. It's there your creation will be produced and the new cars converted using your design. I understand this must seem much to handle but it's real, and it is happening,... believe me."

"The reason Chloe and I are going back to the airport later today is because I need to purchase it and, with luck, complete said purchase," he informed the now shocked-looking family.

"What about money for the move and a house in which to live, and talking about living, where are we to get the money to survive?" asked Cassie.

"Don't worry about that," Dick replied without batting an eyelid "Either I or Chloe will sort everything out for you."

"Phil," Dick continued "I must point this out to you now as I don't want you to forget it. Once you have the factory up and running and you are more than satisfied with the way your design is being put together, I want you to move back here to be based at the airport. Once there, I'll brief you further what I need you to do."

"Okay, I understand this seems to be too much to handle at the moment for I was where you are right now just a few days ago. Any questions?"

There was the expected silence from his overwhelmed family members so, before anyone could say anything, he continued "Chloe and I have six and a half hours before our meeting, so this is what I suggest. Cassie, you and Phil get all your necessary paperwork together to enable us to purchase two new cars for you. Erica, if you hadn't been so lazy and had done your driver's test just like I told you to do, I would have bought one for you. But hey, toughies. Losers weep."

"Aaaarrrgh... uncle Dickie," wailed Erica.

"No, I'm sorry but it's your own fault. Come along, you and Chloe can go clothes shopping—that should cheer you up. What we need is a car dealership near to a clothing store. Any ideas Cassie?" and she replied "Yes,".

"Okay, you and Phil get all your paperwork and let's go shopping. On our way, and to save time, chuck ideas around about what wheels you would like."

Phil had to go to his boat to fetch his paperwork and said he would meet them at the place in the shopping complex Cassie had mentioned.

Later they had an absolute ball trying on and buying new clothes and shoes, much to Erica's delight. They spent over one thousand five hundred pounds between them.

When Cassie and Phil had finished their clothes shopping, and because Erica hadn't, Dick walked with them to the car dealerships nearby. A new Rover 4×4 bought for Phil and a new Lexus Sedan for Cassie. To say they were elated with their new acquisitions would put it mildly.

"Right, we have time left so maybe we can have lunch and Chloe and I will go straight from here to the airport. After we have finished there, we'll fly back home."

As an afterthought, Chloe asked, "Do any of you need a new laptop?" to which Erica replied "Yes I do, Aunty Chloe."

So before going for lunch, they popped into a computer store and purchased three new laptops, each to their own liking.

Over lunch, Dick said "Remember Phil, no more changes to your design. Just start with getting things together for those three suppliers."

Phil nodded his head and said "Thank you Dick—this is a huge break for me. I can still hardly believe all this is happening but you can rely on me to do my best."

"Good, and it's everything I have ever dreamed of come true and together we will make it."

After saying goodbye, Dick and Chloe left for their meeting at the airport.

## (b)  Maitland Airport

Once in the car, Chloe asked, "What's the owner's name again?"

"Oh, I didn't tell you. His name is Steve Smith," Dick replied, and Chloe asked "Not thee Steve Smith I take it?"

"No, not him. A common name I should imagine."

(Sometime back both had worked in the same building where they had known someone called Steve Smith whom they used to take the mickey out of because of a commercial on the television.)

When they arrived at Maitland Airport, a secretary showed them to a waiting area. There, she asked them to have a seat while she informed Mr Smith of their arrival. Dick being a stickler for punctuality, they arrived dead on time, however, they had to wait the obligatory ten minutes. The secretary came back to show them into Mr Smith's office.

When she opened the door, she introduced them "Mr Smith, this is Mr Shepherd and Mrs Fraser-Rigby." They all shook hands and Mr Smith asked them to sit.

Dick got straight to the point. "Mr Smith, am I correct you still want to sell the airport?"

"Yes, correct. Are you interested in purchasing it yourself, or are you here representing another party?"

"We want to purchase it for ourselves," Dick affirmed.

So they discussed the price and what would be best for the staff and for the airport to keep the business running. They agreed, and the ball set in motion. Mr Smith got hold of his lawyer to make the arrangements and prepare the paperwork, and for Mr Smith the sooner the transaction took place, the sooner he would have the money in his bank account, therefore, the sooner he could retire.

"The greedy bastard," Dick said to himself.

There was a knock at the door and a small, thin, rather sheepish looking man walked into the office holding a file of paperwork and Dick decided the poor chap looked as if he should have been in his grave long since. Mr Smith introduced him to Dick and Chloe as Mr Dumbrill, the Company lawyer, and held out his hand for the file.

"That was quick work," Dick said in amazement.

"That's why Mr Dumbrill still works here. He's much faster and far more reliable than any of the new chaps today," Mr Smith replied smiling at the lawyer.

"How long will this take before everything goes through and Chloe and I become the new owners?" Dick asked Mr Dumbrill.

"I'll see what I can do to expedite things but I would say no more than three weeks."

"That's good. Now, regarding the financial side of things, how would it be if we paid half the amount up front and the rest at the end of the transaction?" Dick enquired.

"What about half the amount now and the other half we put into a holding account, and when all the signatures have been put to paper, I can transfer the second half?" replied Mr Dumbrill.

"If it's good enough for you, Mr Smith, it's good enough for us," said Dick.

"Yes, I agree. I'm all for that," said Mr Smith not even trying to hide his excitement at all.

"Good. How would you like this payment, Mr Dumbrill? Credit or debit card, or would you prefer a bank guaranteed cheque?"

"As this transaction is to go through now, a Debit Card, in my mind, would be best. So, instead of putting the balance into a holding account, I could telephone you and we transfer the balance. Would you agree to this?"

"Yes, Mr Dumbrill, that would be fine."

The lawyer produced the documents and, as Chloe had worked

for many a year in a Buy-to-Let office, she was familiar with the workings of ownership transfer, therefore, Dick and Mr Smith left the two of them to do the work while they ambled over to the Boardroom. Mr Smith cracked-open a bottle of champagne to drink a toast to the transaction.

"I'm not a champagne drinker as I don't like the stuff. But in the circumstances—Cheers Mr Smith."

"Please, call me Steve. May I get you something else instead?"

"That's kind of you. If you don't mind I'll have a whisky and water please and... my names Dick."

They discussed the takeover. Dick told Steve to make sure when he announces to the staff about the takeover, their jobs would not be in jeopardy and wanted this point put across for he would need their expertise to carry on running the airport.

"Steve, the one person I would like to meet as soon as possible is your right-hand man. The one who looks after the place when you're not here."

"A brilliant one he is too. His name is Deon DuToit. He is of French origin but when he speaks, you wouldn't notice it as his mother was South African and he grew up there. I'll call him now, shall I?" Steve asked, and Dick said "Yes, please do."

The door opened and in walked a middle-aged chap who stood about six-foot tall. He was a handsome man of slender to athletic build and one could see he radiated a confidence which impressed Dick and hoped the two of them would get on well together. It was obvious Deon wasn't one of those who has their heads shoved so far up their own backsides they do not know whether they should cough or fart.

"Ah Deon, thanks for coming. Deon, I'd like to introduce you to Mr Dick Shepherd." They greeted each other and shook hands prior to sitting down at the boardroom table where Steve continued. "The reason I called you in is that I have some important news which, for the moment, is to stay within these four walls, please. Once you hear what it is, you'll understand the secrecy."

"As you are aware, I have been trying to sell the company for some time now. This morning Mr Shepherd and his partner, Mrs Fraser-Rigby, have purchased the airport and Mr Dumbrill is of the opinion he will have the paperwork completed within three weeks. Maybe I'll out of here within two. Right now, Dick wanted to meet the person who runs the place when I'm not here and that is you. The good news is, Mr Shepherd wants you to carry on running the airport as is, but I'm sure he will put you in the picture and work things out together."

As he finished speaking, Chloe entered the boardroom with Mr Dumbrill, who closed the door behind them.

"Chloe, meet Deon DuToit, he's Steve's right-hand man and will carry on running the place for us once Steve has left," Dick informed her. He continued "Just a notion Steve... would it be OK with you if I filled Deon in on what we will require right now?"

"Great idea. What do you say, Deon? You will work with Mr Shepherd from now on and I'll just be here to help as and when needed."

At this, he paused, looked at Mr Dumbrill and said "I take it all the paperwork will be ready by then? I wouldn't want to stay any longer than that. What's your opinion?"

"Well, I have everything in hand which I hope to have completed within a two week period and I do not foresee any problems if you wanted to leave straight away. All you must do when the time comes, is to put your signature to paper. I could even send someone there to you with the papers for you to sign, if you like, but it's your decision and yours alone to make. How do you two feel about it?" Mr Dumbrill asked Dick and Chloe.

"I've no objections," Dick replied, and Chloe said "Neither have I, but what about you, Deon? How would you feel about Steve leaving right away?"

Deon deliberated for a moment and looked at Steve. "I have no objections if you leave now, Steve. I run the airport when you aren't here, so it makes no difference to me. Therefore, yes—I'll be okay with it if you want to do that."

"Well, Steve, I believe the old proverbial ball is now bouncing around in your court. I speak on behalf of Chloe and myself but it's your decision and I'm sure either way will make no difference to us," Dick said and raised his glass to Steve.

"So are you two drinking alone?" asked Chloe.

"Oh, fu... sorry," said a rather embarrassed Steve. "What may I get you?"

Deon stood up and said "Please allow me to do that. May I get drinks for everyone?"

All glasses charged, they toasted to the sale and purchase of the company, Maitland Airport Services.

"I suppose you would like to know if I've decided yet," said Steve. "What I'll do is phone my wife, bounce it off her and take it from there. In the meantime, enjoy your drinks and I'll be back." He walked to his office, closing the door behind him, and telephoned his wife. Not long thereafter the door opened and with a huge smile of relief, he made his announcement "As of this moment, I am retired."

As Steve walked towards them, they all stood up and clapped and, one by one shook hands with him. Mr Dumbrill was the first to speak to him.

"Now you go home my boy and live a wonderful life with your family. Don't you fret about anything and I will call you when everything is ready."

After more congratulations, Steve made his excuses to leave so he could pack all his personal things.

The rest of them sat back down at the table and Dick said as they only had just over an hour left, before having to board the homeward-bound aircraft, they should discuss a few points here and there. After this he assured Deon he would not interfere at all how he ran the Airport. He would have full powers over everything and Dick asked Mr Dumbrill to construct a letter of appointment to legalise the position. The only people who could overrule anything in any way shape, matter, or form, would be Dick, Chloe and Kerri. That would be the only obstacle he would have to contend with should the occasion ever arise. However, Dick assured him the likelihood of it happening was remote.

As time was against them, he apologised to Deon and said he would have to plan for another time to walk around the airport and meet the staff. It was his intention to meet each one and not by way of all and sundry meeting in a hangar with him standing up in front of them speaking a load of crap. He regarded this as impolite.

Dick's philosophy was in a situation like this, the personal touch was the correct and only way in which to show respect to one's employees, and to get theirs in return. Not like some A-holes he had had the misfortune of working for in the past. Those pigs, those utter boneheads—the so-called employers who found enjoyment in causing their opposition to throw money away. He despised people like this who were all just money-orientated and who also thrived on the downfall of their fellow man. This person would never enter his home, no matter what the circumstances.

Goodbyes all around, Dick and Chloe left to board their plane.

Chapter Five

Joel's Next Briefing

IT WAS A pleasant enough flight and before long it was over and they found themselves in a taxi taking them home. During the drive home, Chloe's phone rang, and she answered it. Dick overheard the conversation as he was sitting right next to her.

"Hello," she said, and there was a pause. "Well, you can go screw yourselves. I gave you my letter of resignation and not even wild horses could drag me back to your offices. Piss off and don't you dare call me again, ever? You bloody useless people," she said and ended the call. Chloe looked at Dick and with a face like thunder, said: "Those damned arseholes want to know why I'm not in the office or at any of my calls."

Dick had to laugh and said "Calm down dear and put it behind you. The beautiful part of it all is... you never have to go back there, right? So relax, and when we're home, you can crack open a bottle of wine. Not that you need it,... I mean, you've been drinking all bloody day," he teased her.

"What the hell are you talking about? I only had one glass of champagne in the boardroom."

"Look, I was only joking, trying to put a smile back on your dial after that stupid phone call, that's all."

They arrived at the house, paid the fare and before going inside, Chloe apologised to the taxi driver for her outburst. As they walked in, they noticed the dining room light was on. They peered around the corner and saw Joel sitting at the table and on the table was a bottle of wine, together with a wine glass, and a glass of whisky and water.

"Hello and welcome back," Joel said "Please have a seat as I'm only here for a short while. I'm here to congratulate you on the purchase and to pour Chloe that drink she so needs."

"Thanks Joel," she said and sat down "that's thoughtful of you."

Dick said he needed to stretch his legs, so he stood at the table, picked up his glass and said "Cheers."

"Regarding Phil's invention,... when is he going to contact the suppliers?" asked Joel.

"He should already have made a start this afternoon and I'm expecting him to contact me sometime tomorrow. As soon as he has confirmed the appointments Chloe made, I'm to book flights to wherever. I have asked him to start in Japan so we fly to the furthest point first and work our way back to China, then UK."

"Fine, and it seems you've made a good start. As you two must be tired, I'll leave you for now and see you sometime tomorrow.

Remember, if I'm not here and you need my help or advice, please call me at any time for it has no bearing on us as it has on you," he said, and in a flash, disappeared into thin air.

Dick sat down and he and Chloe talked about their day. "What's the time?" asked Dick looking at his watch "Mmmm... far too late to phone Airbus or any of the others."

"What about that national park or place, or whatever it is, in South America? Where is it again?"

"Oh yeah right, Errmmm.... La Rioja in Argentina. I was only planning on contacting them in four days' time. Still, no time like the present. I think I'll look up the contact details on the web."

"That's right, you go surfing the net as it's the only surfing you know how to do," said Chloe as she giggled.

"Oh ha ha bloody ha" he replied as he switched on the laptop, and while it was booting up, he poured himself another whisky and water.

"Does your child know how much of that stuff you are drinking these days?"

"I don't think so, why?"

"You're damn right she doesn't," Chloe said in a strong voice "She'd tear a strip off you if she did."

"Well please don't tell her. Okay, now where the hell do I start?" he said gazing at the laptop screen and not listening to her. "I suppose Estate Agents in Argentina would be a good place to start. What language do they speak over there, do you know?"

"Yes, they speak Spanish and the currency is the Peso. Oh, and the capital is Buenos Aires," she informed him grinning.

"Okay, smarty-pants. I wonder if I should ask Joel to come and give us more info regarding this. Yeah, I think I will," Dick said, and before they could say Jack Robertson, Joel was there.

"Welcome back," said Chloe "Did you miss us?"

"Miss you," Joel said in what sounded like a confused voice "What do you mean? I was here not that long ago, or had you forgotten?" he asked bewildered.

"Oh never mind, forget what I said" she replied realising he didn't quite grasp she was trying to be funny.

"What would you like to know?"

"Well, Joel, because I have time on my hands, I thought I'd research La Rioja to see if I could get any info which might help. I know you said you would furnish us with all the info we required but I thought I'd give it a head start."

"Fine, let's make this my next briefing and I'll give you the info now. Chloe, I think you should write all this down." As Chloe already had a few pens with her, she fetched a writing pad before making herself comfortable at the table poised to start.

"The town of La Rioja is in the La Rioja Province in Argentina. It has a small airport on its outskirts, but as both your aircraft were specifically designed for smaller more rugged airfields, they can land there. Should you want to make use of any larger aircraft that would be fine, but with some hard braking as they would take up most the runway. However, take-off might prove to be more difficult for them as well, so please bear that in mind."

"Okay, to make it clear," said Chloe and read back her notes to Joel.

"Yes, correct. Also, there you will offload equipment you will need to build your runway, however, the road out of the airport grounds has an archway across it. Get permission to remove it as the loads will not fit underneath it. If they won't agree to that, get permission from the authorities to build a temporary thoroughfare to go around it. This road will lead you around the outskirts of the town and will bring you to the Av Felix de la Cruz number seventy-four, where you need to turn right. Stay on this road which leads you out of town and keep going for about seventy kilometres - and don't worry, the roads are tarred."

Dick didn't interrupt and Joel continued while Chloe jotted down everything she thought pertinent.

"You will turn left off this road onto the Camino Pampa De La

Vega. Carry on for about three hundred and fifty metres and turn right onto a dirt road. Drive for three kilometres before you turn left. Follow this bit of road for under a kilometre and you will get to a T-junction where you will see an old disused road. Follow it to its end, without deviating, for about two kilometres. You will have to re-construct and tar some of these dirt roads."

Dick and Chloe listened and absorbed everything Joel was saying.

He continued "You will now have to construct a new road, heading in the same direction for a further six kilometres. Don't worry—it sounds worse than it will be. This will take you right up to the entrance into the mountain which you, or anyone else, won't see-but don't despair."

As if from out of nowhere, Joel produced a rather large map of the area. They cleared the table and Joel spread the map out which took up almost the entire surface area. Chloe moved round to Dick's left side with Joel on his right standing on a chair. Joel pointed out the roads he had mentioned following them all the way through to the entrance into the mountain. With this, things fell into place.

"If you look over here, this is where your road will end. Coming out of that, and running in a South Westerly direction, you will build at what will be the end of the runway where you will park the aircraft... does that make sense?" asked Joel, all the while pointing at the map with one of his long digits. They said they did.

"The runway from here, to its end, will be seven kilometres long. The ideal length is only five kilometres, but as you have space and as the air at this altitude is not as dense as it is at sea level, there's no harm in having an extra bit of tarmac to play with. Besides, the landing for some of your pilots may be tricky at first for, as you can see, there's only one way in and out. Across this area, your approach for landing will bring you through a wide mountain cutting from the South. Five kilometres from the road number seventy-six, turn left to line up with the runway and the rest should be easy."

Once again, from out of the blue, this time Joel produced a few DVDs which he handed to Chloe. "Look after these. They are for the simulators of both aircraft and they are training programs for the pilots, concentrating on this approach I've explained to you, so I'm sure they will appreciate them."

"Oh yes, they will help," said Dick.

"You won't need to practice."

"What?"

"You don't have to practice because you'll be okay. Extra brain power, remember? But if you want to, I won't stop you."

"Oh, now I know what you're getting at. Stupid me."

"This map is for you. When we get nearer to the time, I'll give you the plans for constructing the runway, the roads, and of the structures which have to be built."

"That sounds great, thanks, Joel. I'll now try to find telephone numbers..." and before he could finish his sentence, Joel handed him a note with a name and telephone number.

"This is your contact. He lives in La Rioja and his English is excellent so you won't have a problem when you phone him. Now, one thing to remember about the runway and that is, on the other side of the arterial road there are electrical cables running parallel to it. You will need to get the local electricity and telephone companies to put up orange aerial marker balls, for visibility when landing. You should also get them to put up red lights on top of the poles that support the cables. On this property, you will have to install PAPI lights. Don't look so concerned Chloe, Dick knows what I'm talking about. Everything okay?"

"Yep," Dick retorted and Joel vanished into thin air.

"I wish he wouldn't do that - it's creepy you know," Chloe said "What are PAPI lights?"

"Those are part of the runway light system. It's an acronym for Precision Approach Path Indicator which is a visual guidance system. I'll try my best to explain it in a way you'll understand. Imagine you're coming in to land at night and it's all dark around you. In front of you is the runway and all the lights are on. These will include the Approach Lighting System, Threshold Lights and Touchdown Zone Lights."

"What's all that about?"

"Never mind about that now, I'll explain all in good time. Now PAPI is the lights you first fly over. If you're too high for your touch—down spot, you will have four white lights. This is not dangerous because you could abort, apply full power, go around and try again but, with all these mountains around us, it could be equally dangerous, if not worse. However, if you are too low, you'll have four red lights to warn you and, if you don't pull up, you could bury the nose into the ground. This is not recommended and the pilots could scrape their poor old shins on the dashboard which will make their eyes water and... no, no, no. I'm talking shit now. Sorry, I couldn't resist," Dick apologised, laughing.

"Don't screw with me while I'm desperately trying to understand exactly what it is you're trying to explain to me."

"Sorry dear. Right, so ideally what you are aiming for are two white and two red lights, and you will be on slope, as it's called. Another thing they do is help you keep your wings in a level configuration and..."

Before he could go any further, Chloe interrupted him, which she was superb at doing. "Okay, that's far too much information for my little brain to comprehend in one fell swoop, but thanks for trying anyway."

"You're welcome. Damn, all this is thirsty work—how's your wine?"

"I still have a half a glass left, thanks."

So he poured himself a large one this time and couldn't care. His daughter was not there and, it wasn't because of contempt, but more out of respect for her feelings. Dick appreciated how much she worried about him because of those nasty diseases that had attacked his fragile body. However, once he had put her in the picture, things might be different. He understood better though because neither Kerri nor her husband did drugs, alcohol or nicotine. He was forever grateful—glad his daughter did not lead the same debauched life he once had done.

It had been wonderful though. All the Bierfests he had played at with the Oompah band. All the various pubs with the jazz band, with his best friends Linda Hobart on vocals and her husband, Robert, on piano, and there was the Rock band with all the biker rallies they played at, amongst others. All wonderful stuff and he had no regrets about any of those times. He had once touched on a little weed which made him violently ill. The next day he could not understand what the hell the drug addicts, or anyone, saw in smoking this stuff, so he decided it was not for him. However, this did not stop him from having loads of fun with the pot-heads for they were good guys. How he wished he could re-live those times again.

He picked up the note Joel had given him with the contact details on it and read it. "Listen to this. The chaps' name on here is Felipe Alonso. Mmmm... Now where have we heard names like these before?" he mused, rubbing his chin with his left hand.

"Yes, I wonder. Well I've had enough for one day and besides, its way past my bedtime," she said as she stood up.

"Okay dear. I'll stay down here and pore over this map."

"Yes, and in doing so, no doubt you'll pour more whisky down your throat as well?"

"How did you guess?" Dick grinned at her.

So she made her way upstairs to bed, while he settled down to... pore, or was it pour? He wasn't sure, so to save pondering, he did both.

True to his word, Phil phoned the next morning and told Dick he had confirmed the appointments for Japan in eight days' time, China in ten days' time, and back in the UK two days later. A round trip of five days. He also said, as he wanted to keep things as secret as possible, he did not inform each individual supplier about the others. This, he hoped, would keep industrial espionage at a minimum for he was paranoid with his invention and greedy businessmen. For him, all businessmen were greedy, money-grabbing bastards and back-stabbers to boot. Not that

Dick ever disagreed with this philosophy—quite the reverse, in fact.

Dick asked him to e-mail all the details so he and Chloe could book flights and hotel accommodations. He also said Phil should come to them on the sixth so he could go with them to the factory up North. Thereafter, the two of them could travel together to the airport on the ninth in case something was awry with them travelling up to London on the same day, from different directions, as Phil was six hundred and forty kilometres away.

They ended the call and Dick switched on his laptop, which was in his bedroom, to check his e-mails and see if the info had already come through. It had, so he printed it out and set about looking for flights and accommodation, but before doing this, he unplugged his laptop from the forty-two-inch screen and, unplugging the sound system, keyboard and mouse, together with the battery charger, took the laptop downstairs and put it on the dining room table. Chloe switched on her desktop computer, which they called the dinosaur, and both set about surfing the net.

"Any preference on airlines?" she asked.

"Any of the international ones will do."

"What about hotels?"

"Erm,... why don't you concentrate on the airlines and I'll look up hotels. I'd want to find hotels as close to the businesses as possible and, hopefully, they won't be over-booked."

"Okay, and what days and times are you looking at?"

"I want to fly direct from Heathrow to Tokyo on the ninth of February. Try to get one as early as possible as the flight takes around twelve hours."

"Will do," said Chloe, and they both typed away searching for the required information.

"Here's one, but it only departs at one-thirty in the afternoon and arrives there, local time nine-thirty in the morning, whatever that means."

"If it arrives at nine-thirty and it takes, let's say or let's allow, two hours going through Passport and Custom controls, I suppose it would be all right. Yes, go for it and I'll book the hotel rooms."

"You sure now?" she asked and Dick nodded "Right, I will book them. Shit."

"What?"

"The bloody prices are almost ten thousand pounds each."

"I suppose this time last week I would have told them to stick their seats where the sun don't shine. But, as money is now of no concern, go for it."

Chloe booked the seats and set about booking a flight from Tokyo to China. While sorting through all the flights, she had an idea. "I've thought of something. If money is no object, why don't you hire one of those executive jets to fly you around wherever you need to go?"

"Brilliant. Now why didn't I think of that?"

"Perhaps because you're an idiot?" she teased, and he chuckled and carried on with his search.

So Chloe turned her attention to looking up private executive jets for hire and said "Okay, here's one. It's called 'Executive Aircraft Company' and you're looking at about one hundred thousand-plus pounds for a complete round trip starting and ending at Biggin Hill Airport. Shall I book them?"

"Yes please. Also give them the days, times and places of our meetings so they can advise us of all relevant departure times, but I'm sure they will ask you for that, anyway. Oh, and remember to cancel the other lot, will you?"

"Okay, and as it's Biggin Hill, I can take you guys there if you like - it's not far."

"Yeah, fine by me, and we'll save money on a taxi fare," Dick joked, and they both found it a tad bit funny.

Sometime later they ordered a Chinese takeaway and carried on working while munching away at their food.

Aircraft booked, hotels booked when Dick thought of something important. "Hey, we haven't booked a flight to France yet, have we? You know, for our Airbus appointment tomorrow?"

"No, I don't think we have. Shall I ask that executive compa......?"

This time it was his turn, and before she could finish, he interrupted her (which made a pleasant change) "Excellent idea. It will save all the airport security nonsense. A pity we didn't think about this the other day. We could have used them to fly us to Maitland Airport. Too late now though."

Chloe placed the call and made the arrangements for the following day. "What address am I to give them?"

"Tell them we're going to Airbus. Say we want to fly to Aeroport Toulouse-Blagnac and say to park on the Airbus side. They may have to get permission from the Tower but they'll know what to do."

"Please spell out those frog names for me."

"Give me a minute and I'll write them down for you. It's easier."

As soon as they had finished, Chloe booked a taxi for 9:00 a.m. next morning as they didn't feel like driving themselves to the airport.

"What are you going to wear tomorrow?" she asked.

"Oh, my dark suit, I suppose. Why?"

"You have all this money at your fingertips, right?"

"Right."

"So why do you still insist on wearing those suits you know to be older than your daughter? I mean, why the hell don't you buy a few new ones, for goodness' sake? You could have dressed more appropriately the other day at Maitland Airport, but no, not you. You have to wear all this ancient clothing that looks like crap and besides, with your new body, the suit was ill-fitting and made you look ridiculous," she said giving him the old shifty eyeball.

"Eerrr... oh... I don't know... erm... I'm not bothered. If they don't like what they see, well stuff em is what I say," he said without a hint of embarrassment. For him, his suits were still in great nick for their age as he had always looked after them.

"When last did you try the other one on?"

"Don't know. About four or five years ago, maybe."

"Right, stop messing about. We've still got plenty of time before the shops close and the shopping mall is down the road."

"No, I don't..." Dick began but, mid-sentence Chloe held up her hand ordering him to stop right there. "I won't go with you to France if you don't dress appropriately. Besides, it won't take more than an hour, for shit's sake. Now get your arse into gear and let's go." By the tone in her voice, he decided not to argue and gave in.

Later they were back home with their spoils, but they took much longer than what Chloe had expected, but Dick, though, didn't mind. New suits for him, and shirts, ties and shoes, including an assortment of casual clothing to boot. Chloe didn't do too badly either. Between them they had spent well over five thousand pounds—the suits being the most expensive items – but who cared?

They made their way upstairs to sort out exactly what they would wear for the trip and put aside the clothes they would pack. Afterwards, it was back downstairs to first, pour themselves a much-wanted drink each, before carrying on working.

"You know, the next time we go out, I want to replace this bloody dinosaur," Chloe said with a venomous look at the old desktop computer.

## Chapter Six

## The Airbus meeting

DICK COULD NEVER go anywhere first thing in the morning without having had his breakfast. So, having made an extra-early start, he and Chloe had just finished fifteen minutes before the taxi arrived. At 8:55 a.m. they left for Biggin Hill Airport and the traffic was its usual nightmarish self, so they only arrived at 9:40 a.m. and Dick paid the driver. He asked him for his telephone number for they would want him to come pick them up on their return from France. As he could not give the driver the time of their return flight, he would phone him from France.

At Biggin Hill, Sheila, the company PA, took them through to the office. There, they met the Office Manager and the pilots. After the introductions, she asked if they had any baggage.

"No, just my briefcase," replied Dick.

As departure was at 10:00 a.m., they boarded the plane. The flight was pleasant the likes of which neither of them had ever experienced before. This was the life and they decided it was, without a doubt, the only way to fly.

"Soon you will be in ownership of your own plane and I'm sure it will be even better. What do you say?" Chloe asked him.

"Oh yes, and I can't wait either,"

Chloe cogitated and asked: "If Joel, or whoever it was who gave you this ability to fly any aircraft anywhere in the world, any time of the day or night, why aren't you flying?"

"A great question, and one I cannot answer right now."

"I well remember Joel shitting on your head asking you why you are not using your brain. So why aren't you using it? and make no excuses."

"I'm not making excuses, but I've got so much on my mind at the moment I never even debated it. Right now I'm trying to get all my ducks in a circle which is more than enough to get on with, and as for flying a plane... well you need all your marbles about you... and it's been a long time. It's not the same as just jumping into a car, driving off, and hoping for the best. So... no, I'm not making excuses."

"Ducks in a circle? Don't you mean ducks in a row?"

"No, I'm different. Anti-establishment if you like."

"Oh all right then," Chloe said with a smile "I forgive you."

"Gee thanks," he said with a rueful smile back at her. "Oh there's something I would like you to cast your educated eye over, please. I meant to give these to you before but I forgot." He opened his briefcase, took out his scribblings of different names he had mulled over for the company name, and handed it to her.

As she read through, he heard her muttering 'No' 'No' 'No'. Then there was a soft expletive which got his attention.

"What the hell is this?" she asked in surprise.

"What the hell's what?"

"This," she said pointing at a name in the scrap book.

"What's wrong with it?" he asked nonplussed "It's only the spelling that's incorrect. I mean, most of the bloody kids of today don't have a clue how to spell, anyway. So why not?"

"Why not? Look, man look," she exclaimed "Look at the first letter of each word. Write them down but next to each other, and see what you get." She felt she had to get her point across somehow, but trying not to raise her voice too much.

Dick had no need to write them down because before him, they stood out like a bulldog's balls. The acronym KKK smacked him right in the face. "Oh for five six seven's sake" he moaned, furious with himself for not spotting what he had just read. "Well we can't have that, now can we?"

"Okay – If you have Maitland Airport Services, why don't you have Maitland Electric Car Manufacturers?" she now suggested.

"Yep, I can live with that," he replied feeling relieved "I had an inkling you would come up with something."

"Yeah – and I wish you would come up with something," she chuckled to herself. "Mmmm... and you're the one with extra brain power," she said, giving him a naughty smile which made him smile.

As they had finished their hot drinks on the flight, Helen served a light lunch which was delicious. Local time in France was one hour ahead of England. So they were due to arrive at their destination at around 1:30 p.m. and their appointment at Airbus was for 2:00 p.m., perfect timing.

Dead on time they arrived at the French airport where the pilots received clearance to park at the Airbus facilities. This made things much easier for them, so before an Airbus representative met them, Chloe gave Dick an appraising look and said "You look so much better in your new attire. It wouldn't surprise me if some Frog girls made passes at you."

"Oh yeah right. This I've got to see."

"Perhaps I should inform them of your new appendage?"

"No, don't you dare," he replied smiling.

The onboard hostess opened the door for them to disembark. They both thanked her and Dick said "We'll see you in a few hours, I guess. I forgot to ask you your name."

"It's Helen, Mr Shepherd."

"Thanks, Helen. Listen, I'm apologising in advance but I have no idea how long we'll be. If they don't like us, we'll see you in five minutes, but if they do—who knows."

"That's not a problem, Mr Shepherd. Please go ahead and we'll be here whenever you are ready. Good luck with your meeting."

"Thanks again Helen. See you later."

There was a lovely young blond-haired girl at the foot of the stairs who, as they descended, greeted them with a warm smile. She addressed them in English, but with a charming French accent.

"Bonjour," she said "and welcome to Airbus. Please come with me." They followed her to a large building and she took them up in an elevator. They got out at a rather posh waiting room where she offered them tea or coffee. "I'll come back in ten minutes to take you to the Boardroom. Monsieur Bardot and some of his Executive Committee members will wait for you."

Dick wondered if Monsieur Bardot was any relation to the very famous actress Brigitte Bardot.

When she returned, she led them through a door and down a long passageway. They arrived at the reception where she pushed a button on the wall and a lift door opened. They travelled up two stories where they got out, turned left, and walked a few steps down another passageway, stopping in front of a huge set of double doors. She knocked, opened one of them and walked inside with the two of them right behind her.

"Gentlemen, here are Mrs Fraser-Rigby and Mr Shepherd."

After the introductions, they sat at the huge boardroom table. François Bardot, the CEO, started by thanking them for being there and enquired how they could be of service.

"Gentlemen," Dick said standing up surveying them, "thank you so much for seeing us at such short notice. If it's okay with you, I will come straight to the point, but before I do so, I need you to understand one thing. Money is of no concern so, please bear that in mind when I tell you the reason we are here is to purchase four A400M transporters,... plus a simulator to go with them."

He sat back down to a stunned silence, during which all the executives looked at one another, but showed no emotion.

"Well this is not at all what we expected," said M. Bardot. "If we are able to supply these, when would you like delivery?" he asked, to see what sort of response he would get.

"I understand you have had teething problems in the past with your production of these aircraft and, although I stand corrected, there may have been cancellations. If so, I was wondering if you would, by any chance, have any back-orders already in production but where the actual buyer has pulled out of the deal, therefore, would they be available and how soon and for how much?"

"Gentlemen," James Leigh the COO addressed his colleagues. "As you all well aware, we received an order from one of the Southern African countries and they cancelled their order for five aircraft. Mr Shepherd also appears to be aware of this, so why don't we let him look at those aircraft?"

"Look," Dick interrupted "I don't expect you to roll them out onto the tarmac for inspection, although it would be nice, but if you could turn them around in, let's say a year, that would suit our requirements."

"They are all more-or-less at the same stage of production," said James Leigh. "I'm sure they will suit Mr Shepherd's requirements and another year would be more than enough time in which to complete them. That," he said turning to Dick, "includes a simulator."

The scene now set, soon a full-blown discussion was on the go. They all spoke to each other, opposite each other, next to each other, it didn't stop. As it was all in French, Dick and Chloe just sat back and waited to hear the results.

Dick reflected beforehand he may well have struck pay dirt when François Bardot turned to him. "My apologies for all the talk in French and for something I overlooked. The thing is we have had other enquiries regarding these aircraft. You understand that I have to give them some consideration before making any final decision."

"Hang on a minute. Remember I said money is of no object here. As I find the aircraft to be suitable, you can name your price and I'll hand over my debit or credit card to you right now. If it doesn't suit you, I'll make out a bank draft, or however you want the money paid.  Your call. Say how much you want up front even if it's the full amount.  If you do, it must also include delivery of the aircraft to an airfield in England and installation of the simulator there."

Once again there was a moment's silence before Karl Estéve, the Chief Procurement Officer, popped a question. "If I may ask but where is this airfield in England? Not that it's important but it might influence the price?"

"You, gentlemen," said Chloe "might be familiar with the place. It's Maitland Airport."

"Oh yes, we are familiar with the airport. We have exhibited aircraft there in the past," said James Leigh.

"Good, for Dick and I are now the new owners and the papers are being drawn up as we speak. As soon as we return to England, we will sign the final documents. But, in principle, we are the new owners. Deon DuToit, whom you may or may not have met, will continue to run the place for us."

"Yes, we have met him but what about Steve Smith?" enquired

François Bardot.

"Steve was glad to sell," Dick replied, "He's thrilled to be on early retirement."

"Ahhhhh,... early retirement, eh" Martyn Callejon, President of Production, said grinning.

Once again an in-depth discussion took place. As this was on the go, the secretary opened the door for another lady to enter who pushed a trolley which contained tea or coffee dispensers and also included light snacks.

"Would anyone like anything stronger?" James Leigh asked "Chloe, Dick, would you prefer a glass of wine or beer...?"

"Thanks very much but when doing business, gentlemen, I make it a rule not to drink alcohol until all proceedings are over, so I will stick to having tea. Sorry, Chloe, I suppose I speak for myself but if you want a glass of wine, please feel free."

"No thanks. I'll have tea."

They sipped their hot drinks and had something to nibble on. The discussions continued and Hans Weimar, the CFO, got up from his chair and said "Please excuse me for a moment. I'm just going to go do some sums and we can discuss the figure I come to for your approval—assuming the sale will go ahead."

Although he was addressing Dick and Chloe when he asked, he

looked towards both François Bardot and James Leigh. They both agreed he should first come back with the numbers before they continued. Hans later returned and handed his summary to François and James for them to scrutinise.

"May I have your attention please," François announced. "Hans has given me a figure James and I agree with. So, if Chloe and Dick are also happy, I think we may have a deal. For the supply and delivery of four A400M transporters, plus the installation of one simulator, the amount we have agreed upon is nine hundred and forty-five million eight hundred and eight thousand six hundred Euros." He jotted the numbers down on a piece of paper which he handed to Dick and Chloe.

"That sounds like a fair enough price. Any discount for cash?" Dick asked which made them all laugh and which seemed to relax the tone.

"Hey, but wait a minute," Dick continued "You said you had five aircraft available. What about the fifth one? If we decide we want this one and you are prepared to include it in the deal, any further discount?" he asked again and this time they chuckled.

"You're serious about this aren't you?" James asked him.

"You're damn right I am. We'll take it if the price is right."

Once again Hans stood up and made his way to the door. "I'll be back with an update," he said and hurried out of the Boardroom.

"How would you like the payment made?" Dick now popped the question for all to consider. "I'm prepared to give you the total payment right now and I assure you, there won't be any problem. Use one of my cards and we'll stay here until your bank has confirmed the money transfer... simple."

Hans returned, handed the update to François who announced "The new amount for supplying all five aircraft is one thousand one hundred and sixty-eight million three hundred and fifty-one thousand eight hundred Euros. However, although you were joking, Hans has suggested we round the figure off by giving you a discount of three million three hundred and fifty-one thousand eight hundred Euros. This brings our price to one thousand one hundred and sixty-five million Euros. If you will accept this, we can shake hands and draw up the paperwork."

"That's wonderful," Dick said pleased.

So they stood up and shook hands with François, and then with all the others. "Okay,... now I have to ask once again. How would you like the payment made?"

Hans Weimar was, by now, in the picture and suggested "Well, let's try the credit card and see what happens, Ja?"

Dick took out his wallet and handed over the card mimicking Hans by also saying "Ja."

Hans once again left the room but returned and asked "Forgive me but to what company name should I make out the receipt?"

"Mmmm... make it Maitland Airport Services please," Chloe told him.

While Hans was out the room, more talking was going on and "So what are you going to use the aircraft for?" Karl ask Chloe.

"I think you better ask Dick" she replied and with her usual excellent knack in the art of interrupting Dick, she did. "Karl asked what you going to use the aircraft for?"

"We have a new car manufacturing business venture on the go. Soon, you will accept it because – and don't laugh – it will revolutionise the world. As I will move a lot of the product around the world, these aircraft suite this purpose and yes, I said the world," he added as he encountered several sceptical looks.

"I decided it would be, if not cheaper, easier to use my own mode of transport rather than relying on any freight airline companies for certain deliveries. Believe it or not, the idea came from you and that's why we are here."

"From us?" asked Martin confused.

"Yes. When looking for transporter aircraft, I noticed your company saves time and money by moving your own pre-built aircraft around from factory-to-factory in a... is it the Beluga aircraft?"

"Yes, it is," replied Karl.

"Once I saw the Beluga, I investigated your company more. That's when I found the A400M which I found impressive and that's why we are here today. So there you have it."

Dick lied to them for it had been Joel who suggested the A400M, but he didn't care for they were none the wiser and it was none of their business.

Hans returned with copies of the transactions, including other paperwork, and informed everyone the money transfer was complete. He handed the receipt over to Chloe and said it was the quickest money transfer he had ever witnessed.

"Congratulations," Hans said to Dick and Chloe "you are now the proud owners of five brand new uncompleted A400Ms plus one brand new simulator, which we still have to install." Dick wondered if this was Hans's German attempt at humour as they all, once again, shook hands.

"Gentlemen, I said this when we were first introduced but please allow me to say it once again. Thank you for allowing us to impose upon you at such short notice and thank you for selling your lovely aircraft to us. If there are no further questions or paperwork to sign, I think Chloe and I should be on our way. We still have a lot to get through before the sun rises tomorrow morning."

"Ah yes," Martyn asked "when would you like us to deliver and install the simulator?"

"Good question. I will be away in the Far East for a while, so I would say not before the fifteenth of this month. Any time which suits you after that would be more than fine."

"Okay,... why don't we settle on the twentieth of this month?" asked Martyn.

"For me that's perfect. It also affords me a little extra time to plan the installation area at the airport. I'll inform Deon tomorrow and please mark the delivery for his attention. When the installers arrive, they must also ask for him as I will want him to oversee the installation."

"We will take care of that for you, and good luck with your venture," said Martyn.

Dick put his hand in the inside left-hand pocket of his jacket and retrieved business cards which he handed out to them. "My apologies. Our new stationery and cards are being printed so this card is the only one I have on me at the moment. It's the one I used for the band I used to be in. Still, the main thing is they have all my pertinent contact details on them should you want to get in touch."

"Would you mind asking your secretary to phone our pilots informing them we are on our way?" Chloe asked Martyn.

As he was the closest to the door he obliged. "I'll get her to contact them right away."

"Gentlemen, until we meet again, I bid you Au revoir," Dick said trying out his best French accent.

"Dick, you speak French," François laughed.

"Si, Si 'señor,"

"Oh please don't get him started? He only knows a few words in a few languages. If we carry on, we'll be here all bloody night," Chloe said, at which they all chuckled, shook hands and said goodbye.

The nice young secretary arrived, and when the last farewells were said, she showed them the way to their awaiting aircraft. They thanked her and shook hands with her before mounted the stairs. Once onboard they said hello to Helen and asked her to convey their apologies to the pilots for having taken so long.

Helen replied saying although she would, it wasn't necessary as it was all part of the service. She added, "As it has taken quite a long time, I take it your venture was a success?"

Dick and Chloe replied in unison "Very successful thank you."

"Do you think I can make a quick phone call to book a taxi before we take off?"

"Yes you can, Mr Shepherd. Please use our onboard phone over there," Helen replied pointing to a phone affixed to the side of a cabinet.

"Please call me Dick."

"Thanks, Mr Shepherd but company policy does not allow me to."

"Understood," he acknowledged and called the taxi.

"Now can I offer you two busy bees anything to eat or drink?" Helen asked when he returned.

"That's kind of you. Please may I have a large glass of white wine? Sauvignon Blanc would be nice," Chloe jumped in first.

"I'll have a whisky and water please,... with a few blocks of ice."

Their drinks served, Helen said "Once we're airborne, I'll bring you a menu as I'm sure you must be famished by now."

"He's always famished. Even when his stomach is full, he's famished. He's a bloody eating machine is this one," Chloe said to her and she and Helen giggled.

They sat back to enjoy the flight. Dick said to Chloe they had forgotten to ask the nice young lady, who met them at the airport, what her name was.

"Shall I find out for you?"

"No, don't be silly," he replied, and Chloe beamed at him.

Helen served a wonderful three-course meal, including a few more drinks, before arriving back at Biggin Hill Airport.

"I'll see you in a few days' time," Helen remarked as they said their goodbyes.

Their taxi was waiting, and they arrived home just after 10:00 p.m. that evening. By this time they were both exhausted though still on a high at their success. Dick said they should have one more drink before retiring for the night so, sipping their drinks, they pored over some finer points which had transpired during the day.

"I've just remembered. At the time I said nothing but why didn't you ask them not to install the jet engines in the aeroplanes?" asked Chloe.

"Well done on noticing and not saying anything. When I sat down, I thought about it and decided not to go to the lengths of explaining about engine replacements for fear of a rejected order. In this case, it would be best to leave well enough alone. In any event, we might need to use the turbo-props if Phil's motors are not ready, although I don't foresee that happening."

"What time is our appointment for?"

"One o'clock tomorrow afternoon."

"And what time must we leave here? I take it we are going in our own car? What I can't get to grips with, we've got all this bloody money and like your clothes, you're still driving that piece of crap," she teased with a hint of laughter in her voice.

"Hey, hang on there. Since when has EMO let us down?"- the letters being the first part of those on the number plate. "Besides, as with my clothes which were, as you pointed out, more important, I haven't had time to look for another car. So while it still works, I'll use it."

"Oh, whatever,"

"Allowing for the traffic, we should leave here no later than eleven o'clock in the morning."

"Well on that note, I'm taking my drink to bed with me as I want to get my act together for tomorrow and besides, it's......"

Before she could finish, Dick saw a golden opportunity to once again repay her by interrupting... "Yes,—it's way past your bedtime."

"Exactly" she said, kissing him on his cheek. "Good night, dear."

As she was walking towards the stairs, he called to her. "Please remind me to phone Deon tomorrow before we go. I need to tell him about the simulator."

"Okay, Mr Brainy. Don't forget to phone Deon tomorrow,"

"Ohhhhh... piss off will you."

He could hear her giggling as she negotiated the stairs in the dark, trying ever so hard not to spill her drink. He downed his drink as he wanted to have another one before he too hit the sack. So at the dining room table, he jots down notes for the next day's meeting with BAE Systems.

Now due to the fact his Dad had flown Wellington Bombers during the Second World War, he hoped BAE could execute his order for him. The Wellington Bomber, designed and built by Vickers-Armstrongs Ltd they, along with many other well-known names, closed by various mergers which took place over the years.

The start of the mergers came about by none other than the Government and had ended up with BAE Systems as they are today. Therefore, if he could do a deal between them, it would please him no end because it would mean an indirect link with both his Dad and the VC10.

As usual, he was up bright and early. After seeing to his ablutions, he made his way downstairs to make breakfast and it wasn't long before Chloe joined him in front of the TV to watch the world news as they munched away.

"I see the Government have at long last come to their senses. They cancelled the Knighthood they gave to that bloody Zimbabwean dictator," Chloe announced.

"And about bloody time too. They had no reason to have given it to Bob McGabe,... damn fools," Dick retorted "and I'm glad the Zimbabwean people have come to their senses too for they've kicked the old fart out of office."

When they had cooled down after hearing the news, Chloe asked: "So what time did you say we were leaving today?"

"I think we should leave no later than eleven-fifteen."

"Why so early?"

"I'm worried about the traffic for it sometimes becomes a bloody nightmare. Besides, I hate being late for anything."

This afforded them two hours to get dressed and to sort out what to take with them. Dick looked at his notes and noticed he had written a reminder to himself. He picked up the phone and dialled the number and the pleasant voice of the lady on the switchboard greeted him, saying "Good morning, Maitland Airport. How may I help you?"

Dick pleased with this for he remembered how, in the past, his experiences with other receptionists had been far from polite. "Hello, may I speak to Mr Deon DuToit please?"

"I'll put you through."

Dick spoke to Deon about the Airbus simulator with delivery expected on the twentieth of the month. He instructed him to find the best spot for it and to allow enough room for a second one.

"Who were you on the phone with?" Chloe asked him as she walked into the lounge.

"I've just spoken to Deon about the delivery of the simulator."

"Oh, yeah. You asked me to give you a reminder, didn't you?" she said with a wry smile. "Sorry."

"Yes, and because of your Tom-foolery last night you also forgot about our time of departure this morning. But never mind, Mr Brainy over here didn't."

"Sorry," she said again as she turned around and made her way back upstairs.

"Before we go, don't forget the Satnav," she shouted down to him.

"I've got it, thanks."

As she came back downstairs, she said: "Okay, I'm ready when you are."

"Oh yes," he said, hinting with sexual overtones.

"In your dreams buster,"

"Blast," he exclaimed funny "What a come-down. I suppose I must visit Mrs Brown then."

"Mrs Brown? Who the hell is Mrs Brown?"

"I believe she has five lovely daughters," he replied, laughing at her.

128

"Ohhhhh... stop being so bloody stupid, will you? It's far too early for that."

"It's never too early,"

She glared at him as she couldn't think of a fitting reply.

They gathered up their things, along with a bottle of Spring water, locked the house, and walked the short distance across the backyard to the garage. When Chloe opened the main garage door from the inside, Dick gave the car a quick once-over. After inspecting it, he decided Chloe had been right and it was perhaps time to do a trade-in.

But what to buy or not to buy? Now that was the question.

Chapter Seven

The BAE meeting

THE FIRST PART of the motorway the traffic wasn't at all bad, but when approaching the Farnborough off-ramp, things took an ugly turn as there was a huge traffic jam.

"Just as well you left earlier," said Chloe.

"Well, these days it pays to do so, what with all these boneheads on the roads, you can't take chances any more."

Arriving at their destination with only five minutes to spare, the young lady behind the reception desk greeted them with a big smile on her face.

"Mmmm... she reminds me of the weather announcer on the television. The one I refer to as Miss Smiley," Dick whispered in Chloe's ear.

They approached the receptionist and introduced themselves. "I'll phone Mr Kingsley's secretary."

"Thanks so much," said Chloe, and they both turned away to look out of the huge window which protected them from the elements.

It didn't take long before they heard the voice of the secretary. "Hello, I'm Gina, Mr Kingsley's Personal Assistant. Please follow me and I'll take you to the Boardroom."

Gina led them to the lifts and took them up to the third floor where they followed her down a short passage. She stopped outside a door, knocked and walked in. There was only one person in the room, whom Gina introduced as Mr Ivan Kingsley, the Chief Executive Officer. They all shook hands and three other people walked into the room. Gina introduced them as well - James Denham, President and CEO of BAE Systems. Nicholas Wharton, the group MD of Program Support, and Perry Lynden, the Group Financial Director

"I will chair this meeting today," said Ivan Kingsley. "So how may we help you?"

Dick started out similar as he had done at the Airbus meeting. "Gentlemen, you'll wonder at what I'm about to ask you be ludicrous, however, I will ask you to please not dwell on the matter for too long for if you cannot oblige, we will need to know as soon as so we waste no more time. This way, I can approach another aircraft manufacturing company."

"Before I go any further, please let me assure you money does not come into the equation. Should you be in a position to supply what we require, I don't expect you to rip us off either.

The first thing we need to establish is if you still manufacture aircraft, and if so, where?"

"Yes, we do," replied Mr Kingsley. "Although our suppliers are scattered around the world, they are not too far afield."

"Good. In that case, would you by any chance still have the plans for the Super VC10?"

There was a stunned silence. "The Super VC10," Ivan Kingsley said in amazement "Now there's an aircraft not spoken about since the Air Force grounded their fleet. Sorry, but I can't say if we do. Can anyone here?" he asked the others.

"Not to my knowledge," James Denham replied, as did the other two.

"That's a bugger. Is there perhaps anyone in your organisation who may know? One can often find someone who's been with the company for years on end, and although he or she has never climbed the ladder too far they do, however, have more knowledge about things everyone else has long forgotten. Surely you must have someone like this?"

There was silence as they mulled over the matter. "Wait a minute," Nicholas Wharton exclaimed, "Lyris might know if we have such a person." He turned to Dick and Chloe to explain "Lyris Milton is our Human Resources Director. If you'll excuse me for a moment, I'll ask her to find out," he said and got up and left the room.

"Mr Shepherd, what is it you want should we have these plans?" asked Mr Kingsley.

"Please call me Dick, and this is Chloe."

"Thanks very much. My name is Ivan and these two gentlemen are James and Perry," nodding in their direction.

"Thank you," Dick continued. "Now that the formalities are out of the way, I'll carry on with the ludicrous part I mentioned at the start. What I want you to do is to build five new aircraft based on the original design concept, meaning the outside cannot change."

"However, the inside must be by today's standards. The cockpit must have state-of-the-art avionics, along with all wiring, pipework etcetera. So before I go any further with what I want and how I want it, if you have the plans, can you do it?" Dick asked of a semi-stunned three gentlemen.

"Yes," Ivan replied without hesitation. "With the plans and money, anything is possible."

"Wonderful," Dick replied feeling more assured. "All things being equal, how long would it take to build and supply these aircraft? For me, I would like it to be as soon as possible without sacrificing quality."

"A fair estimate would be the closest we could give you at the moment," James informed them.

"Mmmm... okay," Dick mused "What do you classify as being a fair estimate?"

"I would say nothing earlier than four years," James replied, "but miracles have happened."

"They have, and for me, four years is fair enough, however, should you pull a rabbit out of a hat, even better. You know, like... two years. Remember what I said 'Money is no object'" he reassured them.

"As Nicolas has not returned, would you still wish to carry on with the project with the assumption we have plans?" James asked them.

"Well I don't foresee a problem," Chloe said with a smile on her face. "If you don't have the plans, then you've been told a wonderful story."

Laughter filled the room, which helped to create an even better atmosphere. Dick explained to them about his Dad, the Wellington Bomber, the connection between two, and the Vickers Super VC10. He also explained about how he had fallen in love with the aeroplane as so many others around the world had done.

"You know, it angered me when those bloody terrorists blew up the plane on the apron at... mmmm," Dick cogitated. He couldn't for the moment put his finger on the name of the place.

Ivan came to his aid. "Oh yes, I remember the incident well. It was on the runway at Dawson's Field in Jordan in September 1970. They blew it up as it stood there."

"That's it. That's the one, and I was pissed off with those bastards. I'm sorry, I seem to have digressed. Okay, as I've said, I want the outside design to be that of the original Super VC10 version of the plane but the cabin, and especially the cockpit, must be by today's standards. The only reservation I have about the cockpit is I want to keep the design of the allegro type steering wheel column. I don't want the type used in modern day aircraft. It's called a side stick, correct?"

"Yes, correct. It's called a side stick."

"Thanks, James. Also, I want the cockpit area to be a little bigger with sleeping quarters behind it, however, all those interior designs will come as and when required. Yes, I could go to other companies who make large private jets today and buy them off the shelf, but there's one major flaw. None of them are VC10s."

He now noticed he had their full attention. "If you have the plans, do you or I have to get permission? I mean from any one person or from any other organisation or company in order for us to have these aircraft built?"

They looked at each other for an answer. It was James who broke the nanosecond of silence to say, "If we have the plans, no we don't have to seek permission from anyone because we will hold the full rights. So no problem there."

Dick breathed a sigh of relief as getting permission could well take a good while, but now he worried in case there were no plans and it would take ages to produce new ones. He was so wishing Joel could be there to hold his hand. "Don't be so damn stupid. Think positively and there won't be a problem," he said to himself.

When the door opened, he believed it to be Nicolas returning with an answer. However it was Gina again, and she was pushing a similar trolley as the one they had used at the Airbus meeting. She offered them tea or coffee and placed plates of biscuits on the table. While she did the pouring, everyone at the table muttered to one another. Once finished, she left the room.

"What type of material do you foresee us using to build the aircraft?" Ivan asked Dick as they were having their refreshments.

"Now that's a good question," Dick said but before he could carry on, the door opened again. He turned his attention towards the door as Nicholas entered with a medium sized gentleman who had loads of wrinkles on his face. He also walked as an old man, giving his physical aspect of being bent forward. Dick understood how this felt for he had been there himself not so long ago.

"This is Patric Butland, one of our Production Managers who's been with the company for many years."

Before he could carry on, Ivan spoke, "That's right. Patric was with the company before I even left school," he said to light approving laughter from the others.

"Sorry I was so long but I took quite a while to find him," Nicholas informed them. "Lyris sent me to one person who sent me to another person who led me to Patric."

Dick found it hard to contain himself for he noticed Patric was pulling a trolley behind him, the type used for carrying goods in boxes which might be too uncomfortable to carry in one's arms. There were a few boxes on the trolley and Dick got up and walked across to Patric to shake his hand.

"I apologise gentlemen," Dick said, not caring about his actions. "I don't want to appear to be presumptions but, if these boxes contain what I think they do, well, I'm more than excited at the moment."

Nicholas now addressed Dick "I feel I must fill you and Chloe in what's going on. The rest of you may also not know of the fact that when Patric's retirement became immanent, he approached Management to see whether he could stay on. So as you can see, we kept our man. This is most fortunate as he is the only one who stayed on after the last takeover and who is still with us. He is now the last person within the entire company who had any dealings with the VC10."

"In fact, he cut his teeth on them as a successful apprentice within the company. When he found out there would be a merger, Patric was telling me he took it upon himself to make copies of the last remaining plans. He did this in case the company destroyed the originals, and guess what?" Nicholas asked the curious faces looking at him "The company destroyed them." There was a look of amazement from all present.

"So with us in this room," he continued "we may well have a person to be better than Nostradamus himself. Who could have foreseen we might need these plans again?"

As he spoke, he pointed at the boxes on the trolley, looked up into Dick's eyes, and turned to look at his colleagues for approval.

"Fantastic," said a relieved Dick, "I think Patric deserves a large bonus for that."

"Whatever possessed you to do this?" James asked Patric.

Patric had a deep resonant voice whose tone was strong and positive. By this, they realised he was a well-educated and knowledgeable person.

"When I started here as an apprentice working on the VC10s, I often wondered what it would be like to own my aircraft, but as the years went by, I realised this was never likely to happen. That's when I came up with, what I call, a pretend plan. I would own my aircraft in my head. So I buried it in my imagination where it would be with me forever," he said with a smile and continued.

"The day came when the Company announced they no longer required anything regarding these wonderful aircraft anymore, and because I was not prepared to take any chances, over a full weekend I made copies of the plans as I would not allow my aircraft to die. For me, it was still far too young to have that happen to it," Patric said with utter conviction.

"I know this sounds like it's coming out of the mouth of a madman," Patric continued "but I had to live out my fantasies. Besides, it's kept me going all of my working life. May I inquire why you need these plans?" he asked, in case he might never see them again.

"Before we get there Patric, I have to know why on earth you never took them home with you?" asked Ivan.

"Take them home with me?" Patric replied dumbfounded "That would be stealing. No no no... these plans belong here, with the company. That's one reason I wanted to stay on. It's not only because I love what I do these days, even though I'm tied to a desk, it's because I felt I had a duty to look after these plans and documents because nobody else seemed to care."

"Well Patric, if ever there were anyone more grateful for your actions, I can assure you it's me," Dick said with a huge grin. He shook Patric's hand once more.

"Well, that throws a whole new light on the subject. Shall I explain to Patric why we need these plans and why we are so excited we have them?" asked Ivan.

"Yes," was the consensus.

Ivan continued. "Patric," he said "Dick and Chloe are potential customers who want us to build five Super VC10s for them."

Upon hearing this news, Patric's entire face lit up like one gigantic neon sign. If his smile had grown any bigger, it would have disappeared behind his head. "I hope you don't mind but may I please give both of you a hug?"

Chloe stood up. "Oh go on then," she replied and held out her arms to him.

Dick also stood up to await his turn for a hug. He could not get out of his head the idea of another person on the planet who shared his great love for this aircraft and found his respect for the man grew even more.

"I now know why God has put me on this planet and for what purpose," Patric announced, moved.

"Yes, and you'll be able to play out your fantasy in two years' time," Dick was quick to respond.

"Gentleman," Dick once more addressed the team "I know Patric is not on your executive team so, because he is the only one left in your company with experience regarding these aircraft, you consider making him part of the production team? Assuming we are all agreed to going ahead with the project."

"I sure would appreciate it because it would be an honour to have such a dedicated and devoted person working alongside the younger people of today. You never know, Patric might be able to teach the rest of the team a thing or two," Dick said looking at Patric, at which they all chuckled.

"No question about it," Ivan said without hesitation. "If Patric is up for the challenge... yes." He now addressed his colleagues "All in favour raise your hands."

All hands went up. "As you can see, Patric, the vote is unanimous. Now whether you want to either accept or reject it, the decision is up to you," Ivan said to him.

"Rejection has never been part of my vocabulary," Patric said still sporting a huge beam on his face, "especially with my aeroplane."

"You know, I don't think I've ever seen anyone hold such a joyful smile for so long,... ever," said Perry grinning.

"Yes, and should this go ahead," Patric replied, "I'll be ecstatic for the rest of my life."

They all smiled.

"Well you'd better practise, Patric, for I can assure you the build will go ahead," Chloe said and Dick nodded his head in approval, clapping his hands and the rest followed suit.

"I know I shouldn't have to ask this but, to satisfy all, what sort of condition are the plans in?" James asked him once they had all settled down.

"A good question, Mr Denham, but they are in almost mint condition, and if you don't mind my saying so, it's because these are my babies."

"If you are on the team, Patric, you had better call me James. You are welcome to call us by our first names, and I speak on behalf of everyone."

Before anyone else could say a word, Dick said he was in total agreement. He hated the ridiculous formalities associated with the corporate world—a world he felt he could do without, but he if he wanted all the lovely aircraft he so desired, there would be times when he would have to deal with it.

Gina popped her head in, and Ivan gave her the signal to speak. "Sorry to interrupt. May I organise more tea or coffee?"

"Yes please," Ivan acknowledged on behalf of everyone. She later returned wheeling the trolley and dispensed the drinks.

"Now we know the plans are in perfect condition, do you think this will affect any production time?" Ivan asked the team.

"That's something we must work out," James replied "although I don't think this is the right time to do so. What I think we should concentrate on first is to talk to Dick and Chloe further about what they want of the aircraft. Would you mind?"

"No, not at all," Dick replied "I don't mind. Errmmm... where would you like to start, inside or out?"

"Well, why don't we start with the outside?" Nicolas suggested. "A good enough place to start and I think I'll get Gina to take down the notes." He went out of the room only to return a short while later followed by Gina with a notepad and pen in hand.

Dick continued "Nothing is to change on the outside. The overall appearance must be the same. If you find it necessary to make any changes, you must clear it with Patric first," he added and Patric smiled his thanks.

"However, I want to know if it's at all a viable proposition to have raked wingtips or winglets fitted. I would ask your design team to look at that. If there has to be a dramatic change for whatever reason to accommodate the added extras, forget it. I'll stick to the original design."

"Now, what I want is four commercial type aircraft with an optimum maximum capacity of one hundred and thirty-four seats. However, we could reduce this depending on the final interior design we come up with. I think I will need to work with your design team on that. I also want the probe-and-drogue system installed for in-flight refuelling."

"The fifth aircraft is to be a refuelling air tanker, but I only require the one centre refuelling pod. Nothing on the wings. For obvious reasons, I won't require the probe-and-drogue system on this one and, for the moment, I think we must install a minimum of thirty-eight seats in this one, or as much the design team think would be practical," Dick informed them and proceeded.

"I would like to use lightweight and high durability composite and advanced aluminium alloys. Now regarding the wings. Because of problems with rust on the originals, I want you to use carbon fibre epoxy composites and titanium graphite laminate. Whereas, regarding the airframe, I want you to use composite materials. Oh yes, I would also like you to please strengthen the floor."

"Right, now remember," Dick continued "one of the big airliners built using composite materials for their airframe, they did this to allow a twenty percent more fuel efficient frame than its predecessor. I want us to please also aim for that goal, therefore, I must add the final product must be at least ten percent overall more efficient than the original Super VC10 and with today's materials and light-weight avionics this, I'm sure, is more than possible to achieve." Heads nodded in agreement all around the table.

"Now we get to the cockpit. For obvious reasons, the avionics must be up-to-date state-of-the-art equipment but, I want the original control column and no side-stick and we will have to design around it. Also, and again as I stated earlier, I want the overall cockpit area to be bigger. I think it can be increased in size because the old avionics took up so much more space as compared to what its modern day equivalent does. You've noticed how big I am, so every little helps... as the actress said to the bishop," Dick said, creating a few smiles.

"Oooo yes, I know," Chloe added and blushed.

"Steady madam," Dick said turning to smile at her. He continued "Also in the cockpit, I want the four-seat configuration allowing for supernumerary seats. Two, or even three, if possible."

"A what?" Chloe asked in amazement.

"It's an extra fold away type seat. Nothing fancy."

"Who will sit on those?" she asked.

"Anybody."

Upon hearing this, Patric raised his hand. "I'll be that anybody person for I don't mind getting a numb bum," he said, which made them chuckle once more.

"Another thing you may recall I mentioned earlier was, I want a rest area behind the cockpit. This must be big enough to accommodate someone of my size, but we'll get there when we sit down for final briefings."

"Oh I forgot. I would like updated versions of the Rolls Royce Conway turbo-fans, or whatever Rolls Royce can replace them with. However, I would like them to be near fifteen percent lighter and fifteen percent more fuel efficient thus increasing the range by about fifteen percent. If you achieve this, we should look at current figures of, empty weight of around one hundred and fifty-one thousand pounds. So, if we achieve the efficiency goal, the current weight should reduce to around one hundred and thirty-eight thousand pounds."

Gina was scribbling while the others were giving Dick their undivided attention.

"The engine's output power was around twenty-one-odd thousand pounds of thrust. The new ones, therefore, should put out around twenty-four to twenty-five thousand pounds, if not more. Next, and for now, about the ICAO codes. I'd like the call signs of each aircraft to be Kerri one-zero-one, Kerri two-zero-two etcetera but we can always cross that bridge when we get there," Dick informed them, spelling out Kerri for Gina's benefit.

Dick took a sip of his tea, which was by now lukewarm, but he didn't mind. "Is there anything else you require from us right now or have you got enough to start with?"

"I think we may have enough to plan the processes, however, there is a small matter regarding payment," Perry put in.

"The money side of things is no problem at all. Should you want a down payment now, no problem. Should you want the entire amount now, still no problem. The ball's in your court to play with. Also, what I've done is I've drafted a basic contract which I'm sure your Legal Department will put this into a proper form and I will have my attorneys go through everything before we reach a final agreement. Now, how would you like to have payment and how much would you like up front?"

"We'd have to do a proper costing on this but does anyone have an inkling what each unit might cost?" Ivan asked to his colleagues.

"As you say," Ivan said as he looked in Chloe's and Dick's direction "we must sit down and work this out. But if I were to hazard a guess, I'd say we'll be looking at around a hundred million plus per aircraft."

"Right, so let's say we give you a down payment of, errmmm... two hundred and fifty million pounds to get the ball rolling. Is that enough or would you prefer more?"

They looked at each other for approval of the amount. "I'm sure it will be enough for us to get on with," said Perry. "Once we've done the costing, I can let you know. If we need more, you can send us the balance."

Dick looked at Chloe who nodded and he said: "Yes, that's fine with us."

"How would you like to make payment?" Perry now asked Dick "Would you like to use a debit or credit card? Or would you prefer to use a bank draft?"

"I don't have a chequebook or bank draft on me. Would a credit card suffice?"

"That would be fine," Perry said and Dick took out his wallet and handed over the credit card. "Make the receipt out to Maitland Airport Services please," said Chloe.

"Will do," Perry replied as he left the room.

"Maitland Airport Services you say," James said looking at Chloe.

"Yes, Dick and I are the new owners. We are just waiting to sign the final papers, but yes... we are the new owners."

"We've held a lot of static displays there," James informed them "for potential buyers when they've held their annual air show. What's happened to...?"

James hesitated and Chloe stepped in saying "Steve Smith? He's now retired and Deon DuToit is running the place for us."

"Which reminds me," Dick said as he interjected "I forgot to ask you to include delivery of the aircraft to the airport. Damn," he now exclaimed "I also forgot to ask you to build and install a simulator. Is it possible to do this for us, please?"

"Yes, we can," James replied. "When we do the correct costing, we'll add it in and you'll be able to pick it up from the itemization on the quotation sheet."

"Thank you. I appreciate that."

The door opened and Perry came in, walked over, sat down and handed Chloe a sheet of paper. Clipped to it was a printed receipt from a cash point machine. "It's all gone through. I've never handled such a large transaction being transferred so by credit card before. Amazing," he said.

"Well, you've not been using the right bank," Chloe said causing them to grin.

"Now what I suggest," Dick said "as I'll be in the Far East for a few days, have your legal people draw up documents. When I get back why not get one of your drivers to come to our home where Chloe and I can sign them? Then once we've done that, he can bring them straight back. Any objections?"

"That can work for us," Ivan acknowledged. "By then we should have the correct estimated cost as well and you can settle the balance at your convenience."

"We can send the card machine with the driver if you like?" Perry added.

"It's one of those machines requiring an internet connection and we'll show him how to operate it," said Ivan "but only with your approval."

"That's fine," Dick acknowledged. "Well gentlemen, we've been sitting in your lovely boardroom now for the last six hours, so should there not be anything else, we'd like to wend our weary way home as we still have a load of other work to get through."

No one else had questions, so they shook hands all round. Gina showed them the way to the front door where they said their thanks to her for all her help and support before starting the slow walk to the car.

"I think you should buy a new car, and soon. These people will see us in this heap and wonder what the hell's going on. You spend all this money and driving a car that's what, sixteen years old?" Chloe said sounding embarrassed.

"You're right. As soon as we've caught up with ourselves on all the other stuff, we'll buy a new one."

The traffic on the way home was a total nightmare, caused by two road traffic collisions which caused an eight-kilometre tailback and slowed things down to a snail's pace.

"Still, at least we're moving," said Chloe.

## Chapter Eight

### (a) The Argentine connection

THEY ARRIVED HOME just after 7:00 p.m., which wasn't bad at all considering the traffic problems they had suffered.

"I'm starving," Chloe said sighing "we should have stopped for takeaways."

"Can't you phone someone?"

"Would you like Chinese again?"

"Good idea," he replied.

"You want the usual, I suppose?"

"Yes, please."

While Chloe looked up the telephone number, Dick switched on the laptop. He got out his paperwork before contacting Felipe Alonso about the purchase of the property he required.

"Could you use your mobile to call for the takeaways as I'm going to phone Felipe?"

"Okay, you got his number?"

"Yep."

Dick dialled the number, and he'd be lucky if he got through the first time.

He was right. After the fourth try, he at last made contact. A woman answered the phone but he could not understand her. In English, he tried to get her to put him through to Felipe. She said something to him, which he could not make out, then there was a click and thought the line disconnected, and as he was about to re-dial, he heard a voice.

"Hello, this is Felipe speaking. Can I help you?"

Dick was glad to hear him speaking English although with a strong Spanish accent. "Hello Felipe" he replied and introduced himself.

After a short conversation, Felipe asked him if he had a video conferencing program on his computer, and if so, which one. Once they had sorted out which one to use, they both hung up. In a short while, he called Felipe on the video conferencing system and Felipe answered.

Dick advised him to make sure he had enough paper and a pen handy as he would need to make extensive notes. Straight to the point, he explained everything he required, and also stressed money transfers were not a problem. Felipe, however, was a little perplexed about this due to the strained relationship between the two countries. However, Dick assured him there would be no problem at all and told him to have a little faith.

He asked Felipe about getting permission from his Government regarding building a runway, and if they enquired why, he was to tell them of his plan to establish a car manufacturing company. They would transport the cars by air to other countries, and once sold, the outside currency would boost their economy.

Although some information was not one hundred percent true, it was enough for the enquiry. He asked Felipe for his e-mail address so he could send him all his contact details and would include an entire description of the items he wanted to purchase. He told Felipe he would fly to Japan on the ninth and said he would appreciate it if he could have feedback by the eighth no matter how little there was. Felipe agreed to this, and they said their goodbyes.

No sooner had Dick hung up when there was a knock at the door.

"That'll be the takeaways," Chloe called to him.

He got up, grabbed the money she had put on the table, and walked to open the front door. Before him stood an elderly Chinese man with a big packet in his hand.

"Chinese" he announced as he held the packet out towards Dick.

Dick stopped himself from saying 'Yes, you are'. Instead he said 'Yes, thank you.' Bag exchanged for money, and saying "Good night", Dick closed the door and took the bag to the dining-room table. Chloe already had the plates and cutlery out so, helping themselves to the various dishes, they sat down to eat.

"So what's on the menu for tomorrow?" Chloe asked him with her mouth full of rice.

"Any pun intended?"

"Hey," she uttered before realising what Dick had said "Oh... mmmm... no," she giggled.

"Now let's see," Dick mused for a moment "We don't have anything on the go at the moment. With luck, we may just have a quiet day."

"Now that would be great," she said. "Wait a minute," she exclaimed.

"What?"

"We can use the time to buy a new car. It will save me the embarrassment the next time we go visiting people in high places."

"I see," Dick replied with a hint of sarcasm.

"No, you won't see. You will go."

"Okay, don't give me a thousand words—I'll go."

"Pour you a whisky and water, dear?"

"What," Dick uttered in surprise "Do my ears deceive me or have you offered to pour moi a drink? Why the sudden change?"

"Well, you've been working so hard and I've just shouted at you. So I decided to offer to pour you a drink as a sign of truce."

"Now that's what I call patronisation."

"Do you want a bloody drink or not?"

"Ahhhhh... that's better," Dick replied smiling "that's more like it, and yes, you can pour me a drink, please."

After she had handed him his drink, she called it a night. "Right, I've had enough so I'm off to bed." And so saying, she kissed him on the cheek and made her way upstairs.

Sipping his drink, he searched the internet for a decent car. Because of his size and build, it had to be on the larger side of the scale, and as these things are never easy, he searched and searched until he gave up. About to throw in the towel, he spotted a new 4×4 from a reputable manufacturer.

"Hello, I could fancy that," he said to himself.   "If they've got one in stock ready to drive away, it's mine for sure."

He finished his drink, and he too made his way to bed.

Early the next morning, they followed their normal routine except Chloe joined him about an hour later than usual. The landline telephone rang and it was their landlord, Adrian, asked if he could pop in as he would be in the area.

They agreed and told him they needed to leave the house at no later than 11:30 a.m. that morning. He said he would try to be there earlier, and as it was, he arrived at 10:00 a.m. and Dick answer the door.

Adrian wondered about Dick's appearance... had he lost weight or was it a different hairstyle? Puzzled, he decided not to ask and said "You're looking good. I'm glad to see you looking so well. Hello Chloe," he said as she came into the open-plan living area.

"Hello, and to what do we owe the pleasure?"

"Well," we received your notice to vacate the premises and, as you have been such loyal tenants, we wanted to find why you're leaving? I suppose we're curious if you're leaving because you're moving of your own accord, or is it due to their being anything wrong in how we have treated you...?"

"No, no, no..." Chloe interrupted in her usual forthright fashion. "We've been more than happy living here and more than pleased with your handling of the property and our tenancy."

"Chloe and I have a golden opportunity to buy and run Maitland Airport, so that's what we will be doing. In fact, we have already purchased the place and will move into a house on the property. Also, the General Manager will run the show on our behalf."

"Cup of tea or coffee, Adrian, or do you want to have a quick look around instead?" asked Chloe.

"No thanks. I called to check if things were okay between us, that's all. So, on behalf of all of us, may I wish you everything of the best in your new venture. It sounds great. I hope I have the balls to do something like that when I reach your age," he said and they all had a good old chuckle.

They walked towards the front door, but before they got there, Dick said "Adrian, you already have keys to the house but as we have a spare set, take these. We'll be travelling backwards and forwards for a while, so if you or one of your partners wish to gain access to the house, you'll have an extra set giving you you independence to show other potential tenants around the place, and by all means please do so, but phone beforehand."

"That's kind of you," Adrian replied as they shook hands. "We'll miss you as our tenants," he said as he turned around and walked towards his car.

After closing the door, Dick turned to Chloe and said in suppressed excitement "Right,... shall we do this thing?"

"Oh... you've changed your tune from last night. Everything okay?" she asked, but with a hint of laughter in her voice.

"Yep, I'm a new man this morning, ready to jump onto my trusty steed and ride off into the sunset."

"Yes, and you're also a stuffing looney—just as I've always

suspected. But hang on, I'm just going to make a quick phone call before we go."

"Who too—your psychiatrist?"

"Now that's a great idea—I'll book an appointment for you, shall I?" she said and they both giggled.

"While you do that, I'll check to see what has to come out of the car. I'll do that in case we get another one today and they take poor old faithful EMO as a trade-in."

"Oh... boohoo," she said, mocking him while making her phone-call.

Although he had quite a soft spot for the car, he was aware of many people around the world who got attached to theirs. Dick was not one of them.

He recalled an article in a tabloid. It told of a devoted mad-hatter in the USA who insisted on being buried with his car. It also told of a lunatic in England who married a big boulder—or was it a rock? Either way, it was still pure lunacy.

"Oh well, to each his own, and if that's what floats their boat... then so be it," he mused. "Now those are the whackos Chloe should make appointments for to see a psychiatrist. I wonder what she would say if I demanded she buried me in a VC10?" he asked himself. "Wait, a minute. I have a damn good idea what she'd say...," and laughed.

Dick give the car a once-over and noticed the right back tyre half-deflated, so he pumped it up to a little higher than normal and hoped it would last for this, the last ever potential trip they would make in it.

## (b) Demise of EMO

They arrived at the car dealership and the salesman said he was busy. Dick looked around and saw there wasn't another customer, or any other single person, anywhere in sight other than themselves.

"If any salesperson working for us tries his luck like that, he'll be out on his bloody ear," Dick said to Chloe grinding his teeth in fury.

Unable to resist, Dick confronted the salesman head-on. "Would you prefer if we turn around, walk right out of your life, then I drop your manager a line informing him he overworks his staff?"

"Oh please no," replied the snivelling little prick "It was idiotic of me to have behaved like that. Please accept my humble apologies," he now said offering his hand. "My name is Ramsbottom. Nick Ramsbottom."

Although they shook hands, Dick felt like ramming his boot up Nick's bottom. So because of his rudeness, he introduced himself as Mr Shepherd and Chloe, as his partner, Mrs Fraser-Rigby. "Let's see if the little prick remembers her name."

"How may I be of service to you?" Nick *the pric*k asked Dick.

"I want one of your new top of the range 4×4s and I want to drive it away today. I also want ten percent cash discount off the sale price," Dick said playing hard-ball because of the way he had been treated "and, how much will you give me for that piece of shit over there as a trade-in?" he said pointing at his beloved EMO. Chloe couldn't help but smile.

Dick took the paperwork for the car with him, including the service history. In doing so, they completed the deal for a new car within two hours. On their way home driving their lovely new car, Dick said "Not that I care, but I wonder whether EMO's left back tyre deflated altogether. That would be one for the books," and Chloe agreed.

"I hope you realize I'll never drive this car," she said.

"Why ever not?"

"Because it's far too big for me."

"But you've driven me before," Dick replied giggling.

"Oh... ha bloody ha."

"Well, once we're fooling around at the airport, you'll have plenty of room to try it out if you like. Just please don't drive it into any aircraft, especially if they're on the runway full of people."

"Now would I do that?" she said looking all wide-eyed and innocent.

"I wouldn't put anything past you—and don't give me that stupid look."

She ignored him and instead asked: "I don't feel like cooking, do you?"

"No."

"Well, why don't we stop off and get two of those horrible greasy burgers? We haven't had one for about three months now."

"Okay, we'll buy nice cheap, non-greasy, non-fattening burgers, together with non-greasy fries and lovely fizzy sugarless drinks. This is so we can spoil the interior of our nice new expensive car," he said with a smirk on his face.

"Yes... that's it," she said "That sounds about right."

However, as they had no intention of eating in the car, they took their burgers and drinks home and ate them there. Hunger pangs satisfied, they set about doing housework. Afterwards, they sat in front of the TV to see what was showing, and if good, it would make a wonderful change. They had just found what might be an interesting documentary when there was the usual flash of light and Joel appeared in the middle of the lounge floor, obstructing their view.

"Hello, you two," he greeted them. "Stay where you are but switch the TV off for a moment. I'm only here to say how satisfied we are with your progress so far."

"Thank you," Dick and Chloe said in unison both looking well pleased with themselves.

"If there is anything you want from us, please ask," said Joel.

"Well now yes, there is," Dick replied "My daughter has similar health problems to those I had before you fixed them for me. I would, therefore, be more than grateful if you could fix her problems. Please understand not only will you be doing it for her, but you will do it even more so for me and also, when looking for pilots, I want my daughter to be a candidate, to fly anything and be damned good at it and perhaps being one of the best. Are you able to give her the same flying abilities you gave me,... maybe more?" Dick asked and waited with bated breath for the answer.

"Yes, we can. Once you have explained to her what's what, I'll introduce myself to her, then we can mend her body just like we mended yours. How does that sound?"

"I will be forever in your debt."

"No need for that. Once she knows of the facts, I'll inform our doctors when to expect her, and what about Ivan? There's no point in just doing the one. We may as well do both at the same time—or have you other ideas?"

"No, I have no qualms."

"Then once you have decided who you will select as your other pilots, we'll see what we can do." Joel now turned his attention to Chloe. "What about you? Would you also like to have the ability to fly an aircraft?"

"Me," she exclaimed feeling surprised by the question "Thanks for the offer, but no thanks. That's not for me. I'll leave it to the others, thank you very much."

"Okay, in all fairness I already knew the answer, but I had to ask. Is there anything else you would like us to do for you, health-wise or physical changes?"

"Oh hell no, but thank you. I have no health problems. I'm okay with the way I am."

Joel said "But if you have a change of heart, call me." He looked back at Dick with his big black almond-shaped eyes and asked: "So when do you intend on speaking to your daughter?"

"The best time would be the evening of the fourteenth. I'll work out a time. What I propose to do is, once we've come back from China and have seen the British company, Phil flies back home by twelve noon on the fourteenth. On our way back, we stop off and meet my daughter at the airport nearest to her. I can't remember its name off-hand, but when I speak to her, I'll find out."

"Well then, if there's nothing else for now, I'll let you enjoy your relaxation time," and once more he disappeared in his usual fashion.

The two of them, once again, sat back, and as Dick was about to relax, he asked, "Have we booked a flight for Phil as he's supposed to be here tomorrow?"

"I haven't. I was under the impression you did."

"Oh stupid me. Okay, I'll call him."

Dick picked up the handset, phoned Phil, advising him to get all his stuff ready as he was to fly to them the following day.

"But I'm already packed," Phil said as he had, in fact, been waiting for Dick's call.

Dick could only apologise and informed him he would soon email the information. Once received, Phil had to print the ticket and boarding pass.

"For goodness' sake," Chloe snapped "Why don't you get the executive guys to fly down there first thing in the morning. They can collect Phil and after they've landed, get one of their drivers to bring him here from Biggin Hill, and when you see them on the ninth, you pay the bill before you fly out. Saves all the hassle you are about to go through."

"Aren't you the clever one then? That's a far more sensible route to take," he replied, feeling rather stupid for not thinking of it himself.

He picked up the phone to arrange with the Executive Aircraft Company to do what Chloe had suggested. Once confirmed, he emailed Phil the info, which included the pickup point.

Job done, he sat and relaxed.

The following morning Kieran Michaels, from Michaels Realtor's, phoned to say he had viewed the three factories mentioned. He had also found another factory outside Blackpool and decided with the info he had, it might meet their requirements. Although it had closed down ten or more years ago, the left-over stock was still in storage.

"That sounds great, Kieran. What about housing?"

"Mr Shepherd as I say, this factory I have found fits the bill. When they built this factory, they had in mind to build a small Housing Estate for their employees and families."

"This sounds too good to be true," Dick cogitated, then said "I'll come up there tomorrow and plan to be there by nine o'clock in the morning. Do you by any chance have contacts with any recommended building companies?"

"My brother is a qualified Civil Engineer. He works for a rather large and well-known building company and it's only five miles from the car factory."

"You, young man, are the bearer of good news. Now this is what I would like you to do. Get hold of your brother, tell him I'm going to fly up there tomorrow and arrange for him to be there. If possible, he should also bring his Managing Director and perhaps also one or two of the other Executives. Can you organise this?"

"As soon as we end our call, I will phone him to see what I can come up with and I'll phone you back within the hour with whatever news I have, Mr Shepherd."

"That sounds great. Let me give you my mobile number because I'll be busy on the landline."

This now done, they ended their call.

"Change of plan," Dick shouted to Chloe. "We, my dear, are flying to Blackpool tomorrow to view a factory which has a small Housing Estate attached. So I'm going to contact the Executive fly-boys to book us a round trip or whatever they call it."

"What time do you want to be there?"

"I'd like to be there by nine o'clock in the morning."

"So what time must we be at Biggins?" she asked giggling.

"Biggins," he repeated "Biggins indeed," he said again while chuckling. "Right, when I speak to them I'll get an answer."

He phoned and booked the flight. They said if he wanted to be at the factory by 9:00 a.m., wheels up by 7:30 a.m., landing around 8:30 a.m. This gave them about twenty minutes travelling time by car. Dick liked this and agreed and told Chloe about the arrangements.

He now phoned Kieran to ask him to meet them at the airport and asked him to be their chauffeur for the day—if he didn't mind. Kieran agreed but said he was still waiting to hear from his brother.

"That's okay. If you can't organise it, we must do it again another time. But it would be great if they could be there."

"I'll do my utmost, Mr Shepherd, and I'll phone you the moment I have news."

Call ended, the two of them settled down to do paperwork and decided to create a filing system as things got out of hand with papers everywhere. Everything around them seemed to explode into life travelling at a hundred miles an hour.

"Let's hope things don't go tits up," Dick considered, then said to Chloe "We've got time on our hands, so why don't we go down to the Mall and have lunch there? Let's get away from all this work for a while."

"I'm all for that, and I can do a little shopping at the same time."

"Oh... brilliant bloody suggestion that was," Dick said sounding deflated.

"Don't moan about it. It was your idea, and as I have accepted, it's too late for you to change your mind. So, put that in your pipe and smoke it."

"Yeah, whatever. But we must be back by 'two thirsty' to allow for Phil's arrival," he said, and she commented "There you go with your 'thirsty' bit again. Right, that's fine. What time do you want to leave?" she asked, and he said "Now,"

"Now?" she repeated parrot-wise, to which he pointed out "Yes, now. If we don't go now, you won't have enough time to do your shopping."

"Ohhhhh... all right, let's go."

He grabbed a bottle of cold Spring water from the fridge before they made their way to the garage. As it was a clear warmish day, he experimented with the sunroof in their new 4×4 and they sped off as happy as two school kids who hadn't a care in the world.

Chapter Nine

The Car Factory Purchase

THEY ARRIVED BACK home just after 2:00 p.m. where they found a message on the answering machine from Kieran. Dick picked up the phone and pushed the re-dial button. "Hello, Kieran. It's Dick Shepherd. Any news?"

"Good news, Mr Shepherd."

"Okay, don't keep me in suspenders. I hate bouncing around for too long," Dick said in his usual facetious fashion.

"Well, not only is my brother coming around tomorrow, he's got the MD and the Production Director to be there and, I've also arranged for the owner of the property to be there as well. I hope it's all right with you?"

"Abso-bloody-lutely," Dick exclaimed. "That's brilliant. I can't wait to meet everyone. Are you still on for meeting us at the airport?"

"Yes, I will be there."

"Just to inform you, we are travelling in a private jet, so we won't be coming through the normal terminal."

"Oh that's okay—I'm familiar with the place and I'll meet you there."

"Thanks, Kieran. We'll see you tomorrow at about eight-thirty in the morning."

"Yes, Mr Shepherd. See you. Bye,".

There was a rumbling noise outside followed by a knock at the door. As Chloe was the nearest, she opened it and Phil greeted her.

"Oh hello there, and how was your trip?"

"Yeah, wonderful, thanks. It's the only way to travel," Phil said sporting a huge grin on his face. "Whose idea was that?"

"Not your uncle's."

They both grinned.

"Come on in, the master is waiting inside perched upon his throne. No, not the upstairs one."

"I heard you say it's the only way to fly," Dick said to Phil as they shook hands.

"Damn right it is. I hope it's the only way we will travel from now on?"

"Ummm... well no," Dick replied. It was now his turn to keep someone in suspense.

"No?" Phil exclaimed in surprise "Please tell."

"We'll explain all, but first take your bag upstairs, sort yourself out, pour yourself a drink, then sit down and relax."

Phil hurried upstairs, did what he had to do before hurrying back to a drink already waiting for him. Dick beckoned to him to sit down and picked up his own glass. "It's been a while, so cheers and welcome back." The three of them clinked glasses in salute.

"A lot has happened since the last time we met," Dick said and explained.

"Well, we purchased Maitland Airport and tomorrow, the three of us are flying to Blackpool to see the factory I'm hoping to purchase. That will be the birthplace of your machine, together with the cars we will manufacture, or in most cases, convert. But that's not the exciting bit," and he took a sip of his drink.

"Remember I said to you when production is running and you're happy with the staff you are to move to Maitland Airport?"

"Yes, I do."

"Well, now this is the part that will knock your socks off because it's something you will enjoy doing, and for a long time, I might add."

"What is it?" Phil asked, unable to contain himself.

"Okay, I'll put you out of your misery, shall I?" Dick teased "We purchased five Airbus A400Ms," Phil's eyes widened "and that's not all. We also purchased five Super VC10s. How do you like them apples?"

The expression on Phil's face outshone the brightest of moons. "When do I get my hands on them?"

"Steady on now Fido,... patience," Chloe said laughing.

Between Dick and Chloe, they brought Phil up to speed on what they bought, and delivery dates. Therefore, the sooner they were up and running in the factory up North producing cars, the sooner Phil moved to the airport. Dick also told him about the next days trip and the time schedule.

"I take it Kerri knows what's going on?"

"Well... errmmm... no, she knows nothing yet, but I will speak to her about it on the fourteenth," he said, explaining his idea about meeting up with his daughter.

After further discussions and a couple more drinks, they all retired for the evening as it would be early risings for them all.

The following morning, bright and early, they arrived at Biggin Hill Airport in good time for their flight. Before boarding, they walked to the office, but no one was there, so they walked out to the aircraft. Standing at the bottom of the stairs was Helen.

"Good morning Mr Shepherd. Good morning Mrs Fraser-Rigby and good morning Mr Upton."

"Oh, you met my nephew?"

"Yes, Mr Shepherd. He was on yesterday's flight."

"Oh," Dick replied feeling stupid. "Um... question. I wanted to pay the bill, not only for today but for the fourteenth, and there's nobody in the office. So how do I pay?"

"Now don't you go worrying about things like that," Helen assured him. "You'll be back tonight and you'll also be back again in a few days' time. So there's plenty of time yet, Mr Shepherd."

Reassured, they got onboard the aircraft, and before addressing Chloe, Dick and Phil, Helen gave the all clear to the pilots. "While the pilots are getting ready for take-off, would you like a cup of tea or coffee?"

The hot drinks served, and before they had even finished, they were airborne. A little while later, Helen served breakfast, so they all tucked in. Touchdown was just past 8:30 a.m.

"Mmmm... perfect timing chaps," Dick said to himself in approval.

They said their thanks to Helen and once again Dick did not give her an exact time when they would be back so he clarified a contact number with her and said he would call when they were on their way back.

As they walked down the stairs, they heard a voice addressing them, "Mr Shepherd, Mrs Fraser-Rigby?"

As Chloe was in front, she felt she should reply "That'll be us."

"I'm Kieran Michaels of Michaels Real Estate Agents," he introduced himself.

They shook hands and Kieran led them to his car. The drive to the factory wasn't bad considering they drove in rush hour traffic and they arrived at 9:10 a.m. and Dick approved.

Kieran drove into the grounds of a disused factory and they saw four people standing a few yards from where Kieran had parked the car. Dick assumed these were the gentlemen from the building company, and the owner. They got out of the car by which time the others had moved towards it to meet the newcomers. Kieran introduced them all to each other.

"You didn't travel all this way to view one side of the building. Shall I show you around?" Bill Mowday, the owner of the properties, asked.

"Yes please," replied Dick.

"Okay, follow me and I'll explain as we go along. I take it because these gentlemen are here you will want them to make alterations to the place?"

"Yes, I'm doing it this way to save time. If I like the properties, and purchase them, I want these gentlemen to do the job, if they feel they can handle the task."

"I've always maintained there's no job too big or too small for our company," Tom Schaffer, the MD of Creative Civil Engineering, advised him.

Dick was hoping this would be another promising start as it had been in their dealings with all the other companies, but how wrong he was. As they were almost halfway through the factory side of things, Eric Twelvetrees, the Production Director and Tom's right-hand man, got fidgety and showed signs of being an impatient man. For the moment, Dick let it ride and tried to concentrate on looking and listening to what Bill had to say about the premises without being put off by Eric's antics. But he contains himself no longer and led Tom to one side.

"For shit's sake, Tom, what the hell's his bloody problem? For the last three-quarters of an hour, I've had to endure nothing but his excessive moaning or complaining. I've never come across someone with such a lack of patience before. What's wrong with this twat? If he carries on like this, one of two things will happen. One, he pisses off or two, I move out with my entourage and the whole deal goes down the stinking tubes and I'm sure Bill will be ecstatic by this news."

Still annoyed, Dick interrupted Tom. "Hang on a moment. Should we carry on and should I award you the contract, that miserable bloody bastard stays well away from the properties. You will assure me he has nothing to do with my project. If I award the contract to you, I will make bloody sure it's a condition, and should he poke his nose in anywhere along the process of the alterations, there will be a penalty clause I will exercise. So, what's it to be?"

Tom apologised and pulled Eric to one side and ordered him to either go sit in the car for the rest of the walk-around or to catch a bus back to the office. Dick didn't care one way or another which option Eric wished to choose, but he acknowledged his approval to Tom. One man down, they carried on with the inspection.

"What was that all about?" asked Chloe.

"I had enough of that twat, so Tom has ordered him to piss off. I can't understand why he was here, what with all his bitching and complaining and being so impatient about everything. It was off-putting."

"Yes, I noticed something like that. Well, he's gone now so you can relax" she said while rubbing her palm up and down his left arm in a soothing gesture.

There was a load of body shells of old cars there and Dick overheard Phil asking Bill about them. "What's the deal with all these old cars?"

"These were the left-overs when the factory closed down. Because they're glass fibre, you'll find that a lot, if not all of them, will be salvageable. There are as many chassis, but what sort of condition they're in I'm not too sure as powder-coating was still in its infancy back then. Now should you wish to use them, I'd recommend you go back to bare metal to check for any imperfections before applying another layer of protective coating."

"So these come with the building, do they?" asked Phil.

"Yes they do."

"Okay, so if they come with the building, will we be able to carry on where you left off, then sell them on to Joe public? I mean, must we get permission from anywhere?"

"To answer your first question, yes. Then as to your second question—well, that's part of the deal. So should anyone give permission, that person is me, but you don't have to put them on the road if you don't want to. You can scrap them if you want. However, they are yours to do with what you want, should you make the purchase?"

End of discussion, they looked at each other before turning their attention back to casting their eyes around the place.

"Are you absorbing all this?" Dick asked Tom. "I mean, if we moved in here tomorrow and I furnished you with plans of how we want the building and the grounds, will your company be up to the challenge? Either you can or you can't, so please don't waste my time? If you can't, please say so now so I can organise another contractor who can," Dick said crossly, for he was still mad at Eric.

"Dick, I can guarantee you my company is more than capable of undertaking this task," Tom assured him. "Yes, some may say it's a challenge, but I don't see it that way. For me, it's a task and I'm more than ready to take it on, should you award me and my company the contract?"

After completing their walk-about looking over the inside of the building, Bill led them outside. They asked more questions and relevant replies were given by Bill, Tom and Joe.

When they had finished, Bill suggested "Shall we take a peek at the Housing Estate?"

"Yes," Dick replied. "That's a good idea."

As the Estate was close to the factory, they walked the short distance while exchanging ideas with one another about the factory and the grounds.

"You will spend a lot of your time here," Dick said to Phil. "Therefore, as you will be in charge, you must make sure you get what you want and where you want it to be."

"You going to put me in charge? I'm the number one bloke here? What makes you think I can do that?" Phil asked, feeling apprehensive.

"If I for one moment thought you couldn't handle the job, I would not put you in charge of the project. But you can do the job, so you will be the Managing Director of Maitland Electric Car Manufacturers until I call on you to move to Maitland Airport."

Phil paused for a moment and one could see he was going over things in his head. "Okay, that's great. I'll do it."

"Good, I like the positive waves you're putting out. You've got nothing to lose but everything to gain because you will be at the forefront of the birth of your invention, the wonderful device that will make a lot of businessmen, the so-called powerful businessmen in the world, pissed off."

"Therefore, I predict a lot of them brought to their stinking rotten knees because of it, and while I'm on a roll. We must make sure we take away the misery the poorer community are suffering, then place that misery onto the plate of the Corporate World. It must also include the worlds' Government Departments. Mmm, perhaps not all though."

"Those a-holes are guilty for the collapse of many a small business around the world. Not to mention the misery they have caused millions of householders. Let's give the poorer community a little happiness before they too are drowned."

By this time they had reach the outskirts of the Estate. One could tell a lot of undesirables kept on visiting the place because of all the visible broken windows and broken brickwork, not to mention the rubbish those boneheads had left behind, including lots of old syringes. One could also make out that most of the dog-ends were the remains of cannabis joints. But all-in-all, Dick approved.

"Tom, what are your views on this?"

"There's a lot more going on here than meets the eye, Dick. Casting an educated eye over the place, I see lots of minor damage to most of the rooftops and walls. We will have to carry out a thorough inspection of the Estate before I can give you any an idea of the cost. But, work wise, it's nothing we can't handle."

"Good," Dick replied. He turned his attention to Bill whom he took to one side and out of earshot. "Now Bill, as I understand it, you own all the rights to all the property including the factory, the inventory and the Housing Estate. So, if I were to ask you how much you want for everything, lock, stock and barrel, what's your asking price?"

"Ten million pounds Sterling for the factory and ten million pounds Sterling for the Housing Estate and yes, that's lock, stock and barrel," Bill replied without hesitation.

Dick thought for a moment. "You have a deal," he said extending his hand, and they shook hands to seal the purchase.

"How many houses are there?" Dick asked, and Bill said "Two hundred at last count."

"Excellent. Oh,... and tell me how much you want in the way of a deposit, then as soon as we have all signed on the dotted line, I'll transfer it," he said while they walked back to the others.

Dick appointed Kieran to handle the sales transaction, including everything associated with the buying and selling of properties. He now called Tom and Joe to one side. "As we have agreed upon a deal, tell me how much you think it will cost and how much time you need to give me a quote plus, how long you think it will take you to complete the project."

Tom sized up the situation for a moment. "The paperwork has for obvious reasons not gone through yet, and as Bill is still the legal owner, he must tell me if we can start by walking around the entire property, including going inside all the houses. Also, I'll need at least three days before my estimators can come up with a realistic cost, and a realistic time frame."

By now they had joined the others.

"Bill, are you averse to them coming onto the properties to do the necessary?"

"No, not at all. I think you must treat the place as yours now, but what I will do is write a letter explaining what's transpired. You may be here at night and get a friendly visit from the local constabulary, so it may come in handy."

"Brilliant" Dick acknowledged. He handed out his outdated business cards (for which he apologised) to all concerned, should they need to contact him. In an aside to Chloe, he asked if she would please make a mental note to organise letterheads and business cards as soon as possible. She nodded and said she would get onto it when they got back.

He told Tom and Joe they would be overseas for several days which should afford them enough time to work out their quotations so they should be ready with these by the time they returned and Tom promised to have it sent to Dicks e-mail address.

On the way back to the airport, Dick asked Chloe to contact Helen. He told Kieran he would send an aeroplane, if need be, to Blackpool to pick him up and fly him to Biggin Hill. They would sign all the paperwork, and transfer the deposit, after which he could fly straight back home.

Although he didn't show it, Kieran was all for this idea. He agreed with a brisk and cheerful readiness as he hadn't been on a plane trip in a while, let alone an Executive Jet.

"Would you by any chance have one of those new portable card reading machines that work on the internet you could bring with you?" Dick asked Kieran.

"We received one from our Bank only last week to try out."

"That's great. Please bring it with you."

When they arrived at the airport, they said their goodbyes to Kieran and "Now don't forget that card reader," Dick reminded him.

"Don't worry, Mr Shepherd, I won't."

They were all greeted by Helen as they mounted the steps into the plane and said "Hello" to the pilots.

"Please make yourselves comfortable, and may I bring you your usual drinks?"

They all said "Yes please."

With their drinks served, Dick said "Cheers to another great purchase completed" and they clinked glasses.

"You realise that once they start work, you must move up here," Dick said to Phil.

"Yes, I'll pack what I need and drive there. A tiring distance but nothing I can't handle."

"I remember you driving over three times that distances in one go in the past," Dick replied, smiling at the memory.

The aircraft taxied onto the runway, clearance issued to the pilots and they, once again, took to the skies. On arrival at Biggin

Hill, Helen opened the door for them, and Dick went straight to the office to settle all outstanding bills. He also booked and paid for the flight to fetch Kieran on the morning of the fifteenth and received a departure time of 11:00 a.m. They said if passenger Kieran could be there by 10:45 a.m., it would be fine, so he sent a text message to Kieran informing him of this. When finished, they left Biggin Hill Airport, arriving home just after 4:30 p.m., which meant they had, for once, missed the rush hour traffic.

By 5:00 p.m. they had all settled down and Chloe asked if they would like anything for supper. As they were still full from what they had had on the plane, they abstained, but said if hunger pangs grabbed hold of them later on, they would find something in the cupboards or fridge to nibble on.

Just as they were sitting down with their drinks, Dick noticed a flashing light on the answering machine, so he pushed the button to listen to the message. "Hello Mr Shepherd, this is Felipe Alonso here. I must inform you I have good news and some bad news, so please call me when you can. Thank you."

"Damn, what now? I hope it's nothing too serious" he said and started up the laptop. Once logged on he dialled Felipe's conference call number hoping he would answer which he did.

"Hello, Mr Shepherd. Thanks for calling back."

"So what's the bad news?"

"I think I should give you the good news first."

"Okay, shoot,"

Felipe told him because they accepted everything, all was in hand.

"I beg your pardon?" Dick said in surprise. "Do you mean to tell me you have purchased all the property I require? Have received permission from the Government for me to build a runway there? How the hell did you do all this in such a short space of time?" Dick asked and found he could not contain himself, so before Felipe could say anything, he continued. "If that's the good news, how the hell can there be any bad news, for goodness' sake?"

"Nothing to worry about," Felipe assured him. "Only I've had news from my contacts in Government saying El Presidente would like the first car off the production line, as a thank you token, but I'm sure he wasn't serious about it," he said and Dick could hear his amusement.

Dick thought about this for a moment because in his mind most of the South American Governments were conniving bastards. "Mind you, ninety-nine percent of all Governments around the world are like that, so what's the difference?" he said to himself.

"No, get a message back to him and say I think it's a tremendous idea but I won't present him with the first car off the production line. I will, however, present it to his wife."

Pleased with his counter-offer, Dick smiled with relief knowing there was no bad news.

"Okay, Mr Shepherd," Felipe acknowledged laughing "When I finish up with my paperwork, and if I complete it tonight, I'll email the information to you so you have it by the time you get up in the morning."

"Thanks, Felipe. I appreciate your hard work very much, and I'm serious about giving the car to El Presidente's wife. So please make sure you get the message through to him."

"Okay Mr Shepherd, I will and thanks for the business."

"You're welcome Felipe, and we'll see you soon. Bye for now," Dick said letting out a huge sigh of relief. "The bugger got me there all right."

Both Chloe and Phil had a good old chuckle for it wasn't often anyone could catch Dick out by playing a practical joke on him.

"You haven't met Joel yet, have you?" Dick asked Phil.

"No, I haven't."

"Shall we do the introductions now?" Dick asked Chloe.

"Well look what you put me through. So... hell... yes" Chloe said, dragging out the last few words to emphasise them, and Joel entered.

"Oh bugger me," Phil exclaimed which put smiles on their faces.

"Hello Phil, I'm Joel."

"Shit, I'm sorry."

"What... do you think I'm ugly? I can assure you we think the same about you," Joel said, at which Dick and Chloe packed up.

"Relax and listen," Joel said as he concentrated his big black almond-shaped eyes towards Phil. "Your machine is brilliant, and I have brought documents with me for you to study," and, from out of nowhere, they appeared in his hand. He continued

"These will give you the plans in which to create the different sizes you will require, not only for the cars, but also for the A400Ms. Included will be the ones needed to drive the generators which you are to install inside the mountain," Joel explained. He noticed a confused look on Phil's face, but he left it for the moment and carried on.

"Also included, you will find the drawings for the various gearboxes you will need for each different item, and because you can read plans, these won't be a problem for you. Now... do you have questions?"

Silence greeted him.

"He's asking you, Phil," Chloe shouted at him.

"Oh sorry, I apologise," Phil said all bemused "I'm still overwhelmed. Mmmm... no. I have none at this stage thanks."

"I can tell by the look on your face you have no clue regarding the mountain."

"Mountain? What mountain?" Phil asked in bewilderment.

"You've got a lot of explaining to do, haven't you?" Joel said turning to Dick.

"Yes, I have. I'll fill him in when you've gone."

"Well, if you have nothing else, I'll be off," he said and, just as he finished saying the last word, he disappeared. This had by now become the norm for both Dick and Chloe but was mind-blowing for Phil who, however, said: "Okay, that was interesting."

For the rest of the evening, both Chloe and Dick explained everything to Phil. He now understood why he had to report to Maitland Airport once the factory operation was up and running and being controlled by good people.

The following day after breakfast, Dick checked his emails where he found Felipe had been true to his word and all the information he required was there. He also found, although there were a few buildings on the main property, nobody lived there any more.

What had happened was, years ago when the children had grown up, they had all left the farmstead to live and work in the cities. When the parents had passed away, the place became dormant, and the children were glad to sell. All they wanted was fifty million Pesos, which was less than four million pounds.

"What a bargain," Dick thought, not that it made any difference.

The piece of land he required across the road was not for sale, however, as the farmer found himself on hard times, he was more than prepared to lease the ground on a long-term basis, and only for one million two hundred thousand Pesos per annum, less than seven thousand five hundred pounds a year.

"Another bargain, but heigh-ho, who cares?"

Dick wrote a short note in reply to Felipe's email asking how he should make payment. He suggested, because his credit card was acceptable, they should make use of it and, if he was in agreement, he would give one-third of the numbers over the phone, the other third via email and the rest over the conference call website. This, he hoped, would minimise the fraud situation.

Dick remembered to contact his daughter and arranged to meet her at Brickner Airport at 6:00 p.m. of the fourteenth. Kerri was excited about this as they hadn't seen each other in over a year and yet, they only lived four hundred kilometres away from one another.

"Still, the internet has its uses, thanks to Skype," he thought.

He instructed her where she was to meet them at the airport and told her she was to follow the way by looking at the signs. Failing that, she should ask someone. But, knowing his daughter, there wouldn't be a problem because, it was a case of, like father like daughter. He was proud of her.

While Dick thought about the trip, he dropped a bombshell. "Why don't you come with us tomorrow?" he asked Chloe.

"Bugger me," Chloe cried out in surprise, "I thought you'd never bloody ask."

They spent the rest of the day getting ready for the trip.

"Listen," Dick said to them before they retired "I'm having one more drink because drink and altitude, or just alcohol has no adverse effect on my body any more. Ha ha ha ha ha."

"Even if it still did, it wouldn't stop you, now would it?" Chloe said, as she looked him up and down.

"Mmmm... oh yes it would," he replied, trying to get himself out of the predicament he had laid for himself.

"Yeah right," she said scoffing at his remark "and I suppose you're not talking tosh now either, hey?" she replied, making them all giggle.

"What time must we be at the airport tomorrow?" asked Phil.

"They advised me wheels up is at three o'clock tomorrow morning, so we must be there by two-thirsty."

"Oh bugger," Chloe remarked "I wish you had said sooner. I'd better get to bed now."

"You said two-thirsty. What does that mean?" enquired Phil.

"It means it's time for another drink, whether then or now. But may I suggest it's now?"

"Oh, okay, I suppose I'll have another one as we can always have a snooze on the plane."

"Yep, a good idea. So why don't you have one for the road?" Dick asked Chloe.

"As long as you get up and pour it."

Dick got up and poured the final round for the night before they all went to bed, knowing they would get less than seven hours sleep.

## Chapter Ten

## The Japanese and Chinese Connections

WITH ALL THE hustle and bustle so early in the morning, they were at Biggins, as Chloe now referred to it, by 2:30 a.m. A new face greeted them in the reception.

"Good morning all. My name is Tony and I presume, sir, you are Mr Shepherd?"

"Yes, I am. Good morning to you too, Tony."

"I take it, Mr Shepherd, you have your luggage with you?"

"Yes,... we've left our suitcases outside the door."

"Fantastic. I'll get Peter to load them on-board for you."

"Thank you, Tony. Please check for me what the outstanding balance on our account is as I would like to pay for it now."

"Would you like to include this trip, Mr Shepherd?"

"Yes, please."

Tony opened Dick's account and did the checks and transfers.

"Thanks, Mr Shepherd. Your account is up to date and may you have a pleasant trip."

"I've parked my car outside and here are the keys in case you need to move it. I'll pick them up from here on our return."

"Okay, Mr Shepherd. We'll take good care of it for you."

Helen greeted them as they walked towards the plane. "Good morning all" she said and smiled.

"Good heavens," Chloe said "don't you ever take any time off young lady?"

"Yes I do. When we get back from this trip, I'll be taking a week off."

"Well, as much as you deserve it, we will miss you. Are you going somewhere exciting?"

"Yes, my partner and I are going down to Cornwall to visit my parents."

"Well, I hope the two of you have a fantastic time."

"Thank you, I'm sure we will. Shall I bring you the usual?"

"Yes please."

As they relaxed into the comfortable plush chairs, they sipped away at their hot drinks. "Mmmm... a Russian tea would go down well," said Dick.

"I told you so," Chloe said annoyed "It makes no bloody difference at all with you—always have to bring alcohol into the picture," she scolded him. Both he and Phil burst out laughing.

As the checking of the account had taken a little longer than expected, wheels up were after 3:00 a.m. However, the pilots informed them they hoped to get a little help, not too much though, from part of the Jet Stream. If so, they would make up for any lost time. A little while later Helen came to show them the breakfast menu.

Although the pilots had been hoping to make up flying time they did not, however, land until just after 12:00 noon the following day, but Dick wasn't too fazed by it. There wasn't only one supplier of the items he required - it was just that this one was far more convenient. Anyway, that's what Dick had understood Joel to mean.

After clearing Customs and Security, a middle-aged Japanese man met them and introduced himself as Mr Chiriku. As he did this, he put both hands together and bowed before them, which Chloe and Phil both reciprocated.

"To hell with this," Dick mumbled to himself. "The only person I bow down to is Her Majesty the Queen." Instead, he held out his hand to Mr. Chiriku, who grasped it with both of his, and shook until the two of them became one big giant dildo for the gyrations seemed to increase in speed. "Bloody hell," Dick said to himself in surprise "Steady on there, China bell."

Although Mr Chiriku conversed in broken English, they understood him. The drive was pleasant enough, and they arrived at their rendezvous at 12:50 p.m. This gave them time enough to get to the Reception and introduce themselves. A tiny wee Japanese girl led them to the Boardroom where she opened the door and beckoned them to enter.

"Here's more bloody corporate crap which I don't need," Dick grumbled to himself "but I'm stuck in the middle with it. I swear, someday someone will sit down and write a song about these bloody idiots with clowns to left and jokers to the other."

Chloe led the way into the boardroom, followed by Dick with Phil bringing up the rear-guard.

"Oh no, what's going on in here?" Dick said to himself.

A gentleman seated at the head of the table stood up and addressed them in his broken English. "Good afternoon. My name is Yoshiro Hoshino, President of Nippon Robotic and Smelting Works. This is Tadao Fukuhara, Executive Director. This is Hideki Kimoto, Corporate Planning Director, and this is Tetsuo Inouye, General Affairs and Finance Director. Please,... sit down."

As the putting together of the hands with the ever bowing movement of the torso was going on, Dick decided not to be disrespectful, so he played along. "Okay, I'll put my hands together as they do but I'm damned if I will ever bow. If they don't want to shake hands, well, stuff them as well" he muttered under his breath.

Although this behaviour for him was over the top he did, however, admit to himself he would rather it happened this way. His experiences in the past with some companies in the Western world, were unforgiving. "Those blokes can learn a lot from this," he cogitated.

"Gentlemen, and lady welcome to Japan and welcome to our business. How can we help you?" asked Mr Hoshino.

Dick addressed them, making sure he didn't speak too fast, but also to not sound disrespectful. "Thank you so much for allowing us to be here today and I hope we can do business together. We are starting a new motor car manufacturing company, and what we would require from you is to supply and install all the required automated components."

"Also, my colleague Mr Upton, has a new design for a particular machine. He would, therefore, require you to make and supply some inside workings, plus the outside casings and has all the plans and drawings for you to follow. So, would you be able to manufacture, supply, and install the items we require?" Dick asked as he handed over all the drawings to them.

They put their heads together and conversed in their mother tongue. "We apologise for speaking in our own language but we need to understand what your requirements are and, if are you another businessman who's not sure how the business world operates. We have had many people in the past who have cost us money and we, therefore, cannot take any chances but, we wish you no disrespect," said Mr Hoshino.

"That's understandable, Mr Hoshino," Dick replied. "Please be aware there is no problem with finances. In fact, we will put down a deposit of any amount you feel you would require.   I wanted to go to another supplier, but we have it on good authority you are the best."

They continued to discuss affair's at length. Mr Hoshino, who did all the talking on his Company's behalf, asked permission to send one of his employees to pay the factory a visit. This was to work out the production line and the factory floor.

Dick was more than pleased with this idea and said it would be tremendous to arrange this without delay.  "To have someone there with the knowledge of a factory layout is most welcome. Someone who can help, advise, and guide our team about the floor plan, sounds good. Gentlemen, if you feel you need to send two or three people, please do so. They can stay as long as necessary and all expenses will be to my Company's account."

"Mr Shepherd, we specialise in the total overall design of car manufacturing factories. May I suggest we design the entire plant for you, including the office block?"

"Yes, please do that. How soon can send your party out to do some investigating?"

Mr Hoshino spoke to his team and after some deliberation came back with an answer. "We can send an advance party out in two weeks' time."

"That's excellent," Dick said feeling well pleased. "May I at this stage say our contact man will be Mr Phil Upton here. Also, may I give you a down payment of, shall we say, two million American dollars by way of securing your business?"

All the members of the board accepted Dicks offer and they produced the paperwork without a hitch. Due to the lack of an interpreter, the discussions, together with the production line design, lasted until 8:00 p.m. that evening.

Happy about proceedings, Dick stood up and thank them. With their habitual bowing and putting together of hands, they bid each other farewell.

They arrived at the hotel before 9:00 p.m., booked in, and an old-fashioned page boy led the way. The hotel had a Casino and lots of restaurants and shops so, because the next day's flight was at 1:00 p.m. the following afternoon, loads of fun lay ahead of them. However, as Dick and Chloe were about to leave their room, they heard and noticed the familiar soft sound and light of Joel's arrival.

"Hello," they said together.

"Hello," Joel greeted them. "Don't look so surprised. Even although you're on another continent, if you need me, call. Not that I was expecting you to have had any problems, I wanted to congratulate you on how you handled everything."

"Thanks, Joel" said Dick.

"Are you enjoying yourself, Chloe?"

"Yes, thanks, Joel. I can't wait to have something to eat. I'm starving."

"Well, I won't keep you any longer, so congratulations once again," Joel said and disappeared.

"Are you going to phone Phil's room and tell him we're ready?" asked Chloe.

"Yes, I'm about to do so."

As Phil was the closest to the lift, they met him outside his room.

"Joel paid us a fleeting visit," Dick told him.

"Oh yes. Did he want anything in particular?"

"No. He came to say we handled the meeting well, then he pissed off."

"Oh all right, but he does seem to get around, doesn't he?"

"Yeah, he sure does," Chloe now replied.

"After we've eaten, I'll find a hole in the wall and draw cash for us to use in the Casino," Dick said to Phil.

"Oh good, I can't wait."

They entered the lift and pushed the ground floor button which took them straight to the Casino area. Because of the size of the entertainment complex, they meandered in and out around the place taking in all the wonderful sights. They continued walking about when Chloe's eye caught the familiar sign of a good old American ranch-style Steak House. "Good spot Chloe," Phil said, and they made their way over and sat at a table.

They placed their orders and found the food to be as good as advertised. Although they had never set foot inside this Steak House before, it somehow seemed to be familiar to them, and why? They had no idea.

After consuming their meals, they decided it was now time to find the actual Casino itself. The time had now come for them to not only waste someone else's money but to have loads of fun spending it.

They found their way inside and all thought whoever had done the layout of the last Casino they had visited many years ago, must have done the layout for this one for it looked ever so similar. But they didn't spend too much time wondering about it as it was now time to get the ball rolling.

After enjoying themselves, the time came for them to retire for the night and Dick wonder if Joel had anything to do with the million dollars Phil won on one of the slot machines.

The next day, they made sure they were well in time for the flight. Take off was scheduled for 1:00 p.m. and the duration of the flight to be one hour, but because they would travel in a Westerly direction, they would gain one hour. This meant although they had left Tokyo at 1:00 p.m., they would arrive in Shanghai at 1:00 p.m. the same afternoon.

Chloe's head was in a spin. "We've arrived before we've even left," she said, which made little sense to her at all.

After clearing Customs and Security, a Company driver greeted them. Instead of clasping his hands together, he only bowed and introduced himself as Cheng. They drove in silence until they arrived at their next destination, Rare Earth Manufacturing Company. The driver showed them the way to the Reception area where a petite girl greeted them, only this time she was Chinese.

"Xiawu hao, good afternoon," she said in Chinese and English, but with a charming accent.

Dick admired people like this for he only spoke his mother tongue. He sometimes wondered how well he understood English as it is one of the more difficult languages to master, but then he was more than streets ahead of the vast majority of the people in his own country. The people who classified themselves as being part of the so-called modern-day society.

They followed the petite girl two floors up and, a short walk later, she showed them into the Boardroom. Dick wondered if the man who greeted them was the father of the petite girl for the only difference between the two of them was their sexes.

"Here we go again, and probably with another long boring introduction."

"My name is Zhuang Zhao, President of the company. These gentlemen are my Vice-Presidents, Lim Jiang, Liang Zou and Hu Ying Tong," he said and, after handshakes all round, Zhuang asked them to please sit.

"Mmmm... not too bad after all," Dick said to himself as he thanked them. "Gentleman, we are here to purchase a running supply of magnets. Is there any chance you will supply my company as we believe it is difficult to get any of these from you, or am I wrong?"

"It all depends on what side of the Corporate ladder you are on," Zhuang said to him.

"We are not on any side of any ladder of any Corporation. We are a single minority family company divorced from the Corporate world."

"Good news," said Zhuang. "It may well benefit you depending on what it is you want."

Phil produced his paperwork, together with the line drawings of all the different shaped magnets and all the sizes of each he would require. The Chinese looked at everything while pondering for quite some time as they exchanged, what Dick assume was, constructive criticisms amongst themselves. In the meantime Dick, Chloe and Phil bided their time as they waited for Zhuang to finish the meeting he was having within their meeting.

"This is a fantastic drawing. I think the magnet you require is the super-strong permanent magnet, is it?" Hu Ying Tong asked Phil.

"Yes please," Phil replied "that's the type I require. Any other type will not work on the machine I'm creating."

"What type of machine are you making?" asked Lim Jiang.

"No disrespect to you or anyone else but, at this moment in time, it's still a secret."

Dick cringed at the sound of what he believed to be an Americanism.

"That's understandable. You can't allow your opposition to have access to your ideas, not that we might be your opposition," Liang Zou said causing them to smile.

"How soon will you start the manufacturing process?" asked Dick.

"Once we have sorted out the cutting dies for the various shapes and sizes you require, I suppose in about one month's time," replied Zhuang Zhao.

"That sounds okay. So when can you ship the first supply?" asked Phil.

"About another month later," Li replied, "otherwise it would not be economical."

"Once again that's fine," Phil advised them. "When the first supply of the small magnets is ready, can you airfreight enough magnets for one machine? You can see the quantities on the line drawings."

"Yes, we see and I'm sure that won't be a problem," Zhuang assured Phil.

Phil thanked them as he handed over a copy of the factory's address in Blackpool and said they must address the package for his attention.

"Because of the weight," Liang pointed out, "I think it will be more expensive than you may expect."

"That's not a problem," Dick informed him "let us worry about that side of things. Now, talking about money. How much would you need as a down payment for the manufacturing and the supply? Will three million American Dollars be enough to start with?"

The Chinamen looked at each other and said a few words in Mandarin without letting their facial expressions give anything away (not that Dick minded).

Zhuang replied, "Three million American Dollars would be more than enough to get the job started. It should be enough for about three months supply, but we will keep you informed all along the way."

"That's tremendous," Dick acknowledged.

They had been conducting their business for quite some time and Dick, Chloe and Phil had to leave by 5:20 p.m. to travel to the airport. The rest of the time they spent sorting out the upfront payment and just general chit-chat about the manufacturing processes, and to satisfy Phil, why the scales of the production time seemed to be so long.

The time came for them to depart, so with the usual bowing motions, they shook hands and thanked everyone. The young lady showed them the way to the car where Cheng was waiting to drive them back to the airport. This time, however, it wasn't in silence for they chatted about the meeting. As Chloe and Phil nattered away, Dick phoned Helen informing her they were on their way.

"Will the magnets be good enough to do the job?" Chloe asked Phil.

"Oh yes, more than good enough."

"And what sort of life span do they have?"

"Well, I hope forever."

"And is that possible? I mean, you must understand I don't fully grasp the workings of a magnet. The way I understand things is if you put something metallic to it, it will stick to it, right?"

"In a nutshell,… yes. With my lot, it's more complicated than….."

"Okay, enough is enough for my little brain," Chloe chipped in. "When it's all up and running, you can show me and I'll be able to get to grips with how it works. Deal?"

"Deal," Phil smiled in agreement.

They arrived at the airport and said goodbye to Cheng before walking the short distance to the aircraft.

"Hello. Did you have a good meeting?" asked Helen.

"Yes, but a dry one," Chloe replied "so a glass of the old vino will go down a treat."

"What will the boys have?"

Dick liked the way Helen said it as she wasn't supposed to interact with the clients in any informal manner. He thought perhaps she was just settling down to the process of getting to know them.

"I'll have my usual please," replied Dick.

"I'll have a glass of wine as well please," said Phil.

Drinks served, they drank a toast to Phil and the up-and-coming success of his machine. When they were well into the flight, Helen served a few more drinks along with their supper, or was it going to be lunch? Maybe breakfast perhaps? Still Chloe remained confused about the time factor and lost within the time-frame itself.

"Oh well, it doesn't matter. We'll be home in a few more hours' anyway," she said to herself. "Don't forget you have to drive when we get home," she said to Dick "so you'd better make sure not to have another one."

"Oh creeps I forgot" he replied as he tossed back his drink before trying to get some shut-eye for the rest of the flight.

However, he was just about to nod off when he heard Chloe ask "When you are piloting your own plane, are you going to be drinking like this as well?"

"Oh hell yes," he replied at which both he and Phil just had to giggle.

When they arrived at the airport, and while their luggage was being offloaded, Dick walked straight to the Reception where he saw Sheila behind the desk. "Good morning young lady. How are you?" he asked, and she said "Good morning Mr Shepherd, I'm fine thank you, and how was your trip?"

"Great thanks," he replied. Sheila handed over the car keys and asked: "May I be of help with another booking, perhaps?"

"Yes you can. I need to book a flight for two days' time, the thirteenth, and book it for the day, please. I've no idea how long we will be but we need to go to Derbyshire, East Midlands Airport. The appointment is at nine o'clock in the morning,".

"That's not a problem. If you need to be there at nine o'clock in the morning, wheels up should be, I would say seven-thirty, if that's okay with you?"

"Perfect,... and our trip on the fourteenth—I've already paid for that, have I?"

As she used Dick's credit card to pay for the necessary, she looked at their file and confirmed his account was once more up to date and handed the credit card back to him.

"Thanks, Sheila and we'll see you on the thirteenth."

Dick walked out of the office and notice Chloe and Phil having a chat with Helen and the two pilots. "All settled and ready to rumble when you're finished."

They settled down in the car and were soon on their way—on their way towards the wonderful M25.

"I wonder if someone will ever one day write a song about this bloody motorway?" he thought to himself.

Chapter Eleven

Toby Manufacturing

THEY ARRIVED BACK home just before 10:00 a.m. The drive, compared to the last few days, was horrendous as the M25 was its normal nightmarish self. The number of big rigs occupying the road was, in Dick's mind, crazy although he understood it was necessary as the goods had to get to the various markets. They took over an hour to get home whereas it would have taken thirty minutes or less in normal conditions.

"Not too bad, considering," Dick supposed.

Once unpacked, Chloe asked them to put their dirty washing in the basket as she was about to get the machine going and the boys obliged.

They sat down at the dining room table where they discussed, and planned, their trip to Toby Manufacturing based in Derbyshire.

"The name doesn't ring a bell with me," said Phil.

"They're a new concern made up of the guys made redundant by some other factories that had closed down, so I had the idea to give them a break and see if they would accept our business."

"They'd be bloody fools if they don't," retorted Chloe.

"Well, another reason I chose them is they are only one hundred and sixty kilometres from Blackpool."

"So what time's our flight?" she asked.

"We'll be flying there on the thirteenth, wheels up by seven-thirty as the appointment's for nine o'clock in the morning."

"Heck, another early bird

"Yeah, but I want to be home by two o'clock in the afternoon as I'm hoping BAE and old Mr Dumbrill will phone."

"Who the hell's Mr Dumbrill?" asked Phil.

"He's the chap at Maitland Airport who is drawing up all the paperwork for the sale and transfer... the usual crap. Ask Chloe—she's more clued about these things than I am. Anyway, he'll send the papers by courier for us to sign."

Dick continued. "I going to ask these new guys if they would, on our behalf, buy Brimstone Car Company in Bristol and must get hold of the Administrators to see if we can purchase the place lock, stock and barrel. This would give us more cars for our production line. I've checked under the bonnet and they're pretty much the same, therefore I foresee no problems with manufacturing."

"So, if we get this place, they are to supply cars the same way as

Toby's is in that there won't be an engine?" asked Phil.

"Yes, and don't forget, I want Toby's running the place. The only drawback is they are just over three hundred and twenty kilometres away, but I'm prepared to live with that."

"Hey,... I've just had an idea. We should find someone more than prepared to supply us with electric motors," Phil suggested.

Dick rubbed his chin and mused "Mmmm... good thinking there Batman. We have time on our hands today so why not now on the internet?"

"Yeah, I agree." With this, Phil got out the new laptop Chloe had bought for him and switched it on, and before he surfed the net, asked: "Where can I plug the battery charger in?"

"Use the one hiding behind the wall-stand," Dick advised as he pointed at it. "Okay, and while you do that, I'll check my e-mails."

Before Dick started, he asked who wanted a drink and Chloe was the only one to abstain. He poured two drinks before he and Phil got going on their laptops. He noticed he had received, amongst others, three e-mails he was expecting from Felipe, Kieran and Tom and started by opening the first e-mail in which Kieran advised him about all the completed paperwork and was therefore ready for signing.

He replied to Kieran saying he would book a plane for him to travel down to Biggin Hill. Once there, a car and driver would wait to bring him to the house where the signing would be done. He also reminded Kieran not to forget the card reader.

He opened Felipe's e-mail and, as he soaked in the information, he had a rush of blood to the head. "Chloe," he whispered to attract her attention, but she didn't hear him, so he tried a different approach "Hello dear," he said.

"Yes, what do you want?" she replied as if she were suffering from PMT (which was unlikely as she was way beyond the point of no return in this respect).

"Tell me, how would you like to travel to Argentina to pay the account for the property we've bought. You'll also need to check out the leasehold we are getting and to sign other papers as well?" Dick asked in a mushy, sucking up manner.

"Oh, now that would be nice, wouldn't it?" she replied in the same manner.

But, as soon as she had said it, their tones changed.

"How am I going to be travelling there?" she asked in a demanding voice.

"Well by plane. How else? or would you rather travel by mule train?"

"No," she exclaimed, "I mean, do I get to go in an executive one?"

He took out his P.U.B. credit card from his wallet and pointed at it. "You've got one of these, correct?"

"Yes, you know I have."

"Well, there you have it. You've just answered your own question, haven't you?" he said teasing.

"Okay, and when would you want me to go?"

"The fifteenth would be a good day, but I'll let you know. You and the crew will have to stay over because the pilots required by law to have a rest period after such a long flight. I reckon the flying time will be at least twelve hours."

"Yeah, that's okay."

"Good. Then I'll send Felipe a reply and tell him what I've proposed, and when I get an answer, I'll let you know."

"Okey-dokey. Mmmm... now who can I take on the journey with me?" she mused out loud.

"Whoever you like, but you'd better book your flight now."

"Yeah, I'll do that right away,".

"Good for you," Dick said in a mocking tone. A slipper went flying past his head missing him by inches. He giggled.

For both Dick and Phil the e-mails, (besides slippers), were flying backwards and forwards. Felipe said it would be a good idea for Chloe to travel there as it should speed things up. He also said it would be a great opportunity for him to show Chloe around the properties as well during the time the pilots had their mandatory rest period.

Dick informed Chloe about Felipe's ideas "Well how does that grab you?" he asked her.

"Not the way you're dreaming of. But yes, it sounds okay."

"Then you'd better arrange the flight for the fifteenth. Make it for whenever it suits you but remember, you will have to stay there for at least eight hours."

"Are you going to be taking me to Biggins?"

"If it's all the same to you,... no. It's because of not knowing the time or how deep I'll be in with the other deals I'm making. You should ask them to send a driver and arrange for the driver to bring you home when you get back."

"Good idea, I'll do that."

"Also, please double-check everything is still in order regarding Kieran's flight on the fifteenth as their driver must have him here around nine o'clock in the morning and, once you have finished, would you get in touch with Kieran to re-affirmed everything with him, please."

"Right, don't worry about it. I'll organise those things now."

Pleased with Chloe, Dick had it all in hand as it now gave him the freedom to concentrate on other matters requiring his attention. "How're your hunting skills doing there?" he asked Phil.

"I've got a few potentials but there are still quite a few leftovers. So, once I've whittled out the ones I don't want, perhaps we can go over the remainder together?," Phil suggested.

"Yeah, I'm good with that, but first I'm just going to send Tom an e-mail and we take it from there."

Dick opened Tom's email. Enclosed was a well itemised account of the repairs and alterations, including what machinery they would need. Tom also gave a time scale of six months, stating the cost would escalate for an earlier completion date. If so, it would be under advice.

Dick was not averse to this at all and replied to Tom informing him of his acceptance of his quote. He asked Tom if he would draw up a contract for them to sign, remembering he should also insert the clause regarding Eric Twelvetrees and his related antics.

He also made a point of advising Tom about the party of seven strong representatives from Nippon Robotics. They would arrive on the twenty-fourth explaining who they were and their field of expertise. Tom's company, therefore, was to work together with them and this too had to be in the contract.

As Chloe was busy with the bookings, Phil and Dick settled down to scrutinize the suppliers of electrical motors. They came upon a well-know Manchester based supplier which was only eighty-eight kilometres away from their factory in Blackpool.

"What a score," Dick exclaimed. "Okay, now here's the deal. Remember, you are in charge of the factory so you will need to move to Blackpool and you must do this as soon as you've done doing whatever it is you still need to be doing at home. Once you're ready to leave, you must first find a place to stay—but I'll leave that up to you. Also, I will not get involved with you, your design, or the supply of the electrical motors because that's your domain. If or when you need any help or money, or whatever, you just have to speak up. I'm only a phone call away."

"Well, why don't I drive here in a few days' time?" Phil now suggested. "I'll stay here with you guys for another few days before driving to Blackpool? While I'm here, I'll find digs and Tom shouldn't be too far ahead of me. Besides, it will break up the long, tiring drive I'd otherwise have ahead of me."

"Yeah, you must get your car there sometime, anyway. So yes, why not indeed,... sir."

They now finished a final comparison of manufacturing companies capable of producing motors for Phil's machine.

"So, this one here is the one we should use?" Phil asked as he pointed a finger at the name on the screen.

"Yes, those are the engineers we need. They're the biggest in Europe but I could be wrong. Okay, I'll have one more whisky and water before retiring for the night. Anyone else want a drink?" Dick asked, but before they could reply, Joel entered.

"Oh hello," they said in unison.

"Hello," Joel returned their greeting. "I'm not staying too long but, to avoid confusion, Phil should use these. It will make life easier for you all."

Joel, as if from out of nowhere, produced a wallet similar to the one he had given to Dick and handed it to Phil. "You have your own credit cards so you know how these work and, you can use the same pin numbers as your own cards."

"Thanks very much, Joel, but what's my limit?"

"Limit?" Joel said "There is no limit. Spend as much as you like, I don't care. Your money is of no concern to us. It means nothing and has no value, so go mad as you humans would say."

"Errmmm... well all right, thanks for that," replied an overwhelmed Phil.

Dick and Chloe could not help themselves from having a giggle. Joel, meanwhile, said he would be in touch and made his usual instant disappearance.

"Well that sorts out a lot of hassles with putting petrol in your guzzler," Chloe said to Phil.

"Yes it does, and now I can identify with you. Great," Phil said with a silly grin on his face.

Dick decided they should have another drink to congratulate Phil on his newfound wealth.

"I suppose I can use these cards to pay for anything else I may need up North?"

"Yes," Dick assured him. "It will save me having to come up there."

Chloe said to Dick "I've confirmed everything and Kieran should be here around nine o'clock in the morning on the fifteenth."

"Thank you."

After chatting about nothing in particular, they all finished their drinks and went to bed for they had to be up at the crack of dawn to be at the airport by 7:00 a.m. the following morning.

Once again on arrival at Biggin Hill airport, Dick went straight to the reception area and Toni greeted him. He handed over the car keys and Toni wished them a pleasant flight.

"Mr Shepherd."

Dick turned around to face him again, "Yes Toni."

"You may not know this but you have a new hostess for today as Helen is on leave."

"Oh yes, Helen said so. What's her name please?"

"Her name is Claire, Mr Shepherd."

"Thanks, Toni. Until the next time, cheers for now."

They walked over to the aircraft and the hostess who was standing in the frame of the door, greeted them.

"Good morning all and welcome onboard. My name is Claire and I'm your hostess for this trip. Please take your seats and I'll serve breakfast once we're in the air."

They thanked her as they made their way into the cabin area of the aircraft. Making themselves comfortable, Claire took their breakfast orders after take-off

"You know, I've just realised we had nothing to eat last night," remarked Chloe.

"Did you switch the washing machine off?" Dick asked her.

"I did, and I folded up all the washing once it was dry, but because you had your nose inside a whisky bottle again, you didn't even notice, now did you?"

"All in the line of duty, my dear, all in the line of duty. Someone has to make sacrifices you know."

"Yes, and you're talking shit again, aren't you?" she retorted.

"Now, now,... relax and eat your breakfast like a good little girl."

"Aargh... bollocks," she now snorted. Phil was having a good old chuckle as he listened to their conversation.

They landed at East Midlands Airport just after 8:30 a.m. and the pilots taxied the plane to the private sector. A middle-aged woman met them, who introduced herself as June, and said she was there to take them to their destination.

They looked at each other dumbfounded as they hadn't arranged for any transport.

June grinned and said, "Because of your frequent flying with us of late, we decided to surprise you and supply transport to your destination."

"Phew," Chloe exclaimed "you had us worried there for a moment."

"That's kind of you," Dick said as he handed her their destination address. "We were going to go by taxi."

She punched the postal code into her Satnav, and they set off... into the morning rush hour traffic. "Oh well, here we go yet again," Dick said to himself.

They arrived at the Toby Manufacturing factory at 9:00 a.m. where Dick thanked June for her service.

"I'll be waiting here for you when you on your...," June tried to say but Dick interjected.

"For goodness' sake woman, we could be here all bloody day. Why don't you give me your mobile number and I'll make sure one of us calls you at least a half an hour before we are ready. After all, even the pilots don't know how long we will be."

June fumbled around inside her purse, found what she was looking for and handed over a business card to Dick.

"Now you go home or do shopping, perhaps even go for a swim, or whatever else you like and we'll call you later."

"Thanks, Mr Shepherd, I appreciate that."

"You're most welcome" Dick replied and watched as she drove away.

"Go for a swim," Chloe chortled. "What the hell was that all about?"

"I don't know, but I had to say something," Dick said while shrugging his shoulders. Phil and Chloe chuckled.

"Go for a swim," Chloe repeated as she shook her head from side to side still giggling. "Go for a bloody swim. What next?"

They entered the building and walked over to the reception desk where they introduced themselves to a man whom they took to be the receptionist. He phoned the CEO's personal assistant advising her of their visitor's arrival.

"Please forgive me as I don't know what I'm doing. I'm only standing in as our receptionist was bursting," said the stand-in male receptionist in a rather hushed voice, and why? They did not know.

They shared a slight giggle but said it was nothing to worry about. Before they sat down, the lift doors opened and yet another young man greeted them. Dick muttered to himself "Hello, what's this then, no women?"

The young man introduced himself as Billie and asked them to please follow him. However, they didn't get into the lift, instead they walked through a set of double fire doors. A short distance down a corridor led them into, not a Boardroom, but just a normal small, cramped meeting room.

Seated at the table were four men, one of whom stood. "Hello, I'm Sterling Hoskins, Chairman and CEO of the company" he said, and the others now stood up.

Dick was not at ease. His hateful experiences in the corporate world of yesteryear suggested something was not quite in place. He could, however, be wrong and hoped he was.

"This is Struan Munroe, Finance Director. Josh Leeson, Operations Director and Torbin Burch, Business Development Director,".

They introduced themselves and shook hands before being seated. Although still uncomfortable, Dick decided his overnight hectic lifestyle might be the cause of his uneasiness. He, therefore, forced himself to relax and to get on with the reason they were there.

"Gentlemen, the reason we are here is to purchase as many of your new cars yet to come off your assembly line. Yes, we know you are a new concern and yes, we also know you need to get your rolling stock out of the factory as soon as in order for you to break even but, more so to keep the ever-present wolf away from knocking at your door."

While Dick sat there and being proud of his opening statement, he took a chance at saying what he had because he didn't know much about this business, anyway.

There was a moment's silence, so he carried on. "There is, however, one small snag. Although we want you to supply the cars as you have designed them, we require you not to fit and supply the motors, the actual engines."

He could see the looks of astonishment developing on their faces so before they could butt in he, once again, carried on.

"Don't worry because those cars you want to sell to the dealerships in the normal way will have the engines. Oh, and just in case you are wondering... no, we will not put another internal combustion engine into your cars. It will, however, be an electrical one."

Dick now didn't carry on as he wanted to see what would happen next. The face of uncertainty said it all.

"Ummm... this might sound ridiculous but please understand this is all confusing for us. You've just dropped a bombshell," said Sterling. "You say you don't require the engines, right?" he now asked, at which Dick nodded his head in response.

"So, does this mean you'll still require the gearbox?" Sterling asked in a rather uncomfortable way, at the same time trying not to sound stupid.

"Well, we could not operate the car without it."

"Now this electrical motor, will it connect to the gearbox?" asked Torbin.

"It will," replied Phil.

"Okay, let's create a scenario," Sterling said "Yes, we supply the cars to you and yes, we deliver them to you minus the engines. Do you expect us to sell the cars to you at a lower rate, or are you going to purchase the cars, minus engines, at the price which would include the engines?"

Although Sterling had asked this question hastily, he was sincere but appeared troubled.

"Once I've explained everything, I guarantee you will not under any circumstances wish to refuse our proposition. But first, gentleman, before we carry on I must ask if you would sign a secrecy clause? If yes,... I'll explain further. If no,... we get up, walk out of here and will never see you again, but I can assure you of one certainty and that is, you will soon see other cars on the roads with our electrical motors in them. So what's it to be?"

They deliberated among themselves for a spell before Josh said: "Do we have to sign this secrecy clause now, or are you going to give us more to go on?"

"Yes and no," Dick replied "and I'll give you something else to consider. Being in the car industry you must know about the Brimstone Car Company in Bristol that's gone into administration resulting in its imminent closure, correct?"

"We have," replied Torbin "but what's it got to do with us?"

"Good question," Dick said to his bemused potential suppliers. "All I want you to do is to get hold of the Administrator and tell them you want to buy the business, lock stock and barrel."

"What," Sterling exclaimed. "Even if we wanted the business, we can't afford it, so that's out of the question."

"Only if you don't believe. No, I'm not referring to your religious beliefs. I'm referring to your inner selves. If you don't believe in your inner self, you won't achieve much in life," Dick said, and once again there was a silence.

Time enough for Dick to reflect on why he had been uncomfortable. These were new guys on the scene. Guys who had never sat around a typical Corporate Boardroom table before and this put him at ease, so he carried on.

"Please guys, your position is not unique. I've been where you are today, so here's what I would like you to do. However, you don't have to do it, but I would like you to do just one thing. Phone the administrator and ask him how much it would take to purchase the business. Are you prepared to at least do that?"

"Would you mind if I and my colleagues left the room for a minute to discuss this?" asked Sterling.

"No, not at all. I would have been surprised if you didn't." They left the room looking rather bamboozled.

"What the hell are you playing at?" asked Chloe.

"Sorry, I'll explain once we're on our way home but, just for now, I'm having fun. I've realise these guys are new to the somewhat corrupt Corporate world, so I want to give them a small taste of what it's like and what they should expect and yes, I am being a bastard, aren't I?"

"Damn right you are. Now get on with it, will you," she said as Phil chuckled in the background.

"And don't you encourage him," she said to Phil. This only made him laugh even more.

The door opened and they returned, but minus Struan.

"We've had a chat about this and Struan, as we speak, is phoning the Administrator to find out what the cost is. However, we have a concern and that is, we don't know if you are genuine or not. I don't want to offend, but the fact is, we don't know you. We don't know where you're from or what you do. In fact, we know nothing about you at all., therefore, we don't know if we can trust you or not," Sterling said uncomfortably.

"Gentlemen, in Casinos, yes I gamble. In business, however, I assure I don't and you can trust me on that. We'll answer your questions after I have put you in the picture."

There was a slight pause then Dick continued. "What if I put a proposition on the table? We pay the full amount for the Brimstone Car Company, should it be up for sale, but ask you to run it as if it were your company? Then all you do is to charge us an administration fee, or whatever you want to call it, and you supply the cars as and when we need them. No catch,... I promise. Sounds too good to be true, doesn't it?"

"Okay," Josh now said, "you want us to supply these cars in the same format as ours?"

"Yes," Dick replied, at which there was another moment's silence.

"Sorry, but this is too much for me to handle," Sterling said still confused by it all. "I'm still not convinced. I mean, put yourself in my shoes. Would you trust me?"

"No bloody ways would I trust you, and to make sure, I'd kick you out of my office. So what are you going to do now? Are you going to kick us out or are you going find out how much further we can go with this meeting?"

While the three of them had a further discussion amongst themselves, Chloe reached over to Dick and whispered in his ear "You're a sadistic bastard, aren't you?"

Struan returned to say the company was up for sale but at a cost of six and a half million pounds.

"Gentlemen, if you get the Administrator on the phone again, we will purchase the business on your behalf," he said in all sincerity. "We'll put the business into your name, as the Controlling Body, and also, give you a further six and a half million pounds to get yourselves out of the red which will put you well back onto the production line. Now should you accept this offer, you will always, from now on, deal with Phil here. Guys, the proverbial ball, as they say in the classics, is in your court."

"Come on guys. This is a once in a lifetime opportunity and is your only chance to make it big—so don't blow it. Now what would you like to do? Kick us out or welcome us into your business world?" Dick asked in all good faith.

"Once again Dick, this is strange for me so if you don't mind, I'd like to have a further discussion in private with my colleagues," Sterling said looking at him in bewilderment.

"Yes, that's understandable," replied Dick.

So again they left the room and Chloe, once more, turned her attention to Dick "Will you stop it now," she said with a face like thunder.

"Ohhhhh... just relax, will you? It's a learning curve for them and will one day come in handy, so let them make hay while the sun shines, will you?"

"You can be such a bloody shit sometimes," Chloe said with a wry smile to which Dick replied "I know dear. You taught me well, didn't you?" and the three of them giggled like school children.

The intrepid businessmen returned, but all of them were wearing poker faces which made it hard to read the situation.

Still, Dick wasn't too bothered by it, and asked: "So what's the verdict, gentlemen?"

"Consensus between us wants us to follow our heads and say there's no deal, but our hearts say otherwise. I now speak to you as head of the team and on behalf of all of us, we have followed our hearts and would like to come on board with you," Sterling announced.

Was there another probable Americanism in Sterling's reply?, Dick mused, but if they wanted to join forces, then that's what counted. So he stood up, and they all followed suit. "Congratulations guys. You will not regret your decision," he assured them and they shook hands all around.

"Now, Struan, let's get the Administrator back on the line shall we?"

Struan lifted the telephone and dialled the number which he had written on his notepad. "Hello, this is Struan Monroe again. We spoke earlier when I asked you how much you were asking for Brimstone Motor Company? Well, I will hand you over to Mr Dick Shepherd of Maitland Electric Car Manufacturers desirous of purchasing the company. Hold on please."

Dick took the phone and said "Good morning, my name is Dick Shepherd—and I'm speaking to?..... Thank you, Mr Sellers. As Mr Munroe said, my company wishes to purchase Brimstone Motor Company lock, stock and barrel and I'll pay the asking price. I understand from Mr Munroe you will only accept payment if representatives from both sides are present. Also, I forgot to mention we will purchase the company in the name of Toby Manufacturers who will run the business on our behalf. As we will pay cash, would you have the relevant sale and purchase documents prepared and ready for signature when we meet. Mr Munroe will fax you all the details later today. So can I suggest we meet tomorrow at three o'clock in the afternoon at the factory's offices?  Excellent, and I look forward to meeting you. Goodbye."

Dick turned his attention to Struan Munroe and said: "Am I correct in remembering you are the Financial Director?"

"Yes, I am."

"We call him Doc," Sterling advised them. "He dropped out of varsity after two years of studying medicine."

"Do you by any chance play a musical instrument?" Dick asked him.

"No. Why?" Struan asked confused.

"Oh, no particular reason. Just curious, that's all."

"Okay,... in what format would you like payment of your six and a half million? Example, would you like the total amount to go through straight away? If so, do you have one of those new portable card reading machines?"

"Yes we do. It seems to be the in thing at the moment."

"Then who's the one to draw up a contract? Because the sooner that's done, the sooner I can use this thing?," Dick said as he waved his credit card at them.

"Torbin, please have a contract drawn up... like... mmmm... now?" asked Sterling.

Torbin stood up, but before he could say anything or even leave the room, he was reminded not to forget about Brimstone Motors. Dick handed Torbin a printed out A4 sheet of paper containing all the information required for the contract. "Here, take this as you will need it," he said and Torbin took the sheet of paper and left the room.

"While he's doing that," Dick continued "may I suggest we talk about what it is we require of you."

"Yes indeed," Sterling replied in a manner in which Dick understood him to be much more at ease.

"As Phil's going to run the factory in Blackpool, he will always be your contact because it's his motor which will go into your cars so, I will now hand over the next stage to him."

Phil looked disconcerted at this as he was himself not used to handling this side of things, so he cleared his throat and advised them of his requirements. "I want the small, medium, and large cars, plus the 4×4. I'm not fussy about the colours of each as that will be up to you, however, every single vehicle you supply to us must have the complete bells and whistles concepts one could fit into them. Top-drawer stuff with no variants in that regard."

"I want to keep it clean and simple. It will be easier on your production line, and on mine. The reason for this is that the fewer interruptions we have on the production lines, the more cars we can turn out, and the more cars we turn out, the lower the cost and the quicker Joe Public will buy them. Gents, we want to flood the market with our cars as soon as possible."

"Will the public be able to afford the prices of these new cars?" enquired Sterling.

"The average small car price, at the moment, is around eight to twelve thousand pounds per unit," Phil replied. "We, however, are striving to sell your..., I mean our small cars, at an absolute maximum of seven and a half thousand pounds per unit, no more. So there's a significant difference there."

He continued "When the public realise they don't have to buy petrol or diesel any more well, which way they will go? You guys will be so busy, you'll be working a twenty-four-hour shift and that, gentlemen, is a guarantee."

"I take it your production line is geared up for this?" asked Dick.

"Yes, it is," Sterling replied, "however, we will need to use more staff once we get going."

"That's great," Dick responded "then may I suggest you get onto it for time is of the essence, and remember, you do not have to fit the exhaust system as it's not required."

"Ah yes. Good point. Thanks" Sterling acknowledged.

Phil continued. "I will draw up a full set of specs for you and hope to have this e-mailed to you within the next week. I'm doing this so you can start next week, or thereabout, your planning and scheduling. Questions anyone?"

Before anyone could say anything, the door opened and Torbin entered. "What I've done is I've used a standard template of old, but it does the job, so I hope you don't mind."

"No, not at all. May we peruse it now?" and Dick placed the contract between himself and Chloe so they could go through it together. On reaching the end they nodded at each other and Dick asked: "Right, where do we sign?"

The signing part now over, Chloe asked Struan if he wouldn't mind organising their card reading machine. Within a moment he was back with the machine in hand, so Dick handed over his credit card to him.

"Also, on a Toby Manufacturing letterhead, can you draw up something explaining to them our company is buying Brimstone Motors? That is, on behalf of Toby Manufacturers who will run the business—or words to that effect," Dick asked Torbin.

Transaction completed, receipts handed over together with a copy of the contract and signed secrecy clause plus a letterhead addressed to the Administrator. "That's it. We're done for now. I'll ask our driver to collect us in half an hour, so if you have any more questions, please ask them now."

As there were no questions, Dick phoned the driver and Chloe phoned Claire to say they would be there within the hour.

"Before you go, and now we have cash in the bank, may we please take you to a late lunch as a thank you?" Sterling asked them.

Although they grinned at what he had said, Dick turned down the offer, however, he did say they should do it another time as they still had a lot to accomplish that day, and because they would fly to Maitland Airport the next day, they were rather short of time. So they chatted about nothing in particular.

As time waits for no one, there was a knock at the door. A young lady entered, went up to Sterling and spoke to him. He thanked her and told them their driver had arrived, and while they shook hands, Phil mentioned he would occasionally pop in unannounced.

In the foyer, June greeted them with a warm smile. They got into the car and had an uneventful drive to the airport.

"There now," Dick said to June. "You have to admit it was far better than sitting in your car for these past four or more hours waiting for us, not so?"

"Oh yes, and it was most kind of you. Thank you."

"You're welcome," Dick replied. He had the notion to ask her if she had by any chance gone for a swim but decided against it.

Claire greeted them, welcomed them onboard and, before long, they were in the air. While making themselves comfortable, she served them their drinks. With yet another pleasant flight under their belts, Claire wished them a good evening.

"Thanks, Clare. See you tomorrow," they said in unison.

They arrived home at 3:20 p.m. and, because Dick was expecting two phone calls, he checked the answering machine. He preferred messages being left on the landline, rather than on his mobile, as he favoured using the mobile for emergencies only.

There was one call from BAE advising them of a driver coming to the house and should be there by 8:30 a.m. the following morning with the documents for Dicks scrutiny and signature.

"Good show," Dick said to himself.

As he was getting his laptop out, the phone rang. He answered it and it was Mr Dumbrill who advised him of a courier being on a 6:30 a.m. flight to London the next morning and should be at the house by no later than 9:00 a.m. With him, he would have all the papers necessary for signing. He also said should Dick have any queries, he was to phone him and he would guide him through the entire process.

"What a nice man," Dick said as he put the phone down.

They spent the time recounting the affairs of the day before getting everything together they needed. He phoned his daughter to ask her if she and her hubby would like to fly back with them and spend a few days there before going back home.

She sounded excited and was hoping her Dad would fill her in as to the goings on, but Dad would not budge. He said he would explain everything once they were at the house.

Dick too was excited, but he didn't show it.

Chapter Twelve

(a) The Signing

THE FOLLOWING MORNING they were all up early and come 8:45, there was a knock at the door. Dick opened it and there before him stood a young lady who had dyed her hair blond. Failing that, then she had spent an awful amount of time dyeing the roots of her hair black. Whichever it was, he didn't know and didn't much care either.

"Hello Mr Shepherd, my name is Susan Dench, from Maitland Airport. Mr Dumbrill sent me here with these documents for you to sign. I hope I'm not too late?"

"No, please come in. Oh, wait a moment. Is that your taxi over there?"

"Yes it is," she said looking puzzled.

Without another word, he walked over to the driver and spoke to him.

"Good morning,".

"Mornin' Gov, how can I help you?"

"Your passenger will pay you when you take her back to the

airport but she will be here for at least three quarters of an hour. So, I will give you one hundred quid now, and this is from me, then another one hundred when you leave because I need you to wait here, please. Is that okay?"

"For that kind of money Gov, I'll stay here all bloomin' day if you likes."

"No, that won't be necessary. Anyway, she shouldn't be more than three-quarters of an hour."

"Cheers Gov, ta,"

He walked back to Susan who was still standing at the front door. From there, he showed her the way to the open-plan living room and introduced her to Chloe and Phil.

"Would you mind entertaining Susan while I pore over these documents?" he asked Chloe.

"There you go, poring away over the documents again," she said to him which made him smile. She turned to Susan, "Okay young lady, come with me" in a mother-hen manner, and asked, "Cup a tea?"

By 9:15 a.m., Dick had completed reading and signing the documents and found no reason at all to phone Mr Dumbrill as the entire document was self-explanatory.

"Forgive my butting in Susan, but what is Mr Dumbrill's first name?"

"It's George, Mr Shepherd."

"Thanks, and you can call me Dick, that's Chloe and this is my nephew, Phil."

"Thank you," Susan replied looking a tad embarrassed.

"Okay dear," Dick said to Chloe "you need to come over here and sign each page, please."

The signing now complete, he handed the big white sealed plastic envelope to Susan and told her to guard it with her life. They all said goodbye and thanked her and Dick walked her to the door. "Wait here for a moment. I want to see the taxi driver again."

Dick told the driver because he had already paid him, he need not accept payment or a tip from Susan, to which the driver agreed. He informed Susan what had transpired whereupon she thanked him as she got into the taxi. The taxi driver said "Cheers Gov" to Dick, and he drove off.

He closed the front door and, when he reached the kitchen, there was yet another knock. As Phil was now the closest, he opened it and said "Good morning" to the young man on the doorstep.

By this time Dick had turned around and there he saw what he could only describe as a spotty hermit standing in front of Phil.

Although well presented the poor chap had, however, a serious acne problem. "Shame," Dick thought to himself. "Oh well, I suppose someone has to have them."

"Good morning sir, I'm Robert Wilkinson and I'm here representing BAE. I've got the documents which need your signature please."

"That will be for my uncle," said Phil as he beckoned him to enter.

Phil took him to the open-plan living room where he introduced him to Chloe and Dick.

He opened a briefcase removing a huge wad of paperwork.

"Oh creeps. We'll be here for another bloody hour," Dick said to himself.

However, Dick was wrong for it turned out the spotty hermit was a qualified junior lawyer and he explained what they needed to do. Thanks to him the whole process only took twenty minutes, much to everyone's delight.

"Shot," Dick exclaimed. "All done?" he asked Robert.

"Yes, that's it. I'm now in the position to give you a message from the Board of Directors,... The wheels are now in motion," he said with a wry smile on his poor acned face.

"Wonderful" Dick replied and wondered whether he should

shake the lad's hand again or not (for fear of contracting whatever it was flowing around within his bloodstream). He did, and Robert was on his way back to his place of employment.

"'Das ist gut, Ja?', as the Germans would say because 'dust' is good for them, 'nein?'" Dick said to both Chloe and Phil. "Right, I'm just going to check my e-mails and then we must think about getting ready as wheels up should be at noon."

"So how's your German?" Phil asked him.

Dick could feel the laughter stirring inside him and couldn't resist replying "My German's fine. Why, how's your one?" he asked, and Phil chuckled "Oh, ha-bloody-ha."

Dick opened an email from Tom which advised he had attached the Letter of Acceptance and a copy of the Contract to the email and also advised him of the cost of doing the complete job which would be eleven and a half million pounds. However, he still reserved the right to charge any extras, as he had mentioned before in an earlier conversation, should they arise. It appeared from various intense scrutinies a few anomalies may well pop up from time to time.

Dick printed out the Letter of Acceptance and the Contract and phoned Tom to inform him everything was in order. If payment was to be up-front, he should send his card-reading machine with Kieran the following day. Tom advised Dick he had one and he would get it dropped off with Kieran in the morning.

Tom also said he would put two teams in on the job, one for the factory and one for the housing estate. If there were no hiccoughs along the way, they hoped to complete the job by the fourteenth of July. He said this, along with the other items, were all in the Contract for Dick's perusal.

Before he replaced the phone in its base, he asked Tom to concentrate on the factory floor area where the assembly of Phil's drive units would take place. They required the space while the work on the factory, and housing estate, was still in progress.

Dick now prepared himself for the trip to Brimstone Car Company.

"Come on then. If you don't want to be late, I suggest we leave now," Chloe shouted up the stairs to them.

"Okay, on my way," Dick called back.

"Me too," Phil echoed.

### (b) Brimstone Car Purchase

"We should make good time if this stays as it is," Phil said as the traffic was surprising steady.

They did, for the traffic behaved itself for a change. As a result, wheels-up was at 11:50 a.m. and Claire did her usual serving trick. After dropping Phil off, Dick asked Claire to convey a message to the pilots. As their appointment was for 3:00p.m., he would appreciate it if they could depart as soon as for Brickner Airport and to advise them about his daughter and son-in-Law accompanying them back to Biggin Hill, therefore, wheels-up should be no later than 6:15 p.m. Claire conveyed the message and said to Dick all was in order.

Once the plane had landed and had parked at its designated spot, Phil got off.

"Cheers Phil. See you on the eighteenth."

Before Phil was even in his car, they were back in the air. They arrived at Brickner Airport a little earlier than expected and Dick told Claire they should be back around 6:00 or 6:15 p.m. They now set off in search of the taxi rank and the drive to the factory took a little over fifteen minutes.

"Please give me your contact number. We'll need you to come and fetch us again around five-thirty this afternoon," Dick said to the taxi driver.

"If you likes Gov, I could just be 'ere then."

"Thanks, but give me your contact details anyway in case we're finished sooner rather than later."

The driver searched amongst his papers and found a card which he handed over to Dick. "Cheers Gov, I'll sees you later," he said before driving away.

"He must be that other bloke's cousin," Dick thought to himself.

They walked to the front door and rang the doorbell. Moments later, the door opened and before them stood a tall, elderly cadaverous-type man in an ill-fitting dark suit and Dick swore he was using formaldehyde as his aftershave or deodorant.

"Good afternoon" he greeted them in a thin, dry voice and it took all of Dick's strength to stop himself from laughing. "You must be Mr Shepherd," the man said.

"Why must I be?" is what Dick wanted to say but instead his reply was more polite. "Yes I am and this is my partner Mrs Chloe Fraser-Rigby" he informed the cadaverous-type man and wondered to himself "Let's see if the waning brain can handle that one."

The old man led them to the Boardroom where they met two other people who were sitting behind a mound of paperwork strewn all over the desk.

"Hello, I'm David Sellers and this is my associate Lyn Miles. I see you've already met my Dad."

"Oh crap, I'd better mind my p's and q's," Dick thought to himself "Yes, I'm Dick Shepherd and this is my partner Chloe Fraser-Rigby."

As there was so much paperwork on the desk, David suggested they sit at another table. Once they were all seated, David said:

"Now, we believe you want to purchase this company lock, stock and barrel."

"Yes we do and we will put up the funds for and on behalf of Toby Manufacturing."

"So Mr Hoskins said, and that's fine with us," David acknowledged. "I received all the details from Mr Hoskins and therefore expecting this deal, and as per your instructions, the documents are ready for signing, and to confirm, the purchase price is six and a half million pounds?"

"Yes, that's right. When would you want payment and can I pay by credit card please?" Dick asked to which David replied, "We were hoping to receive payment now and yes, we can accept a credit card."

"Okay, let's do it."

"But before we do," David advised them "I must ask Lyn to fetch our card machine first. Magic things those. They save such a lot of time and effort," he added, at which Lyn got up and excused herself. "While we wait for Lyn to come back, we can go over the transfer papers and sign them, if you find all's in order?"

"Yes, okay," Dick replied.

David added. "I hope you don't mind but, as the funds are coming out of your account, I must insist we put your name or names on the documents."

"No, I don't mind at all," Dick agreed.

As they read through each page, they put their initials at the bottom and, on two separate pages they had to put down their full names, address and signatures.

"You realise that part of the deal is taking on all the staff?"

"No I didn't," Dick replied "but that is a blessing in disguise as it saves me from recruiting new staff."

"Well sir, fret no more," David responded "I spoke to the ex-owner and he informed me not only he but all the staff are over the moon at this news. Would you like to meet him?" he asked, and Dick and Chloe responded in unison "Why not?"

David excused himself and left the room. Soon, he reappeared with whom they assumed to be the ex-owner. Not a tall man— only about one metre seventy-five centimetres – and had a receding hairline. It seemed he tried hard to lose the blubber around his midriff, only he wasn't succeeding, but in a strange way it suited him.

"This is Jonathan Styles," David said introducing him to both Dick and Chloe, so they shook hands and sat down. David gave the three of them some alone time and said he and Lyn would join them once she had returned.

Dick began by explaining to Jonathan what they required and what was about to happen. He told him Phil would come and see him sometime on the morning of the eighteenth, and although he would deal with Sterling Hoskins, it would be Phil who would be the person in charge overall. Also, with the new ownership, Jonathan would be the General Manager of the business and it would be up to him to get the staff back and working as soon as possible.

Jonathan asked them if they would like to look around the factory, to which both Dick and Chloe accepted, so he led the way through the reception area and out onto the factory floor.

"This place is spotless," Chloe commented.

After a quick tour, they returned to the office to find David and Lyn had returned. Dick handed over his credit card and, in no time at all, Brimstone Car Company had a new owner.

"So when can you can you come back to work?" Dick asked Jonathan.

"Now,... and do I keep my original office?"

"Well, if you're not going to use it for anyone else, then yes, it's still yours. I suppose I can approve of that for, although Phil will be your boss, I'm Phil's boss."

"Thanks, Dick. As soon as you leave, I will make phone calls."

"For goodness' sake man don't let us stop you. Get on the blower straight away,".

With this, Jonathan walked back to his office while Dick and Chloe strode around the place. At one stage they bumped into David, and Dick asked: "What are you planning to do with all the paperwork?"

"When I'm finished, with your approval, the originals go to Toby Manufacturers with a copy to Jonathan."

"That would be perfect, however, I'm having second thoughts about how we've gone about this, but it won't affect you, only Toby Manufacturers. So, what I suggest you do is, as you've got my postal address, send me the originals instead. Don't send anything to Toby's," Dick said and David acknowledged the instruction.

They carried on walking around the office area, sizing it up, before going back out into the factory area. Chloe once again remarked on how clean and tidy the entire building was.

"Yes, I think we're lucky with this one," Dick said, and his mobile phone laughed at him. "Who the hell's got my number?"

"Well, answer the bloody thing and find out," Chloe snapped.

"Hello."

"Hello Daddy."

"Sweetie-pie," Dick exclaimed—as he always did when he heard his daughter's voice. "How are you, sweet child o' mine?"

"I'm okay, Daddy. Is everything still on for tonight?"

"Abso-bloody-lutely," he reassured her. "Chloe and I are already here but we'll only be at the airport at about five forty-five this afternoon and I'll explain everything then."

"Okay, we'll see you there."

"Indeed you shall, my meadies child. Love you," he shouted into the phone. (Like most people do when using mobile phones,... they must shout.)

"Love you too Daddy. Bye,"

"Your child is the only person on this planet who can make you go weak at the knees, isn't she?"

"Oh, I hadn't noticed," he replied silly.

"Yeah right. Stop talking shit, will you," she said with a smile on her face.

Dick knew what she meant, but he didn't like to show it for, not only did he love his child, he adored her and no one would take that away from him.

"Don't you think we can go now?" Chloe asked him, to which he replied "Yeah, I suppose we can. Let's go back to Jonathan's office, see how he's doing and say goodbye. Then we go."

"Come on then," she said in agreement.

They found their way back to Jonathan's office and, as they entered, they heard him on the phone and assumed he was talking to one of the staff members.

"Okay, I've got to go now. The new owners are here in my office," he said and put the phone down. "That was my secretary, and she's excited about her job. She'll be here first thing in the morning to help me get in touch with the rest of the staff. I've also got hold of the three other chaps on the original Director's Board, but one of them doesn't want to come back."

"Is he an integral part of the business?" Chloe asked, to which Jonathan replied "No, he isn't."

"So you won't miss him?" Dick now asked.

"Mmmm... no, not at all," Jonathan affirmed.

"Well, I wouldn't worry about it," Dick said "but it prompts me to ask: Did you asked yourself if you need the other ex-board members? Look, although I don't regard it as being important, it might be something to think about, but we leave it in your capable hands,"

Dick picked up the desk telephone and phoned the taxi driver who said he had driven into the driveway and was about to park the car.

"Okay Jonathan, it's been nice meeting you and here's to some lovely new cars being sold soon. Phil will be here in two days' time and he'll guide you along," Dick said as they shook hands before walking out of the office.

They turned a corner in the passageway and saw David and his father, who were on their way to see Jonathan to finish up their side of the business, and they said goodbye. Once again Dick noticed the smell of formaldehyde permeating the air.

They arrived at the airport in good time, paid the driver who, on dropping them off, said "Cheers Gov" and they turned and walked into the building. As they did so, Kerri took them by surprise for she was hiding behind a pillar, jumped out and said "Boo" in their faces. Dick kissed her on her forehead and gave her a big bear hug, but without squeezing the living daylights out of her.

"Hello, my sweetie-pie."

"Hello to you too, Daddy" she replied, and after what seemed like an eternity to the others, they relinquished their hug.

"Hi Dick," Ivan said from behind him, so he turned around and they shook hands.

"Got your licence yet to fly the drone?" Dick asked Ivan.

"No, not yet. I received a letter from the authorities but they say it will take another week and a half."

"Well, I suppose you are dealing with those overworked and

underpaid Government servants,".

"Dick," said Chloe.

"Yes, dear?"

"This chap wants to know if he can take their luggage to the plane."

Kerri and Ivan only had one big travel case between them and the porter picked it up and took it to the waiting aircraft.

"Right you two, shall we board the plane?"

"Daddy, what's going on? Since when can you afford to fly around in a private jet and why don't I know anything about it?" Kerri asked her father as they walked arm-in-arm towards the exit of the building leading them to the aircraft.

"Patience my child. I will reveal everything."

"Okay, but what's going on with your hair?" she asked in amazement as they got to the door.

There she stopped, had a good look at her father, looked at Ivan, then looked back at her father. "Daddy, what is it you're not telling me? Are you working out in the gym with your health condition the way it is? Look at you," she exclaimed in surprise. "You're different somehow, but I can't put my finger on it, or am I dreaming?"

They carried on walking and once again he assured her he would soon reveal everything.

"Forget about getting anything out of him," Chloe said to her "You know your father, right?"

"Oh yes, I know my stubborn father all right. I'm still convinced it was his stubbornness that saved his life when he was in the hospital, you know."

All the while he said nothing and only listened to what they had to say. As they approached the stairs to the aircraft, Dick showed Kerri and Chloe to board first, and as they climbed the stairs, Chloe introduced the two newcomers to Claire.

"Hello, welcome on-board. Please make yourselves comfortable."

"Oh my goodness me, this is so nice," Kerri said in approval. "From now on when we go on holiday, this is how I expect you to take me," she said to Ivan with a broad smile on her face.

"No," he replied, "I'm expecting you to take me travelling in style this way."

"Oh, come now children, there's time enough for that," said mother-hen Chloe.

They sat down and Claire approached them. "May I get you something to drink once we're airborne?"

"My usual, please," Dick replied, and Chloe echoed, "Yes, and my usual as well, please."

"And you two?" Dick asked his daughter and son-in-Law.

"A fruit juice for me, please?" Kerri asked, and Ivan requested the same.

Once airborne, Claire served the drinks and Kerri demanded in a loud voice, "Daddy, what are you drinking?"

"It's only whisky and water, my child."

"But you shouldn't be drinking that stuff, what with your ill health,... and what about the medication you take, the anti-coagulant? Alcohol doesn't mix well with it, you know."

"I warned you about what would happen when your child found out about your drinking," said Chloe.

"Steady yourself, my sweetie-pie. I will explain everything to you, and once I've have, your mind will be at ease."

The poor child just looked at her father with a blank but fuming stare. "So when are you going to put me in the picture and out of my misery?"

"I promise once we get home, I will reveal everything. I don't want to say anything now as there are too many ears around. So, are you well, my child?" he asked, hoping to get away from the present subject... himself.

For the rest of the flight, and the taxi home, they spoke about family issues and no word mentioned about the up-and-coming future events.

"I'll see you tomorrow," Claire said to them as they prepared to disembark.

"No, you won't see me," Dick said in reply.

"Oh, are you not going to Argentina then, Mr Shepherd?"

"No, I'm not. Only Chloe is."

"And maybe perhaps another one," Chloe added.

"You've been mumbling about someone else but I didn't realize you were serious about it," Dick commented, and Chloe said "I know, and I wouldn't tell you either."

"Why's that then?" he asked her, to which she replied "Ohhhhh... I don't know. No particular reason."

All the while Kerri was trying her best to understand what was going on but thought it best not to say anything.

"Oh, all right then. You enjoy your time with your mystery guest."

"Thanks, I will, and by the way, I must be at Biggins at nine-thirty tomorrow evening so the driver will fetch me at around nine o'clock" said Chloe, reminding Dick of her movements. "See you tomorrow Claire, bye," she said while descending the on-board retractable stairs.

"Okay, that's fine with me" he said to her. "Who am I to argue?" he said to himself as he too descended the stairs with Kerri and Ivan.

Dick walked into the office to double-check everything was still okay for the early morning flight which Kieran would travel on. All okay, they set off on their car ride home. Once at home, he suggested they sort out the sleeping arrangements first, and unpacking, before settling down at the dining room table with the obligatory drink.

Dick and Chloe told Kerri and Ivan everything.

Chapter Thirteen

The happiness of Kerri

A GLASS OF wine for Chloe a glass of whisky and water for Dick, mugs of coffee for the "kids", they settled down to what Kerri regarded to be... story time. The two of them listened with intent, absorbing everything being said to them, all the while sipping at their coffee. At some points their eyes would light up, at others, huge frowns would develop on their foreheads. Sometimes they would even wriggle around on their chairs— whether this was due to their being uncomfortable or even nervous tension, wasn't clear.

It was very unusual for Dick's daughter to just sit for almost an hour and fifteen minutes without her saying or doing something, but she was so engrossed, even to the point of speechlessness.

From out of the blue, Kerri said "Sorry to interrupt Daddy but can we have a break? I need to pee and I'd like another coffee, please."

While she was upstairs, Ivan got up to make another two cups of coffee, and also to replenish Dick's and Chloe's drinks.

"Would anyone like something to nibble on?" Chloe asked, and

Dick said "Good idea, methinks." With drinks and nibbles at the ready, they all sat back down at the table.

"Okay, you can carry on now please Daddy," said Kerri, smiling at him.

So, Dick obliged and carried on from where they had left off and got to a stage where he looked at Chloe. "Do you suppose it's time for... well,...?" Chloe understood what he was getting at, and she replied, "Yes, it's got to happen sometime, so why not now?"

At this, Dick got up and put another chair in a strategic spot.

As he did so, Kerri asked "Time for what, Daddy?" and he replied "Time for this" and, as he sat down, Joel entered and appeared seated on the extra chair. "Hello all" he chirped.

"Hello, Joel" Chloe and Dick responded.

Ivan flung himself back into his chair in surprise and Kerri let out a gentle scream while clasping her hand over her mouth. "Fucking hell, and all the while I didn't understand what to make of this," she muttered through her fingers.

Dick didn't like his daughter to swear and had always made it a policy not to swear in front of her. "Sweetie-pie, your language" he reprimanded her in strong but quiet voice while gritting his teeth and giving her a stern look.

"Sorry, Daddy."

"Ohhhhh for fuck sake," Chloe exclaimed "Please get out of that old-fashioned style of yours. Kerri's approaching her thirties and married now for,... how many years, and if she's a chip off the old block, what else do you expect of her? You old wanker," she now said with a smile.

"Hello you two, my name is Joel," he said ignoring what was going on between Dick and Chloe.

"Wow," Ivan uttered "Is this for real?" he asked as he looked at Joel.

"Yes it is," Dick assured him "We heard Joel introducing himself to you," he said to them but looking at Ivan.

Joel looked at Kerri and Ivan with his big black almond-shaped eyes and carried on where Dick and Chloe had left off.

"Now Dick, regarding what you asked me about having added benefits given to them, shall we carry that out?"

Kerri said "What are you talking about, and if it's about us, please explain, daddy?"

"Remember I explained to you about Joel and his team fixing all my ailments and giving me a new body? Well, they are more than prepared and willing to do the same for you. In addition, you will both have the ability to fly any aircraft, anywhere, day or night. Fantastic, right? I want you to take them up on their offer, sweetie-pie, because I need you guys to help me with this quest Joel and company have embarked me on."

"I agree with your Dad, Kerri," said Joel. "You have nothing to lose and everything to gain."

Upon hearing this Ivan was excited. "To pilot a plane, that would be great. Come on Kerri, we have to do it. Your Dad did it and hell, you even commented on how good he looks."

Kerri pondered for a while, at the same time searching for reassurance from her father. So he got up, moved around the table to her side and put his arms around her. "It will all be just fine, sweetie-pie. Please trust your old man on this one" he said and dropped a kiss on the top of her head.

He put one hand under Kerri's armpit, prompting her to stand up, and led her to the empty area of the dining room floor asking Ivan to join them. The three of them stood there and Dick, once again, gave them his reassurance. "Just stand here and when Joel prompts you, please hold his hand."

He sat down while Joel walked over to them. Each of them held onto his outstretched digits, and Joel turned to Chloe and Dick and said "We'll be back."

"Cheerio," Chloe called out.

Kerri was about to say something when they disappeared into

thin air.

"Shall we watch a little television and get pissed?" Chloe asked Dick.

Dick wanted to reply "But we don't have a little television." Instead, he settled for "What an excellent idea."

After watching the usual crap and getting through a few more drinks, Chloe asked: "What time will they be back?"

"Not before midnight."

"What's the time now?" she asked, and Dick said "It's just on eleven-forty, so perhaps another half hour. One for the road?"

"Go on then. Isn't it wonderful I don't have to get up early in the morning?"

"Yes, you do. Kieran should be here by no later than ten-thirty."

"Oh darn," she said. "I forgot about him."

They sat back, sipped their drinks, and carried on watching the never-ending crap being shown on the TV. "Still, I suppose it passes the time," Chloe said, stifling a yawn.

She said she had had enough and, therefore, decided to go to bed to read her book, so they kissed each other goodnight. Dick had the idea to get well pissed, but he decided against it. Instead, he flicked through the channels and found was crap after crap.

"What on earth do I pay all this money to these people for? They've got a million and one different channels and there's stuff-all on them. Even the naughty channels are crap. Just as well it's not my money," he said, remembering Joel's words: "We don't deal in money....."

"Why we can't practice things this way, is beyond me."

While he was still pondering certain points of view, there was the familiar soft light and sound and the travelling duo arrived back with Joel.

"Hello you guys and how did it all go?" he asked Joel.

"The doctors said it was a success, but more so your daughter."

"Please convey my heartfelt thanks to them for me, Joel."

Joel raised a hand in acknowledgement, said he would, and vanished.

Dick looked over at Kerri and Ivan and they both smiled. "Grab a drink and come sit over here," he said pointing at the second couch.

Ivan got coffee for Kerri and himself while she sat down and discussed their new improved bodies. Dick told them it would take a few days for everything to rectify itself and settle in.

"Yes, they said. I'm so excited and I can't wait to tell Mum. This has to be the most insane thing I've ever experienced, but what about that lighting? Imagine using it with my photography work. Hell, I'd show some of those so-called photographers what it's all about."

"Well, why don't you ask Joel? Maybe he'll oblige?" said Dick.

"I should cross one hurdle at a time. Let this experience first settle in, for I'm just so excited. Thanks, Daddy," she said and, getting up, gave him a big hug.

"You are so welcome my child, however, it's not me who you should thank—it's Joel."

Ivan returned with two mugs of coffee and handed one to Kerri. "I can't wait to get into the cockpit of a plane," he said beaming at Dick.

"What plane?" asked Kerri.

"Hell, any plane."

"Well now, isn't that fortuitous."

"What do you mean, Daddy?"

"What I haven't yet told you, I'm having a simulator delivered and installed on the twentieth from Airbus. It's the A400M. Have you heard of it?"

"Well I've not, but Ivan might."

"No, I've never heard of it."

"That's not too surprising as it's a transporter, not a commercial airliner. It's only been flying a few years now if that helps."

"Mmmm... no, it doesn't," replied Ivan.

"Well, I reckon the simulator should be available by the end of the month for trials—for testing, and this is where you two come into the bigger picture," Dick said while they kept looking at him.

"I need the two of you to resign from work, with immediate effect, and hand in your notice to your landlord," Dick instructed them. "You must tell him the place will be available to him on the first of March. Now before I go any further, let's sit at the table so you can make notes because things are going to get interesting in your lives."

So they all got up and made themselves comfortable at the table.

Dick started things off by saying "There is a chap at Maitland Airport who, at the moment, is running the show for me. His name is Deon DuToit and although I want the two of you to be there and in charge, you must let him continue to run the show. The reason being is because neither of you nor I have the foggiest notion of how to run an airport."

"Also, and not to being disrespectful to you in any way Ivan, Kerri is to be number one in charge over there and yes, if you like, being your boss. But I'm sure you will understand this is for obvious reasons."

"Yes, Dick, for I would do the same if I were in your shoes."

They heard stirrings from up above and, in no time at all, Chloe was back downstairs as she was longing to hear how they were after their stint with Joel.

"May I pour you a drink, Chloe?" Ivan asked her.

"I'll have a cup of coffee with you two."

"Yes," Dick pointed out "and you won't get any sleep tonight if you do."

"Mmmm... you right. Bugger it, I'll have a half a glass of wine, please," she said. Ivan got up to get another round of drinks for all of them.

While they had their drinks, they told Chloe of their sojourn with Joel. Afterwards, Dick informed Chloe just how far he had got with filling them in about Maitland Airport.

"Daddy."

"Yes, sweet child o' mine."

"When do you want us to move there and where are we going to live?"

"There's plenty of housing at the airfield and I suggest you move into the ex-owners house. He should move before the end of the month."

"Okay, but what about Mum?"

"What about her?" Dick mused looking rather vague "Mmmm... well now,... let's... errmmm...,"

"Daddy!"

"Sorry my child—only teasing," he said sporting a big smile. "You should invite your mother to move with you. I mean, you're not going to leave her behind, are you?"

"No," she replied "but you don't mind if she moves in with us?"

"Of course not, sweetie-pie," Dick said re-assuring her. "She's your mother and you may one day need to care for her, as you may also one day need to care for these two geriatrics sitting here in front of you."

"Erm... Dick," Ivan said "I don't mean to jump the gun but what about my Mum and Dad?"

"Fair question, but you've asked it way too early. There are plenty of other bridges we must cross before we go down that path. All will fall into place as we go along. So please, don't worry about it yet as it will happen when the time comes."

"Okay Daddy, but you are going have to help us with the move. Money-wise, I mean" she said. Before Dick replied, Kerri jumped out of her skin for, in a flash, Joel reappeared in his usual flamboyant manner.

"I'm not staying but—here, you can explain," Joel said handing Dick a familiar looking wallet, and in a flash, disappeared.

"You'll get used to that," Chloe said to them.

"I hope you don't mean crapping myself," Kerri said, and they all chuckled.

Dick opened the wallet and peered inside. Noticing two familiar —looking cards, he scrutinised them before handing them over to Kerri and Ivan.

"You two are already in Joel's favour as he is giving these to you to use, as and when you need to. You can spend as much as you like and on anything you like."

"What does P.U.B stand for?" Kerri asked, at which Chloe and Dick both smiled.

"No, it doesn't stand for the obvious. It stands for Phoenix United Bank," he told them.

Kerri looked at the cards and gave her head a little shake from side to side. She, one by one, handed them over to Ivan who asked: "What pin numbers do we use?"

"The same ones you use for your current cards," Dick advised them.

"And what about statements and who pays...?" asked Kerri.

"Not to worry about anything like that at all. Nothing, zero, nil, nought, zilch and yes, even diddly squat. You use as and when. When you get home, buy a new car, as a test, then phone me."

"What kind of car?" she asked her father.

"Yes, Joel would say anything you like but I, as your father, have reservations about a certain sports car you've been admiring for a few years now. Well, that's a definite No-No and will remain so until you have had advanced driving lessons. Once you can prove to me you can handle the raw power output the car has to offer, then we have a deal," Dick said, and for a moment, sat there in silence. Sizing up the situation he extended his arm towards her to shake hands on the matter.

However, because Kerri's response wasn't quick enough for him, he continued. "If there is no deal, I take those cards back. It's as simp...."

Even before he finished the sentence, she grabbed hold of her father's hand, shook it, and said "Deal".

As he looked at her, he realized what Chloe had said earlier was true. Kerri was just like her old man—a chip off the old block – which made him a proud father.

"Right," Dick said standing up "I'm off to bed. I have to get up early because an Estate Agent will be here at about ten to ten-thirty in the morning with papers for me to sign. You two are using my bed tonight and when Chloe leaves tomorrow, you can move into her room until she gets back."

"Where are you going to?" Kerri asked Chloe.

"I, my dear girl, am going to Argentina for a few days," Chloe boasted. "Your father is letting me loose among the Argentinian men as I need to sign papers on his behalf."

"And good bloody luck to those guys too is all I can say," Dick said, and they giggled.

"Daddy," Kerri said in the way which always melted his heart as she was about to ask him for something. "Why don't we use these cards tomorrow and buy a car?"

"You can do that but, you don't have all the papers here with you to prove who you are. Not so?"

"Damn," was all she said.

"All right, sweet child o' mine, give me a hug and a kiss as your old man must now do impressions of sleeping." So they all decided to retire for the rest of the night.

By 7:00 a.m. the following morning Dick was up and about getting breakfast ready when there was a knock at the door.

"Who the hell is that at this hour of the bloody morning?" he said out loud to himself.

Upon opening the door, before him stood two things, which was the only way he could described them. Thing number one greeted him.

"Goo mornin' sir. We's sorra t' distur-byo so earla in de mornin' bu' wee wus wonderin' if yo 'ad any ol' clothes or furnichin's or anytink along dem lines dat jou weesh t' trow oot. An' if soo, may wid be abel t' tak dem orf yore 'ands fer yo?" the thing asked in an alcohol and nicotine infused voice.

The accent was unrecognisable. Dick wonder what the thing had done to its mouth for he had seen nothing like it before. What was it trying to say, for goodness' sake? Before Dick said he found it hard to understand him, thing number two spoke, but in a deeper voice.

"De missus an' I ar' down on orr luck, see, an' wee wold grea'ly appre-shates to recei' yo kin'ness sir."

To his amazement, Dick found he understood this thing better and wondered if it were perhaps a hint of Irish he detected in his accent? So he studied his form and looked from him to the other one and back again. "Well, where the hell's the bloody missus then?"

"Why sh bee stand'n der, sir" he replied in a confused manner. "Sh be de on' dat spoke t' yo when yo open'd de door sir," he said sounding surprised.

"Bloody hell. Shit, imagine waking up in the morning finding that thing lying next to you. Aaaarrrgh... wake me up from my nightmare," Dick screamed inside his head.

Instead, he told them they should return on the twenty-seventh of March and said he would see if he had anything for them hoping they would never return.

"Do you have a car or a truck or some other mode of transport perhaps?"

"Wee 'as 'n 'orse sir," replied the wife.

"I beg your pardon,... a what?" Dick asked with raised eyebrows.

"N' 'orse sir, wit a kaart," replied the bloke.

"Oh, you mean a horse and cart."

"Yit sir, a 'orse 'n kaart."

("Well why the hell didn't you say so in the first place, you twat," is how Dick wanted to reply.). Instead he remained diplomatic and said, "I'll see you next month."

"Tanks a loa sir," they seemed to say in unison.

He closed the door and walked towards the kitchen. On his way, he heard himself mumbling away to himself. "Why me, for goodness' sake? Why me and why so early in the bloody morning? What the hell have I done to deserve this? The sight of those things would be enough to drive a man to drink,".

"Who was at the door, dear?" Chloe asked as she proceeded to walk down the stairs.

"Oh bugger me, you don't want to know."

"Hey?" Chloe said, confused by his reply.

"You don't want to know," Dick repeated feeling as if the bottom were about to fall out of his world. However, something jogged his memory, and he said: "Remember the movie where the shit monster came up from out of the toilet?"

"Yes, I remember it. Why?"

"Well, believe it or not, that was him,... and his bloody wife was with him as well, for shit's sake," he said yet again pathetically for it felt as if the world had now fallen out of his bottom.

Chloe burst out laughing.

"Who would ever think the scene would ever play out in real life?"

"Yeah, and it sounds like it will haunt you for the rest of your life as well," she answered, while trying to suppress her giggling.

"You'd better bloody well believe it," he blurted out "and you'll see for yourself if they come back on the twenty-seventh of March."

"Why would they do that?" she asked looking puzzled.

"Because they were looking for handouts of any sort. Furniture, clothes, whatever and, to get rid of them, I told them to come back then," he said, heaving a big sigh.

"Oh well, they may not come back at all so don't worry about it."

"Breakfast?" he now asked her in his normal voice.

"Yes please."

As he was serving up the breakfast, a sleepy-eyed Kerri walked into the kitchen and gave her father a nice good morning hug. "Morning Daddy."

"Morning my sweetie-pie. Breakfast?"

"What you got?"

"What you see before you, my child."

"Okay, but no bacon for me please."

"Morning Chloe," Kerri said from across the room still hugging her old man.

"Shall I dish up for Ivan as well?"

"Yes please, Daddy."

Ivan came downstairs and said good morning just as Dick offered the breakfast plate out towards him. He said thanks, and they all sat down at the table to have their breakfast together.

"A long time since something like this has happened," Dick

mused.

"Hey," Chloe exclaimed "why don't you tell them about the shit monsters who came a-knocking at the door this morning," she said while grinning.

"Oh no please don't start," Dick groaned.

After breakfast, they attempted to tidy up the downstairs area. Once finished, they one by one made their way upstairs to attend to their ablutions.

"What time did you say he's coming here this morning, Daddy?"

"He should be here no later than ten-thirty,... why?"

"I know it's cold out there, but it's a cloudless day so I was wondering—why don't we do something today?" she asked, once more in the loving way she had when wanting something from her father, and the weakling Dad asked, "What do you have in mind, my child?"

"Are there any castle here we haven't visited yet?"

"Mmmm... I don't know. Why don't you log-on to the internet. You never can tell, you might just find something you were not even aware of."

"Good idea. May I use your laptop please?"

"Be my guest," Dick replied. "Now listen, when you buy

yourselves a new car or cars, you had better buy new laptops."

"Oh yeah, that would be great," Kerri said looking at Ivan. "Why don't we go to Leeds Castle?" she asked him.

"But you've been there already," remarked Chloe.

"Yes," Kerri replied, "I've been there twice before and Ivan's been there once."

"Look, it's a nice place to go to and I've been there..." and before Dick finish, Chloe blurted out "Five times before."

"Flipping heck, is that how many times we've been there?"

"Yep," Chloe replied "and I'm not going there again. No, no— don't misunderstand me. I don't mean now. Wherever it is you go to today, I won't be going with you because I need to do washing and ironing before I pack for tonight's trip. So please, if you want to go there again, don't let me stop you."

"Sweet child o' mine, I'll let you decide. Sorry Ivan, if you want to chuck in your tuppence worth, please do so. I'll let the two of you decide and I'll be your taxi driver. How's that sound? But if you want to go to London, I'm not driving. We'll do *training* instead," he said and emphasised the word training.

There was another knock at the door which made him check the time. "If that's Kieran, he's twenty minutes early, which is not a bad thing. However, if it's not, then it can only be those fucking shit monsters again."

As Chloe was the nearest to the door, she got up to answer it. "So,... it's not that difficult to swear in front of your child, now is it?" she said as she tapped him on his left shoulder.

"Damn," Dick bellowed to himself "You stuffed up there, you twat."

"Hello, young man. Come in, and how was the flight?" Chloe asked Kieran as she led the way to the dining room.

"Terrific," Kieran replied. "What a marvellous way to travel," he said as he noticed the rest of them sitting at the table.

"Good morning Mr Shepherd, I hope I'm not too early."

"No, not at all. It's being late I cannot abide. Meet my daughter, Kerri, and her husband, Ivan."

They shook hands and Dick asked them to please clear the table. He needed the table-top area for the documents Kieran had brought for him to sign.

"I suppose you are yet again going to pore over the documents," Chloe said with a slight hint of sarcasm as she smiled at the hidden meaning.

"No, not now. It's far too early and besides, I'll be driving the car in a little while."

The others just looked at them and decided it must be a joke between the two of them.

"I take it you have the card reading machines with you?" Dick asked Kieran.

"Yes I have," Kieran confirmed, and bent down to retrieve them from his attaché case.

With the reading and signing of the documents, together with the money transfers being carried out, he finished. This included Tom's required amount to get the building process in motion. Kieran gathered up all the papers and placed them in their separate protective plastic sleeves. He now placed them, together with the card reading machines, back in his attaché case.

"Thank you both so much for the business Mr Shepherd and also, thanks for laying on the flight for me. I will brag for as long as my colleagues will allow me to."

"You're so welcome, Kieran, and thanks for taking care of your side of the business for us. We appreciate it."

They shook hands, and Kieran said his goodbyes to the others as he left.

"Well, we are now the proud owners of a derelict car factory just outside Blackpool," Dick announced, to which Chloe added "Yes, and not forgetting two hundred houses."

"Indeed," Dick said with a satisfied smile on his face. "Have you now decided what it is you want to do, my child?" he now asked.

"Well I'm not interested in going into that madhouse called London."

"Hallelujah and praise be to God," Dick said, and Chloe sang "Yeah man" just to round it off.

The following short silence broke by Ivan speaking to Kerri. "You want to go to Leeds Castle again, don't you?" he asked, and she said "Errmmm,... yes I do," she admitted.

"Well, what are we waiting for?" Dick asked. "Let's get dressed and get the hell out of here before God gets here and bitch-slaps me for saying what I did," he said causing her to giggle.

They spent a lovely day at Leeds Castle and were back home by 5:30 p.m. where Chloe gave Dick a message.

"Phil phoned. He wants to inform you he has already secured two Employment Agencies to recruit the labour force he will require at the factory, but whether he uses both agencies, he's still unsure. He also said there's no need to call him back."

"Ta for that, and so are you all packed?" he asked Chloe, who said "Almost done. Just a few more items, then I can sit back and relax."

"And the driver will be here b...?" Dick asked, but he didn't have to finish the question as Chloe did her usual thing and said "about nine o'clock".

Dick settled down at the table and switched on his laptop to check his e-mails and schedule.

"Oh this effing tablet," he heard Kerri complain., and Dick asked "What's wrong with your effing tablet?"

"I've no idea but it always does weird things neither Ivan nor I can fathom out how to fix," she replied, and Chloe suggested "Well, why don't you go down to the shopping Mall and purchase the two laptops now, instead of waiting until you get home? You can afford it, or had you forgotten?"

"Oh yes. Hey Daddy, please takes us there. They should still be open," Kerri said to her dad, who said "Okay, let's go, and perhaps we can get takeaways." As they got up to leave, he said to Chloe they would be back before her taxi arrived.

Once they returned, Dick carried on where he had left off while Kerri and Ivan set up their new toys. Sometime later there was a knock at the door.

"That will be for me," Chloe said, at which Dick picked up one of her bags and walked with her to the car.

Bags packed in and she was off.

## Chapter Fourteen

## La Rioja

WHEN CHLOE ARRIVED at Biggin Hill, a young man met her and took her luggage to load it onto the plane. Chloe got onboard and Claire led her in and helped her make herself comfortable.

"May I get you your usual?" asked Claire.

"That would be nice, thank you."

Before long they were in the air and on their way to Maitland Airport. Arrival was close on an hour later and they taxied to the private sector of the airport where Claire advised Chloe the pilots wanted to top-up the fuel tanks. They would normally ask the passengers to disembark while this took place, for health and safety reasons, but they turned a blind eye this time.

When the door opened, it wasn't Cassie who walked in, but Deon. "Hello, Mrs Fraser-Rigby. I thought I'd pop in to say hello. Here's your sister-in-law," he said while holding out a hand in Cassie's direction.

She had a dumbfounded expression on her face because Deon added, with a smile on his face, "Mr Shepherd phoned to inform me and asked if I would chaperone his sister to the plane."

Chloe looked at Claire who was smiling. Cassie walked in and Chloe stood up and they gave each other a kiss and a hug.

"Enjoy your trip and see you soon."

"Thanks, Deon" Chloe replied just as Claire was about to close the door behind him.

Cassie sat down, made herself at home, and Claire served the drinks.

"Please call me if you'd like something to eat."

"Thanks Claire, I will," Chloe assured her. "That damn brother of yours is always pulling surprises, the bastard," she said to Cassie.

"Yes, and I assumed he'd grown out of it. Okay, please fill me in. What's on the go?"

As they had a twelve-hour flight ahead of them, they asked Claire to bring them something small to eat with more drinks. Chloe brought Cassie up to date on what had been happening after which they grabbed a snooze.

Arrival was due at 8:05 a.m. and they were dead on time. Chloe had arranged the hotel booking for themselves and the crew and had also organised a people carrier as she was not happy about driving on the wrong side of the road. The pilot, John, had offered to do so. Passports and security checks all done Allan, the co-pilot, who understood a small degree in Spanish, said they were okay to leave and got directions from the desk clerk and they set off after loading their luggage.

On the way, Chloe said "I want to please make one thing clear to all of you. I don't care what your company policies are, but I would like you all to call me Chloe and my sister-in-law is Cassie. Besides, no one will find out, not so?" she added. They all thanked her and had a slight giggle about how she had put it.

They arrived at the hotel and booked in but, although Chloe and Cassie shared a room, the others did not. All rooms came with free Wi-Fi, together with cable television and included private bathrooms but, they only serve a continental breakfast, however, they served additional drinks and snacks at the bar. As a bonus, the Hotel also catered for off-road secure parking. "There's never any trouble here", the front desk clerk assured them.

The Hotel was just under half a kilometre from the main square, so if they wanted to have an evening meal or even lunch, they could go there. It was close to 11:00 a.m. by the time they had settled down, so Chloe decided to inform Felipe they had arrived. When he was ready, he was more than welcome to come over to meet them.

"I'll be there at eleven-thirty," he said.

The phone rang in their room, and as Cassie was the nearest to it, she answered. It was the front desk calling to tell her, in broken English, Felipe had arrived. Chloe said to tell him they would meet him in the dining area, and once ready, they would set off to meet him. When the desk clerk saw them, he showed them to where Felipe was waiting.

"Hello Felipe, I'm Chloe and this is my sister-in-law, Cassie." He stood up, shook their hands and waited for them to sit before he sat down again.

"Right young man, where are these documents I need to sign?"

He opened two big strengthened envelopes and took out a mound of paperwork which he placed on the table. "As this is an international transaction, the Government demands all these papers need signatures and I will guide you through the process. Another reason we have to do this is because you're British," he said, and they all giggled. "Shall I get drinks?"

"Yes please."

It took the best part of another three hours to get through everything. They noticed it was bloody hot outside, so it was just as well the Hotel was air-conditioned. If it wasn't, they would have sweltered as they studied the small mountain of documents before signing.

"Felipe, what's the temperature out there?" asked Cassie.

"It's only thirty-three degrees centigrade today."

"Bloody hell" both girls exclaimed together.

"Why, what was the temperature when you left the UK?"

"It was a cool nine degrees," Cassie informed him.

"That's a big difference. You should make use of the Hotel's swimming pool."

"Good idea," Chloe replied. "When can you take us to see the properties?"

"May I suggest we don't do it now because it will only get hotter out there? So, to make things more comfortable for you, I say we go first thing in the morning, say seven o'clock?"

"Fine by me," Chloe said and Cassie agreed.

Because the hotel does not serve lunch or supper, Felipe suggested a few restaurants in the town and also recommends a few tourists places they might like to visit.

As he was about to leave, Chloe remembered a very important issue. "Oh yes Felipe, Dick wants you to please organise a meeting with some of the Argentine Government officials. He was wondering if it can happen here? His reason is, he would like to take them around the properties to show them what he proposes to do. Remember he's going to supply the world with a new revolutionary type of car which should make your Government a lot of money in the form of taxes."

"I'll get hold of my contact and see what he can come up with then I'll inform you," said Felipe.

"Thanks, and please also advise Dick what you find out."

"Okay, I will. I now need to get these documents off to the officials so they can do their thing and pass through the legal channels. The sooner I do this, the sooner you get your Title Deeds, and the sooner that's completed, I get paid," he said with a smile. "Did I give you your copy of the Tenancy Agreement?"

"Mmmm... no, you haven't," replied Chloe.

He re-opened his documents container and retrieved a copy which he handed to Chloe. "I apologise. Okay, it's been nice meeting you and I'll come and collect you at seven o'clock tomorrow morning."

"Thanks, Felipe."

"Nice young bloke," said Cassie. "Professional."

"Yes, he comes recommended by Joel."

Chloe and Cassie had a swim in the Hotel pool and struggled through in the heat for the rest of the day before asking the crew if they would like to join them for supper. All agreed and, as it was still so hot, they drove the less than half a kilometre to the restaurant.

Once seated and chatting away, Chloe informed them they would spend the better part of the morning with Felipe so, she invited them to tag along. However, they would be more than welcome to use the car for different excursions of their own. She said it made no difference to them either way, but thought they would be better off doing their own thing.

They all enjoyed the evening very much, so much so it seemed they had formed new friendships, which Chloe appreciated. "Much better this way than the typical corporate way, as Dick would say," she thought. She now understood what Dick was getting at each time he mentioned the Corporate World and how the farts operated within it.

The next morning they were up bright and early to have a good breakfast and also organising bottles of cold spring water for the journey. The Hotelier was more than happy to oblige and even gave them a cooler box of the type which plugs into the cigarette lighter socket in the car.

Felipe arrived on time and when he noticed what they were carrying, he smiled. "That's nice. Now we have two" he said, and they all laughed.

As the crew were not there, Chloe asked the desk clerk to tell them she said they were to have a nice day.

"Si señora, Yo les dare el mensaje."

"Thanks," Chloe replied. "See you later."

"I didn't realize you understood Spanish," Cassie said to her.

"Neither did I" she replied, and they both smiled.

They drove out along the road leading through the town which led them to the one which would lead them to their destination. It seemed to Chloe to be recognisable although she hadn't been there before.

She puzzled about this before it struck home. The description Joel had given them had been so accurate, and he had explained it in such a manner it was as if he had etched it into her brain.

Felipe stopped the car on the tarmac opposite the two sites, they all got out, and he pointed out to them what they had bought. The place, for want of better words, was enormous. A little while later they got back into the car and Felipe drove away, and after some distance, made a left turn which took them onto a dirt road. They now travelled for what seemed an age along this road until they arrived at a large three-building homestead.

"This is your new home. You are planning on moving in, I take it?"

"Oh yes, but that won't be for a while yet," replied Chloe.

"Does the farmstead have its own water supply?" asked Cassie.

"Yes, it does. I'll show you where it is when we get round to it."

There were three main buildings. One was the main house,

another had housed the farm workers in days long since gone, and the other appeared to be a barn, but what it was, they were yet to find out. Felipe first took them to the main house where they discovered it was, in fact, huge.

"It's big because in the days before air-conditioning, they needed the big spaces to allow the hot air to move around," he explained.

The farmhouse had eight bedrooms, of which five had huge en-suite bathrooms plus walk-in cupboards. Another three bedrooms shared general bathrooms between them, which included toilets and there were another two separate toilets at each far end of the farmhouse.

"Dick will love this," thought Cassie.

Although Chloe thought they would have removed the furniture, a shed load was, however, left behind. She had to ask Felipe about this.

"Why is there all this furniture? I thought the place would be empty?"

"I thought so too," Felipe replied, feeling embarrassed.

"Do you approve of the furnishings?" Chloe asked Cassie "Should we keep the stuff or get rid of it?"

Cassie toyed with it for a while. "Well I like it. There's nothing wrong with the stuff and besides, it will save you having to cart it all out of here and to order more. But, however, I have reservations about my brother as he's not in favour of the old-fashioned style."

"Yeah, I understand what you mean. I'll phone him now and see what he says."

She rang the landline, but there was no answer, so she waited for the answering machine to kick in. "Hello,... it's me. Pick up the phone," she said, but there was still no answer, so she rang his mobile.

"Hello, and how are things going in Argentina?" asked Dick.

"Bloody hell, you actually answered your mobile," Chloe said in amazement.

Pleasantries over, she put him in the picture. After careful thought, Dick decided they should rather keep what was there to save on the hassle of buying new items.

"If you're happy with whatever is there, well I'm okay with it. What's Cassie's view?" Dick asked, and she said, "She's all for it to stay, although she said you won't like the old-fashioned styles."

"Oh, erm... okay, what the hell, we'll keep it. Once we've gone through it all, we can always throw out what we don't want or need."

With the problem solved, they said goodbye and ended the call.

"What'd he say?"

"He's agreed to keep the stuff to save on unnecessary extra physical exertions."

They spent quite some time just going through the farmhouse alone. Pleased with what they found, it struck Chloe there was no electricity in the farmhouse, so she made a mental note to ask Felipe about it later.

Felipe took them to an out-building and opened a set of massive doors. "There you are—your water supply," he said, pointing at a pump connected to a huge filtration plant.

"The filter is unnecessary as the water here is pure. The children wanted it, so they had it installed and it's only five years old, still new. Also, it feeds all the buildings."

Their curiosity satisfied, Felipe closed the door and led them to the other building. This one had once been sleeping quarters for the ranch hands. It was even bigger than the main house and the children upgraded it to modern day standards in recent years

"I see it has electricity," Chloe said to him.

"Yes, it has its own generator supply. I'll show you later where it is."

Upon hearing this, Chloe decided not to inquire about the lack of electricity supply to the farmhouse.

"How many can this one sleep?" Cassie asked him.

"I'm not sure, but let's check."

As they walked through the house, they decided this was where the farmer's children must have stayed, for it had a definite young person's touch about it.

"I can move in here with no problem at all," Cassie said to them.

"Yes," Chloe replied "and it seems they've also left behind all the furniture for here as well. Any beds available?" she asked, but there was no reply.

The place was immaculate, considering no one had lived there for the past year-and-a-half, and Chloe said "I'll take it".

"But it's already yours," Felipe said looking puzzled and not understanding her brand of humour.

"Yes, but don't mind me. I'm just being silly," she said, and he shook his head and smile as he carried on walking through the house.

Upstairs, they counted eight huge bedrooms with en-suites, and downstairs, fourteen bedrooms, seven having en-suites and seven having separate bathrooms including toilets. Three single toilets placed in strategic spots around the house with one huge kitchen, and one huge dining room.

From there they walked into a large sized living room area, and besides the furnishing, it had a huge high-end variant sixty-three-inch plasma television set still clinging to its wall mount bracket. It also had a veranda which seemed to encapsulate the entire house, or referred to as a hacienda, for it was more like one of those than a farmstead.

They decided the place housed forty-four people with ease, and with a comfortable squeeze, a lot more. After spending even longer on this building than the main farmhouse, Felipe took them across to the last one. It didn't seem like much from the outside so they weren't expecting much from it either. He opened a doorway and led them inside.

The building was one huge area, so much so the square metres were difficult to work out to the untrained eye. However, it housed a swimming pool at the one end, which was not too far off Olympic size, a stage at the other end with a dance floor in front of the stage, and a seating area which held sixteen round tables and each table had ten chairs.

"What the hell's going on here?" Chloe asked in surprise.

Felipe looked at them and shrugged his shoulders. "I've no idea," he replied, and they stood in their positions to study the area again and again.

"I'd better take pictures of this entire property for Dick to study," said Chloe.

"Good idea," Cassie replied "The swimming pool is so green it looks as if you can use a lawnmower on it."

As this building was not too far from the foot of the mountain range, they decided it would be easy enough to climb a short way up. This was to afford them a bird's-eye view of the place. They negotiated the rocky surface, which had brush growing on it, however, they failed to notice an old crumbling footbridge in the distance.

"Nice fauna and flora," Cassie said to Chloe, who agreed.

As they gazed at the vastness of the property from their slight vantage point, Chloe kept herself busy taking many photos. They also wondered what had gone on there in the years gone by.

Had this been an old cowboy ranch once owned by a rich farmer? If so, was he a nice guy or was he perhaps an eccentric tyrant? Did Butch Cassidy and the Sundance Kid, once sighted in Bolivia, cross the border to come and perhaps hang out here within the safety of the good guys or the eccentric tyrant? The type portrayed by the Hollywood moguls for so many years now, giving one a probable false impression what happened on ranches or rather, haciendas, like this one?

The history, Chloe thought, was so immense for this place she had no option but to like it.

"What's that silvery white light up in the distance over there?" Cassie asked as she pointed in the direction towards her right-hand side.

They all gazed at it and because it didn't move, Felipe said he thought it might be a star.

"A star" both girls seemed to exclaim together.

"It's only... what? What's the time now?" Cassie inquired, and Felipe said "Two minutes to twelve."

"Two minutes to twelve on a bright cloudless day with no pollution in the air and you say it's a star. Like, No Way José," Cassie cried out. "How the hell would you be able to see a star at this time of the day on a day like today?"

"I can't say," he replied as he shrugged his shoulders.

"It's a god-damned flying saucer you blind fools," Chloe said as she continued snapping away at the scenery with her camera.

They stood there and studied it a little longer. "Yes, it's a likelihood for we see quite a few here from time to time," Felipe declared.

"Well now, there you have it. Problem solved," said Chloe.

"Okay ladies, what would you like to do now?"

"Is it possible to go back and see the other property again?" Chloe asked, "There's nothing to see, but I'd like to take a few photos of the area."

"We can and yes, there isn't anything there to see—only a vast piece of open land."

Chloe said, "Well let's negotiate climbing back down this bloody mountain and drive in that direction and see what it brings."

As they were driving, they all kept an eye on the white shining light as it came towards them. It appeared to be round and flat and also the size of a small building.

The flying machine dipped down towards the ground at a phenomenal rate before it levelled out at about eighty metres and shot right past them. Then it seemed to just disappear, perhaps even crashing into the mountain because, to their knowledge, there was no entrance.

"Did it crash into the mountain?" asked Felipe.

"No," Chloe replied with certainty "it flew inside it."

As they now turned right onto the tarmac road, they headed toward the leasehold property, and when they were in the middle of it they found it was now on their left-hand side. As Felipe pulled over, he pointed out the property to them—a vast area of nothingness.

"I think that's where Dick's having part of the landing lights installed, or whatever the hell you call them," said Chloe.

"I suppose if I ask you to explain, you'd just laugh at me wouldn't you?" Cassie asked her.

"Oh yes, you're damn right there. You'd have to ask your brother."

"Okay, no problem."

By now it was well after noon and the temperature was climbing even higher, so Chloe said she had had enough and asked Felipe to take them back to the hotel. As they took a leisurely drive back, they absorbed, what for them were, new sights. They, therefore, only arrived back at the hotel just on 3:15 p.m.

"I'm knackered," Chloe pointed out "I think I'll have a lie- down. Perhaps we can have supper at the same restaurant again," she suggested.

"Yeah, that sounds good," Cassie agreed "but I think I'll first go for a dip. What time is our flight?"

"As far as I can remember, I think it's six o'clock tomorrow morning. We'd better check and inform the front desk"

They each walked off to do their own things.

The crew arrived back at 5:30 p.m., just in time for all of them to go for an early supper, and at 8:00 p.m., the crew retired for the night. Chloe and Cassie, however, thought they would spend a few more hours in the bar and have a few more drinks. That turned out to be a big mistake.

The hotelier served breakfast at 5:00 a.m. the following morning. In the dining room sat three bright-eyed and bushy-tailed crew members, while two sorry-looking ladies each had the mother of all hangovers.

Chloe and Cassie didn't remember most of the flight back to Maitland Airport as they slept almost all the way there. Saying their goodbyes to Cassie, the plane departed for Biggin Hill. Chloe thanked the crew for everything, and the driver took her home where she arrived at 10:40 p.m.

Chapter Fifteen

(a) The Father and Child Reunion

"WELL THAT'S CHLOE on her way, I suppose," Dick said to his daughter and son-in-Law.

"Okay Daddy, now that's she's gone, please explain why and what she is going to Argentina for?"

"The property I purchased, together with the Leasehold, I need the documents signed, sealed and delivered because I want to get the contractor in there to build the roads as soon as possible. Then on completion, they need to level out the ground, and the area is massive."

Ivan asked, "How long will it take?"

"I'm hoping not longer than two years, however, I'm going to pump in as many hands as I can and try to work a twenty-four-hour day."

"Yes, and seven days a week, I suppose," said Kerri

"And why not?" replied her father. "Now if you need to, please write this down. The last owner of Maitland Airport should leave before the end of the month, therefore, I want you to move in on the last day, which is the twenty-eighth. What you must do is to hand in your contractual notice for where you are staying and tell the Landlord you will be out before then. If he so wishes, he's more than welcome to let the place out to other potential tenants. Now the reason I say this is, I don't want you to leave the house empty while it's still in your name,... Capire?"

"What?" Kerri said to her dad.

"Capire," he repeated "It's Italian for understand—Capire?"

"Please pronounce it slowly."

"I'll try but whether I'm saying it correctly, I've no idea, but it's something like... CA-PEE-RAY, and that's about as close as it gets," Dick said, and wrote each part down on a piece of paper and handed it to her. "Right, now read it out and when you've got the hang of it, say it fast."

"Now," Dick continued "I need you both to be there as a presence, as it were. I want the employees to understand you are representing the employer until he gets there, and as I say, Deon will run the place, although he will have to answer to you. Is that okay?"

"Yeah, fine by us," Kerri replied while looking at Ivan.

"Good," Dick acknowledged "Now one thing I'll need you to do is to find a house there for Chloe and me. There are quite a few to choose from, but I'll put Deon in the picture and he can appoint someone to take you around. I don't want him doing it as he already has enough on his plate."

"All right—that should be fun," Kerri said smiling.

Back on his laptop, Dick caught-up on some sports news, but an unusual article caught his eye which he had to read.

"Listen to this. These poor kids being turned into so-called martyrs by, first, being brain-washed, then having bombs strapped to them by these bastards who are far too chicken to do it themselves, it's just sickening. It's no wonder Joel and his family want to put an end to us all. Now listen to this as it's bloody funny," Dick said and read the article out loud "A suspected suicide girl was arrested in Muda Lawal market in Nigeria but the Police Superintendent, Mohammed Haruni, said, and I quote: 'It was unlikely the girl was a suicide bomber as she did not detonate any explosives when she was attacked'. So how's that, then?"

They all laughed.

Dick got up to pour himself one last drink before retiring for the night. "I hope I don't have those bloody things knocking at the door again tomorrow so early in the morning."

"Just don't answer the door," said Kerri.

"Yes, I'll take that advice. Thank you, my child." Looking over a few more non-interesting articles, he finished up and made his way to bed.

The following morning there were quite a few e-mails sent to him overnight. The first one was from the Chinese suppliers to inform him everything was still going according to plan. He answered thanking them for letting him know.

The second one was from Phil to say he was making the stop-over at Brimstone Cars to meet the guys, so he was not too sure what time he would arrive at the house. Dick replied advising Phil he was taking Kerri and Ivan to Biggin Hill the day prior to his arrival and their flight was at midday, but he'd be back home by no later than 12:30 p.m. He also said Chloe would be back later that night so they'd all be together.

The third one was from Nippon Robotics informing him they had organised their seven strong advance party. Everything had been set for the twenty-fourth and they would stay at the same hotel as Phil. Dick replied saying he would pass the message on.

"Morning Daddy," came the beautiful tones of his daughter's voice.

"Good morning sweet child o' mine. Had a good kip?"

"Yes, thanks. Have you had breakfast yet?" she asked, and Dick said, "No, not yet."

"Would you like whatever it is I make?"

"Go for it, my child."

"Tea?" was her next question, and he replied, "Yes please, sweetie-pie. I'll have Red Bush, thanks."

Ivan came downstairs and they all sat down to eat what Kerri put in front of them.

"Thank you, my child. Have you two got anything planned for today?" Dick asked, and they looked at each other for a second.

"Mmmm... no, nothing," replied Ivan.

"So it's a nice relaxing day, is it?" Dick teased.

"No Daddy. We must do something,".

They mulled over ideas and, as Dick could never get enough of the Duxford Museum, he asked them if they would like to go there.

"Why Duxford? What's at Duxford?" enquired Kerri.

Dick told them about the Imperial War Museum in Duxford, and what else was there. As they all liked aircraft so much, they agreed to go and, once they were ready, they were on the road. Although not a perfect day the weather was, however, kind to them. This meant they could walk about the place without getting sunburnt or, as it wasn't raining, mud on their shoes.

"You guys fancy a flip in a Tiger Moth?" Dick asked them.

"Hell yeah," Ivan exclaimed, so they each had a turn.

"Remember the experience as I'm sure you may never fly that way again," Dick said to them.

After 2:30 p.m. Dick's mobile laughed at him, so he decided he'd better answer it. When he saw the number, he knew it was Chloe. "Hello, and how things going in Argentina?" he asked, and she filled him in.

They enjoyed the rest of their time at the Museum looking at all the old warbirds, and on the way out, Ivan had to buy certain items in the shop. On the drive home, Dick suggested they either go to a restaurant or get takeaways. They all settled for Chinese takeaways.

Back home while having their meal, for some unknown reason a discussion about the gay society came up. Dick heard himself say to them that, in the past, they had had many gay friends, both male and female. He said they were all good, humble people with some as mad as hatters and others level-headed. He never forgot a special brother and sister team both he and Chloe once had the pleasure of working with within the banking industry. She was straight and he was gay although it wasn't obvious.

"Their names were James and Gina Slack and both were as mad as they come but loveable. Gina had just re-married and James, within the next year-and-a-half, about to marry his long-time partner."

"Chloe and I are still to this day waiting for a bloody wedding invite from him, the bastard. But I must tell you a hilarious story Gina once told me."

"She said at one stage, when the two of them were in their late teens to the early twenties, between them they had bonked every bloke in Dartford," he said. They all laughed out loud. "I miss those two."

At 9:00 a.m. the following morning, Dick phoned Deon to let him know the plans. "Morning Deon, how are things with you, the staff, the airport?"

"Good,... going along like a dream and as per your request, I got to see Chloe the other day when she popped in here to pick up your sister."

"Oh yes, and thanks so much for doing that. Right, now remember Airbus are delivering the simulator on the twentieth, but that's not the reason I'm phoning you. I want you to please check for me if Steve has moved out. If he has, I need my daughter and son-in-Law to move in there at the end of the month. Also, I need you to please give them a quick tour as I want them to find a decent house there for Chloe and me."

"That's fine, Dick. Steve moved out two days ago and said they couldn't wait to move into their sea-side cottage."

"Well, I'm pleased with the man," Dick replied trying hard to hold back on the sarcasm.

Deon continued "Now as far as other properties go, I'm not too sure if you're aware of this but, they built a lovely huge home for the President of the Company. Just before the family were to move in, he and his wife lost their lives in, of all things, an aircraft accident. So if you like, Dick, I can organise this home for you."

"Now that's ironic—the President of an airport and his wife losing their lives in an aircraft accident. It cannot get worse than that. Okay, as far as his house goes, it sounds perfect so I'll take it, thank you. However, I have one concern. You're a busy chap there, so I want you to get your best man on the job, please. I don't want you wasting your time on unimportant matters."

"Yeah, understood, and I have the right person for the job. It's a lovely middle-aged woman and damn good at her job."

"Okay, I'll leave it in your capable hands. Oh, and one last thing. As my daughter and son-in-Law will be there representing me, I have given them strict instructions you are still the man running the airport and for that, they are to respect you. However, they still have free reign over the place and, should you have a problem, please speak to my daughter."

"Thanks, Dick—I appreciate it and yes, if I'm in a pickle, I will speak to her."

"Knowing the three of you, I have every confidence you'll work well together. Right, I'm hoping to be there when the simulator arrives. If all works out, I'll organise the two of them to be there which will give you guys the opportunity to meet."

"Yes, I hope you can organise it."

"Okay Deon, once I've seen in what direction my workload's going to take me, I'll inform you. Cheers for now," Dick said and replaced the cordless phone back into its base.

By the time he had ended his call, the other two had come downstairs with their one big travel case. "When you get home, don't relax too much because I have changed plans.
I want the two of you to be at Maitland Airport with me on the twentieth when the simulator arrives. What I'll do is, when I drop you off at the airport this morning, I'll book a plane and we'll pick you up on our way.

"What time will you pick us up?" asked Kerri.

"Once I've booked the plane, they can advise me then I can let you know."

"And what time are we leaving this morning?" she asked.

"I'd say eleven bells would give us enough time and don't forget to type out and send the letter to your landlord. Now if you remember, I suggested you take it to him and speak to him in person about it. It may just make things easier."

"Yes, we'll do that, and once we've dropped it off, I can buy myself my dream car," she said, with a smile on her face. Dick gave her *the look*. "Just kidding," laughed Kerri.

While they were having their discussion, the landline telephone rang. "Ah, the talking telephone" Dick said as he got up to answer it. "Speak to me."

"Hi," Phil responded and giggled at the way Dick had answered the phone.

"All set for your journey tomorrow?" asked Dick.

"Yep, but before I meet up with the guys at Brimstone, I've been wondering about changing the name to incorporate both companies as one. The name I've come up with is Brimstone and Toby Motor Works and I had an idea to run it by you first. So what you say?"

"I don't mind. Listen, Kerri and Ivan are here so let me ask them," Dick said, and explained to them what Phil had come up with. They were not averse to the new name and, in fact, said they rather liked it.

"Consensus dictates your new name is a winner, but I'd get hold of the guys at Toby's first and find out what they think for they may not like it. If it's okay with them, I take it you will get them to do the necessary regarding letterheads, signage, business cards etcetera?"

"Yes, I'll get onto them, and if they approve, I'll do as you suggest and get them to handle it. Also, as I'm meeting the lawyer, the same one Kieran used to handle the takeover bid, I'll get him to do the legal bit. Is that okay?"

"Yeah," Dick replied "I've got no problem with that. Whatever you decide and in whatever direction you go with this, I don't mind at all. I'll even say if you want the two factories to be independent of one another, then hell yes, go for it."

"Yes, good idea. I shall bear it in mind."

"Good, and please give my regards to Jonathan."

"Will do."

They carried on speaking about the two companies, chucking a few more ideas around, settling on a few major changes which they both agreed upon and, therefore, would adopt.

The time came for them to go to Biggin Hill Airport. When they arrived at around 11:30 a.m., a helpful hand collected their travel case and loaded it onto the plane. Dick walked to the reception area and saw a face behind the desk he did not recognise.

"Good morning Mr Shepherd," said the new face "nice to see you."

"Ugh,... I hate that expression," Dick said to himself.

"My name is Emily and how may I help you?" she asked in a friendly but professional manner.

Dick gave her all the information regarding the trip on the twentieth, including what the pilots would need to file on their flight plan for the day. She advised him Kerri and Ivan should meet the plane at 8:45 a.m. for departure around 9:00 a.m. to Maitland Airport. Dick paid the account and walked back to Kerri and Ivan with the information.

It was now time for them to board the plane so Dick gave Kerri a kiss on her forehead, together with a gentle hug, and then shaking Ivan's hand, they said their goodbyes.

The rest of the day was a quiet and relaxing one for Dick which he took full advantage of as he knew it wouldn't last. He heard rumblings and rattlings at the front door which was Chloe entering. The time was 10:40 p.m.

"Hello dear, and how did it go?" he asked her "No wait," he uttered "Sit down and relax. I take it you would like to have a glass of vino first?"

"You're reading my mind again," Chloe said while smiling. "You must forgive me but I'm shagged out. There's a lot to get through, including photos, and I don't feel like going through all of it now."

They relaxed, enjoying each other's company and agreeing they would leave everything for the next day.

The following morning, Chloe downloaded the photos onto her computer and showed him the major points of the properties.

"You will never ever grasp the enormity of the properties and of these buildings. Why someone would build places like these in the middle of nowhere is mind-boggling. For example, why on earth put this huge swimming pool inside the building? Well only they know. Here, look at this," she said, pointing at another screenshot.

"That is the en-suite to the second bedroom. Not the main bedroom—the second one. I cannot impress upon you enough just how big these buildings are and I sure as hell still can't get over it."

"Well, I don't mind at all," Dick replied. "When the first lot of Contractors start work, some of them can sleep in these houses and all of them can make use of that recreational area. Or do you have any other ideas?"

"Well I suppose it's one way of filling up the bedrooms."

"True, because we won't be living in them."

"Here, look at this one," Chloe said, once again pointing at the screen "from what I understand, this would be your entrance, you know, when you're coming into land and maybe this is the entrance you will take, and this is where you'll be putting lights up," she said, although in a confused manner, but Dick understood what she was trying to explain to him.

"Oh yeah, you've got it spot-on. By the looks of it, it's better than I was hoping," he now said making her feel more at ease about her lack of knowledge.

Chloe got up to make herself a cup of coffee while Dick abstained. He flipped through the photos with a fine-toothed comb as they gave him a good insight what to expect once he was there. Although grateful for the pictures she had taken, they couldn't give answers to all the questions he now asked himself, but in good time he would quench his thirst for answers.

## (b) Phil's Re-deployment—Part 1

The time approached in the morning when Phil had to say goodbye to his mother and niece as he had a few hours drive ahead of him. His first stop would be at the Brimstone Car Company where he arrived at the factory at 9:20 a.m., which was not too bad considering the weather had not been nice to him on his journey. At the reception desk, he met two presentable young ladies whom he guessed to be in their mid-twenties.

"Good morning, I'm Phil Upton and I'm here to see Jonathan Styles."

"Oh yes, Mr Styles is expecting you," said one of the young receptionists "I'll let him know you've arrived."

He looked around the area to familiarise himself with the entrance and of what he could see of the parking area.

A man came up to him and said with a welcoming smile "Hello Phil, I'm Jonathan." They shook hands, and he invited Phil to his office where they first discussed how the staff were settling back into work again. "I said to Dick, and my prediction was right, all those who have returned are ecstatic about having their jobs back."

"How many not returned?" Phil asked, and Jonathan said "One chap Paul, who was on the old executive side, but we won't be filling the post again. On the production line, however, we have nine who have not returned, but with the way we have to supply the cars to you, those positions are redundant as they're no longer necessary. So it's a win-win situation."

"Okay, Jonathan,  what are they doing at the moment? I mean, they're not producing cars yet, are they?"

"Oh no. We don't foresee the production line running before the end of the month. Still lots to sort out and I want the entire factory area cleaned and, where necessary, a lick of fresh paint on the floor markings."

"Great," Phil said "there's nothing like good housekeeping. A place for everything and everything in its place,... right,".

"Correct, and besides it always helps with those blasted Health and Safety factory inspectors. They drive us insane sometimes."

"What, only sometimes? They drive me insane all the time," Phil said, at which they shared the joke. This was a good thing because it helped to break the ice and created a more relaxed atmosphere. "I now have good news. I will only require delivery from you in about five to six months' time, however, that must not stop you from your production work."

"Sure thing, Phil. Would you like to meet the other two ex-Directors who have now come back to their original jobs but now as Managers?"

"Well, I suppose now is as good a time as any," smiled Phil.

Jonathan picked up his phone, dialled the reception asking Randi to find the two chaps in question and ask them to come to his office. There was a knock at the door and in walked a chap similar in shape, height and build as Phil. He introduced himself as Brendan Green, the Office Manager.

After the normal pleasantries, they sat down only to hear another knock at the door and in walked the second chap. He stood about one metre eighty-five centimetres tall and well built, so Phil decided he must spend a lot of time in the gym. "I must keep an eye on this one," he said to himself as Alec West, the Factory Manager, introduced himself.

"Where would you like to begin?" asked Jonathan.

"First,... to tell you what it is I want from each of you. Second,... to spend time with each of you while you explain to me what, how, and where you carry out your job. Then afterwards,... I'd like to announce for all to hear an important decision I've made.

Phil explained what he wanted from them off the production

line. He also wanted to know when they expected to get rolling stock loaded onto the trucks for delivery up North although he had already given them a time span.

"The quality of the finished product from you is to be of the highest standard, both inside and out, and if you had in your original design over two or three variants of the car, we only want the one designed of the highest quality finish."

"So, you only require one variant of the car?" asked Alec.

Phil replied, "We have no need of a half-a-dozen different variants of the same car on the road. The only difference is to be in the colours and I suggest you stick to only four shades, or maybe even less. Now, as there will only be one common interior, you must make sure the outside colour scheme is comparable, or rather, compatible."

"What about the seats?" Alec asked. "Are they to be vinyl or leather?"

"I will only accept plush leather," Phil instructed them. "That also applies to the door cards and dashboards. These things are to be the real deal if you know what I mean."

They looked at each other for a while before discussing further Phil's ideas regarding the fittings, which included the sound systems and the overall extras on the inside of the cars. They tossed their ideas around before agreeing on the designs and colours.

Phil said because they were Managers, they would get the first three cars off the production line as company cars. However, he wanted Company advertising slogans on the outside of the two front doors.

"What slogan do you have in mind?" asked Jonathan.

"I will leave it in your capable hands, but before your creative juices start flowing, I must inform you of a name-change. The name of your set-up here is changing to 'Brimstone Motor Works'. So, using this new name, underneath it in a smaller typeface, you must add the wording 'a subsidiary of Maitland Electric Car Manufacturers'. The overall design I will leave up to you."

Because Phil had decided to keep Both Brimstone Motor Works and Toby Manufacturing as two separate entities, he saw no reason to mention the discussion he had with Dick about a possible amalgamation of the companies.

"Further, you are to have as a logo Maitland Electric Car Manufacturers which will appear on both front doors. The rest of the wording, and the overall design, I'm leaving up to you guys to deal with."

"Also, because of the company name change, I need you to organise new signage, letterheads, business cards etcetera as soon as possible, please. But for the time being, you'll just have to use your own cars. All right, now I'd like to start with you

Brendan, if that's okay with you?"

"Fine by me, Phil. Would you like to follow me?" Brendan said, and they excused themselves from the others.

In Brendan's office, they made progress through all the boring things keeping an office running on a legal level. Most was beyond Phil for he was a hands-on person on the mechanical engineering side. For him, though, he had to put on a brave face and pretend he understood everything about those items placed before him. Once they had gone through it all, Brendan took him around the entire office area and introduced him to all the office staff members which, as it so happened, included the most important person in any office environment... the tea lady.

"These gentlemen 'aven't brought yo' a nice cup o' tea yet, 'ave they Mr Upton?" she asked him.

"No, they haven't," he replied trying hard not to giggle.

"Oooo,... I'll put the kettle on straight 'way then," she said. Phil suppressed an insane desire to say it wouldn't fit her but, as he was the new kid on the block, decided against it. So instead, he smiled.

"Milk, Mr Upton?"

"Yes please," he replied, and he was just about to walk away when she asked yet another question.

"An' sugar?"

"Yes please," he replied once more, but again as he tried to walk away, she asked yet another question.

"One spoon or two, young man?" she said. He thought for a moment and wanted to say "One spoon and two milk please", but chickened out and said, "Yes, two please."

"Yo' goes abouts ya business young man, an' I'll brings ya cuppa t' ya."

At last he had a good old chuckle to himself while he and Brendan carried on with their walk-about. Impressed by the general layout of the office, Phil asked Brendan to take him to Alec's office.

"Thanks, Brendan. I'll see you a little later on."

Phil walked into Alec's office, where he sat down and Alec put him in the picture on how many staff they had on the floor. He also showed Phil a plan they had come up with regarding the shift pattern once the production line began.

"Sorry, I forgot to ask this earlier but are they servicing any of the machinery?"

"Yes, Phil, they are," Alex replied. "I've given them strict instructions everything is to operate as new as I won't tolerate failures once the line runs."

"Fair enough I suppose."

"Phil, would you like to meet the staff?"

"Yes please."

They got up and, leaving the office, walked towards the factory door entrance. As Alec opened it for him, what he saw was a huge mess scattered all around him. "What's going on here?" Phil enquired.

"Please don't worry about this," Alec assured him. "Everything is being stripped down for cleaning and, once it's all back together, the floor will be cleaned and re-painted."

"Okay, now that makes sense," Phil said feeling relieved. While standing there he heard a familiar voice. "Excuse me young man but may I serves yo' ya tea here, or shall I serves it for yo' in the office?"

"That's kind of you. I'll have it here, thanks."

The nice old duck now gone, he sipped his tea. "Mmmm... tastes like crap," he said to himself, but still drank it while Alec continued informing him what else was going on, on the floor.

When finished drinking his tea, Phil found a place to put the cup down and they continued to walk through the factory. As they did so, he shook hands with most of the staff, including all the Foremen. As impressed as he had been on the reception area, so was he with the factory floor and he paid Alec a rightful compliment.

"Would you now organise to gather all the staff together so I can make my announcement please."

Alec got hold of the main Foreman, informed him what was happening and instructed him to get everyone together, asking them to come through to the factory area. It didn't take long before everyone was there, and because they didn't have a podium, Phil made use of a plastic container used for the glass milk bottles, donated by the nice old tea lady, and hoped the damn thing wouldn't collapse under his weight.

While carrying out his balancing act upon the unsteady crate, he introduced himself, but to those he hadn't already met. He started off by welcoming them all back to work and informed them about the general operational plans. He also said there was nothing for them to worry about as the factory would go on *ad infinitum*.

"If only they knew how true that statement is," Phil said to himself.

"Right folks," he now continued. "In closing, the other day, when my uncle put me in charge, I sat down and had an idea about how I could make you all happy again. You know... the way things were before the untimely closure of this place. So, the idea I came up with, well... if it doesn't get you going, nothing will. Therefore, please allow me to ask all of you as a whole, a question."

He paused to looked around at all of them, and as he asked his question, he slowed his speech rate down.

"What would you say if I said to you I'm instructing your paymaster to give you a double salary cheque at the end of next month, as a welcome back bonus?"

Because the staff let out an almighty roar and applauded his announcement, he found he had to raise his voice before he got to the last few words of the sentence. The hubbub seemed to go on for a full minute, and once they had settled down, he said to them he felt lucky to have them on-board and looked forward to working with them for many a year to come.

He lied, but he had to. Phil was a firm believer in being *slapped* with the truth rather than being *kissed* with a lie and, therefore, had no option but to *kiss* them for the truth was not relevant to them in his changing world. He said goodbye to them and, together with Brendan and Alex, walked through to Jonathan's office, all the while ever so grateful the old duck's rickety milk crate had not collapsed under his weight.

"Will you now please ensure the double salary payment goes through next month," Phil instructed Brendan.

"Yes, I will attend to it, Phil."

"Thank you. Right, are we finished for now?" asked Phil.

"For now, yes," replied Jonathan.

"Well, seeing none of you wants to take me to lunch, I'll hit the road," Phil said as he smiled.

"Oh yes. I apologise. Let's do that, shall we?" Jonathan replied feeling rather embarrassed.

"No, no—I was only joking guys. I'd like to but please let's do it the next time. At the moment I've got too much on my plate, however, may I suggest you take your partners out tonight for a bite to eat to celebrate the relaunch of the company and put it on the expense account," Phil said, and they thanked him.

They shook hands with him and said goodbye. As he got into his car, he reflected upon his visit and concluded they were a nice bunch of people and hoped it would stay the way it was and wondered if, over the coming years, they would stand together through thick and thin. While deep in reflection he almost jumped out of his skin for Joel made an unexpected appearance seated in the front passenger seat.

"Hello, Joel," Phil said after he got his composure back.

"Hello, Phil," he said, returning the salutation. "I must compliment you. Nice touch, instructing the paymaster to issue a double salary. Good psychological move that will get the staff motivated again."

"Thanks, Joel, I appreciate that."

"You're welcome. As this was always only going to be a short visit, I'll let you get on your way now," Joel said, and the passenger seat was once again vacant.

Phil drove to Dick and Chloe's home where he would stay for a few days before driving up to Blackpool. The place where he would live and, therefore, become his home. His new home for at least the next year at any rate, but he couldn't help the excitement flowing through him when, in his mind, he viewed the drive-unit he had designed.

He now realised he had become impatient about the time he would have to spend waiting before he could assemble the first one.

"Patience is a virtue, Phil... patience is a virtue," he said to himself while navigating his way along the next leg of his journey.

Chapter Sixteen

The Airbus Simulator

"SO WHEN ARE you expecting Phil to arrive?" Chloe asked, and Dick said "I'm not too sure. He's first making a stop-over at Brimstone factory to meet the staff, and that will take a few hours at least, and who knows how long it will take him to get there. I mean, you realize what that road can be like?"

"Yes, I do. Rather him than me."

"Too true."

"Dick, we must do shopping today as we are running low on everything."

"I agree, and if Phil is to stay here for a few days, it's only right we feed him."

Chloe chuckled. "I'm sure he'd appreciate it,".

Later they were on their way to one of Dick's favourite haunts... the Superstore. He hates shopping but appreciates the fact it's something he has to do, however, there are two major bug-bears for him. The one being screaming, undisciplined bloody kids and the other being the smell of old people, especially the unwashed ones. Those two things could drive him mental although he appreciates the fact they have as much right to be there as he does. What he can't understand is how they all seem to have the uncanny ability to know what day and time he will be there.

"The mind boggles."

They completed their shopping as soon as possible and made their way home to pack everything away. They had only just finished when right on 5:00 p.m. there was a knock at the door.

"Well, that must be him," said Chloe, and Dick got up to open the door with a big smile on his face "Hello" he greeted Phil "you look shagged out."

"Hi," Phil replied in a tired voice "That bloody traffic gets no better," he retorted. "It's not so much the amount of traffic on the road, it's the bloody idiots who think they own the damn road. Where do these people come from? I'm sure a chimpanzee could do way better than those bloody fools."

"Never mind. Sit down and relax and Dick will bring you a drink," Chloe said giving him a welcome hug.

Phil sat himself down at the table and told them all about his visit to Brimstone. He explained about his meeting with the entire workforce and informed them about the welcome bonus he'd given to them.

"That's a nice gesture and I hope they appreciated it," said Chloe.

"Yes, they did and I got quite an ovation for it. Also, I've said to Jonathan the three of them as Managers will get the first three cars off the line as company cars."

"That's fine by me," Dick said nodding in approval.

Looking very smug, Phil told them about Joel showing up to express his approval. Delighted with the news, Dick and Chloe said, "Good old Joel" in unison.

Phil explained to them what was on the go within the factory, the office area, and what he perceived the working relationships would be like and did not forget to tell them about the dear old duck who was the tea lady. He warned them to stay well away from the tea, at which they all had a good chuckle.

The following morning they were up early. At 10:00 a.m., Dick phoned his daughter, as a reminder, and told her she and Ivan were to meet him at Brickner Airport at 8:30 a.m. the following morning for the trip to Maitland Airport. They had to pack their bags as they would stay for the night before flying back on the evening of the twenty-first.

He booked a flight for the next day and wheels up to be at 8:00 a.m. He informed the Secretary they would all be staying over but it wouldn't be necessary for the plane and the pilots to remain there.

"Okay, you two," Dick now said to Chloe and Phil "this is what I have planned for the next few days, so please listen. Tomorrow we are going to Maitland Airport, via Brickner Airport, where we will pick up Kerri and Ivan and the five of us can watch the off-loading of the Airbus simulator, if it's not already there. Once we have done that, I want you, Chloe, together with Kerri to go with Deon's PA to look at and choose which of the houses we will live in and you, Phil, I'd like you to accompany me as we go about meeting the staff."

"What's Ivan going to be doing?" asked Chloe.

"Well, I've had a slight change of plan as I want Ivan to stay with the guys who will install the simulator. I need someone, other than Deon, to learn how the outside operates. This must include everything about the computer room and the air conditioning unit, but not only that, he must also make sure it's installed in the correct place because we will need to make room for the other simulator when it arrives in due course, and while I think of it, don't forget to take those DVDs Joel gave you. Deon will have to put them in a safe place for us."

"What time are we leaving?" Chloe asked Dick while handing over the DVDs to Phil.

"Because we're picking up the other two at eight-thirty in the morning, wheels up at eight o'clock. Also, we'll stay over-night and come back on the twenty-first at five o'clock in the evening. We, therefore, should have ample time to look around and see most things at the entire airport."

"Wunderbar," Phil said in the crappiest of German accents.

"So you can speak German as vell?" Dick imitated him.

"Like you, he does try, but then at least he didn't pronounce it wonder-bra," said Chloe smiling.

Phil telephoned Sterling Hoskins at Toby Manufacturing. After announcing himself, he agreed to meet at 9:00 a.m. on the morning of the twenty-second. He also made similar arrangements for the same day at 2:00 p.m. in the afternoon with Torque Motors Engineering in Manchester. The rest of the day they organised the books and the paperwork of all transactions so far. All agreed it was a thankless task although realising it was a necessary one.

"As I didn't get to watch the game on Saturday, I think I'll catch up on it now. Are you guys going to watch?"

"Dick, what game is it?" asked Phil.

"It's France versus England in the Six Nation's rugby," he replied. Phil abstained as he still had loads to organise, but Chloe said she would join him in a while.

"Are England at the top of the log?" she asked.

"I don't think so. But if not, they'll be there at the end of this game, although I foresee it being a tough game."

They settled back, with eyes glued to the TV to watch the game, at the end of which Chloe said: "Not a convincing performance, was it?"

"France equals good game, England equals nightmare," Dick exclaimed in annoyance. "That was a piss-poor show," he said now sounding disgruntled.

"Okay, where are they now on the log?"

"After that loss, only third, but it doesn't matter anymore because of the loss, Ireland have now won the trophy. So, as next week is the last round, all England can do is to play their hearts out, win the game, and get their pride back."

"Yeah, they seemed to have lost them," Chloe said, while referring to a pride of lions.

The following morning with bags loaded, they took off, and because they had breakfast at home, they didn't bother with anything onboard the plane. At Brickner Airport, Dick's daughter and son-in-Law boarded the plane, and after saying their hellos, together with hugs and kisses all round, in no time at all they were in the air once more. Before long, they were on the landing approach to Maitland Airport. They disembarked, and the pilots flew back to Biggin Hill Airport as planned only to return the following evening.

Nobody at the airport were expecting them, but Dick didn't mind in the least. He thought it would be a good opportunity for him to see how things were operating, while in a state of incognito, for only a handful of people had met them. In the reception area, he walked up to the desk where he asked a large middle-aged lady to contact Deon for him.

"May I say who's calling please?" the Receptionist asked in a professional manner, to which he replied, "It's Dick Shepherd."

Picking up the phone, and while dialling Deon's secretary's number, a look of surprise seemed to cross her face. She may well have had an idea who he was, but couldn't be certain.

Moments later Deon's secretary arrived. "Hello, Mr Shepherd. I'm Mimi Rodgers, Deon's secretary. Please follow me."

On the way to Deon's office, she shook hands with Chloe who introduced her to the others. Arriving at the door, Mimi invited them inside whereupon Deon stood up to greet them.

"Deon, let me introduce my daughter, Kerri, to you. This is my nephew Phil, and son-in-Law, Ivan."

They all sat down and Dick asked if the simulator had arrived. Deon said it had. "I've just got back from the hangar and I'm going back there later."

"Good, but before you do," Dick said "I have one or two things to go through with you. First, we'll all be here for the next two days and fly back tomorrow evening so, I need you to ask someone to book us in at a hotel, please. Then,... I think we need to organise the girls first so they can do their house inspections."

"Also, I want you to show Ivan and Phil the simulator as I'd like them to be there all the while as I want Ivan to watch and learn as I've decided I don't want you to be there all the time. You have far too many other important issues to get on with," Dick said to an ever-attentive Deon.

"As your priorities for today are only with the simulator, I need someone to show me around the office so I can meet as many of the staff as possible. But that's not a criterion because as I say, we are here for two days. I had George in mind being a good person to show me around the place, or do you have any other ideas?"

"Mmmm..., George has taken a few days off," Deon informed him "but not to worry for I have someone else who can do the job for you. I'll get Bill Butland who is my right-hand man here and, like me, he knows the place like the back of his hand."

"Fine by me," Dick said, whereupon Deon got up and left his office saying he would get hold of Bill.

"Now you all heard what I want you to do, and we've all got our phones with us, so we are only a phone call away from each other."

"That's all good and well, Daddy, but you never have yours switched on."

He took it out of his pocket and switched it on. "I hope the battery lasts," he said with a smile on his face.

"You can be so unbelievable sometimes," Chloe said to which he replied, "Oh yes, but you love me anyway,".

"Yeah right," she said smiling.

The door opened and in walked a young lady who seemed to be about the same age as Kerri. She was pushing a trolley upon which there were the obligatory tea and coffee jugs together with cups and saucers. She pushed the trolley to one side and said they should please help themselves, and as she made her way to exit the office, they said thanks to her. They now crowded around the trolley to pour themselves drinks acting as if it would be their last.

"Why are we acting like this?" asked Dick.

"We get it from you, daddy,".

"Thanks" her father replied, at which the others smiled.

Moments later Deon returned introducing Bill to all of them. He said the person he wanted to escort the girls to the housing section was, in fact, over there at the moment and would take her about fifteen minutes to get to them.

"How far away is it?" Chloe asked in surprise, and Deon said "It's on the other side of the runway. At this time of the day we have to travel the outskirts,"

"Well, in that case, I see no reason to hang around here," Dick said. "Come on Bill; let's get to know each other while you show me around this place. You guys have fun and I'll see you whenever. Deon, please don't forget to ask someone to book rooms for us."

"I'll get onto it right away."

"Didn't you say you wanted me to meet the staff with you?" Phil asked Dick.

"True, but wouldn't you prefer inspecting the simulator? If not, please join us."

No argument at all as Phil said: "I'll take the simulator this time thanks."

"That's what I thought, so I'll see you all later."

Bill took Dick through a maze of corridors including offices and introduced him to an array of different personnel who all seemed engrossed in the work they were doing. The layout of the building wasn't the best in the world, but neither was it the worst, while the open plan section was a hive of activity. Dick couldn't work out what it was they were all busy at, so he decided if Bill would not enlighten him, he would not bother asking him either. They spent a good time on the walk-around and Bill introduced Dick to many staff. Afterwards, Bill led him the way to the hangars housing various aircraft belonging to many people and or businesses.

"What time do you have your lunch break?" asked Dick.

"Around one o'clock. It depends on the work-flow and air traffic."

"Well it's almost twelve-thirty so I think I'll get them all together and we'll go for lunch. Why don't you and Deon join us?"

"Thanks, that would be nice."

"Can you recommend any good restaurants?"

"Yes, I'll get my PA to book a table, shall I?" asked Bill.

"Yes please."

"We also have a Company people carrier we use for occasions like this. Shall we make use of it?"

"Why not?"

A little before 1:00 p.m. they had all assembled in the reception area. Before they bundled into the car, Phil told Dick his mother was on her way to meet them.

"Fine, get the address from Bill and ask her to meet us there."

"Erica and her boyfriend are with her."

"Yeah, that's all right. I don't mind that mad niece of yours."

"Don't forget she's your grandniece." They both chuckled.

A short drive later, they arrived at the restaurant and Dick's sister Cassie, showed up with her grandchild Erica and the boyfriend in tow.

"Please excuse me guys but this is part of my dysfunctional family," Dick said to both Deon and Bill as he introduced them. In retaliation, his sister punched him on the arm. "See,... proof positive."

They all enjoyed a slap-up lunch at the end of which Dick stood up saying it was time to go. When they arrived back at the office, he asked if there was somewhere they could use as he wished to have a family meeting.  Deon showed them to the Boardroom and said if they needed anything, to just give his secretary a shout.

"I recognise this room," Chloe said to Dick as they all filed in.

"And so you should."

"Okay folks," Dick said to get their attention. "Please grab a chair and sit down. While all of us are together, I'll instruct you who will do what and why." So in tandem, both he and Chloe explained the situation so far and who might do what soon.

"The first thing I want you to do, my dear mad sister, is to get your stuff together and move in here. Kerri and Chloe have been to see the houses and they can put you in the picture as to what is available."

"Daddy, we're not finished over there yet and need to go back."

"Do you need to do that now or can it wait until tomorrow?"

"I suppose we can do it tomorrow."

"But what about Cassie? Can she make it tomorrow?" asked Chloe.

"Sorry,... no," Cassie responded, "I can't make it tomorrow."

"Well, that settles it," Dick informed them. "We'll go over there right now."

The lady who had taken the girls over to the housing area earlier was back on hand. This time, as there were so many of them, she said she would take them across in the mini-bus.

"This is Poppy," Chloe said introducing her.

They spent another couple of hours looking at houses and, by this time Dick had had enough. "Please hurry you lot and make up your bloody minds what houses you want to live in. It's doing my bloody nut in, for fuck sake" he emphasized and, as he said The F-Word, he realised his daughter was standing right next to him. "Sorry for swearing, sweetie-pie."

"Don't be silly, Daddy. It's fine."

Housing problems sorted out and Poppy, armed with the info regarding who wanted what house, they now all piled back into the mini-bus. They drove back to the office block where, upon arrival, they found it was time for those who worked the day-shift to go home.

"Bloody hell,... I feel I've accomplished nothing today," Dick said loud enough for all to hear.

"Yeah, I understand what you mean," replied Chloe.

"I have an idea," Dick said to them. "You girls go to the hotel because I want Phil and Ivan to stay behind here with me as I want to catch up on the simulator installation."

"All right, but how do you propose we get there?" asked Chloe.

"Well, I'm sure Cassie won't mind dropping you off." So the two girls fetched their bags and loaded them into Cassie's car, and they were off.

"Now I need to organise the people carrier for us."

Deon fetched the keys and gave them to Dick. However he, in turn, handed them over to Phil.

"Deon," Phil said "I need you to guard these DVDs for me. Do you perhaps have a safe in your office?"

"Yes I do. My office is a short detour to the hangar, so I'll show you where it is and, pop these in."

"Should anything untoward happen, you will need them.

Verstehen sie?" Dick said and a deep loud *JA* emanated out of Phil's mouth which made them all smile.

"Deon, the boys and I will be here for some time so please, I don't want you to feel obliged to hang around here. You need to go home to your family at a reasonable hour, otherwise your wife will think I'm a hard task-master, or worse still, a bastard. You know, a typical corporate boss, and 'I don't want that' to coin a phrase by a certain singer."

"Thanks, Dick. What I'll do, I'll take you over there, show you around, then Ivan can take over and I'll come back here and finish up."

"Good idea, Deon and please forewarn the security staff we are still here."

"I'm sure someone has already told them. But I'll mention it, anyway."

Later Deon said his goodbyes, so the three of them, together with the Airbus night-shift foreman, walked around the area. He explained to them, in his best English, what was what and how it worked. Over the next two hours they all got on well with each other, which included the engineers.

"I like what they've done with the false walling," Dick said "It seems the air-conditioning unit will cope well."

"Yes," Ivan replied "Deon took me to see it. The thing is

massive."

"And it's powerful enough to cope with both units when they're running?"

"That's what I asked Deon, and he assured me it's more than capable. He told me when the air-con guys came around to do their numbers, once they had shown him what size unit they recommended, he ordered them to install the next size up. Plus, there's a backup unit, just in case there's a breakdown."

"Music to my ears. Okay, let's get out of here because, before we go, I would like to meet the on-duty security guys."

After saying goodbye to the Airbus staff, they ambled back over to the office block where they found the door locked from the inside, so Ivan knocked. A big security guard walked towards it and gazed at them for a moment through the window before recognising Dick from the accurate description of him Deon had given.

He smiled as he opened the door. "Sorry about that, Mr Shepherd, but we take no chances."

"Good for you and well done," Dick said, as they shook hands. He introduced him to the other two and asked if he were alone.

"No sir. My colleague is doing a walkabout at the moment and he'll only be back in about fifteen minutes."

"That's a pity. Never mind, we'll catch up with him later. Okay, now what about those workers in the hangar over there? Do they have any security?" Dick asked him, pointing in the general direction of the hangar.

"I apologise sir, but I can't answer that," he said embarrassed for such a big fellow.

"Are your offices open?"

"There is always an On-duty Manager in the office Mr Shepherd - shall I call him?"

"Yes please."

"Hello Mr Clancy, I have Mr Shepherd here and he would like to have a word with you."

He handed the phone over to Dick and, just as he did so, Dick's mobile laughed at him. As he took it out of his pocket, he handed it to a grinning Phil. "Hello Mr Clancy, I'm Dick Shepherd, the new owner of Maitland Airport. I was wondering if you are aware of any additional security we require over in one hangar for a special project that's on the go?"

"Erm... no sir, I don't."

"Is it at all possible you could organise something for right now?" Dick asked, but trying not to sound rude.

"Mr Shepherd, would you mind if I contact the owner of our

Security Company and bounce it off him?"

"Not at all. If he's unaware, please tell him it's of paramount importance we have at least two security guards over there as soon as possible. It's for twenty-four-seven until we complete the project, and as I don't know the completion date, that info I cannot give to you but please allow for two years at least. Also, please inform him I cannot impress upon him enough how urgent this is. Then call me back," Dick said as he ended the call. "Who phoned me?" he asked Phil.

"Oh, it was Chloe."

Dick phoned her, put her in the picture as to the potential problem he had encountered and said he would call again when they were ready to leave.

"You'd better phone your wife and tell her we've got a big problem here, and tell her I can't say how much longer we will be," Dick said to Ivan.

The security guard's phone rang. It was Mr Clancy. "Hello, Mr Shepherd. I've just spoken to Mr Bailey, the owner of the security business. He said if it's not too much of an inconvenience, he should be there in about fifteen minutes to sort out the problem."

"No, it's no trouble to wait. Thanks for your help. While you are on the phone, do you think you could organise any guards for tonight?"

"Mr Bailey has already asked me to do so, sir."

"Great, and thanks so much," Dick said and put the phone down.

"I'm bloody starving. Are there any pizza places close by who deliver here?" Dick asked the security guard.

The guard lent over his desk and pulled out a menu which he handed to Dick. "We use this place all the time sir, and good value for money too."

Dick took the menu from the guard and the three of them checked it over and made their decisions. "Here, what would you like to order?"

"Me sir?"

"Yes, you sir, and order something for your colleague," Dick said to the guard as he handed over a piece of paper to him, and said "Okay, this is what we want, and may I suggest you phone and place the order?"

The guard phoned the Pizzeria and placed the order. When he replaced the receiver, he informed them the food would be there within twenty minutes. The other guard rounded a corner and showed his face.

"Okay, you better tell me your name as well otherwise things could get confusing for me," Dick said to the new face who introduced himself.

"Mr Shepherd, there is a kitchen just down the corridor on the left and, if you like, you could make yourselves a cup of tea or coffee."

He hadn't finished his sentence when they were off like a shot. On the way, Dick shouted "Thank you" to him as he trotted off towards the kitchen. Cups of steaming hot brew in their hands, and while they sipped away, there was a knock at the door. It was Mr Bailey. The guard let him in and made the introductions.

Dick took his wallet out of his pocket and handed over sixty pounds to the security guard. "When the food arrives, please pay for it, leave it here, then come and call us."

"Yes, sir."

They now all walked over to where the installation was taking place. Dick pointed out to Mr Bailey what was there and explained it was too expensive not to have any security guarding the equipment. This too included the safety of the engineers.

"I'm almost certain we'll be able to get two guards in here a little later, even if it means I must fetch them myself."

"All right," Dick replied, "but in your honest opinion, and as a security bloke, are two guards enough for this project?"

"No. I would prefer it if there were three because, when one goes on a lunch or toilet break, there would still always be two on duty."

"Okay, I agree with you, so you must please make sure you put this into place starting now."

"Mr Shepherd, your food has arrived."

"Thanks, we'll be right there," Dick acknowledged the security guard, then said to Mr Bailey "Let's go to the office block and see what's transpired and we can eat our pizzas at the same time."

So they walked back to the office block to devour their pizzas. As they were doing so, Mr Bailey made phone calls organising the additional security required.

Dick now turned his attention to Mr Bailey. "I'm only here for the day tomorrow and what I'd like is for you, and perhaps two of your colleagues, to be here by nine o'clock tomorrow morning so we can walk this entire airport, all buildings and grounds included."

"My reason for this is I want your professional viewpoint as to the security we already have in place. What with the way some mad organisations behave in this world today I can't take any chances. Therefore, I want you and your colleagues to advise me if what we have is adequate and, if not, where in your expert opinion we must strengthen or upgrade it."

"If you are able to identify any areas which you perceive not to be secure, I want you to put the additional security into place. However, if you think you can't handle it, I want you to have balls big enough to tell me. You can then recommend one of your opposition to fill those spots. Okay?"

"Mr Shepherd, I will make sure both I and two of my best work colleagues are here at nine o'clock tomorrow morning and I promise to give this place a thorough going over. However, should the demand outweigh the means of supply, I'll phone you."

Dick looked at him and nodded his head in approval. "What's your name?"

"It's Bill. Bill Bailey."

Dick almost said something to Bill about his name but thought the poor guy had it all his life, and still did, so he settled for a smile instead.

"And my name's Dick."

They shook hands, and Dick introduced him to the other two, greasy pizza fingers and all.

The pizzas now finished, Bill said if they wanted to leave, they were more than welcome to because he had it all in hand. He also told them he would not leave until some positive arrangements were in place.

By this time Dick was dying for a whisky, so he found no reason to argue. He informed the security guards they were using the people carrier and would now be on their way to the hotel.

"Does anyone know where it is?" asked Dick.

"No," replied Ivan.

"I do," said Phil. "Remember I lived here for a few years before you moved me out."

They greeted this news with relieved laughter as the security was a big deal for Dick and it seemed to ease the tension. "I must have a chat with Deon tomorrow about this" Dick said in passing.

As Phil understood his uncle so well, and what he could be like, he had to say a few words. "Now don't get upset with me, Dick. I've seen and witnessed how you can lose it, albeit controlled, and we don't want to lose Deon. So please try to be diplomatic in your approach when you confront him in the morning about this problem. I think you need to remember that this is a whole new ball-game for him and his staff."

Dick looked at him and pondered the point for a while. As he understood what Phil had said, and what he was getting at, he had a slight chuckle before replying, "Well put and yes, I promise. You are correct, and thanks for pointing it out as we cannot afford to lose Deon."

It was now time to leave and because Phil already had the keys and knew the directions, he drove. Once at the hotel, the three of them had a few drinks at the bar before retiring for the night.

On their way to the lifts, Dick had the foresight to ask reception to give each room a 7:00 a.m. wake-up call. "I would also appreciate it if you would send someone to each room to make sure we are all up and about."

"As I finish at six o'clock in the morning, I will inform the day staff sir, but I can't promise anything," the night receptionist replied with a nervous twinge in his voice.

The following morning they were all awoken by a loud knock on each of their doors. As Dick was to find out later, it had been a great idea on his part. "You may give yourself a congratulatory pat on the back."

After hurrying around like headless chickens, they made it to the office by 8:35 a.m. where they found three security guards in the reception area with Deon. Dick walked straight up to them and asked Deon to step to one side as he needed to speak to him in private.

"I'm confused Dick. I can't figure out what's going on."

"Nothing to worry about," Dick assured him, remembering Phil's sound advice. He explained the situation and when he had finished, he noticed Deon was now more at ease.

The main entrance door opened and Bill, together with his entourage, entered the building. They walked straight up to Dick and Bill introduced his colleagues to him. As they had already met Deon, they said their hellos. They now all strode across to the hangar and briefed the guards, and if there was anything at all they needed, they were to ask.

"Now there's just one thing I need to stress to you guys. I understand it will be interesting for you to watch what's going on, and I won't stop you either. However, I must ask you not to interfere with the engineers at all, and although on occasions you will have to speak to them, I must ask you to please keep it to a minimum," Dick said to the guards, and Bill, making his point.

Guards in place, he said to Ivan he must now take up his post with the engineers while the girls made their way back to the houses. Meanwhile, Dick and Phil would now spend the rest of the day inspecting the entire property with the security experts. Dick apologised to Deon, knowing he already had enough on his plate with the running of the airport, but he considered Deon should also be familiarised with not only the good areas but the vulnerable spots as well, should any be discovered.

Just after noon, he received a call on his mobile and recognised a familiar voice. "Good afternoon Mr Shepherd, it's Patric Butland here from BAE Systems in Farnborough."

"Hello, Patric. Please call me Dick will you? for if anyone should be addressed by their title, it's you, sir."

"Thanks very much, Dick, I appreciate that. Just to inform you, I'm overseeing the design team. So as their leader, I'm phoning to ask if we could set up arrangements for you to come to our offices and meet the team to discuss the project?"

"Yes, Patric. When do you suggest?"

"I was thinking the morning of the twenty-third at about nine o'clock, if that suits you?"

"Patric, I'm not in my office right now and I don't have my diary with me, so I'll tell what we'll do. If by ten o'clock at the latest tomorrow morning you don't hear from me to the contrary, I'll be there. Okay?"

"That'll do for me."

"Okay, all things being equal I'll see you in two days' time, and thanks for calling, Patric."

At the end of the call, Dick was well pleased for they had made Patric the team leader of the design department.

By 4:00 p.m., Dick called an end to the proceedings and all met in Deon's office, minus Ivan. There, he asked Deon to appoint someone to manage security as they could not afford to have any lapses and this person was to deal with Bill direct. "I hope you don't mind, Bill but I can't afford to have it any other way."

"Not at all, Dick. That's a good idea. The first thing I'll do is go around the bad areas with him, if you're in agreement?"

"Yes I am, Bill. However I will now, Deon, put the ball in your court, so the sooner you get someone to liaise with Bill, the sooner you have that monkey off your back. Okay, Phil and I will leave you guys with this so please contact me in a few days' time with the information on how you're doing with this, Deon. If you like, you could even get the new person you appoint to phone me."

The others stood up to shake hands, and before they departed, Dick said "To recap one point. My daughter and son-in-law will stay here for now, and for as long as they need to, as I want Ivan to learn as much as he can about the total workings of the simulator. So remember please, if you need anything, just ask Kerri."

They said goodbye and Dick and Phil walked back to the reception to find out where Chloe was. As Kerri had already phoned Ivan, the three of them showed up a little while later.

"Okay, sweet child o' mine. I've said to Deon you two are staying here for as long as you can and Ivan, I've also told him you are to be learning all you can about the simulator. When it's ready to fire up, Deon's got the two DVDs locked up and also, he is to liaise with you, Kerri, should he need anything, okay?"

"Yes, okay," she said and gave her old man a hug.

"Here are the keys to the people carrier. If you prefer something smaller, just ask them. If not, tough," Dick said tossing the keys to Ivan.

"Daddy, what time is the plane arriving?"

"Well, we leave at six o'clock, and as it doesn't take long for them to turn around, I don't think they'll be here before five fifty-five this evening."

"You've still got thirty-five minutes, so why don't we go to the canteen and get something to nibble on and perhaps a cup of tea as well?"

They made their way to the canteen and, on their way, Dick informed the desk clerk where they could find them.

In what seemed like no time at all, Dick said to Kerri "That's our kite. Time flies when you're having fun."

They got up and said their goodbyes, but before they left, Dick spoke to Phil and Ivan. "While Chloe and I are out of the country, Kerri is in charge of the U.K. side of the operation," he said and would, therefore, not put up with any in-house arguments.

"I'm sure there won't be any. I for one am glad it's not me who will be in charge" Phil said laughing and pointing a rude finger at his cousin. Kerri made to punch him, but he was too quick for her.

They all had a giggle at this. Ivan tried to tease her as well but soon buttoned up his lip when she responded. "You carry on and you'll see that when I'm in charge, I'll make sure you're the first one I fire."

Upon hearing this, Dick let out a slight guffaw. "That's my sweetie pie," he said, and Phil announced, "Thank heavens I'll be up North and out of harm's way."

They all chuckled away at Ivan's impending downfall. He looked at them, folded his arms, put a forlorn look on his face, lowered his head down towards the floor, shrugged his shoulders and made a huffing sound. This made them laugh even louder as his acting ability was pathetic.

As Dick walked past him, he patted him on his shoulder twice and said "Never mind" and could have sworn he heard Kerri say she married an overgrown child.

The flight home was, as usual, a pleasant one and the journey by car to the house was uneventful. "I'll send those two a text to say we've arrived," said Dick.

"And I'll pour the welcome home drinks, shall I?" Chloe asked and Dick said, "A splendid idea" to which Phil nodded in agreement.

"I'll get all my things together as I would like to hit the road by six-thirty in the morning," Phil informed them.

"Well then, you'd better only have this drink and no more. You don't want the police to catch you drink-driving, now do you?" Chloe said in her mother-hennish way, to which Phil replied:

"Mmmm... not a good idea."

"And what time are we leaving in the morning?" she asked, and Dick said, "Seven-thirty please."

"Damn," Chloe exclaimed "I was hoping to have at least two glasses of wine before bed time," she pointed out.

Dick said "Well there's always tomorrow."

There were, therefore, no jollifications for they all retired early.

Chapter Seventeen

(a) Phil's Re-deployment—Part 2

BY SIX-THIRTY the following morning, Phil was on his way. He arrived at Toby's by 8:45 a.m., well within the time limit he had set himself. He met Sterling, Struan, Josh and Torbin and they all traipsed into the Boardroom where the discussion took over from where Dick had left off.

"Gentlemen," Phil said, "I might have good news for you. Although everything is as it was there is, however, one small change. Brimstone Cars will no longer concern you because Dick has purchased it outright and has put me in charge of running the concern. So that's something off your shoulders."

There was a moment's silence which Phil took to be a sign of relief. However, Struan had a look of concern on his face. "Does this now mean there will be an impact on the income we were expecting to receive from you?".

"No, nothing has changed except I will run Brimstone, that's all."

"Okay, but how can we take your word for it things won't change further down the line?" Sterling now asked as he too felt concerned.

"You don't, but should you require it in writing... here it is."

Sterling took the document Phil handed to him and after reading it, realised it was a Legal Writ, signed not only by Dick, but also by a reputable firm of lawyers who had prepared the document.

"Happy?" Phil asked Struan.

"Oh yes. Happy, thank you. This is just perfect," replied a relieved Struan.

"Now just for your edification gentlemen," Phil continued. "The name has changed to 'Brimstone Motor Works—a subsidiary of —Maitland Electric Car Manufacturers'. We, however, don't foresee this having any impact on your side of the business."

"Just one more thing before I go. Things are on the go in Blackpool, so I will want deliveries starting in around five or six months' time so please don't let that affect your production time, and because of this lead time I'm giving you, I don't expect you to come back and say there's a problem in the supply of rolling stock."

"No, Phil, I assure you those lead times will not affect our deliveries and I'm sure I speak on behalf of all of us," Sterling said, and the others nodded in agreement.

"Well, on that positive note, I'll leave you guys now and please remember I'm only a phone call away. From now on I'm based in Blackpool which is a damn sight closer than Bristol."

"When will you be moving there?" Torbin asked, and Phil replied, "From here I go to a meeting in Manchester. When I'm finished there, I'll be on my way to what will be my new home."

As Phil had a two-hour drive ahead of him, he had left at 11:45 a.m., which was ahead of his planned schedule.

He arrived at Torque Motor Engineering with plenty of time to spare. As he hadn't yet met anyone there, he wasn't aware of who he would see, what position they held within the company, or what their names were.

"Bugger,... I stuffed up there."

But he was there now, so all he could do was to present himself. A middle-aged, attractive, blond-hair woman with a well-shaped figure greeted him at the front desk.

"Mmmm... these younger girls of today could take a few hints from her," Phil mused as he admired her.

He went about introducing himself to her and she replied in a well-modulated voice "Hello Mr Upton. They are expecting you" and Phil wondered if he should ask her what the MD's name was.

He plucked up the courage and did so. "His name is Mr Joe Kail, and he's the President and CEO of the company," she said in a voice Phil found sexy and he blushed. "Thanks very much," he said and turned away from her.

Someone Greeted him who he could only describe as being an old goat. She stood about one metre fifty centimetres tall and was so round, if she lay down on her side, one could give her a push-start down a hill and she would just keep on going. Phil found it hard to stop himself from giggling but, instead, he greeted her with a smile.

They got into a lift and went to the first floor where she led him down quite a long passage before they reached the Boardroom. She knocked on the door and stood aside to allow Phil to enter on his own. Four people were seated at the table who looked at him as he entered.

"Good afternoon ladies and gentlemen and thanks for seeing me at such short notice. My name is Phil Upton and I'm here representing my uncle, Dick Shepherd, from Maitland Electrical Car Manufacturing."

They all stood up and one lady said "I'm Janet Kuhn and I'm a member of the Managing Board as are my colleagues Lily Davey and Rian Buse, and this is our President and CEO, Mr John Kail."

Phil shook hands with each of them after which they all sat down, and although he felt nervous he did, however, feel confident at the same time.

"How may we be of service to you?" asked Mr Kail.

"I'm here representing my uncle and he is in the throes of

opening a new car manufacturing business but the cars being developed are not your ordinary run-of-the-mill stuff. Electricity will power them. Okay, there are cars on the road that run on electrical supply and I'm sure you understand how these operate in their various forms. However, what you don't understand, and I don't mean to be insulting but, they will operate in a way they never, ever need re-charging."

Lily interjected and asked, "How is that possible?"

"It's simple. I designed and built a drive plant. Now this device will drive an alternator or generator, which ever is required for the purpose at the time, and will supply the electric current needed by the electrical motor, in this case the car and yes, my machine needs no encouragement to turn."

"So, how does your machine work?" asked Mr Kail.

"It's a secret, and still to this day my uncle hasn't been given the full specs. No, not because he does not understand how it works, he doesn't want to get involved in that side of the operation." He lied, but he didn't mind.

They all sat mulling this information over for a while. "How can we be of service to you?" Rian now asked.

"I need a few variants of the different motors you produce. One of them, however, is on the lines of the size you get in a power station but,... well we'll cross that bridge when we get there. For now, we need to concentrate on those motors we require for the cars."

"And will your idea work?" asked Rian.

"With all due respect, I wouldn't be here if I had the notion it wouldn't, and besides if it doesn't, well I'd be sitting on a pile of electrical motors and there'd be a pile of cash in your bank account."

There was a hint of laughter, but nothing to write home about, for these people were your typical corporate bastards who had their heads stuck up their own backsides, and as for laughter? Well, they did not understand the meaning of the word.

"If we were to agree to supply these motors, how many would you want?" asked Mr Kail.

"For starters, I will need ten thousand of each type and I here's a schematic of each one and there are four variants. Now before I go any further I must ask, what one may refer to as being, a delicate question. As my invention is brand new and, therefore not known anywhere else in the world, are you prepared to sign a secrecy clause? With the line of business you're in, I'm sure you understand what I'm referring to and why."

They all sat and looked at each other for a split second and one could see by their expressions they were wondering if they had a well-dressed village idiot sitting in front of them, or not.

Phil continued. "If you are not prepared to do this, please advise right now so you waste no more of my valuable time. My reason for saying this is because I need to place an order for these items now. So, if you don't want our business, that's fine by me as I can always find someone else who will."

They all sat there for a moment, stunned, and because nothing was forthcoming, Phil had an idea which he put to the test. He stood up and addressed them. "You obviously don't want my business, so I apologise for wasting your time," he said, turned around and made his way towards the door.

However, before he reached it, Mr Kail spoke up. "I am sorry Mr Upton, will you please stay a while longer and I'm sure we can sort this out? I hope we can come to an amicable agreement," he said while standing pointing to the chair Phil had just left.

Phil stood behind the chair but, before he sat down, asked "Before we go any further, signed Secrecy Agreement, or not?"

"We can accommodate that."

Phil breathed a silent sigh of relief and gave himself a mental pat on the back. "You getting good at this, well done. Yes, even if I say so myself. I'm sure Dick would be proud of me," he said to himself.

He sat back down, opened his briefcase and took out two folders. "These are the schematics of all four shapes, sizes, power inputs and whatever required outputs," he said, handing them over to Lily as she was the closest to him. "You will want for nothing else should you follow those to the letter and I'll be keeping the other one for now as you won't need it yet."

"Now to give you an example of what I need. The smallest motor I require must be a brushless AC induction motor. It must have near one hundred and twenty foot-pounds of torque and around seventy-one horsepower per unit. Also, with each unit, you must include the motor controller and all the specs you require from me of each motor size are with the schematics. Are there questions?"

"What quantity was it again you said you require of each?" asked Rian.

"Ten thousand of each to start with please, and as I will need the delivery to start in three months' time, can you handle it?" he asked and this time there was no hesitation in their reply.

"We can," Mr Kail affirmed. "There should be no problem with that lead time at all. Now, how do we go about signing this secrecy document?"

"I'm glad you asked," Phil replied once again opening his briefcase. He took out a white C4 envelope which he opened and withdrew from it an A4 sheet of paper. This time, as Janet was sitting right opposite him, he handed it to her. He advised them of the fact it was a legal document drawn up by a reputable law firm pointing out their logo on the letterhead.

Once signed by all parties present, Phil produced yet another envelope which he handed to Lily. "This is a contract I've based on our conversation. Should you want to get one of your legal guys to peruse it, please, by all means, do so."

Lily picked up the contract, got up and walked out of the room.

"When the signed contract is ready, I'm prepared to put down a sizeable advance payment, so I need to know, were you given a card reading machine, the one taking the corporate world by storm?"

"You mean those card readers from the banks?" asked Janet, to which Phil replied "Correct."

Janet now turned her attention to Mr Kail. "That's the machine I spoke to you about at our last production meeting two weeks ago, remember?"

"Yes, I do, and we agreed to get one."

"And did you get one?"

"Yes, we did, Phil, but we don't know how to use it so I hope you can instruct us how to operate it?" asked Janet.

"No problem. Can you give me a cost estimate and what sort of down payment you would want?"

"Mmmm... tough call. Shall I ask Toni to run up a quick estimate?" Rian asked as he looked at Mr Kail who replied: "Yes, please."

"I only need a ballpark figure," Phil said "so he need not be one hundred percent accurate."

"Okay," Rian acknowledged as he left the room.

Phil took a few personalized cards out of his briefcase and handed them over saying "Once you have approved the quotation you can e-mail it please, and if you need to contact me for any reason at all, that's my mobile number on the card."

The door opened and Lily returned handing the contract to Mr Kail. "Everything is in order and, therefore, given the all-clear to sign the document" she advised him. "Is this for me?" she asked Phil as she picked up his business card.

"Yes it is."

A little while later it was now Rian who returned, and he handed an A4 sheet of paper to Mr Kail, who scrutinised it. "The average price per motor, at the moment, works out at two hundred and fifty pounds each, taking into account the smaller ones are lower in cost than the bigger ones. The average price for the motor controllers works out to seven hundred and fifty pounds each, so the overall average price per complete unit and delivery to your factory, at the moment, works out at one thousand pounds each."

"Sounds about right," Phil replied. He retrieved a calculator out of his briefcase to work on a few arithmetical equations for his own edification. "Okay, for starters, according to my rough calculations, we are looking at a cost of ten million pounds for the advanced quantity of one type only, correct?"

"Yes, that's correct," replied Mr Kail.

"All right, and once again, according to my rough calculations, the price should drop as the order quantity increases. Correct?" Phil asked again to which Mr Kail once again replied: "Yes,... correct."

"In that case, how much would you want as a down payment to get the ball rolling?"

"If you could give us say... half, and the balance on delivery, that would be acceptable."

"I'll tell you what I'll do to show you we are sincere in everything we say and do. I will put down thirty million pounds, then we can take it from there, but on one condition." He paused before continuing "The condition is... you are never late with any delivery, from start to finish, and whenever the actual finish will be... well, I'm sorry, I'm not able to say at this point in time."

To this, they all agreed. Phil asked Lily for the card machine and he showed them how to operate it. "Please call your bank now while I'm still here to check if the transaction has gone through."

"That amount of money want transfer straight-away," said Rian.

"I could surprise you at the amount of pulling power we have."

"Okay, I'll check," said Jane. So she slipped out of the room only to return with what appeared to be a printout of a bank statement. "How on earth did you do it?"

"Well... when you have contacts in higher places and no, I'm not religious," he said grinning "but I mean higher places, it's surprising what you can get and what you can make happen within a moment's notice."

Phil wondered if Joel heard him and he stopped himself short from jumping out of his skin when he heard Joel's voice in his ear saying "Of course I can".

"So, work with me folks, and you may just make a fortune," Phil said with a smirk on his face. "Okay, I'm done for now, and as there's a lovely long drive ahead of me, if it's all the same to you, I'll be on my way."

"Not at all, and I hope one day we'll get to meet your uncle," said Mr Kail.

"That's a strong possibility, however, I must warn you I'm nothing like him at all. I'm a pussycat in comparison. He pulls no punches, and he calls a spade a shovel. If he doesn't like you.....," Phil paused for a moment and looked around the room "Please forgive me, ladies, as this is my uncle speaking and not me, but if he doesn't like you, he'll look you straight in the eye and tell you to fuck off. Although, believe it or not, he is a nice person."

The shock by the swear word, and the sentence, showed on their faces. Phil noticed but couldn't give a damn—and why should he? He was not aware of the time frame as to the end of the human population, but the certainty was they would not be around for many more years, anyway. "So, stuff them" he said loud and proud to himself.

Phil had adopted this attitude because he had now witnessed what Dick had tried to explain to him in the past about the people in the corporate world, how they operated and how they treated people whether those people be the public or their clients, but even more so, their own staff members. "Shit, now I understand why Joel and company want to get rid of the arsehole human race. We're all a bunch of fuck-ups" he said to himself.

He shook hands all around and said goodbye for he couldn't get out of the place fast enough to get away from them. However, if they would supply the motors he required, he would eat humble pie.

The start of the drive wasn't too bad but as he got closer to his destination of Blackpool, the traffic had other ideas. He only arrived at the hotel after 6:30 p.m., booked in, and sorted himself out. As supper was still being served, he shot back downstairs to the dining room before it became too late. Afterwards, he decided he would retire early, not only because he wanted to be on site early, but also because he was, by now, exhausted.

"It's been a long day," he said to himself.

Phil arrived on site at 7:35 a.m. the following morning. As Tom had already started at the building site, one of the first things he had installed was two portable offices. He walked straight to the one advertising the company's name on it, Creative Civil Engineering, and decided it could well be the on-site Foreman's office. He opened the door and saw three chaps sitting at a table having a cup of tea.

"Good morning. I'm Phil Upton, the owner of these premises," he said adopting this approach as it would be easier for the introductions and had the idea Dick wouldn't mind at all. "Which one of you is the Foreman?"

A rather large and overweight guy in his late forties stood up and, speaking in a deep voice said "I am and my names Andy. These are some of my colleagues, Ricky and Adam," he replied as they stood up and shook hands. "Tom said Mr Shepherd's the owner and he would come here."

"That's true. Mr Shepherd is my uncle and he, however, won't be here. In fact, it's unlikely he will ever come back here again. He has put me in charge and handed the business over so I'll be here every day from now on, and to inform you, seven representatives from Japan will arrive tomorrow, so can you organise hard hats for them, please?"

"Not a problem. There's a box load of them here which is more than enough to go around."

"Good,... one for me then, please?" Andy opened the box, retrieving a white one which he handed over.

"Thank you. Now, do you mind if we conduct a quick meeting to bring me up to date what equipment, how many staff, and where on site you have already started?"

"No problem. Okay you two, clear the table," Andy said to his workmates. They got out a set of plans, together with other paperwork, and explained the production progress to Phil.

"What's this building over here? It seems to be out of place."

"That's the new electricity supply outlet to the factory and the housing estate."

"Oh yeah, that's great. I'll be putting my own electrical supply output in there, so make sure the electricians run no new cables from the road to here. In fact, once you no longer need the supply from the grid, cut it off as we will not require it any longer once we are up and running."

"Forgive my ignorance, Phil, but what are you going to run the factory and the housing on? I mean, you will need electricity to switch the lights on at least."

"Don't worry about it. Leave it. Later I'll show you what's going on and where the supply is coming from. Okay?"

"Okay," replied Andy.

"So all the electrical supply will come from there and will, therefore, exit this building to the two sites?" Adam enquired looking rather dumbfounded.

"In a nutshell,... yes. Now when can we do a walk-about?"

"Phil, drink a cup of tea while we put all this away, then we can go."

He downed a welcome cup of tea and when finished, they all left the office and stood outside looking at the factory building. As they walked towards it, Phil asked if Tom was due in.

"Yes," Andy replied. "There isn't any reason he shouldn't."

"And while it comes to mind, can you or Tom organise one of those offices for me?"

"I'll check with Tom if there's any available. I'm sure it won't be a problem and I'll phone him right now and find out for you."

"Thanks Andy, tell him to add it to the bill."

Tom arrived around 9:30 a.m. and the three of them made an additional walk-around, but this time it included the housing estate.

"I've organised a mobile office for you which should be here within the next two days," Tom told Phil.

"Thanks Tom. It'll sure come in handy and whatever the cost—well I don't have to tell you what to do."

They spent the rest of the day going over the plans for both sites and also checked up on the progress of the trenches being dug for the new water supply and drainage systems. Towards the end of the day's shift, Phil reminded Tom about the Japanese engineers coming to join forces with them the following day.

Later in the evening, as the Nippon Robotics advance party was staying in the same hotel as Phil, the receptionist telephoned him. They advise him of their arrival, so he went downstairs to introduce himself and there was only one he recalled meeting on his trip to Japan.

Due to the late time of their arrival, the hotel restaurant had already closed, so Phil asked if they would like to go to another one, however, as they had had a rather exhausting trip, they declined the offer and said they would prefer to relax for a while before retiring.

Early the following morning they all met on site, which included Tom and Andy, and discussed the time span needed to do the job. Tom informed them they needed three months to complete the factory side of things.

Although the housing project would run at the same time as the factory, Tom said he did, however, at this early stage, require an additional three months. The intricacies involved required more time, even although they would work twenty-four hours a day six days a week.

The Nippon crew said, although they would work alongside Tom and his crew, once Tom had completed his section of the factory the Japanese, at this early stage, would require a further month to install all the equipment required to run it.

This was all agreed to by Phil.

"One thing I'd like you to organise as soon as you can Tom, is to fit the company name on the outside of the building."

"What name are you looking at?"

"Tom, I will leave the design to you as you are more in touch with those things than me. The name I want is Maitland Electrical Car Manufacturers and it should be luminous at night, please. Whatever you and your design team come up with, I'm sure we'll approve of it. However, if we don't... well I wouldn't worry about it too much if I were you." They both had a little laugh.

"That will be no problem at all. In fact, I'll get the office working on it straight away, shall I?"

"Yes please," Phil affirmed.

So they all put their heads down and got stuck into their various tasks, working non stop.

## (b) The Super VC10 Design Meeting

Once Phil had left, Dick decided it was pointless going back to bed, so he made himself some breakfast and sat at the table. He caught up on some paperwork while eating and wondered what he should take with him. There was nothing of importance and Patric would be there to assist him, so he went upstairs to the bathroom and made so much noise while attending to his ablutions he woke Chloe and she got up.

"If you make the noise a little louder, you could just as well wake up the whole bloody neighbourhood," she said, looking all sleepy-eyed.

"That was my plan," he said with a cheeky smile. "Are you coming with me today or are you going to chill out?"

"Oh damn, I forgot about this bloody meeting this morning. If it's okay with you I'd prefer not to go as all this gallivanting around is catching up with me."

"It's not at all necessary for you to be there, so you sit back and enjoy a relaxing day and no, I have no idea what time I'll be home," he stated before she could ask.

So Dick set out on his journey alone, fighting his way through the traffic with a swear word and a blast of his horn here and there. Now because he had music blaring away through the car's sound system for him, the next great race, therefore, sprang into life.

As always he arrived well before the appointed time of a meeting for he believed there was never an excuse for being late. He walked to the front desk, gave the receptionist his name and said he was there to see Mr Patric Butland. A little while later Patric appeared, and they exchanged pleasantries before going to where the design team was carrying out its work.

It was a large open plan area, not too diverse from the days when graphic designers used huge multi-function drawing boards mounted on stands. Each designer would stand in front of their particular drawing board for hours on end which Dick remembered well. These days the modern-day designer sat in front of a computer screen moving a mouse around and this action was to capture whichever design he or she was working on.

He introduced himself to all of them but only three joined them at the design table. The table itself was large and there would normally be a fair amount of seating places around it, however, there weren't any for this meeting. Patric did the honours and unrolled first one set of plans then, next to it, another set. The five of them focussed their attention on the task at hand.

"As you can see," Patric said, "I've started with the outside of the aircraft as I concluded this would be the quickest to get through.

Once we agree on what you want, we'll send the plans off to the manufacturing side of the company. Any objections?"

"Not from me," Dick replied, and the others agreed.

"The reason I laid out two sets of plans is because one has the refuelling nozzle and the other doesn't because, as far as I can remember, you want one as a refuelling tanker and the other four as a normal passenger-carrying aircraft, is that correct?"

"Yep, one hundred percent correct. I must ask if you have had any thoughts about winglets or the raked wingtips?"

"Yes, and we recommend the raked wingtips as extensive experiments show they are lighter and require less structural modifications to the original wing. Good news, but we also found because of their superior mass properties, they should burn less fuel."

"Wonderful, raked wingtips it is," Dick said feeling excited about the whole proceedings, for it was his aircraft they were designing.

They all looked over the plans and Patric made a comment while pointing at the tanker drawings. "Now there's no probe-and-drogue system, the hose drum units on the wings, as far as I can recall. Is that also correct?"

"Yes, it is as I can see no need for having them."

"So, it's only the one centre-line re-fuelling point underneath and towards the back of the fuselage?" Patric asked to ensure he was getting all his facts correct.

"Yes, that's how I want it as I would prefer a clean wing. But don't forget, this variant is not to have the re-fuelling nose probe either as it's not a necessity," Dick further instructed them.

All the time the three young designers made notes or alterations to those they had already put to paper.

"Now let's talk about the colour scheme you want and what sort of writing or drawings, or whatever it is, you want featured on the outside."

"The colours I like are gloss grey and candy-apple red and this is what I envisage them looking like. The entire aircraft is to be candy-apple red. The raked wingtips, the top of the nose, and a forty centimetre band travelling from the nose to the tail are all to be gloss grey."

"That's something for your design team to work on which they might start on now while we carry on here. But also, on the tail of each aircraft, I want a picture of the Phoenix, although grey, highlighted with the red."

"Understood," Patric replied, "and I'll get the design team to come up with a few ideas of their own and we take it from there."

"Good, but just one other thing. Get them to add the wording

'The Super VC10 Phoenix' at the front just before the nose, in candy-apple red on the gloss grey band. Does that make sense?"

"Makes perfect sense," Patric affirmed. He turned to one of the three designers and sent him off to join the design team.

"At this stage,... anything else you want done on the outside?"

"Mmmm... no, nothing, Patric. What are your thoughts?"

"As far as making any more physical changes, my answer to that is no. As for the paintwork... Well, I'm not much of an artist but, if I were you, I wouldn't put anything else on it. You don't want them to turn out looking like flying bill-boards like other airlines." They had a good chuckle.

"Yes, I agree with you. What about you two?" Dick asked the others.

They seemed hesitant about answering but one said he would give his opinion once they could see a computer image of the design. The third designer returned with the altered design he had been working on which Patric took from him and scanned it before handing it to Dick. "Okay, looking at this, what changes do you want?"

Dick looked at the design and pointed at one section. "Please note this down, as I will require this feature on all the aircraft. Both front doors need to be further down because, on the left-hand side, I require you to fit sleeping quarters behind the cockpit. There needs to be a bed, together with a hand basin and, after that, we get to the left-hand-side entrance door." As he looked up, he saw four sets of beady eyes watching him.

"On the right-hand side, taking up a similar space to that on the left, I want the galley. This must be a super-duper type, with all mod-cons, and not at all what you would find on any ordinary airliner, and following that, we must not forget about the all-important loo. Okay?" Dick said looking at them and pleased to see all their heads nodding.

"After the loo, you get the right-hand side entrance door. Now regarding these entrances, each one must have its own built-in set of stairs of the type that fold away underneath the door but separate from it. Then once it's folded away, it slides by motor-power into the fuselage below the door," Dick said while pointing at the plan of the doors original positions. "I don't want the stairs inside the cabin. I hope I'm explaining it so you can understand? If not, please interrupt and ask away."

"Got it," Patric replied, "we'll get that down and if it's wrong, when you see the revised drawing, we'll change it."

They carried on studying what Dick had told them before he continued. "Should there be a problem and you find you can't have both sets opposite each other, then install only one set. Should that be the case, put the set on the left-hand side in the front and the one at the back on the right-hand side, or vice versa." On this instruction, one of the three designers excused himself and left the room.

"So with these alterations, it will affect the amount of seating space which will fall quite a lot. What I envisage seeing, and what I'm hoping for, is one hundred and thirty-odd seats in the passenger plane, allowing for six crew, and only thirty six-odd seats for passengers in the tanker version, also allowing for six crew."

"Now with the tanker, if you can put in any seats at the back of the refuelling fuel tanks, please do so and as many as you can. Right, now regarding all seats. You must take into account the space between each seat and must allow for someone of my height and stature to sit and relax in that space in comfort. But I mean... relax."

"I have suffered in the past on some of these over-packed bloody airlines which cater for the smaller person to get more bums on seats in the cabin. Therefore, and for obvious reasons, there will only be one class on these aircraft."

They continued their discussion by trying to decide on the colour scheme of the carpets and the seats and also, what sort of overhead packing space Dick required. They spoke about each seat having an inbuilt television mounted in the back, and not forgetting where they would position the front seat televisions. But for Dick, these he classed as luxuries and not necessities.

The lunchtime break now approached and Patric had received a message to pass onto Dick saying Ivan, James and Perry had invited him to lunch. Although Dick didn't mind, he would prefer lunch with Patric, on their own, where they could speak about flight and, perhaps, even its history. But he decided it would rude not to accept.

When the extended lunch was over and, as he would never remembered the way back to Patric and the team, Gina offered to show him the way. But out of the blue, Dick heard Joel's voice in his mind "You should have more faith in your abilities" he said, so Dick told Gina not to bother as he had remembered the way.

"Come and have a look at this," Patric beckoned to him as soon as he came in.

They sat in front of a monitor and he stared at quite a few intriguing paint designs. They were far more interesting than he had ever imagined, and after studying each design, the one he chose was of the entire aircraft being gloss grey. The nose cone and tail fin not candy-apple red but rather more of a plum colour. The band, running down the side of the aircraft, would start from below the cockpit windows and finish up just short of the tail and, because of the rear engine pods, the outer engine casings also had a band running its length. The top of the fin, including the extra fuel tank, were gloss grey and the two colours, together with the design, complimented each other to such a degree he had no hesitation in selecting that design.

"Nice,... and I like it. Now all you need to do is to find a picture of a phoenix and drop it in on the tail-fin, and to reverse what I told you before, the Phoenix will now be highlighted in plum with gloss grey," he said to the young graphics designer.

The two designers came back to the table and carried on with the design. They tried to work out how many seats they could fit into the cabin area available after making provision for the sleeping quarters, galley and toilet.

"At the back," Dick carried on "we need to allow for another toilet and another galley which must also be of the same high quality, please. Now we get to the two back doors. I will let you work out which side to put the stairs on should space be of a premium if you can't accommodate both. I'm not fussed by that."

Time slipped by with no one noticing and Dick asked if they should carry on and complete the meeting there and then, or should they re-convene at another date?

"If you don't mind, Dick, why don't we complete it now and if there are questions afterwards, I'll send you an e-mail?"

"Agreed," Dick replied, and so they continued.

"What about the cockpit itself?" Patric asked, "I seem to remember you want the most modern up-to-date avionics?"

"Yes, I do. Everything throughout the inside of the aircraft is to be of a modern-day jet airliner. The only thing I will not have is a side-stick. I don't care how your designers do it, but I want the allegro-type steering wheel column, which the original aircraft had. I cannot see myself using a side-stick configuration. That's the thing the young computer junky uses, and it's not for me, thank you very much,".

They scanned through everything once more when he remembered a critical item they had not accounted for. "I don't want the same air-conditioning system you get in modern day aircraft. I want mine designed around the older airliner that allowed for smokers, which should be on these plans." When he said this, the three designers looked at him in astonishment.

"No, don't worry – there's definitely no smoking allowed on my aircraft. What I'm getting at is this. As I am not serving the public, per se, and as I'm not in competition with other airline companies, I'm therefore not interested in the fuel bill. I want fresh air coming into the cabin as it was in days gone by and you three, if you can't follow what I'm talking about, then ask Mr Butland... he understands."

"Oh yes, so tomorrow, I'll show and explain to you what Mr Shepherd is talking about."

Dick continued "Now with the periscope, you should upgrade it to modern-day technology and don't base it on the old design. I don't want people standing up in the cockpit looking through it to see how the tail-fin is behaving as they did on the original. Perhaps you can install a camera or three and link them up to a screen in the cockpit."

"Much better idea and I'll change the plans," Patric acknowledged. "Okay, I do believe we have everything for now."

"Yes, we've accomplished quite a lot. Oh hang on, I've just remembered one more item and that is the names on each of the aircraft. The tanker is Big Dick and the others are to be Chopper, Little Willie, Moom and Meadies Child," he informed them writing the names down on a piece of paper. These names brought a rare smile to the faces in the room.

It was now 7:00 p.m. and Dick gave his thanks to the team for their dedication to the job and said he hoped to see them again someday soon. He said his goodbyes and Patric walked with him to the front reception area. As it was a fair distance, they spoke about nothing else but the VC10, both being excited about the project. They shook hands and said their goodbyes.

While driving out of the premises he phoned Chloe, using the hands-free system in the car, informing her he was on his way. When he got home, he decided not to do any more for the day, so he relaxed for a while and had the obligatory whisky and water (or two), before retiring for the night.

The following day they spent planning the up-and-coming trip to Argentina. This included the Argentinian Government members meeting in La Rioja. As a goodwill gesture, they decided it would be a good idea to purchase various gifts, but because of the strained relations between the two Governments, they decided not to buy anything too British in case it may offend.

They drove to the outskirts of London, and not the city centre itself as they deemed it to be far too dangerous and unwelcoming these days. They parked the car, and walking around, they looked at the shops and stalls of the various street vendors from all around the world strewn over a vast area.

"Hey, look at that," Chloe cried out pointing towards a typical African Mart.

"I think if I'm thinking what you're thinking then let's think no more for it's a brilliant idea of mine you thought of," Dick said in his usual silly way which caused them both to giggle.

They bought wood carvings of different African animals—giraffe, rhino, elephant, Cape buffalo and lion, together with quite a few more.

"If we carry on like this, we will have to make two trips to the bloody car," Chloe exclaimed, and Dick said "Yeah, just looking at this lot, we have more than enough."

"Then may I suggest we get the hell out of here now?" she demanded rather than asked, and he agreed.

On their way home, they made sure they did a stop-over at the Superstore to buy enough wrapping paper and Magic Tape.

As they walked towards the car, Dick said "Why don't we get fish and chips? Saves having to prepare something when we get home."

"Good thinking there, Batman. Let's do that."

After eating their food, they set about wrapping the gifts on which they prided themselves on being the perfect choices. On completion, and putting them to one side, they relaxed and prepared themselves to enjoy the rest of the evening.

"Pleased with yourselves aren't you? And so you should be," and there was Joel, appearing out of nowhere as usual.

"Hello Joel," Dick and Chloe said in unison. "Thank you," Dick said "Are you happy with what we accomplished today?"

"More than happy. So far everything seems to be going to plan, and in good time too, but there's one important thing you must understand. Everything you are doing is not to satisfy me or my family, it is to satisfy you and your family. Have a good evening and I'll see you again soon," and, in his usual fashion, he disappeared.

Dick and Chloe looked at each other and grinned. "Happiness is," said Chloe, and they raised their glasses to Joel.

"What time are we getting up in the morning?" she asked him.

"Well, wheels-up is at three o'clock tomorrow morning and it's about a twenty-minute drive to Biggin Hill allowing forty-five minutes for our ablutions. So,... I guess I'll get up at one o'clock. Want me to wake you up?"

"Yes please, but only after you come out of the bathroom."

"I'll do that small thing for you, and I think I'll pack all those gifts into the car now. I don't want to be doing that at two o'clock in the bloody morning."

"Yeah, good thinking there, old man."

"Yes,... and up yours, old girl," he said joining her in the banter.

Together, they set about preparing the house for being empty while they were away by getting the inside security lighting arranged. When finished, Dick set about checking all the paperwork he would need to take along with him before filing it back into his attaché case. Afterwards, they packed a bag each for the trip.

As soon as Dick found himself with a few moments to spare, he phoned his daughter to remind her of their early leaving and, while she was in charge, she was not to take any crap from anyone. If she felt they were on the losing side of anything, she was to phone him at once, anytime, night or day.

Chapter Eighteen

The Argentine Government Officials Meeting

AS THEY WALKED into the reception area at Biggin Hill, Dick stopped dead in his tracks as someone caught his eye.

"Hey... look who's back," he said to Chloe pointing at Helen.

"Good morning," Helen said with a broad smile.

"Hi Helen, nice to see you again," Chloe walked up to her and they exchanged hugs.

"Had a good break?"

"Yes, thanks, but it's good to back again."

Dick didn't go in for those sorts of niceties, except in exceptional cases, so he smiled at her and shook hands. "We've brought more luggage this time but nothing too heavy."

"That shouldn't be a problem," Helen assured him "Where is it?"

"It's being loaded as we speak."

"Is there anything I can help you with before we board, Mr Shepherd?"

"Yes, please, Helen. There are two things. Can you inform me if we've got any bookings in the pipeline? Also, as I'm not too sure if we're going to in La Rioja for one, two or three days, I need you to advise management and tell them I will pay for any extras on our return."

"I'll sort it out for you now, so why don't you get on-board and make yourselves comfortable."

"That's sweet of you," said Chloe.

"See you on-board," Helen said and walked off towards the office.

As they boarded the plane, Chloe popped her head inside the cockpit. "Hello strangers, another nice long flight," and John replied "Hello to you too. Nice to see you both again. Yes, it will be a long one so you two just sit back, relax and enjoy it."

Helen appeared and making sure all was in order, closed the door behind her. "I've organised everything and they assured me, so long as you've got the money, you can stay as long as you like."

"Oh, he's got the money all right," Chloe said with a giggle.

They were well on their way when, after breakfast, Chloe asked Helen to come and join them.

"I don't for one moment care what your company rules are. I want you to come and sit here because Dick's going to join John and Allan as he wants to speak to them, and bring something to drink and two glasses please."

The two girls now set themselves up to do what girls do well when there are no men around.

"Have fun," Dick said and walked through to the cockpit. There was a jump seat near the pilots and he made himself at ease albeit in a most uncomfortable position due to his height and long legs.

"Hi, you two, mind if I come and join you for a while?"

"By all means," John replied, "and if your backside goes numb sitting there, you can always shove a pillow under it."

Dick spoke to them about the cockpit and the avionics in the aircraft. He had a good reason for this as he would soon need to hunt for pilots and the particular brand of pilots needed were those accustomed to flying around the world, and as a bonus with these two, they had already had a glimpse of the greater area of the future runway. Therefore he decided this trip to be as good a time as any to tell them what he had in mind.

"Without seeming to brag," Dick said to them "what I'm about to tell you will come to life once I get to the proposition I want to put forward to you."

He explained to them about the Airbus A400Ms he had purchased and about the simulator being installed at Maitland airport. He continued "I've also got on order, and they may well be delivered within the short period of two years' time... five Super VC10s."

Both John and Allan turned their heads towards him with looks of total amazement, however, before they made any comment, he carried on.

"Although they are the genuine aircraft and airframe in their outside appearance, they will modernise the inside for me—and that will include the avionics."

Although lost for words, their eyes lit up like neon signs.

"Now here's the deal," Dick said "I'm still looking for five pilots for the Airbus's and I will need a further two for the VC10s, so here's something for you guys to consider. Would either or both of you be interested in any of those available positions?" Before they had time to answer, he said: "Right, I'll now stretch my legs and pour myself another drink," and was out of the cockpit. He hadn't walked two paces when he heard, as did the girls, a joyful shout from the cockpit which put an instant smile on his face.

"What the hell are you three up to in there?"

Because Chloe explained to Helen what the future would bring, he knew he could answer the question without confusing her. "I've just asked them if they would like to fill any of those vacant pilot positions we have," he said looking smug.

"I take it they have agreed?" asked Chloe.

"I've no idea. I still have to find out, but judging by the hullabaloo in there, the answer may well be yes. What do you say?" he asked, and they both agreed the answer would be a resounding "Yes."

He stayed with the girls for a wee while longer, to give his poor old bum a rest, before returning to the cockpit.

When he got himself ensconced once more, he asked: "I take it by the noise in here you have decided?"

"Yes, we have but we have a question," Allan replied in repressed excitement.

"And what would that be?"

"You said you have two vacancies left on the VC10s?"

"That's correct, and I suppose those are the two positions you would like to fill, right?"

"Neither of us would want anything more," replied John.

"That is what I had in mind," Dick said with a self-satisfied smirk and shook hands with both.

"This is what I suggest we should do. It's not a good time to talk about this now, but once we're in La Rioja, there will be times when we can sit down and chat about the whole deal in a more sensible way. Okay?"

"Sounds great," said Allan.

"Good. Now as I've got a meeting tomorrow with some Government officials, I want to get some shut-eye, so I'll see you later," Dick said, leaving behind him two thrilled pilots.

They arrived at the Major Alfaro Airport just before 12:20 p.m., and when Helen opened the door, a lovely temperature of thirty-two degrees centigrade, a humidity of twenty-nine percent, and no wind at all, greeted them.

As the crew would sort out the aircraft's parking facilities, Dick asked Helen to leave them to it and to go with them. He had not only organised a car for Chloe and himself but a people-carrier for the crew for the duration of their stay. So, he would get the car hire company to hand over the keys for the people-carrier to her. This allowed them to come and go as they pleased.

Chloe remained in the office to attend to all the paperwork for the cars and Dick and Helen were about to leave when a greasy looking man came prancing over to them and introduced himself as Jorge, the Airport Manager. With his limited English, they made out that, since there was hangar space available, they may park the plane in there. The space would be available for at least the next year or two, maybe even longer, and for a fee, it was available to them for as long as they wished. This made Dick and Helen exchange expressive glances and stifle giggles.

As Dick wanted no come-backs, he took hangar space for a week which he paid for in advance. Once satisfied, he and Helen walked back to the aircraft to inform John and Allan about the arrangements. Jorge, in the meantime, was to rustle up labour to fetch a tug which would tow the aircraft into the hangar, under the watchful eyes of the pilots.

Once they hangared the plane, the doors were closed and locked and a key handed over to John. They now all walked back the short distance to the terminal where Chloe was waiting for them. They handed over their passports, and security checks carried out before they left the airport, and as Allan remembered the way to the hotel, he drove the crew in the people-carrier while Dick and Chloe followed behind them.

Upon arrival, a girl greeted them Chloe did not recognise. She was just as efficient as the previous girl had been and, once they had all booked in, Allan thanked her in Spanish. Once finished, they walked to their rooms and dropped off their suitcases where Dick called Felipe to inform him of their arrival. Felipe said he had to make telephone calls first and would not be long.

Dick knocked on Johns Hotel door and told him once again they were to come and go as they pleased and also told him to collect all receipts and said he would make sure to reimbursed them for all of their expenses.

Chloe and Helen each had the other's contact numbers in case any emergency crop up on either side.

When Felipe arrived, the Government contact was with him whom he introduced to Dick and Chloe as Juan. They all walked through to the dining area where they had a short briefing about the following day's meeting.

"The reason I took so long to get here," Felipe said, "was because I had to wait for Juan to phone the Government offices to tell them you had arrived."

"That's understandable," replied Dick.

Juan said although there would be five dignitaries at the meeting, El Presidente himself would not be able to make it.

"It would have surprised me if he had been due to the short notice I gave you," Dick replied "Juan," he continued "Chloe, and I have brought them some small gifts as a token of our appreciation. Would that be okay?"

"As long as there are no bombs or poisonous objects in them, I suppose it should be fine," he replied with a smile on his face, and the others enjoyed the joke.

"Just two other things," Dick asked "Have you organised a go-to person for me and have you found us a Civil Engineering Company?"

Felipe said smiling, "What I decided, because I have already dealt with you, I will be your go-to man, if you agree."

"That's fine by me. Here, let's shake on it and we can sort out your fee later."

"No problem," Felipe replied "and I hope you don't mind, but I've asked Juan to help."

"Two for the price of one, well that's brilliant," Dick exclaimed "No, I approve and, as I say, we'll sort the fees out later. Now what about the Civil Engineering guys?"

"I have found a reputable firm and have planned for them to be here by ten o'clock in the morning of the day after tomorrow. We can take it from there," said Felipe.

"Brilliant,"

"Dick," Juan said, "I've been wondering about those gifts you have brought. May I suggest I take them and I'll give them to the security people who will accompany the officials so they can check them before handing them over."

"That's a good suggestion. Yes, we'll do that."

They were just settling down into further discussions when Helen came up to tell Dick and Chloe the crew were going sight-seeing.

"You guys have loads of fun and we'll see you... well, when we see you," said Chloe.

So the four of them sat around the table and continued discussing the up-and-coming meeting before digressing onto anything and everything else. By this time, it was getting close to 5:30 p.m.

"We must decide what we want to do about supper," Dick said, looking over at Juan and Felipe. "It would please us if you and your partners joined us tonight, and will you book a table at the best restaurant, please?

They both agreed, and Felipe said he would pick them up at seven o'clock while Juan would phone the restaurant. Dick said they would be ready and waiting so they shook hands all round and said, "Hasta la vista".

Dick and Chloe walked back to their room to unpack their cases and to relax for a while before getting ready.

As the Government officials meeting was to start at the Town Hall at 9:00 a.m. the following morning, Dick stayed away from the booze and they got back to the hotel at just on 11:00 p.m.

When dropping them off Felipe suggested "If you like, I'll pick you up at eight-thirty in the morning.

"You're on, thank you very much. Until then, good night."

Dick was up bright and early, and because of the warm weather, swam in the not too large a swimming pool, but it was adequate enough for him.

After breakfast, Felipe arrived dead on time and, with his help, they bundled all the gifts into the boot of his car. Dick held onto his briefcase and he and Chloe got into the car. They took off at a slow speed and he wondered what time they would get to the

Town Hall. Three minutes later they pulled into the car park and he looked over at Felipe in bewilderment.

"You've got to be bloody joking. We could have walked here," he said in bemusement.

"Yes, but not carrying the gifts," said Felipe.

Juan pulled up and Dick said they should now transfer the gifts into the boot of his car, which they did. This done, they all stood around chatting about anything just to pass the time away. Then nine o'clock came and went, as did nine-thirty, and Dick could not contain himself any longer.

"What time are these bloody people supposed to be here?" he asked fuming.

He himself was a stickler for punctuality and had no patience with this kind of behaviour. For him, if someone would be late, the least they should do was to call to advise them of the situation. Felipe apologised but Dick understood it had nothing to do with him. At nine thirty-five, three aircraft flew overhead.

"That's them," Juan blurted out in relief and Dick said, "I suppose it'll take them another goddam hour to get here."

Chloe put her hand on his arm to calm him down. "Hang in there, old boy. It's not the end of the world... yet, and you realize this is Argentina?" she said which made him smile and relax a little.

"Thanks dear, that's just what I needed," he said putting his hand over hers. Forty-five minutes later, the Government officials arrived. "Ahhhhh... at long bloody last."

"I bet you won't mention it when they step out of their cars," Chloe joked.

"You're damn right I won't," he replied, and they chuckled.

The five officials got out of their cars and were first met by the Mayor of the town who had come out to greet them. To show respect, Dick and company hung back a little until Felipe or Juan were given the go ahead to usher them across.

"Bugger me, I'd like to see these arseholes swim when the shit hits the fan," he whispered to Chloe, and she punched him on the arm.

Juan spoke to one of the security guards and took him over to the car where they peered inside the boot. Dick did not hear or understand what was going on, so he didn't bother about it.

Juan returned to join them and after another five minutes the delegation came over to them and Juan started the introductions.

"Allow me to introduce Mr Shepherd and Mrs Fraser-Rigby," he said. Turning his attention towards Dick and Chloe, "This is Señor Bautista Lopez, Chief of the Cabinet of Ministers. Señora Paula Ramos, Minister of Foreign Relations. Señor Thiago Perez,

Minister of Labour, Employment and Social Security. Señor Santino Ruiz, Minister of Industry and, Señora Rosario Ortiz."

"Shit, I thought he'd never bloody stop," Dick uttered to himself, but smiled and shook hands with each of them, followed by Chloe.

With the formalities over, Felipe suggested they drive straight to the farmstead and take it from there. They all returned to their cars, and just before they set off, with Felipe in the lead, one of the security guards gave him a walkie-talkie to keep in contact, should it be necessary.

As Chloe was renowned for her lack of a sense of direction, to her amazement she remembered where they were and what would appear around every corner. Felipe took them around the entire farmstead and explained what was on the cards, and as for Dick, this being the first time he was seeing the property, Chloe hadn't been wrong when she had said he would love it.

They found quite a large table on the inside of the main farmhouse where Dick laid out a plan for the entire area. This included the so-called factory buildings for manufacturing the cars.

He took them through the plan pointing out what buildings would go where, which included the runway. This also included the piece of property on the other side of the road. Dick slowed his speech rate and Felipe and Juan translated for him as none of the officials spoke or understood English, or so he was led to believe.

They spent quite a few hours there, driving on roads not suited to the vehicles they were driving but Dick took it with a pinch of salt. They drove out onto the tarred road and stopped in almost the same spot Felipe had stopped at when he had shown Chloe and Cassie the property.

After looking around and studying with intent, the officials didn't seem to mind, and although they were standing on a single carriageway, the little or no traffic would not interfere with anything.

They got back into their cars but, before they drove off, one of the security guards came up to Felipe and said something to him to which he agreed.

This time Felipe sped off, and the speedometer seemed to creep higher and higher the further they got down the road. He said, "I must apologise for travelling so fast but these people want to get back to the airport because they need to leave as soon as possible."

"You mean they want to get out of this place quicker than what they got in," Dick said, and Felipe smiled.

"But what about the outcome?" Dick now asked, and Felipe replied "Don't worry because they have all the final documents with them. You are to sign these, together with the officials, at the airport. That's the main reason we have to go there with them."

"Okay, we won't rest on our laurels just yet but, once the signing is over with and they have gone, perhaps we can have a celebratory drink or two." A general cheer of approval reverberated around them.

They had spent a long time out in the hot sun, but nobody minded and, when they arrived at the airport, it was close to 2:00 p.m. and they trooped into the terminal building, which was empty save for the Manager and a desk clerk whom they asked to show them to a private room.

The manager showed them into the small lounge and, once they had all settled down, out came the documents. Translations galore were the order of the day, together with a million and one decisions which both sides agreed to. After they had completed the signing, Felipe said Señor Lopez had asked if El Presidente's wife was still to get the first car off the production line.

"Please tell Señor Lopez this will happen but, on one condition, and that is I get to hand over the car in person."

They all had a good laugh, and a handshake offered to seal the deal.

"Juan," Dick called across the room to him "what about those gifts we brought for them?"

He came over and told him two of the security guards were checking them while the documents were being signed, and they should arrive at any moment. True to his word, the security guards entered the building bearing the gifts.

"Tell them the largest one is for El Presidente," he said, asking Felipe to translate this for him.

With many thanks for the gifts and one final round of handshakes, the officials were off. Dick decided he wanted to stay to watch the planes take off, but Chloe wasn't having any of that. She wanted to take him up on his word about going for celebratory drinks.

He, therefore, gathered together all their copies of the signed official documents which he put in his briefcase, and they left the building. As they did so, besides the Manager and desk clerk, he had an eerie sensation they were being watched over by an extra pair of eyes, and when they drove away, he felt grateful it was now all over and done with.

"Thanks, Felipe, and you too Juan," he said with relief. "We'd never have been able to get through it all without your help. You have both earned your money today, speaking of which, please inform us of your fee per hour and how you would like the payment made."

There was an embarrassed silence, so Dick jumped in with an idea. "Tell you what. As I have not hired you, and as you won't be working every legal hour, why don't we pay each of you a retainer of say.... twenty-five thousand pesos a month?"

He wasn't the one driving, so he views both and smiled to see the looks of astonishment on their faces.

"What," Dick teased "Is that too little?"

"No, no," Juan replied "The offer is more than generous, which I cannot refuse."

Dick now said to Felipe. "I'm aware of the fact you're driving, but I can also see there's no traffic around either, so there's no reason you can't speak." They all chuckled.

"I had nothing to say but, I too cannot reject such a generous offer and Chloe, would you mind if I use a swear word?"

Before she answered, Dick interjected, "She can teach you a thing or two about swearing, so don't mind her."

"In that case... Yes, I fucking accept your offer" he shouted, and they all laughed again and clapped their hands at his excitement.

As they rounded a particular corner, within the city limits, Dick noticed part of a sign outside a building which read El Banco. "Stop please Felipe, and go there now," he said pointing at the bank. Felipe made a U-turn and parked the car right in front of the bank. "Please wait a moment. I'll be right back."

After some time Dick returned with two folded C4 envelopes in his hand which he handed over—one to Felipe and one to Juan.

"This is a down-payment of your first month and I suggest you both give us your bank details before we leave so we have them on file. Besides, it's much safer than sending sensitive information over the internet. This means we can transfer the money into your bank accounts every month until we complete the job."

"Also, I have arranged with the Bank Manager here, when the money transfer comes through, he is to contact you. What you need to do now is to go to the bank and introduce yourselves, although I'm sure you already met him, and give him your contact details and yes, he does 'spik 'a da English," Dick said in his best Spanish accent, which was pathetic.

"So come on, let's go."

Dick walked them in, saw the Bank Manager, waved at him and pointed at Felipe and Juan. He turned around and walked back to the car to wait for them and said to Chloe "Nice lads those two are."

"Yes, they are," she replied.

That night they had supper with the crew and, mentioning no names, some of them imbibed a little too much.

Early the next morning Dick was well into his swim when Chloe came to tell him Felipe had phoned. He said the Contractors wanted to bring their meeting forward to 9:a.m. that morning.

"Yeah, I don't mind at all."

Chloe informed Felipe while Dick did one more length, which took his one metre ninety-seight-centimetre frame about two seconds to accomplish. He got out and took his well-exercised body back to his room quite chuffed about his early morning routine. As it was already after 8:00 a.m., they got dressed and, while waiting for Felipe to arrive, they had their breakfast at the same time.

"He said he would pick us up again, did he?" Chloe asked Dick.

"Yes, he did."

"Whew,… that's all right then."

Felipe arrived with two other blokes, and Juan brought up the rear. Introductions made and, as the engineers spoke English, it made things a helluva lot easier all around.

"Let me introduce Dick Shepherd and Chloe… sorry Chloe but I've forgotten your surname," Felipe said in some embarrassment. Chloe just smiled at him and said, "It's Fraser-Rigby, but don't worry, Chloe will do just fine."

"That's right," Felipe said, still embarrassed. He continued "This is Rafael Morales, the Director de Operaciones of Josue Castillo Construcciones Civile and this is their MD, Manolito Delgado."

Felipe pronounced the names in a way they understood him, which was not at all difficult. They now chatted away before setting off on their journey back to the building site.

"I've got to come up with a name for this area," Dick said to Chloe.

"Well, I'm sure you'll come up with something appropriate soon," and Chloe laughed at what she said.

As they approached the area of the planned road extension, Dick exclaimed "I've got it".

"Well whatever it is, I don't want it, so keep it please," Chloe joked.

"No," he said stifling a laugh "From now on I will call this area *The Argentine Area 51*."

"Oh yes?" Chloe questioned in amazement "and what about the Americans? I mean, won't they take exception to that?"

"I don't give a flying you-know-what, about those bastards," he said sounding annoyed. "They don't own this planet although those bloody corrupt and bullshitting career politicians might say they do. But they don't, so stuff 'em."

Chloe was ever so sorry she had mentioned the word *Americans* for it was a rude one in his vocabulary. Did he love them? Did he hate them? No, was the answer in both cases, but did he care about them? Now that was the question.

No, he did not care about them because of what most their corrupt Corporate Companies had done, and still do, but not only to their own country and its citizens but also too many millions of innocent people around the world.

To cap it all, the so-called bloody American Presidents, together with most of the Congress, turn a blind eye to what had been, and still was, happening all around them. Or was it because they too had a hand in it? Maybe the answer sometimes may well be a resounding... yes, and it was the norm for them to indoctrinate their citizens daily.

"Perhaps the special interests have a lot to do with it," Dick mulled. "Tossers. Who the hell wants to befriend the American so-called hierarchy? Another bunch of stupid people who have their heads so far up their own arses, they cannot fathom out whether to cough or fart."

Dick remembered he had loads of cousins over there. Cousins whose origins stemmed back quite a few hundred years. He would, however, admit at least seventy-five percent of the ordinary American man-in-the-street was a different kettle of fish altogether, and from the little he understood, a decent enough upstanding people they were too.

It would be great if, at their next General Election, the American voters opted for someone who was not yet another corrupt career politician. A non-political figure who cared about the citizens and their country. Someone with a huge set of balls. Perhaps someone who would, at long last, drown-out the voice of the extra opposition within America known as the corrupt, biased, and lying mainstream media, once and for all. Perhaps this same President would also wash away the *filth* surrounding the Washington area but then, only time would tell.

"Well, before Joel pulls the plug on them," Dick said to himself.

Felipe stopped the car at the first location, as did Manolito, and they all got out.   As the wind wasn't blowing anymore, Dick produced a plan which he laid out on the bonnet of the car and there, he explained what it was he wanted done at this part of the site.   From there they moved on to the next location and, once again with the map perched on top of the bonnet, he explained that part of the site.

The runway was now the next important issue on the agenda. "Can you gentlemen build a runway for aircraft to land on and can you construct the runway here, bearing in mind it needs to be seven kilometres long?"

"No," replied Manolito "our company cannot do anything like that but we have a friend who is, in a small way, a competitor of ours, but one of his specialities is building airport runways.   In fact, he, and his father before him, and his father before him have built most the runways here in Argentina.   So, if you like, we can get him involved with this project—no problem."

"That would be acceptable, but what about the ILS or the DVOR or the DME or the NDB or even PAPI's?" Dick asked. He understood full well they wouldn't have the foggiest notion what he was talking about.

"If what you are asking has anything to do with the runway, the best person to speak to is our friend Ricardo," Rafael replied with a nervous twinge in his voice. "He's the only one who will understand what you want."

"Mmmm... Ricardo," Dick mused "Now that's a good name. Why don't you get him on the phone?"

While Rafael was calling Ricardo, he continued talking to Manolito, telling him about the layout of the runway and his requirements. "The most important thing is that you waterproof all the electrical cables and or lighting and even plumbing, and I mean one hundred percent waterproofed. No exceptions."

"Understood, and with us, Dick, that's normal operating procedure. If you agree for us to take on the job, when would you propose we should start?"

"Immediately," Dick replied nonchalantly. "If you can guarantee you will hire trustworthy sub-Contractors, whom you can guarantee to come in and do the jobs you don't specialise in well, we can draw up a contract as I would like construction to start, not as soon as possible, but right away."

Manolito cogitated for a moment. "From our side, Dick, it's not a problem, and if Ricardo cannot start straight away, there is enough for us to get on with before he moves in."

"Fine, but let's say I said I want you to carry out the construction as we discussed, how soon can you bring in your equipment ready to start?"

"Give me five days," Manolito replied, "but I have one concern."

"And what's that?"

"Well, we haven't even given you a quote yet," he said with a worried look.

"That's true, but what if I told you it's an open chequebook?"

"Mmmm... and when do you propose to write out the first cheque?" he asked, and they both laughed, which helped ease the tension somewhat.

"When we get back to town, we can go to the Bank and I can make a transfer, if they are still open."

"No, they won't be open by the time we get back, but we are staying in town for the night, so if you want to do it tomorrow...?" and Dick interrupted him saying "Okay, we'll do that. How much do you want to secure the contract?"

"What would you say to twenty-five million pesos to start with?"

"Are you sure that will be enough?"

"Enough," Manolito said in astonishment "How much do you want to put down?"

"Well, why don't we make it a nice round figure of thirty million pesos?"

Unable to believe his ears, Manolito said "That's wonderful, and perhaps we can draw up a temporary contract in the meantime?"

"Okay, when we get back into town, we can draw up paperwork to sign and have a drink afterwards to seal the deal. When Chloe and I leave, Felipe and Juan are our men you can contact for anything. Those two will represent me when I'm not here, all right?"

"Maravilloso," Manolito exclaimed "sorry, I meant to say wonderful." He was over the moon for this contract would set their firm up and get them out of the red.

Rafael walked towards Dick with his phone in his hand and said Ricardo would like to speak to him.

"Hello Ricardo," he said and explained what he wanted. By the sound of Ricardo's answers, he was sure this was the right bloke do the job, but he needed to make sure.

"Can you be here by around nine o'clock tomorrow morning?"

"Sorry, but that's not possible because the next plane is only in two days' time."

"All right, and if I sent my plane there to fetch you, would you be able to come?"

"For sure," Ricardo replied surprised, "that will be no problem."

"Okay, just give me a moment because I need to speak to my pilot."

Dick used his own phone to call Helen's mobile, and she passed him over to John who said there would be no problem, however, because of the distance and because of the opening and closing times of the smaller airports, he suggested they leave that evening.

"Yes, good point, but let me check if anyone from here wants to go for the ride."

Dick relayed the information to Manolito who said he would like to go. This would allow him to explain the project to Ricardo while on the plane.

"Good idea, and you can take the plan with you," Dick suggested "That would give him an even better idea."

"Yes, I agree,"

Dick handed Rafael's phone back to him saying "Okay, tell Ricardo you're on your way tonight and he must be ready to leave at first light tomorrow."

Dick reverted to John and asked him to get the plane ready for the journey.

"I've worked out our planned route. It's a three thousand two hundred kilometre round trip, so all things being equal, we should be back here by eight o'clock tomorrow morning."

"Perfect," Dick replied. "Okay, we are about to leave here so we'll bring Manolito straight to the airport but allow for two other passengers."

"No problem, see you later," said John.

Dick pulled Felipe and Juan aside. "I would like you guys to go on the trip, and don't worry about expenses, I will cover those."

"Yes, I'll go," Juan affirmed as did Felipe.

"Well, it's time for you to get out of here and you only have five minutes to pack a bag each. You must meet us at the airport in forty-five minutes, okay?"

"Okay boss," said Felipe, beaming.

They all climbed into their various cars and drove off. Dick and Chloe took Manolito and Rafael with them as they were going straight to the airport. Juan drove back into town with Felipe to pack their bags and they got to the airport with just five minutes to spare.

"Damn," Dick said to himself "I'm getting good at all this organising."

When they got back to the hotel Dick invited Rafael to join them for supper which he accepted. Pleased with this, it meant he had more time to talk further about the Argentina Area 51 after they had had their supper. When they had finished and had returned to the hotel, Chloe excused herself and made her way to their room.

With the opportunity, Dick produced yet another map of the runway area as he needed to point out a few things to him. Before they started construction of the runway itself, deep holes would have to be dug, two abreast across the width and two hundred and eighty spread down both sides of the seven-kilometre length of the runway.

"In each hole, there is to be a one hundred and fifty thousand litre fuel tank, and each tank, with all its pipework and fittings, must be made of stainless steel. Each one must also have an electrical operated shut-off valve operated from ground level, once covered."

"Once you finish working on each tank, you must build a strong protective covering to encapsulate them before surrounding each one with concrete, then you can do the back-fill and make sure you compress the soil to its requirements. Now because of the line of business you're in, you understand what I'm talking about, as should Ricardo. Oh yes,... you must not forget about lightning conductors,... that's important."

Rafael, for a moment, looked as if he was in a trance.

"Are you able to do this?"

"Yes, Dick, I'm sure we can, but why so many?" he asked with a puzzled frown.

"Don't you worry about it. You concentrate on the job at hand and, if you can do the job, just remember the runway will be on top of those tanks, therefore, the work has to be precise and the final product has to be flat and level and you must make sure the tanks are all at a deep enough level. Questions?"

"Yes,... how much time have we got?"

"You haven't. I wanted the job completed yesterday, that's why I want you to start now," Dick replied as he stressed the point. "Entender?"

"Si, entiendo completamente:"

"Good," Dick said well pleased "So, this means you can get organised first thing tomorrow?"

"Si, I mean yes Dick."

"That's good, Rafael. Tomorrow I will give you all the plans for the entire project from the first road build to the last building, okay?"

"Si, that will be okay. Grazias Dick" Rafael replied, now with an excited look on his face.

They had one more drink each and a further chat about the project before retiring for the night.

The following morning Dick, Chloe and Rafael met in the dining area for breakfast and, after 9:15 a.m., in walked the travellers and the crew. They all said 'Hello' and Rafael introduced Dick and Chloe to Ricardo.

They all jumped into the cars and set off. "On the road again," Dick mulled and said to himself "I'm sure there's a song in there somewhere."

He heard Rafael speaking to Ricardo in Spanish and assumed he was telling him everything about the previous night's discussions. As Felipe was driving, Dick asked him to start at the farmstead so he could, once again, make use of the large table on which to spread out all the plans.

Once there, he set about giving his instructions regarding the entire operation, and as they now had all the plans for all items and components, there should be no time wasted on any of the projects. By now they should've asked all questions and, therefore, all answers given.

On a final note, speaking to Ricardo, he explained everything about the tower. He also spoke about the Navigational Aids Integrator which must also include the Instrument Landing System, Doppler VHF Omni-directional Range. The Distance Measuring Equipment, the Non-Directional Radio Beacons and the Precision Approach Path Indicators.

"I assume you want all the most modern up-to-date equipment?"

"Yes, and nothing less, including all the bells and whistles, and you're a clever man Ricardo. Please don't forget the valley area over here," he said pointing at the map.

There was a moment's pause. Dick continued. "When I'm not here, Felipe and Juan will be in charge, so if you need anything at all, get hold of them and if there is a problem, they will refer it to me, okay?"

"No hay problema, Dick," replied Ricardo.

After spending a lengthy time there, Dick said he had had enough and it was time for them to fly home. He asked Chloe to phone Helen to get ideas from the pilots what would be a good time to leave.

He now turned to Manolito saying, within full hearing of all present, they must now go to the Bank to sort out a money transfer for him and, as Ricardo would sub-contract, he would allow for that payment.

Back at the hotel, Dick said to Chloe "Although happy with the way things have gone so far, I might ask Joel for his opinion."

"Mmmm... yes, I suppose it wouldn't hurt," she replied, and quick-as-a-wink Joel appeared.

"Now what seems to concern you?" Joel asked Dick.

"Well, I'm not concerned about anything. I had an idea to check with you if, what I'm doing, I'm going about it in the right way."

"Fair enough, Dick. I've told you before why we chose you and don't forget what I said to you the other day, but what I haven't mentioned to you is one of the main reasons. It's because we don't have to hold your hand and guide you. It's as simple as that."

"Thanks, Joel. That reassures me."

"Good, now let me put you in the picture. There are millions of people out there who, although they have twenty-twenty vision, they see nothing. Also, there are millions of other people out there who, although they have acute hearing, they hear nothing, but there are even more millions of people who have 'closed minds' and are not interested in even trying to open them, that is, to grasp what they are doing or what is happening all around them. People with one, two, or all three of these attitudes or behaviours are of no use to us, either in the singular or collective form."

"So don't fret my friend, for none of these examples I've just given applies to you at all, and that's what makes you unique. That's why we don't have to hold your hand."

"Thanks once again Joel," Dick said looking as pleased as Punch. "Every time I speak to you, my confidence level grows. It's as if my inner ability is making my aura much stronger, giving me the knowledge on how to do what I'm doing and how I carry out my actions."

"Well, I'm glad that's happening, but it's nothing more than I expected. Now, just to further put your mind more at ease. When, or if, we see you're going off-track, and so far you haven't – I will inform you, otherwise just carry on the way you are. I can tell you are at last using that mind of yours although there are still areas of it you need to use. But don't let that worry you yet as they will all soon fall into place. Happy?"

"More than,... and thank you once again," Dick replied while sporting a slight grin.

"And what about me, Joel?" Chloe asked giggling.

"Well now, where shall we start........?"

"Oh... no," she stated "Please don't go down that road as I don't want to be embarrassed, thanks," she replied, and Dick giggled.

"Okay, are we contented and more relaxed now?"

"Yes, thanks, Joel," she said.

"Like Dick, you are using your mind and your abilities and, until now, have been coping well. You are an intelligent woman, so just carry on as you are, but don't get complacent. There is more room for improvement and capable of so much more, and again, if we see you are slipping at all, we will inform you. So, until the next time..." Joel said, and he disappeared in his usual fashion.

"Well, for both of our sakes, you did the right thing by asking Joel's opinion," said Chloe.

"Yeah, I'm glad I did."

While Dick still mulled about Joel's visit, John called him to advise him he had sorted everything out. Once the account at the airport settled, they were ready whenever he and Chloe wanted to leave.

Money transfers done and goodbyes said, booking out of the hotel completed, car hire and airport accounts settled, they were ready for wheels-up just after 4:00 p.m.

"John," said Dick just before take-off.

"Yes."

"Why don't we fly over and check out the property we've purchased?"

"I'll check with the tower and see if we can," John replied. A few moments later he announced they would make a slight detour.

Once airborne, Dick walked back to the cockpit. Using his index finger as a pointer while looking out of the window, said "See that valley down there? The cutting that winds its way through those mountains, and see how it turns to face that big wide-open area then runs parallel with the mountain on the left heading straight towards the other mountain in front of it?"

"Yes," John and Allen both acknowledged.

"Well that's the corridor you will have to follow before landing on the runway," and both looked at Dick as if he were bonkers.

"You kidding, right?" Allen asked with a perturbed look on his face.

Although John had understood what Dick had explained, he wanted to have another look at it. He spoke to Allen about it and they did two more circles around the area.

"If you don't mind," John said to Dick "I'm going to go a little lower so I can get a better mental picture of it all."

"Yes, please," Dick said in agreement "I too would like that."

Two more times they circled around the area and, once their curiosity satisfied, they set their course for home. With nothing else said, and with a huge grin on his face, Dick made his way back to the cabin to relax and enjoy the flight. As neither he nor Chloe was hungry, Helen served drinks and some light snacks.

Chapter Nineteen

The Big Move

(a) Kerri and Cassie

"I WONDER WHAT my dad wants us to do there once we move to the airport?" Kerri asked Ivan.

"Well, listen to this. He wants me to learn and to get to understand the Airbus simulator but I don't understand why."

"So when we get there, are you to spend most of your time with the installers?"

"Yes, I've got to get inside the engineer's heads, as your old man put it."

"I sure as hell would like to know why."

"Yes, me too," Ivan agreed.

"Okay, I suppose there's no point in speculating, so we'd better get on with this packing," she said to Ivan "Mum," she now called up the stairs.

"Yes,"

"Have you packed yet?"

"Yes, I started yesterday. Why?"

"Oh, fuck," exclaimed Kerri.

"What now?" Ivan said surprised.

"Mother's got a head-start on us."

"Well, we'd better pull our fingers out. What time are the removal guys going to be here?"

"Seven-thirty tomorrow morning so, no playing on skateboards and no flying the drones. Which reminds me, you'd better check with Deon what the score is with your drones when we get there."

"You're right. I think I'd better."

The flat boxes they had purchased online now assembled, they packed those items Kerri's mother had already wrapped in bubble-wrap, and by 11:30 p.m., they had completed everything.

"Got your bag, Mum?"

"Yes, my child."

"Got your bag, Ivan?"

"Yes, my child" Ivan mocked. He didn't notice Kerri had seen a small ball lying on the floor close to her left foot which she picked up and threw at him. Much to his delight, she missed.

"Okay, shall we go?" Kerri now asked.

They locked up the house, got into the hire car and drove to a nearby hotel. Kerri had planned it this way with everything packed and ready for the morning, therefore, the following morning, and before the removal van arrived, there would be no need to do another thing.

She had also planned for a car-carrying company to pick up their cars the day before, so on the day of the actual move, they would drop the hire car off at the airport and fly-out to Maitland Airport.

When her Dad found out about her idea, he couldn't help but comment to himself "Yes, that's my clever child".

The removal guys arrived dead on time (ha-ha) thirty-five minutes late. "Why are you so late?" Ivan asked the chap who approached them first.

"Apologies but the blasted Satnav took us in a different direction."

He seemed genuine in his answer so Ivan accepted his apologies, thinking, as they had hired nothing but the best in the business, he expected nothing less. While mother and daughter waited outside, Ivan remained indoors to instruct the guys what had to go and what had to remain behind.

When the van was almost packed, an army of cleaners arrived and cleaned the upstairs. When they had finished with the cleaning, the downstairs area was available for them to start.

With the van now locked and secure, the driver said they would be on their way and would meet them later at Maitland Airport.

"What time do you think you'll get there?" asked Ivan.

"I'd say around one-fifteen this afternoon but it all depends on the traffic."

Once the cleaners had finished, the three of them did a walk-around inspection of the place to make sure everything was in order. While they were doing this, the Landlord arrived. Satisfied with the results, Kerri paid the cleaners and thanked them for their good work.

"Hello, here are the keys, three bunches," Ivan said, handing them over to the Landlord.

"You've done an excellent job here."

"And what else did you expect?" Kerri demanded, more than ready to bite his head off if he made any smart-ass comment.

They said their goodbyes to the house and the Landlord, got into the car and drove to the airport. They handed over the car and walked the short distance to the aircraft waiting for them. As there were only three with no luggage, the Aircraft Company laid on a smaller twin-engine, propeller-driven aircraft for the short haul.

Kerri was undecided about this, but thought better of it and climbed on-board. The flight took an hour for them to get to Maitland Airport.

"Hello all," Deon smiled in welcome as they got off the plane.

They introduced Kerri's mother, Rachel to Deon who led them to the office area. Once there, he handed over the keys to their respective cars, and by turning around, he pointed through the reception window to show them where their parked cars were.

"Is there anything you want to do, or is there anything we can help you with?" asked Deon.

Kerri asked, "Is Poppy going to assist us with getting into the house?"

"She is, and I thought she would have already been here. I can only surmise she has something else to sort out....."

Before he could finish, they heard Poppy's voice behind them. "Good morning all. Sorry I'm late but I had to wait for a certain aircraft to land" she said, and they all smiled at her.

"I suppose I'd better check how the simulator is getting on," Ivan announced.

"Oh no you're not," said Kerri, laying her foot down with a firm hand. "You'll only do so once we have settled into the house," and everybody laughed.

"Damn," Ivan exclaimed in a hushed voice.

"I believe you have your own transport here?" asked Poppy.

"Yes, we do," Ivan replied, "they're all out there."

"What I suggest,... you all follow me and I'll give you a run-down how we traverse the airfield while killing no one," Poppy replied causing them to grin.

"Later Deon," Ivan said as he raised his right hand in a goodbye gesture.

While they were walking to the cars, Poppy told them she had organised another three houses for them to look at, if they wished.

"Well," Kerri replied, "Cassie and Erica are to move here as well but I'm not sure when?"

"Perhaps you can phone her and ask her if she wants to come down here and have a look at the houses and choose?" Rachel suggested.

"Good idea Mother. I'll phone her when we get to the other side."

Poppy briefed them how they were to approach and travel around the airport perimeter and also when safe to go across the runway. They all jumped into their cars with Kerri's mum going with Poppy. They travelled at the safe speed required and arrived at the house almost ten minutes later, which seemed an age to them.

"Come in," Poppy invited them. "As your furniture hasn't arrived yet, I brought refreshments for you, and here are your keys. Sorry, but there's only one set.   If you require another, someone will have to have them cut."

"Okay," Ivan replied, "I can do that sometime, thanks."

"Why don't we have a cup of tea," Kerri suggested, "after which we can view these other houses and I can let Cassie know at the same time?"

"Yes, let's do that," said Rachel.

 "Fine, then we can all go in my car, or even walk" said Poppy.

When they had finished having their tea and biscuits, they walked off to view the other houses. Kerri telephoned Cassie, and from each individual house, she gave her a description.

"They all sound good but, from your description, I think the second one appeals the most."

"When can you get down here?"

"I have to wait for Erica to get home first, so we'll be there as soon as we can."

"Okay, I suppose time doesn't matter. I mean, the houses aren't going anywhere."

"Yes, I suppose," Cassie replied. "Okay, I'll meet up with you guys' later."

While Kerri was on the phone, Ivan's phone rang and it was the removal chaps saying they should be there within the next fifteen minutes.

"We'd better get back to the house as the van has entered the airport grounds and on its way."

"What," Kerri remarked in amazement "they must have done low flying if they are already here."

"They left almost three-and-a-half hours ago, you know," said Ivan "and besides, we've spent two hours looking at the other houses."

"True, I suppose we'd better go then."

They were back at their house and switched Poppy's kettle on for another cup of tea. Rachel was just about to rinse the used crockery when the removals van arrived. The off-loading began and in less than an hour, they had placed everything in their designated areas.

By this time Cassie and Erica had arrived, and while the other three continued unpacking, Poppy took them to show them which of the houses they would like. When they arrived back at Kerri's home, Poppy was no longer needed for the rest of the day, so she was on her way. Before leaving she handed over two sets of house keys to Cassie as she had rejected one house but hadn't been able to decide between the other two.

"So, when do you think you will move in?" Kerri asked her.

"I must wait for your father to get here because I need him to pay for the packing and the removal people."

"No, nonsense. You organise whoever and whatever and I'll pay for it and if you can do it now and move tomorrow, all the better. Besides, I'm sure it'll make my Dad happy."

"Okay, let me see what I can come up with."

"Don't go for the cheapskates as money's no problem," Ivan shouted at her from the other side of the room. "Get the professionals in."

A little while later Cassie looked at Kerri, and with a frown on her face, said "I can't understand this. This company are prepared to go to my house, pack everything up right now and load and move us before eight o'clock tonight, but it comes at a price."

"Let me speak to the person," Kerri said holding out her hand for the mobile. "It's a woman," said Cassie handing the phone over.

Kerri introduced herself and asked the woman what her name was, in case she needed to call again. She introduced herself as Mrs Robson. Kerri requested her to please send the removal men over to the address Cassie had given her and also asked her if the Company had a Bank card-reading machine. Mrs Robson confirmed this and Kerri instructed her to make sure the driver, or the person in charge, had it with them. Therefore on completion of the job, she could transfer the full payment.

"You'd best be on your way," Kerri advised Cassie who was gaping at her in utter amazement. "They will be at your house soon, about four o'clock this afternoon she said, and you've still got to finish packing up all your odds and ends. So, I'd pull finger if I were you."

"Would you like me to come with you?" asked Rachel.

"Yes, that would be nice, if Kerri and Ivan don't mind."

"It's not for them to mind," Rachel replied and they giggled.

"No, that's fine with me Mum, you go. Cassie, you'd better give me the name of the Company and their telephone number, just in case." Cassie looked it up on her mobile and Kerri loaded the info into her own phone, adding the contact name of Mrs Robson.

"See you later," they shouted as they drove away.

Kerri phoned the removal company back and Mrs Robson once

again answered the phone. Kerri said, if she felt it was necessary, they were more than welcome to add a labour force to the team to make the packing up and removal even quicker.

When they had left, Kerri and Ivan carried on with their own unpacking, sorting out what would go into which of the rooms. Ivan, in his wisdom, moved the big heavy fridge on his own. Fool he was because as he placed his right hand underneath it, he slipped causing the fridge to smash down hard on his hand. The pain was not received in good humour.

"Aaaarrrgh," he screamed out loud "Fuck, fuck, fuck," he now said as the pain intensity grew and grew.

"What the bloody hell have you done," Kerri asked as she approached to see what the commotion was all about.

"I've just squashed my hand under the fridge," he said through all the pain. "Can you please try to lift it so I can get it out?" he asked in agony.

Kerri lifted the fridge just enough for Ivan to extricate his hand from under it. He stood there suffering the intense pain, caused by a few broken bones and cuts allowing blood to spout.

"I think I'd better get you off to the hospital and quick."

"Yes, I agree with…" but before Ivan could finish, they startled as an alien, and not Joel, appeared as if from out of nowhere. Although his head was very much like Joel's he was, however, much taller. He, therefore, appeared to be a little thinner than Joel.

"I apologise if I scared you but I'm one of the 'doctors' who operated on you. Now before you take Ivan off to the hospital, let me look at what we can do for him," he said speaking in a voice completely different to Joel's.

Before they could say or do anything, both Ivan and the 'doctor' disappeared. Kerri just stood there dumbstruck as this all happened in mere moments.

"Well that was surreal," she said aloud. "I wish they wouldn't make themselves known like that as I tend to shit myself." Realising what she had just said, she burst out laughing. "Well, I can only assume they will do a far better job than our lot at the hospital," she thought.

"Okay... and then there was one," she once again spoke out loud. This time, however, standing with her hands on her hips and looking around the room. "No point in procrastinating. I may as well get on with the unpacking."

When they completed the repairs to Ivan's hand, they returned. "I do again apologise if I unnerved you earlier on but I have some favourable news" said the 'doctor' in an ever so soothing sounding voice. "Ivan's hand is as good as new" he said, and before they could say "Thank you" he disappeared into thin air.

"Let me look," Kerri said as she grabbed hold of his hand and scrutinised it. "Mmmm... I wish our doctors were that good."

"Yes, and perhaps Joel's family will take over from ours. You never know."

"Yes, perhaps. Now don't you go doing damned foolish things like that again," Kerri said in a stern voice. "Idiot."

Ivan stood there stunned gazing at Kerri as she gave him *the look* before she turned around to resume their unpacking.

While engrossed with their unpacking, Erica's boyfriend Robert, knocked at the door.

"What the hell are you doing here?" Ivan asked rather surprised.

"Erica's Nan sent me over to let you know they have arrived."

"Who has arrived?" Ivan asked feeling confused

"Erica, her Nan and Kerri's mother."

"What," Ivan exclaimed in astonishment. "That's impossible."

"Well I can assure you the impossible has happened," Robert said with a smirk.

"Hey" Ivan shouted into the next room.

"What" Kerri cried out.

"They've arrived,"

"Who's arrived?"

"Cassie, Erica and your mum, that's who."

"Don't talk crap, Ivan" was Kerri's immediate response.

"Well if I'm talking crap, will you please tell Erica's boyfriend that." Kerri walked through into the living room where Ivan and Robert were. "There you are. Please tell him he's talking crap," he said pointing a finger at Robert.

"Do you mean those removals people have done it all already?" Kerri asked Robert.

"Yes they have. All done and dusted."

"Bloody hell, that's incredible. I must phone Mrs Robson and thank her for getting it organised." While on the phone to Mrs Robson, Kerri made her way over to Cassie's abode to pay the account.

Both Kerri and Ivan thought it better not to mention anything about the accident and by midnight, they completed so much, both houses were now liveable in. The rest of the stuff would find their rightful places in due course.

After a restless night, Kerri and Ivan got up early, had breakfast and drove to the airport offices to report for duty.

Because Erica had to go to college, Cassie offered to play taxi driver and came by to ask Rachel if she would like to keep her company.

As Kerri had popped a wad of notes into her mother's hand before leaving, Rachel asked Cassie "How would you like to go shopping?"

"Nana,... don't you have any alcohol before you come and fetch me," Erica said before getting out of the car at the College grounds.

"Who me? now would I do something like that?" Cassie teased looking all innocent.

"Wait a minute," Rachel said to Erica "Here, take this fifty pounds to get a taxi back home, if that's okay with you Cassie? We can then have more time to shop."

Erica gave them a dirty look, grabbed the money out of Rachel's hand and slammed the car door behind her. As they drove off they burst out laughing. The two of them behaved like silly school girls and giggled most of the way into town, and in the shops, and all the way back home.

In the meantime, Kerri and Ivan had arrived at the office and, as they didn't know the place or the business, approached Deon. They asked if he would take them around the airport to meet as many of the key personnel as possible.

"That's not a problem, but if it's okay with you, I'd prefer to get someone else to do that as I'm snowed under."

"We should have thought of that before, but can we at least spend about a half-an-hour with you first as we have quite a few questions?" asked Kerri.

"Yes of course. Please, grab a chair and make yourselves comfortable."

So Deon spent time with them answering as many of their questions as he could. He put them in the picture what his job entailed as Kerri, being in charge in Dick's absence, needed to understand this. She listened and realised she had a helluva lot to learn, and soon.

As he had done with Dick, Deon asked Bill Butland to show them around and introduce them to the most important people. At around 10:00 a.m. Kerri's mobile rang, it was her father wanting to know how they were getting on. She filled him in on everything and what progress the two of them had made so far.

"Daddy, what is Mum going to be doing?"

"Don't worry about your mother or Cassie for now. When I get there, I'll brief them what I want them to do, so when next you bump into them, tell them to enjoy their holiday," he said, which made Kerri giggle.

"Okay, sweet child o' mine, I'll be in touch from time-to-time and I'll see you at the end of the month. Please call me if you need anything."

At 1:00 p.m. they had a break and Bill took them over to have lunch in the canteen in the break-out area. He left them there saying, if they needed him, they could get Mimi or anyone else to call him and they could tell him where they were and he would come to them soonest.

As it was, Mimi came into the canteen and they asked her to please join them. While having their lunch they spoke about the company although about nothing specific. Towards the end, however, Mimi asked if they knew if there would be any drastic changes regarding the staff situation.

Kerri endorsed what her father had already told everyone that nobody's job would be in jeopardy and all the staff were to carry out their duties as normal.

Mimi heaved a big sigh of relief "When is your Dad going to be moving here?" she asked.

"He should be here by the end of the month, so if I were you, I'd enjoy the peace and quiet while it lasts," Kerri replied, which made them smile.

"Okay, lunch is now over for me," Ivan said to Kerri standing up and bending over, gave her a kiss on the cheek. "I'm on my way to the simulator so, before you go home, come find me."

"Okay, but as we came over in one car, I'd have to do that anyway, wouldn't I,... unless you'd like to spend the night here?" she said. He laughed and stuck his tongue out at her as he turned and walked off.

"Come on Mimi, you can show me a thing or two about what you do. If you don't mind?"

"No, it will be my pleasure."

So Kerri and Ivan completed their first day on the job and were looking forward to a bright and interesting future in their new lines of work.

## (b) Dick and Chloe

After their long flight from La Rioja, Dick and Chloe arrived at Biggin Hill just on 7:00 and were back home around 8:30 a.m.. Dick said to Chloe "I think I should give my child a call to find out how she's getting on."

Once he finished the call, he told Chloe what was happening and gave Phil a call. Phil told him things were running along nicely thank you very much.

"I'm going to put the kettle on," she said. "I'm thirsty. Would you like a cup as well?"

"No thanks, not right now. I'm just going to go through everything in my briefcase and put some kind of order into all the paperwork. You know how much I like paperwork."

"Hello, you two," said a familiar voice, and they looked around at Joel who was sitting at the dining room table.

"Hello to you," Dick said "and to what do we owe this pleasant surprise?"

"You have everything under control and well under way," Joel commented.

"Yes," Chloe answered first "I'm amazed at how smooth it's all going."

"Yes," Dick said "and I don't suppose you've had anything to do with it?"

"Maybe, but then again maybe not. The main thing is all is on the move and that's what counts."

"How much time do we have left?" asked Chloe.

"Plenty of your years yet, so nothing for you to worry about," Joel assured her.

"If that's the case, why have we had to start so early?" she asked.

"To allow the slow working humans time to produce what is required but, to give you and Dick the time to grow and prove your worth—not only to us but also to yourselves, so you can do it all at your leisure and have fun doing it."

"Mmmm...."

"As there aren't any problems I'll be off now," Joel said "I'll only be in contact with you at the end of the month unless you need my advice. So, as I say, have fun."

"Cheers Joel" they cried in unison, and he disappeared in his usual fashion..

The next twenty-three days were uneventful. Dick spent time on the phone to Airbus and BAE Systems giving them instructions saying he required them to supply enough stock of spares-parts and consumables. These he wanted stored, and therefore put into stock, in his own warehouse section at Maitland Airport. He also said these supplies should be enough to service each aircraft over sixty years, even longer. The completed orders must be within the next two to three years, and as this meant extra money in the Company's coffers, they accepted the additional orders.

In the meantime, Phil had sent Toby's the specs they required and said production, once they had completed the tooling, would start around the twentieth of the following month. Deliveries, therefore, would begin on the thirtieth of the same month.

As the factory floor was almost complete the Nippon Company had already made deliveries of the machinery, the first of which would arrive around the eleventh.

The Chinese company had phoned. They left a message on the answering machine saying the manufacturing had begun and had posted the first air-freighted parcel. It all depended on the local Customs people when Phil would receive the parcel containing the magnets.

The scheduled start of the Brimstone production line to produce its first cars was on the twentieth and, as agreed, the first three cars were to be for Jonathan, Brendan and Alex.

Dick thought the electrical motors were in the suppliers stock and ready for delivery and now it appeared the cars might stand around just waiting, so he phoned Phil to ask him to get them to speed things up. He also asked Phil to get in touch with Tom to make sure there was enough outside parking space for the cars. This was to allow for any potential overflow problems.

Later in the evening, the landline telephone rang, and it was Phil. "Hello, you'll never guess what I received when I got back to my hotel."

"Okay, don't keep me in suspenders," Dick said. "What have you received?"

"I've received advance samples of three different sized casings and inner workings of my machine."

"Bloody hell, that was quick," Dick said in surprise. "So when are you going to put it all together?"

"I've already started, although I can't go too far with it yet, but it's looking good. I'll take this, just as it is, to the factory later on tonight and fit the magnets. Can't wait to witness this thing in action."

"Now don't you go burning the midnight oil as I need you to oversee the builders in the morning."

"You know, Tom is fantastic and I don't have to keep on breathing down his neck. In fact, I'm of the opinion he will finish this project at least a month early."

"Damn, things are looking up," Dick said sounding all amazed "Does this mean production will start even sooner?"

"At this rate, and at the speed at which the materials are being delivered, there's no reason not. Also, I'm expecting the motors to arrive any day now."

"Good show and keep up the good work. Now once Chloe and I have settled after our move, I'll come up there for a few days as I'm as curious as you are, okay?"

"Okay by me. All right, until the next time, and say hi to Chloe."

Call ended, Dick replaced the cordless telephone back in its base. He now put Chloe in the picture how things were going and to the progress already made.

"I suppose working twenty-four hours a day, six days a week must make all the difference," she said.

"Well, it must affect it somehow, and Phil believes they may even finish a month early."

"Are you planning to go and visit them?"

"No, not just yet as I want to get our move behind us. You know, I'll phone the same removal company Kerri used to get Cassie's stuff moved and find out if they operate in this area."

"When are you going to phone?"

"I'll phone in the morning and, if they do, I'll ask them to send advance packing cartons."

"Aren't you going to get them to do the packing?" she now asked.

"Yes, I am but I would prefer to pack all my model aircraft myself, for if there are any breakages, I'd only have myself to blame."

"Yeah, it's better that way," she remarked.

After supper, they settled down with drinks and relaxed for the rest of the evening.

The following day Dick phoned the removal company. A female representative would come to the house at 3:00 p.m. and she arrived carrying five medium-sized cartons. Once she had completed her walk-about, she told Dick she would send an e-mail with the quotation attached. He said it would be fine as he would need the paperwork, however, she should consider the company booked for the job and they should be there on the morning of the twenty-seventh.

Surprised at being given the go-ahead without having first

approved the quotation, Dick told her they came recommended and therefore satisfied they would do a good job.

Once she had left, he packed his precious model aeroplane collection. Being on the fragile side, it would take him the best part of the rest of the day, and packing these precious items would also take a lot of tender loving care. Chloe offered to help, but he refused, so she told him what he could do with himself, and flounced off.

The next morning Chloe decided, as she too had a few breakables, some of them from her late mother, she would not take any chances. She, therefore, got stuck into wrapping and packing her own fragile pieces.

"Are you not going to offer your services and help me?" she asked when Dick walked into the dining room and watched what she was doing.

"Hell no," he announced "Why on earth would I want to do that?"

"Ohhhhh you... put the kettle on, will you."

"It won't fit me,"

"If you don't stop, I'll throw something at you," she retorted. He laughed and ducked, expecting a boot to land on the back of his head. It didn't happen, so he whistled off to the kitchen.

A little while later Phil rang again. "I have a problem. The electrical motors are being delivered and I've just realised I don't have a secure enough area to store them in. Any ideas?"

Dick thought for a moment. "I tell you what. Tom already uses a Security Company, so ask him to get extra guys in for that purpose and that purpose alone. Then, designate a specific area. Give him strict instructions the guards in charge of looking after those motors are not, under any circumstances, to leave the area unless changing shifts or lunch breaks etcetera. Ask him if he can organise a movable lock-up storage device, something like a container which you can store all the motors in which will make it secure. Anyway, there are plenty of the other security guards walking the site, even though the builders are there all day and all night."

"Good idea. I'll phone Tom straight away and I'll call you back later on today."

After the call had ended, Dick organised his boxes and stored them in a secure place advising Chloe to do the same.

"Have you booked a flight to Maitland yet?" she asked him.

"Oh hell no, I haven't. I'd better do it now."

"Yes, and remember to ask them to organise a car for tomorrow as the car delivery company are here tomorrow to pick up ours. Or had you forgotten that as well?"

"No, I hadn't forgotten, but I forgot to book a flight."

Once done, he said to Chloe the flight was for 9:00 a.m. on the twenty-eighth, and because the house would be empty on the eve of the twenty-seventh, he had booked them a hotel room for the night.

Later in the afternoon, Phil phoned to let them know three more security guards were on their way, who would operate on a normal rota system. Tom had also organised one of his own lockable containers which should arrive by five-twenty in the evening.

"One last thing," Phil added. "I've handed over the schematic of the factory's power station to Torque Engineering as I want them to look at devising a suitable size motor, and they reckon between a month and six weeks for delivery."

After their telephone conversation, Dick told Chloe how pleased he was with Phil running the show. They now sat back, and after a drink or two, followed by a little relaxation, they made their way to bed.

"What's for brekkers?" he shouted down from the top of the stairs next morning.

"Can't you smell?"

"Not too much fattening stuff for me please."

"Well, what you don't want, just leave."

After a shower and shampoo, he made his way downstairs. There, he perceived what sort of heart- attack food Chloe was beating to death in a frying pan. He looked at the plate, then at the pan, then back at the food. He concluded, in moderation, it should be okay for him to eat, and although he ate the breakfast, he didn't enjoy it but decided not to say so to Chloe.

There was a knock at the door, it was the transport company to collect their cars for delivery to Maitland Airport. Cars now loaded and strapped to the flat-bed delivery truck, together with signed paperwork, the driver and his helper set off on their journey.

"Let's hope Biggins doesn't forget to deliver," said Chloe.

"I shouldn't think they would."

"You said it with a lot of confidence," she replied.

"With the amount of business we've given them, I don't think they would run the chance of stuffing it up now."

"Mmmm... yeah, good point."

As it was now just after midday, he got hold of the bank in La Rioja to transfer the twenty-five thousand pesos apiece to Felipe and Juan. Due to the distance and the time difference, there was a slight problem with the bank draft, but it was all sorted out and the transfers effected.

Sometime later he received an e-mail from Felipe to say both had received their transfers and to say thanks. He also informed Dick everything was steaming ahead at a rate of knots and there was nothing for him to worry about.

"Steaming ahead, you say?" said Chloe.

"Yes, that's what the man said."

"Well, I hope they are not using steam. If they are, they'll still be working there when it's all over," she said making Dick giggle.

By 3:00 p.m., they delivered the hire car and Dick parked it in the garage while Chloe looked on admiring their transportation mode.

"Damn," Dick exclaimed.

"What," Chloe asked in surprise.

"I should have organised someone to come and clean out all the crap in the garage."

"Okay, I'll check what I can find on the internet."

"Gee, thanks ma'am," Dick said in a terrible American Cowboy accent. Why he did this, he did not know but, c'est la vie.

Chloe found someone whom she telephoned, and after explaining the situation to the man on the phone she turned to

Dick and said "I've found a bloke who will come now and clear out the garage, but as it's so late, he will not make the dump in time today, so he will have to store it overnight and take it to the dump tomorrow but there'll be an extra storage fee."

"Tell him I asked what's he waiting for?"

Chloe relayed the message. "He says he should be here in twenty minutes."

Half-an-hour later and there was a knock at the door. Dick answered it and told the guy to go around to the back and he would meet him there. He opened the main garage door, reversed the car out and parked it.   As the guys were sizing up the stuff in the garage, Dick told them to go mad and remove every single movable item.

"I didn't realise there'd be so much," the guy said to Dick.

"So, what are you trying to tell me? Do you want me to throw in an extra hundred quid?"

The bloke looked at him and smiled.  "How can I turn it down, sir?"

They took the best part of thirty minutes and Dick was ever so grateful the trailer they had brought was just big enough. When they had finished, he handed over the cash payment and watched them drive away, thinking of all the memories they were taking with them.

"All done then?" Chloe asked him.

"Yep, all done. I think I'll throw away some of my old clothes. I'll put them in black bags and, on our way to the hotel tomorrow, we can stop at the Superstore and dump them in those recycle bins they have."

"Now that's an excellent idea," Chloe said in agreement "I'll do the same."

Soon, between them they had five big black bags, three of which were Chloe's.

"It's about time you did that, you know," she said to Dick.

"Yes, and you too. But remember, we never had the money before to replace them."

"That's true, but there's a shed load of old clothes there you haven't worn in years. You know, like those old suits you've just got rid of."

"Yeah okay, don't rub it in."

For the rest of the day, they checked and double-checked everything before, once again, relaxing with two drinks before bedtime.

The next morning there was a knock at the door and he couldn't understand why the removal guys were there so early. "Still, in this case, better early than late, I suppose," he thought.

He opened the door and to his utter horror, there in front of him stood the *Thing* and his most undesirable wife. He felt like throwing up as the stench they carried around with them was mind-blowing.

"Oh no. Oh, stuff me. I forgot about these effing Things. What the hell am I going to do now?" he screamed to himself. "They look like two hessian sacks walking about on leg."

"Top o' the mornin' t' ya, sir," said Thing number one, or was it number two? He couldn't tell the difference, so he waited until he could recognise the more understandable of the two.

"Wee ope's ya ken r'members us bot wee wos 'ere foo day's-go. Ya say t' us t' bees 'ere t'day sir, as ya maybees 'as some ol' clothes or furnichin's or summit alon' dem lines, sir. An' ya says te bees 'ere now sir".

Dick decided it must be number two as he could almost understand him. "Where's your horse and cart?"

"Ahhh nooo sir, da 'orse sir, he up n' die on us, sir, an' da missus she no goo' at pullin' da kart, sir" replied Thing number two.

Upon hearing this, Dick wanted to laugh out loud but decided against it. He wasn't an awful person, and he wasn't one to laugh at another man's misfortune, so he decided he would wait until after they had left.

"Please wait here and I'll be back in a moment," Dick said in his best Queen's English.

"Tanks a lo', sir" it replied.

Moments later he returned with the five large black bags of clothes. "I apologise but this is all I have. I'm sure it must be enough for both of you to carry seeing you don't have your cart here with you."

"Oooo tanks ver' mooch sir," said Thing number one.

"It's a piti aboot da 'orse, sir, 'cos we cood've kar-ried more, ya sees. Enways sir, wee 'onts for'et yo' kiness. Tanks a lo' sir" said Thing number two, and they shuffled off.

Dick closed the door, turned around and noticed Chloe standing in the background with tears streaming down her cheeks.

"And tanks a lo' ta ya too, my good woman," he said as he too shared the laughter. When he got himself back in control again he said: "You know, I never could quite make out their accent."

The removal company arrived just after 9:00 a.m. and set about packing what they had to pack. The men seemed professional in both their ways and manners, different to the two who had moved them into the house all those years ago and who were, by 8:30 a.m., already pissed.

Van packed, back doors locked and sealed shut, they said to both Dick and Chloe they were ready to be on their way.

"Will you be driving straight through now?" Chloe asked them.

"No ma'am," replied the driver. "We won't be able to as we would arrive too late, so we'll stop over at one of our secure depots and continue the journey early tomorrow. We plan on getting there at eight o'clock in the morning,"

"Why so early?" Dick asked him.

"We have a consignment we have to pick up by twelve noon to deliver to Penzance by four o'clock in the afternoon."

"Bloody hell," Chloe said, "you guys sure get around."

"Yes, we do. Sometimes we only get home after four days of running around the country."

"Well good luck and have a safe journey," she said.

"And don't forget who you have to contact when you get there," Dick chipped in.

"Mm... yes," said the driver looking at Dick "I have the names here... Ivan Pendry and Kerri Shepherd?"

"That's correct. OK, off you go and drive safely."

The cleaning company arrived and spent an awful amount of time there, enough to drive Dick insane. They were just about done when they noticed the Landlord pulling up outside.

"Good," he said to Chloe "we pay the cleaners then, once we've done with Alex, we can say goodbye to your favourite area."

"Yes, and I can't bloody wait either," she uttered in agreement.

The walk-about completed, they handed over two sets of keys to Alex, shook hands, and jumped into the car. As they drove away from the house, Chloe let out a resounding 'Yes' as they left the area she had always hated so much. The house itself, though, was okay. As they were nearing the outskirts of the dreaded area, Dick burst out laughing.

"Look," he said shaking with laughter, and Chloe said "Where? What?"

"Over there," he said, pointing at two people wearing hessian sacks for clothing and each carrying a few black bags.

They both shared the laughter as this rather shameful joke brought yet another chapter in their lives to a close, and the following day, a new one would begin.

Chapter Twenty

A New Dawn, a New Day,
a New Way of Life

THEY SOON ARRIVED at the hotel close to Biggin Hill Airport. Once they had settled in, they walked downstairs to the restaurant where Dick had an idea.

"Why don't you and I switch off our phones and disappear for two days?"

"You mean go away and say nothing to anyone?"

"Yeah, why not?"

"But won't they worry?"

"I'm sure they will," he said with an evil grin.

"But that's cruel and besides, I'll get it in the neck."

"Well, here's a suggestion. Why don't we ask Joel and get his views on it?" he asked, proud of the idea.

"Okay, that's fine by me because at least someone must

be aware. What about Kerri?"

"It'll be fine."

They mulled about deciding what to do and when they had finished their meal, they walked back up to their room.

"Are you now going to call Joel and......?"

Before she could finish her question, Joel appeared and said, "You should go to the Bahamas for two days and let me handle your family for you."

They looked at him, he looked at them and, behaving like a human, he upturned his hands and shrugged his shoulders.

"What" he exclaimed "Can't I behave like you?" he asked as the two of them laughed at his antics.

"You took us by surprise, that's all," Chloe replied, still chuckling.

"You'd better phone your air-taxi service and see if they can accommodate you," said Joel.

"When should we go?" Chloe asked Dick.

"Go now," Joel cried out.

Dick phoned the office at Biggin Hill and made his request and the receptionist said she would phone him back within the hour.

"I'd pack if I were you. If we were not happy with your progress, I can assure you I would not be sending you on your way to the Bahamas."

Long before the hour was up they received a phone call to say the aircraft would be ready by 8:30 p.m., so if they could be there by 8:00 p.m., that would be perfect, however, it was their decision to make. Dick assured the receptionist, who had phoned back with the information, everything would be fine.

"You're on your own now," said Joel.

"Yes, but hang on a minute, both Chloe and I have had a few drinks during our supper and if the cops stop us....."

Joel interjected. "Do not worry. Nothing will happen, and no one will stop you, so off you go. Come on now, I'm waiting," he said staring at them out of his big black almond-shaped eyes.

"Joel, would you mind if I gave you a hug?" Chloe asked him.

"What, are you nuts? Sorry, but we don't do human

things like that."

"Yes, but you were behaving like one,... now weren't you?"

"Oh, all right. But you make sure neither of you says anything to anyone, you understand?"

"Ohhhhh... stop being such a baby," she said and walking over to him, bent down and gave him a huge hug.

"Okay," Dick said, "that's enough now, otherwise I'll get ideas about the two of you."

"Go on, get out of here," Joel said, as he disappeared into thin air.

As they would fly to Maitland Airport on their way back from the Bahamas, they handed the hire car back in when they arrived at Biggin Hill. Dick paid the additional costs for the overseas trip and cancelled the flight which he had booked for the following day.

They walked out to the aircraft and their favourite hostess, Helen, greeted them. She pointed towards the cockpit and John and Allan greeted them..

"I hope you guys will take advantage," Dick said "and I might give more info about what's on the cards, but that's up to you. You don't have to answer now. Let us first settle down and we'll have a chat later if that's okay with you guys?"

"Yes, fine," John acknowledged.

"Yeah, it's not as if we're going anywhere, is it?" Allan butted in which made them chuckle for they understood what he meant.

"So young lady," Dick said to Helen "have you decided yet whether you will join us once our new aircraft arrives?"

"I've spoken to my partner, who's an aircraft engineer here, and he said if I don't, I must be mad."

"And I quite agree with him," said Chloe.

"An aircraft engineer, you say?" Dick mused for a moment "A pity I wasn't told sooner or I would have asked you to bring him along."

"Mmmm... and the poor guy's at home now on a week's leave. He's peeved at me for taking this assignment."

Before anyone could say any more, Allan popped his head around from his seat and said, "We'll be another minute."

Dick's thoughts were in a spin and his mind was working

overtime. In a flash, he jumped up, dashed to the cockpit and asked the guys to put everything on hold as he was about to make a last-minute change. He dashed back to the cabin and fished his mobile out of his bag. He handed it to Helen and said "Here's my mobile. Please call your partner and ask him to come and join us".

She looked dumbfounded as she took the mobile from Dick's hand. It was an automatic motion, but she handed it back.

"I can't remember the number as I have it on fast-dial on mine," she said with a slight quiver in her voice.

"Calm down Helen. It's not a big deal," Chloe said patting her hand on her shoulder.

"Okay, I'll get my mobile and go over there to speak to him." A little while later she came back looking rather sheepishly at them.

"Is there a problem Helen?" asked Chloe.

"He doesn't seem to want to believe me, not that I can blame him, so I said I'll hand the phone over to one of you to speak to him."

Chloe grabbed the phone out of Helen's hand. "What's his name?"

"It's Mick."

"Hello Mick," Chloe said in her *I'll take no nonsense from* you voice. "Now listen here young man, you are embarrassing the hell out of your lovely partner and you are also wasting our time. So pull your finger out of your bloody arse and get yourself down here now because I can assure you, you don't want my partner coming to fetch you. Do you understand?" she said, stressing the point. There was a slight pause before Chloe ended the call by saying "Good lad. See you."

She turned to the others and said smiling "Well, that ought to do it. He'll be here."

Dick could no longer contain himself as he grinned. "Oh yes, that was typical you, all right" he said looking at Chloe.

This time Dick walked up to see John and Allan. He put them in the picture, explaining he would also need people like Mick with his particular set of skills. They told Dick they knew Mick well and said they regarded him as the best engineer there and rated among the best in the business.

"Thanks for putting me in the picture," Dick acknowledged. "Why don't you guys stretch your legs while we wait for His Majesty to arrive?" he suggested for all to hear.

This brought a chuckle, and Helen said: "Wow, I can't thank you guys enough."

As they were all sitting in the cabin area waiting for Mick to arrive, Dick asked if they had filed a flight plan. John answered in the affirmative.

"Okay, but as we're staying at a resort on Beef Island just off Little Mountain Road, what I want is for you to fly to Beef Island Tortola Airport. Any problems?"

"I foresee none," replied John.

"And I'll see what I can find out," said Allan.

By now a face peered around the door, looking shy and uncertain. Five sets of eyes looked back at him, and they all cheered. As John was the closest to him, he got up and almost pulled Mick inside where he introduced him to Chloe and Dick.

"This is overwhelming for you, isn't it?" Chloe asked him.

"I'll say," Mick replied with a nervous smile.

"Are we ready to go?" John asked looking at Dick.

"Yes, when you're ready."

"Just leave Mick with us," Chloe said, "and he'll soon reason the same way we do."

More laughter reverberated around the cabin.

Due to the time taken up in waiting for Mick, wheels-up was at 9:30 p.m. A little while later, Allan said they should arrive at Beef Island at about 11:30 a.m. the next day, local time.

After a word from Dick, Helen poured a round of drinks, which were to put the still overwhelmed Mick at ease. Dick made sure he sat opposite Mick so they could have a chat while Chloe and Helen listened in.

"Now Helen has told you we approached her, and the guys up front, about our plans and requirements, but what she hasn't told you,... we will also need people of your calibre, so here's the deal. You can, if you like, consider this to be an interview, and if you don't accept the offer, there are others out there who would be more than willing to grab it with both hands."

"I don't expect you to give me an answer right this minute. First, I want us to bond and we'll do so by having two days on the Island together, and when you two are back home, you can talk about it together. Helen has Chloe's mobile number and you can call any time. Okay?"

There was a moment's silence and Dick decided he could do with another drink, so he got up to do the necessary when Helen said, "I can do that".

"Yes, you can because I've witnessed it first-hand. However, you sit there and relax because this gives me the opportunity to stretch my legs. Anyone else like a drink?"

"Yes, please" came the loud answer in unison from the cockpit.

Helen, though, got up and insisted she attend to John and Allan. All glasses having been re-charged, Dick resumed his comfortable position in his chair.

"Mr Shepherd..."

Dick held up a hand as if to say stop and asked Mick to refer to him by his first name.

"Thanks, Dick."

"You're welcome."

"May I please ask a question?"

"Yes, you can... anything."

"What type of aircraft have you got?"

Dick explained the situation to him, also laying out the obvious reasons they would need mechanical engineers like Mick. "For the time being you need to carry on with your current employer, as do Helen, John and Allan, but I must ask you to please keep it to yourselves until I give you the go-ahead. Understood?"

"Oh yes," Mick replied.

"Now to give you an idea when we'd like you to start, should you agree to accept our offer, it would be around the first of February next year. That will be the same for all of you as Airbus should deliver the A400M by the third of Feb.  However, we are still waiting for confirmation of the delivery date for the five VC10s."

"Hey, do you mind if I interrupt?" asked Chloe.

"No, go ahead."

"You'll never guess why we have our favourites taking us on holiday?"

"Is it because they were already on the plane waiting for other customers to come along who cancelled at the last minute?"

"No," said Chloe.

"Okay, I give up. Why do we have our favourites taking

us on holiday?"

Chloe looked at him and said "Remember when you phoned Biggins? Well the receptionist phoned John to ask him if he was available and he said it all depended on who the client was? Well, upon hearing the client's name, he said to her he was on his way but he reserved the right to organise the crew."

Dick looked at Helen and she smiled. "Is this true?" he asked, and she replied "Yep" nodding her head up and down at the same time.

"Well that's wonderful, and I'm honoured."

"So," said Chloe smiling "they have been with us on all our trips ever since and that's why they are taking us today."

They whiled away the time by indulging in normal chit-chat and nothing of real importance. Later they told John and Allan they would try to get some shut-eye.

Dick awoke to the sounds of crockery and cutlery emanating from the serving area towards the front of the plane, so he got up and walked to the bathroom. After attending to his ablutions, he sat down to find Helen had already placed a cup of steaming-hot brew ready and waiting for him. By this time, the other two were awake.

"May I serve you some breakfast?"

"Yes please."

Dick attacked his breakfast with gusto while behaving like a gentleman although one might believe he hadn't eaten in a week. Chloe and Mick, having taken their turns in the bathroom, sat down and had their breakfast.

The approach to the runway was an eye-opening moment and the view, a spectacular one. They approached from a North-East direction, flying over the sea. They passed Scrub Island and Marina Cay on the right-hand side, and over the mouth of Trellis Bay on the left, just before touch-down.

The time was 11:42 a.m., according to Dick's watch, and as there was no hangar space available, John and Allan parked the plane two spaces away from the Airport Terminal.

Dick and Chloe proceeded to the reception area where they introduced themselves. They asked for an invoice for aeroplane parking and airport services for the two days, advising they would leave by 6:30 a.m. on the morning of the third day. Dick also remembered to arrange for some ground staff to be there early enough to fill the plane with Jet-A fuel.

While they were doing this, the other four were getting the luggage and making sure they secured the plane, for security reasons.

Once through Passport Control, they set off to collect a people carrier from the car hire company, and because Mick was the new kid on the block, they elected him as the designated driver. Chloe handed him a sheet of paper with the directions on it.

"Off you go," she said.

They drove out onto the Route Two road, passing the runway on the right-hand side. Afterwards, they turned right onto the Little Mountain Road which would lead them to their pre-booked chalet.

They checked in at the reception desk and given a key and directions to their respective chalets. Once inside the main area, they all realized they would have a great relaxing time there.

"This is a lovely place you booked," Chloe said to Dick.

"I didn't book it. You did?"

"No, I didn't" she replied in bewilderment.

"But where did you get the print-out confirmation sheet from?"

"You gave it....?" Chloe said, now dumbfounded.

For a moment they looked at each other. As if two light bulbs switched on, they said together, "Joel" and laughed. The other four looked at them as if they had lost their marbles.

Chloe put up her right hand and said, "It's a long story and one day either Dick or I will explain."

So they searched out their respective rooms, and being tired from the long over eighteen-hour flight, especially John and Allan, they spent the rest of the day just relaxing at the chalet. They soaked up the marvellous views all around them.

The following morning Dick and Chloe were up before sunrise and they stood on the balcony and watched as the sun started its daily journey. It peeked over the horizon before casting its life-giving rays onto their faces. It would travel the skies over to the other horizon before settling down and resting for the night, and the following day, repeat the whole process all over again.

"This is a new dawn for us," said Dick.

"Yes, and it's a new day for us also," replied Chloe.

They stood in silence soaking up the magnificent view.

"I wonder if this is the start of a new way of life for us?" he said.

As they had all rested well, the next day they did a little travelling around the island. So, armed with a picnic lunch, which the chalet owners had laid on for them, they started off by, first, following the coast road. They took the Route Two as far as the Waterfront Drive turn-off which they followed, passing Paraquita Bay and joining Blackburn Highway.

This coastline road took them to Port Purcell, right around to Fisher Estate where the road became the Sir Francis Drake Highway. They now drove mile after mile revelling in the wonderful scenery and never tiring. They carried on and reached Frenchman Cay, gaining access via the Frenchman Cay Bridge, and there they stopped and had a walk around giving their legs a welcome stretch. A wee while later they were back on the road again. Later, they stopped at Steele Point at the Southern tip of the island where they took an early lunch break.

After lunch, they joined Highway one, which was also a coastal road, and drove all the way to Cane Garden Bay before the road turned inland. This led them to Ridge Road which took them over a slight mountain pass before bringing them down to Parnham Town. Here they re-joined Route Two which led them back to the chalets.

They all agreed it had been a tremendous idea to have done the trip, something the likes of which they would never forget.

Although the drive had taken up most of the day, there was still enough sunlight left for Helen and Mick to go down to the beach. By 9:30 p.m. John and Allan bedded down as they had another long day ahead of them, and by 10:00 p.m., the rest of them also retired after the wonderful day's outing.

As John and Allan wanted to be at the airport by 5:45 a.m. the following morning, Dick and Chloe made sure they were up an hour beforehand. After an early breakfast, organised on their arrival at the chalets, Dick walked up to the reception area to settle the bill.

They got to the airport in good time and, while Dick sorted out payment of the invoices, John and Allan walked out to the aircraft. Once the outside checks completed, poor Mick drew the short straw and had to organise the bowser to oversee the refuelling. Chloe and Helen, meanwhile, set about setting certain things to rights in the cabin before take-off.

As always, the flight was uneventful, and they arrived at Maitland Airport just after 9:00 a.m. Much to their surprise, a beautiful young lady met them while standing with her hands placed on her hips and looking miffed.

"Be prepared," Chloe said to Dick "as, by the look of things, your child will have some strong words to say to you."

Dick approached his daughter with a big smile on his face but, before he could say a word, Kerri ripped off at him. "That's not fair Daddy. Yes, Joel informed us, but why didn't you take us with you?" she demanded.

"I tried warning you but no, you wouldn't listen, would you," said Chloe.

"I didn't take you with us because Chloe and I wanted to get away by ourselves,... just the two of us. We have had no time together since these projects we had to get off the ground. It's been a great responsibility, and we needed space."

"However, as it was, the work got in the way soon after we had boarded the plane so I made changes. But it was still a much-needed break, and on the flight back home, I decided you and your husband should go on the honeymoon you never had."

"Oh yes... and when do you propose we do this?" Kerri asked, still pissed off at her old man.

"When the engineers have completed installing the simulator, we can arrange it."

"Ha,... well I've got news for you, Daddy. They finished while you were away, so we'll take that honeymoon now, thank you very much. And where is it you intend sending us?"

"Well, we can do this in one of two ways. Either you decide and go wherever it is you want to go, or I decide and it comes as a surprise. So, what's it to be? Surprise or no surprise? That is the question."

"Don't be funny with me Daddy because it's not working. Now let me get this right. If we decide, we can go to wherever it is we want to go to—anywhere in the entire world we fancy. But if you decide, we only find out once we get there, right?"

"In a word... Yes. That's correct my sweetie-pie. So once again, what's it to be?"

Still peeved, she pulled away when her Dad tried in vain to pinch her nose.

"Let me speak to Ivan and I'll give you our decision. But I'm still mad, Daddy."

"Okay, okay, that's now over with, so may I please have a

hug?" he pleaded. "Chloe and I are not stopping here right now as we need to unpack and change our clothing. We should be back here at the Airport offices around lunch time."

"Oh... okay Daddy," she said and hugged him.

"Did our cars arrive? If so, where are they parked,?"

"Yes... at the house," she cried grinning.

"I guess I must beg you to take us there rather than ask you, aren't I?" Dick said. Both Kerri and Chloe laughed out loud just as Ivan showed up.

"Ah... good I'm glad you're here," Dick said to Ivan. "You can give us a lift to the house and fill me in as to the progress of the simulator and the progress of your learning."

The crew interrupted them to came and say their goodbyes, having done all the necessary and were now ready to return to Biggin Hill Airport.

Before they all got into the company van, Dick and Chloe loaded their cases. All settled, Ivan drove them across to the other side of the runway.

At the house, chaos greeted them—for the removals chaps plonked everything down higgledy-piggledy all over the place.

"There's no way we're going back over there today," Chloe said to Kerri and Ivan and Dick nodded in agreement. "You'll just have to give our apologies to Deon, please. We can't do anything before first sorting all this shit out."

"Well, why don't we do a de-briefing tomorrow," Ivan suggested to Dick "and, we can be at the simulator?"

"Yep, I can live with the idea."

For a while, they all just looked at the mess and wondered where the best place would be to start.

"Are you two just going to stand there, or are you going to lend a hand?" Dick asked them.

"Neither," Kerri replied "We've got a lot of work to do so we'll see you when you've finished. Bye."

"Sweetie-pie," Dick pleaded, but to no avail.

"It's your own damn fault, you knucklehead," Chloe declared.

"Oh... okay, I'll drink to that," he replied in defeat.

They were just about done with their marathon stint

when, the front door being wide open, Cassie, Rachel, Erica and Robert walked in. They shouted *'hello'* to attract their attention and moments later Dick and Chloe appeared, and the jollifications began.

"Why don't we have a Barbie?" Cassie suggested.

"Great idea, bad timing," said Chloe.

"Why bad timing?" asked Cassie.

"Nothing to put on the fire," said Chloe.

"We've got plenty at home," Cassie informed her.

"No, I don't want to go over there just yet as I'd like to get finished here with some fiddly bits."

"We'll send the kids over and they can do the Barbie for us," Rachel suggested.

"Great idea," said Erica "We'll get the meat now."

"And what about salads and bread etcetera?" Chloe asked her.

"We'll just have to bring that back with us," Erica replied, "Nana, give me the keys please."

"What," Dick butted in "You haven't got your licence yet, and you haven't even been learning either."

"Yes, but I...."

"There are no... 'but I's... in this conversation, mad child. No licence equals no driving... simple," he said, while the rest of them laughed.

"I told you Dickie would take exception to your driving my car," Cassie said to Erica.

"But uncle Dickie, we're on private property."

"Yes, you are one hundred percent correct in your assumption, but who owns the private property?"

"You do."

"Exactly," Dick exclaimed "Even more reason it still means no licence equals no driving.... simple. And how many more times must I say it, for goodness' sake?"

"Oh man, it's not fair," she moaned like a typical spoilt little school girl.

"Nooo,... it is fair," Dick teased her. "Learn, get your driving lessons behind you, apply for your licence and once you've passed,... you may drive. And don't make me say 'simple' again." Once more they all laughed—except Erica.

The problem soon resolved, the food prepared, and they

were ready to eat. During the meal, Kerri and Ivan showed up.

"Are you burning the midnight oil or are you burning the candle at both ends or have you come from home?" Dick asked them.

"No," said Kerri "we've come straight from work."

"Well, sit down and tuck in. So, you two decided yet where you want to go on your late honeymoon, or am I sorting it out?" Dick asked them.

"We had ideas of going to Australia but decided we would like you to surprise us."

"Good," Dick replied pleased. "I'm glad about that because you will have more than enough chances to go to Australia in the line of work ahead of us one of these days. So,... I'll work on the surprise straight away." He got up from the table and walked out.

Sometime later he came back into the large kitchen area and sat down beside his daughter. "I suggest you finish up now and go home and pack your bags with stuff that will last for two weeks. Your flight leaves here at six o'clock tomorrow morning," he said with a smile on his face.

Kerri looked at her father in disbelief.

"I'm serious my child. Pack your bags and get forty winks, will you" he said and, in silence, they got up and walked to the door still in shock.

"Hey," Dick exclaimed "where you're going to?"

"You said we must pack our bags now and get to sleep," Kerri answered frowning.

"No, I don't mean that. Aren't you going to give your old man a hug and a kiss before you go? I mean, because I will not be over there at that bloody time in the morning?"

"Oh, sorry Daddy."

"What about our de-briefing we supposed to be having?" asked Ivan.

"That can wait until we get back" Kerri jumped in before anyone else could answer.

Dick agreed and, after hugs all around, and a kiss from his daughter, she and Ivan left still looking bemused.

A little while later, Dick said he was knackered and would retire for the night, but what he didn't tell them was he would set his alarm clock for 5:00 a.m. the following morning. His reason was he wanted to meet the aircraft when it arrived at 5:30 a.m. and to say another 'proper' goodbye to his daughter.

At 5:30 a.m. the next morning he was over at the main building. While chatting to the security guard, the aircraft arrived and stopped on the apron where the re-fuelling was about to take place. He hurried across to the plane and got on board.

"I didn't realize you were going on this flight?" Helen said looking surprised while Mick looked on in the background.

"I'm not. I've just come over to say 'Good morning' to you guys and to surprise my daughter as she has no idea I will be here to wave her goodbye."

John and Allan left the cockpit and came by to greet Dick. When he had phoned, he made sure they would be the crew on the trip, including Mick as he was still on leave.

"It was my intention to come down here to see you, anyway," said Dick. "I want to introduce you to my daughter and son-in-law as all of you will soon, and for obvious reasons, be working together. Hey, we've got time, so follow me, gentlemen. Sorry Helen, stay here and meet my child when she arrives and please, say nothing to her about my being here.

"Of course," Helen replied, "you do what you guys must do."

He marched them over to the closest hangar and walked in. There he recognised one of the security guards and had a quick chat before going over to the Airbus simulator.

"I haven't seen this since its installation. Shall we have a quick peek inside?"

"Oh yes please," replied Allen.

They climbed the temporary stairs to the simulator entrance and walked inside. A marvellous array of modern-day, up-to-date, state-of-the-art cockpit with the avionics to match greeted them.

"Wow," they all exclaimed together.

"This is pretty bloody cool," said Mick.

"Well, inspect it because soon you guys will train on this, and the VC10."

"I can't wait," said Allan

"I suppose none of us can. Okay, that was always to be a

short and sweet visit, so we had better get back now," said Dick.

They got back to the aircraft at 5:55 a.m., and as they approached, they could hear laughter on-board. "That's my child."

"Daddy, what are you doing here?"

"You didn't for one moment believe I wouldn't come and say goodbye to my most favourite person in the world, did you?" he asked. She walked over and gave him a big hug.

Introductions over with, he told the two of them the crew would come back home the following day and would go back to fetch them when it was time for them to come back home.

Hugs and kisses, and handshakes and goodbyes all around, he got up to leave. On his way out, he handed an envelope to Helen giving her strict instruction to only hand it to Kerri upon landing at their destination—and not before.

He watched the plane climb up into the early morning sky on its journey to a wonderful honeymoon holiday destination. Afterwards, he set about planning a meeting for later on that morning.

Their long flight over, Kerri and Ivan had arrived at their destination. The approach to the runway was to first fly past the island on their left, and away from it. They turned around and once more approached the runway, but this time from a Westerly direction. They could now make out the land on either side, and as they could not see the runway, Kerri asked questions for she noticed they were getting close to the water, too close for comfort. In fact, it got so close that, just before touch down, she could see other holidaymakers sitting outside a pub on the beach drinking their cocktails and waving at them as they flew by.

"Shit that was intense," she exclaimed, and Ivan asked "Where the hell are we?"

"I don't have the foggiest?" she replied. "Helen, where are we?"

"I'm sorry, I'm still not allowed to say, but your Dad said to give you this envelope once we have landed." Kerri opened it and read the contents.

'Hello my sweetie-pie.

If you are reading this, it means you have arrived at your destination, St Maarten, Princess Juliana International Airport. I hope you enjoyed the view when you came into land. Once you have gone through Customs, I have arranged for you guys to pick up a car. So, all you have to do is show them your Passports and Driving Licences.

I have also booked you in at the Sonesta Maho Beach Resort & Casino for starters and you are more than welcome to change to another hotel somewhere else on the island if you so desire. Also, if you would like to island hop, phone the airport for flights or charter planes, whichever suits you.

One last thing. I've also booked the crew in at the same hotel for tonight and have also organised a car for them. Please tell them everything is on the Company, but one thing you have to do for me please, and that is to go to the airport with them in the morning to pay for the fuel. So please arrange with John regarding times etc. for doing this.

I hope you two have a wonderful time and we'll see you when you get back.

All my love,

DD.

PS. Please take lots of photos from the beach as the aircraft come into land.'

"What's that all about?" asked Ivan.

Kerri handed the letter over for him to read, and once he had finished it, it was time to get off the plane.

While the crew shut down the aircraft, Kerri and Ivan set off towards the Terminal to have their Passports stamped and to collect the car. Not long thereafter, the crew joined them and they drove the short distance to the hotel to start their late honeymoon.

"I wonder what your Dad meant by taking photos of the planes from the beach."

"I suppose we'll find out when we get there, but I suspect he wants to get a bird's-eye view of the planes coming into land."

That night in their hotel room, and just before them relaxing, they noticed what they deemed to be the beginning stage of Joel making his appearance, however, it wasn't. It was, in fact, the 'doctor' who came to pay them a visit.

"So sorry to disturb you and yes, I realize we gave this overall assignment to Joel to handle but I was wondering if you would allow me to check your hand. Not that I'm expecting any problems," said the 'doctor' in a very nice sounding voice within their heads.

"Oh no. Please, by all means," Ivan replied while holding

out his right hand.

From out of nowhere, the 'doctor' produced an instrument he for a split second place over Ivan's hand. "Thank you so much for allowing me to intrude on you in your private space," he said. "As I suspected, there are no problems at all as we carried out all the repairs to our usual high standards, therefore there won't be any further check-ups. Goodbye," said the 'doctor', and in a flash he disappeared.

"Well that was very nice of him," said Ivan.

"Yes, and now we can get on with our honeymoon," Kerri said in approval.

Chapter Twenty-One

The Job Assignments

DICK USED THE boardroom to hold a meeting to which he invited Deon to sit in.

"Now we have to think about who does what and how and when," he announced. "First, I would like the three of you, that is Chloe, Cassie and Rachel, to put it into simple terms, about how to learn to operate a radio and no, I don't mean the ones you have in your cars or in your homes. Also, I'd like you to learn how the tower operates and what its function is."

"I will not go into detail now because the experts can do that for me. Deon is only here as an observer so he knows what's going on and, if I'm not around, he will always be here to assist you. Once we have finished here, he will take you to the Training Officer who will put you through your paces."

"And what will you be doing?" asked Chloe.

"I, my dear, am going back to the Bahamas to relax on the beach. No, no no—just kidding. Sorry, I got carried away there for a moment. I must get to grips with the simulator. That's what I'll be doing. I have to get the plane inside my head before Airbus deliver the real McCoy."

"Okay, and when are you going to play with your new toy?" Cassie teased.

"Not now. I have to first sort out office space for myself and I also need to get hold of Phil. Afterwards, I'll spend most of my time on the simulator,"

"You can use my office," Deon suggested.

"Thanks, Deon, but no. I will not impose on your space. There must be a room or space here I can use. I need nothing fancy as I won't be here all the time. In fact, if there's space enough at the simulator, perhaps, I'll use that."

"I'll get our Facilities Manager to find something for you," Deon replied. "In fact, I'll do that now plus I'll get the Training Officer over here to start the ball rolling."

"Thanks, Deon," said Dick.

A little while later there was a knock at the door and a nice looking young man walked in and introduced himself. "Hi everyone, I'm Dominic and I'm the Training Instructor here at Maitland Airport."

Dick looked at him and smiled to himself suspecting only carnal imaginations were going through his sister's mind right there and then.

Introductions over with, Dominic led the girls out of the Boardroom and Dick headed toward Deon's office. When he entered, Deon was on the phone, so he sat down and waited for him to finish.

"That was Michael on the phone. He's our Facilities guy, and he's on his way."

"Thanks, Deon and I'm sorry if I barged in on you like that."

"That's no problem. You are the boss, and besides, my door was open."

"Yes I am, but I don't believe the boss of a company should just barge his way into one of his employee's offices. It's not my style. Besides, there are already more than enough of those arseholes around in the world who feel they may do so, anyway. Way more than enough."

While during a discussion regarding the work flow was in progress, Michael entered and Deon introduced Dick to him. After a few pleasantries, Dick suggested they go over to the hangar housing the simulator, and on entering, he decided this was where he wanted his office to be.

"Deon," Dick said "as I'll not impede on how you run and control the airport, I have decided this is where Michael should organise a space for me. Now please guys don't misunderstand me. I've got a lot of other businesses I have to look after, and I'll be in and out of this place often and as you, Deon are doing such a great job, why should I interfere?"

"However, should you need to contact me, well,... need I say more? But, if I need to go somewhere, you'll be the first I contact. So if you want to get back to your office now, I'll sort things out here with Michael, and for the time being, I'll use the boardroom as I need to get up to speed with what else is going on around me. That will fill in the time while I wait for Michael and his team to create a working space for me over here."

Deon left and Dick, together with Michael, looked at viable areas to create an office space.

"Michael, if possible, I would prefer an elevated area because I'd like to be in line with the entrance to the simulator."

"Well, may I suggest we build your office space all along that wall? By doing so, we can design and build a proper retractable walk-way to the door of the simulator."

"Yes," Dick agreed "excellent idea as that will also lead me to the other simulator."

"You having another simulator installed here?" asked Michael.

"Oh yes, and in less than a years' time, if all goes well."

"So, I imagine you will install it over here, next to this one?" Michael said pointing at an open space next to the installed simulator.

"That's correct."

"Okay, Dick," Michael said and apologised. "I'm sorry, that was a slip of the tongue. I should have addressed you as Mr Shepherd."

"Nothing to worry about, Michael. I would prefer it if you called me Dick, however, if you feel you should address me as Mr Shepherd in front of your colleagues, that's fine by me. But please, at all other times, it's Dick. Understood?"

"Okay, thanks, Dick," Michael replied with a smile though still looking somewhat embarrassed. "Right, as I have a good idea, and am certain it will accommodate both simulators, I'll carry on. I'll do my best to have something for you to look at this afternoon in the way of a drawing plan."

"Great stuff, Michael. I'll catch up with you later."

They now went their separate way. Back in the Boardroom, Dick set about phoning Phil to find out how things were going.

An excited Phil informed him he had put together the first prototype, and it was working beyond all of his expectations. "The speed, the power, the grunt, the torque, and the.... well, whatever you want to call them, it's phenomenal and I cannot get over what I have created. But, because I'm busy with it, I can't get ahead as I'm also tied down with interviews so I need to get help."

"Do you think it would help if someone from Toby's came and joined you for a while?"

"I don't care who it is or where they're from, just so long as they can go through the interview process and hire the people we need."

"I tell you what, I'll come there for a while and try to find the right person to run the factory, because don't forget, I will need you here as soon as possible."

"Oh creeps, I forgot about that," Phil replied sounding rather forlorn.

"Well, the Airbus simulator is waiting for you," Dick said with a slight hint of excitement of his own.

"You mean it's finished?" Phil said with his spirits lifted.

"Yep,... and it's got our names written all over it. Okay, I'll let you get on with it and I'll get myself over there tonight, and please organise a room at the hotel for me."

"Okay will do, and when you get here, you can meet the Nippon guys."

"Yeah, I look forward to that."

Call ended, he walked to Deon's office to inform him what he was planning on doing. He also asked him to check the plans Michael would come up with and asked him to get them to build the office area as soon as possible. In the boardroom, he phoned Biggin Hill to book a plane for 3:00 p.m. that afternoon and also called Chloe to put her in the picture.

Once completed, he made his way home to pack and to make sure he had everything pertinent to the factory and both car manufactures. While he still had time on his hands, he called Jonathan at Brimstone Cars.

"Hello, Jonathan,... Dick here. This is just a courtesy call to find out how the production line is going?"

"Hello, Dick. I spoke to Phil this morning to advise him we would be ready to ship our first load of cars to him on the sixth."

"That's great news. How did you pull this off?"

"I'm not too sure if it was yourself or Phil, or both, who got the staff going or if it's just the fact they don't want to lose their jobs again, I can't be sure, but they have never worked like this before."

"Maybe it's just you, keeping them on their toes," Dick replied and they both laughed. "Tell me, have you painted the signage on the cars front doors yet?"

"Yes we have, and it came out great."

"Excellent," Dick said being well pleased "and you say the cars will be with Phil on the sixth?"

"Yes, they will."

"Good. I'll be able to cast an eyeball over them because I'm on my way there this afternoon."

They carried on chatting for a while longer before they ended their call. There were a few noises outside and the girls burst in through the front door.

"What's all this then?" Dick asked in surprise and Chloe said, looking all coy "We've taken an early lunch, so we came home to wave you goodbye when you leave."

"Yeah, right? What, with you bloody lot, I smell a rat here," Dick said giving them the old shifty eyeball.

"Who, us?" they asked, almost in unison, and Dick said "Yes, you" he exclaimed "What the hell are you up to?"

"Nothing," was the innocent chorus.

"Bollocks," Dick cried out "I know you lot oh so well, and when you get together, you're as thick as thieves you are, so I'll ask again. What are you up to?"

"We've taken an early lunch," Chloe repeated enunciating each word.

"Oh, for fuck sake,... stop talking shit, will you? Just tell me what you're up to."

"Shall we put him out of his misery?" Cassie asked the others, and Rachel said: "Oh, go on then."

"Dominic received a call from home, so he's had to leave and we've got the rest of the day off," Chloe informed him at last.

"So what's the problem?" he asked and, because it concerned one of his employees, he questioned them rather than giving them a mouthful for their unnecessary antics. "Has someone informed Deon yet?"

"Sorry, can't answer that."

Dick picked up the phone and spoke to Deon asking him if he knew of any problem. "Please phone me the moment you have any information on the matter," he said. As the girls were close by, they overheard what he had said to Deon before putting the phone down.

"It seems like his mother's taken ill. I would therefore like it if you guys kept a watchful eye on proceedings please, and keep in touch with Deon."

"It's now time for me to get ready," he said, and off to his room he sauntered. Later, when he had finished, he came back into the sitting-room area and said his goodbyes.

"Now please remember to keep an eye on proceedings. If Dominic doesn't come back for whatever reason, you can get instructions from Deon what you can do in the meantime. I'm sure he will find something constructive for you to do," Dick said as he walked out of the front door.

Once over at the main building, he used the reception desk phone to speak to Deon. He asked him to find the girls something to do to fill in the time until Dominic came back. Later his commute landed, and once parked outside the building, he boarded the plane which was, by then, ready and waiting for him. As he had met none of the crew before, he decided not to get into any idle chatter but concentrate on some paperwork.

He picked up his hire car at the airport and drove to the hotel where he checked in. When he had finished sorting out his room, he drove to the factory, and on arrival, he did not recognise the place. The mobile offices were there, stacked long-ways and buffeted up next to each other, and as there were so many of them, placed in an L-shaped configuration.

While he sat in his car, he became aware most of the working staff were all over the place. They were in and out of the building, with some person shouting obscenities to another group of workers. Although it wasn't his concern, he wondered what they were doing.

A crane here and a smaller one there, materials of all shapes and sizes being moved around. It reminded him of a documentary he had once viewed on the television about an ant living in the Amazon jungle. These ants would carry the leaves of a tree to their nests, scurrying around almost as though they were oblivious to what they were doing.

"Well let's hope this bloody lot are conscious to what they're doing," Dick said to himself out loud.

By now he was standing next to the car's drivers side door, and as he wasn't in any hurry to find Phil, he made a mental note of what was happening in front of him. Because he wasn't paying attention, he failed to observe a big chap in a high visibility jacket and wearing a hard hat approaching him.

"Excuse me sir, but this is private property and you cannot park here," he said. Turning to face him, it was a security guard who had confronted him.

"I'm sorry sir but although this is a building site, it's a secured one, so I have to ask you to please vacate the premises," he informed Dick in a fair but firm manner.

Dick was, however, well pleased at this for it meant security was doing its job. "Hello... private property you say?"

"Yes sir. Private and secured."

"And tell me, who owns these premises?" Dick inquired, and the guard replied: "I'm not too sure of the gentleman's name but he is the uncle of...."

Before he finished, Dick interjected "Phil Upton?"

The guard looked at him and agreed by nodding his head.

"Well, I'm Phil's uncle and I am the owner of these premises."

"Thanks for pointing that out sir but please understand, I don't know you from a bar of soap. My job is important and if I fail, I'm the one who gets it in the neck, and I cannot afford to lose it right now."

Dick held up his left hand and with his right, he dialled Phil's number. "Hi," he said to Phil. "You've got one almighty bloody security set-up on these grounds. Can you come and save me before this huge guy standing in front of me knocks my bloody block off?"

There was a moment's silence followed by slight laughter and within a minute, Phil approached. "Gavin, please meet my uncle, Mr Shepherd, who is your boss.

"Oh dear," Gavin said flushing "I seem to have made a huge mistake."

Dick looked at him and held out his hand. "If you had dealt with this situation in any other way, I would have fired you on the spot. Well done and please keep up the good work."

"Yes sir," he replied as they broke their handshake.

Dick and Phil walked over to Phil's office and, as Dick sat down, Phil handed him a hard hat. "Ta for 'at. Okay, where do we start?"

"Do you want to have a look around the site?" Phil asked, but he looked harassed, so Dick replied: "Yes I would, but what about your dilemma with the interviewing?"

"At this moment, the recruiting agent has set up a room at our hotel. Then starting at eight o'clock tomorrow morning, interviews will take place throughout the entire day, and they have had an enormous response to the ads."

"Well that's brilliant," Dick said, "just what we want, isn't it?"

"It is, but I cannot handle it plus everything else."

"Okay, I have an idea. I can tell you have more than enough on your plate so you stay here and carry on with everything you need to get on with. Then tomorrow, I'll be at the hotel handling the interviews. How does that sound?"

"That's a huge relief for me," Phil said. "I thought I would go out of my tiny little mind."

"No, please don't do that. We need your tiny little mind."

There was a knock at the door which opened and a voice announced: "Some embarrassed security guard said the boss-man is here."

Dick recognised the voice, stood up and shook Tom's hand. There was another bloke standing behind him whom he introduced saying "This is Aaron, Eric's replacement."

"Well thank fuck for that," Dick exclaimed, and they all laughed.

"Shall we all go for a walk-about?" Tom asked them, and Phil said: "Dick, if you don't mind, I have a shed load here......"

"Yes," Dick replied before Phil could carry on "you stay here. I'm sure Tom and Aaron can show me around. So, until later..."

"Thanks, I'll catch up with you in a little while," said Phil.

Dick turned around and followed the other two out of the office. "How's the money flow going, any problems?" Dick asked, and Tom said "No, it's tremendous thank you. I wish every client was like you." More laughter followed which reverberated around the building site dampened by the noise.

"Are the Nippon chaps here?" Dick asked, and Tom said "Oh yes, and you should be proud of them. Those buggers drive us nuts, but in a good way, you understand. When they feel they will catch up with us, they say so in no uncertain manner in our early morning briefings."

"And are you still going to finish on the twenty-fourth?"

"Yes," Tom affirmed, "at the moment we are ahead of schedule and so are the Nippon's."

"I take it you are still pushing the twenty-four-hour day?"

"Yes, Dick, we are. I also pushed to get a one-day shift in on a Sunday which I reckon was a huge score."

"Well, I suppose if the money is there, that's the response you'll get."

"Oh yes," Tom replied grinning "Money always talks, doesn't it?"

Tom led the way and the progress astounded Dick. The layout was such it impressed him to where he visualized the production line in operation.

They walked through to where the Nippon chaps were doing their thing and they stopped to have a chat but, as the language barrier was too difficult with this shift, they didn't hang around there for too long. So Tom led them through to the office space where some furnishings were already in place.

Next up was the completed reception area being occupied by three security guards. Tom let them know in no uncertain terms who his guest was, and as the word had already got around, the three guards had a slight laugh at Gavin's expense.

Dick held up his hand to silence them. "What Gavin did was what I expect you guys to do. So do me a favour and don't laugh at a bloke who's doing his job and doing it to his full potential. Remember, it could well have been any of you," he said, with a hint of annoyance.

He turned around and Gavin was standing in the doorway, so he smiled and winked an eye at him as he walked away. Dick knew full well the other three guards would not know of his actions. As they left the area, he could hear mumblings but could only wonder what Gavin was saying.

When they had finished on the inside of the factory, they walked back outside. It got dark and the outside lighting switched on. Tom led them to another stand-alone building saying it was the new electrical supply house, said this was were Phil would install the machine which would supply the power to the factory and Dick understood what he meant.

They rounded a corner and Dicks eyes scanned an area he perceived to be the biggest car park he'd ever seen. The last time he was there he remembered it being a dumping ground, and while they were standing there a huge truck arrived. Phil was standing on the running board of the cab, instructing the driver where to go to. It was the first delivery of the Brimstone cars.

"Wonderful," Dick said, "Let's follow them."

"Yeah okay, but Aaron," Tom said, "please get at least one security guard so we can show him what's going on."

As the car park was lit up like a Christmas tree, it didn't matter where they parked the cars, and as Dick got closer, he could make out what Jonathan had designed to have painted on the doors of their cars. It read 'Maitland Electric Car Manufactures' and the writing encapsulated a drawn picture of a car.

Underneath, in a smaller typeface, it read 'No Petrol, No Diesel, No Outside Electrical Power Source Required.' Impressed as he was, Dick phoned Jonathan to give him his approval.

Aaron returned with not just one, but two of the security guards, one of them being Gavin which Dick approved of.

"I have an idea," Dick said to Aaron. "Now, even if it's just for the time being, and because there are no cameras up as yet, you erect some kind of hut here. Then, get two at a time security guards in here to keep an eye on the cars. Yes, even if it means getting in more guards from outside."

"Good idea," Aaron replied. "I'll work something out tonight."

"And Phil," Dick asked, "when do you want the factory force to begin?"

"Mmmm..., now, if not sooner, please."

"Not to worry. I'll come up with something."

"Okay guys," Dick continued. "I can tell I'm getting in the bloody way, but I'll be back every now and again. For now, I have to concentrate on hiring a labour force and Tom, when was it you said the housing project would finish?"

"The factory side, by no later than the twenty-fourth of this month. The housing side, at this stage, looks like it will be a month later which is, even if I say so myself, bloody good going, but I plan to bring the boys on over from the factory as and when they finish their respective projects."

"Good idea and fantastic progress," Dick acknowledged "Now it's up to you, Phil to start the next stage."

"Yeah," Phil replied "the motors for the electrical supply house should be here tomorrow or the day after and I can't wait to install them."

"All right," Dick said, "as I've got a lot of preparations to do for tomorrow I think I'll be on my way now."

Back at the hotel, and after having supper, he spent until midnight creating a presentation for those who would be lucky enough to be part of the new workforce. The following morning, both Dick and Phil were up early and, after breakfast, they remained at the table until the people from the employment agency arrived. When they did, Phil got up to call them over.

"This is my uncle who owns the company and he will be here today to assist you guys. I apologise as I'm far too busy to lend a hand, so I'll be on my way now," he said, offering no further introductions.

"Apologies, but the poor chap's under a lot of pressure and I hope I'm not the cause. I'm Dick, and you are?"

"I'm Lucy and this is Martha."

"Tea or coffee before we get started, or are we pressed for time?"

"Dick, I'd first like to glance around the room we have booked. If I'm satisfied, I'll have my tea there," Lucy replied. So they all got up, found the room and gave it a once-over.

"If you're involved with the interviews, may I suggest we ask the staff to organise another partitioning over there," she suggested pointing in the general direction of the windows.

"I'll organise it right away," Dick said with a smile.

Shortly thereafter, a tiny old lady wheeled in a trolley on which were tea and biscuits. Without a word she left it there and walked out and as she left, four young men showed up and, with Lucy's guidance, erected another enclosed interviewing area.

Dick came back and, walking over to the trolley, poured himself a cup of tea, and while balancing the cup on the saucer, walked over to the girls. "This is the way I'd like us to go about the interviewing, please. I take it you two know what my requirements are and, therefore, you know what type of person I'm looking for. So, once you have finished with each applicant and selected one you think fits the bill, I'll interview that person as well before we go any further with them. You two are to sort out the rough from the smooth for me. Okay?"

"You're the employer so yes, it's fine by me," replied Lucy. "And me," said Martha.

"All right. Now those whom you think are no good at all, and are not the personnel I'm looking for, then fine, say thanks and we'll let them know. But if hesitant, write something on a notepad and hand it to that person before you send them over."

"Yeah, I'm fine with that," said Martha, "but what do you want us to put on the piece of paper?"

"I think just an X," Dick replied "but you are also to put one of these small sticky colour dots on their front breast area, for this will help identify the unsure ones for me, and you instruct them to hand the piece of paper over. It will confuse the hell out of some of them. Those you consider okay, won't have any identifiable marks anywhere on their person, so I'll know straight away they are the good ones. Also, have you set out any amount of time for each individual, or how are you thinking about working it?"

"Mmmm... because of the enormous response," Lucy replied "the letter of instruction I sent out to all of them said the interview process would begin at eight o'clock in the morning and would go on until the last person. But I think fifteen to twenty minutes per interview would be more than enough."

"Okay, that's about the best we can do, I suppose," Dick agreed. "Anyone arrived yet, do we know?"

Martha popped her head out the door to have a look before closing it again "Yes, from what I can tell there are already twenty-plus candidates waiting for us."

The door opened and, as Dick was facing away from it, he turned around. "Dick, this is my daughter Gillian and she's going to assist us with calling of the next person, doing paperwork and, well just general dog's body, I suppose," Lucy informed him.

As Dick was by now on the other side of the room, he raised his hand and waved to her. "Hi Gillian," he said greeting her "thanks for coming in and lending a hand". He now turned back to face the furthest cubicle. "Okay," he announced, "I'll use this one and when you're ready, let the games begin."

Time seemed to drag by and the two girls got through sixteen candidates each hour. The reason for this being, those who were unsuitable, received the bad news and, therefore, asked to leave. So, where some took five, six, or seven minutes, others only took a minute, and this helped to arrive at the average. Dick, however, was more thorough and spent, sometimes, twenty-five minutes with an individual some of whom he asked to remain behind.

By twelve-noon, they had seen seventy-one hopefuls, and he had amassed only nine likely candidates for the job, with two perhaps fitting a managerial position. However, the one person he was looking for was the one who would run the show on his and Phil's behalf but so far, no luck. So he got up to tell the two girls he would be back and stepped out of the room. There to greet him was, what looked like, rush hour on Charing Cross station.

"Bugger me," he exclaimed "We'll be here all bloody day and night," he thought to himself.

Dick looked at those within the building and asked for quiet as he had questions to ask them, and those outside, should they not be able to hear him, were to please be patient and wait a while. "Is there anyone among you who has a College or University degree in the auto industry, or perhaps Managerial experience within the industry itself?" he asked and, in amongst the sea of bodies, four hands shot up. "Please come forward and just stand inside the door over there on the right-hand side," he said while pointing a finger towards the door.

He opened the door, peered inside and said to Gillian they were to remain there until he returned. He walked outside and this time it looked like Grand Central Station, New York, in front of him as he couldn't move for all the bodies. However, success was on his side because he got seventeen hands to go up. Once again, he asked those men and women to come forward and join the others waiting inside the room.

They entered and Dick announced to the rest of those still waiting outside they would try to get through the interviews as soon as possible. However, if they could sort themselves out into groups, like all mechanics in one area and all fitters in another, it would be a help. A well-dressed elderly gentleman caught his eye and asked him if he could do the honours for him in organising the troops.

"My name is George Harrelson and I'll do that for you."

"What did you do in the industry?"

"I was the Shop Foreman in that building I've seen you having renovated."

"Mmmm...." Dick mused and had a further conversation with George "Well, don't you go anywhere," he now said as he walked away.

"Certainly, sir."

Dick returned to the room, which now seemed a lot smaller with so many people in it, and informed the girls what he was doing. He re-arranged the previous seating so as not to get those mixed up with the ones he had already seen, but were waiting for a recall. This meant he had twenty-one candidates for Managerial positions, and felt more relaxed.

He grabbed a quick drink of water and asked the first person to follow him. Before he even sat down, he apologised to the candidate and left the room again. He walked to the reception desk, apologised about the crowds and asked if the restaurant was at all busy or available.

"Although it's open, it's never busy at lunchtimes on a week-day, Mr Shepherd."

"Good, I'm glad. Now would you please speak to the Manager as

I would like to send strong candidates in there, and you can serve them hot drinks, together with a light snack."

"I'm sure the Manager would love that."

"Excellent," Dick said "I'll send to you for directions those I want to wait for me in there, Okay?"

"Yes of course, sir. I'll attend to them for you."

After arrangements made, Dick returned to the room to start, once again, the unenviable task of interviewing, and to his pleasant surprise, he could send twenty-four out of the thirty to the restaurant, of which only five were of the original nine. By now it was 2:30 p.m., which he felt was damn good going.

"I think I should do quick fine-tuning," he said to himself.

He got up and, apologising to the girls, called them to one side. "I'm now on my way to speak to those I have put on a potential short list. I won't be long and if you need me, I'll be in the restaurant. Questions?"

"No, not at the moment," they replied, and Dick said "Okay, until later."

On his way to the restaurant, he stopped the Manager and asked him if he perhaps had a more private room he could use and would also pay for and, if so, could they put chairs and another partition in there for him?

"Yes," replied the Manager "please come with me and I'll show you."

"This room will do just fine, if you can organise a partition."

The Manager left and returned a short while later with three of his staff to organise the panelling to create the divider which Dick required.

Dick had, in the meantime, gone to fetch the candidates and, on return, asked them to each grab a chair and to sort out the seating into their relevant groups.

So far, he was pleased with the overall proceedings.

Chapter Twenty-Two

The First Employees

SO THE FUN started and soon Dick had selected General, Finance, Operations, Factory and Sales Managers. Four others, including George, he offered the positions of Factory Foremen with George being appointed the Team Leader. As he also liked the others he had seen, he asked them to remain in the room with him until he had finished.

"Ladies and gentlemen, thanks so much for coming down here today and I apologise for the time it has taken. All of you seated in this area, although not hired you are, however, on a short list, so please do not give up hope. However, all of those in this group I offered various positions within the company and they accepted. As I'm in urgent need of a General Manager, I'm proud to announce Miss Julia Wilson has accepted my offer," Dick said looking in her direction and everyone applauded.

"Julia, would you mind coming up here, please?"

While standing there, Dick pointing to four other people, one of them a middle-aged woman, and he continued. "These four people will be your Managerial staff members and I would appreciate it if those selected would get to know them now, please. Also, I would like a separate meeting here with all of you and I think a good time would be nine o'clock tomorrow morning," he suggested, and they all agreed.

"Okay, I'll get Gillian to come in here with the Contracts she has prepared for the appointees to signed and witnessed. After that, the four Managers, because I've now appointed you based on your individual capabilities within your various fields of expertise, I want you to carry on with interviewing. Those are the rest of the candidates that are waiting, including the fifteen here in the room with us and, should you perhaps see someone who's not within your realm, please send him or her over to the correct person. Is that all clear?" Dick once again asked them, and they all agreed it was.

"What I suggest you do, to save time and confusion, is to form various groups and start from there. Now you five Managers work for,... sorry, work with me, you can't go home until you interview every person, so what I request you do, is to phone home and inform your respective families you'll be home late. If you don't own a mobile phone, you can use mine."

Dick now asked Julia to accompany him back to see Lucy and Martha to explain to them about what had just transpired. He then asks Gillian to take the Contract forms through to where the other Managers were waiting to sign them before they started their interviewing.

As Dick appointed Julia General Manager, it was only right she should sign her Contract with him. Lucy and Martha would be witnesses. He showed her to a seat and Lucy handed her a Contract to peruse before signing. Once Julia signified she approved of the contract, she initialled all the pages before entering the date and signing on the dotted line. Lucy and Martha followed suit, witnessing by also initialling each page and signing at the end.

When signed and sealed, Dick gave Julia a schematic of all the positions available, including the hired Managers, and said she was to take over from there. She also had to remember each potential married employee, the family were to be three persons or less, and the entire staff complement not to be over two hundred personnel. They were to recruit these two hundred by the end of the evening and none was to leave the building until he had addressed them. He told her he had arranged for them to wait in the restaurant downstairs.

As Dick had now conjured up a plan, he sought after the hotel Manager. "What's the seating capacity of your restaurant?"

"Phew... at a push, I can get in around two hundred and thirty-three. I've only ever achieved that once, and it was a madhouse."

"Mmmm... good news. Please come with me to the restaurant."

When they arrived at the entrance, a lot of the successful interviewees occupied the place..

Dick put his hand on the Manager's shoulder. "I must apologise for seeming to take over your hotel like this and thank you for your forbearance and help. Right, I don't care how much it costs, but I want to book the restaurant now for eight o'clock tonight and please allow for two hundred and nine people. I hope you can do it and if you need to get in outside help, please do so. Can you accommodate me? Because if you can't, please tell me so I can make other arrangements."

Dick had played hardball in the hope it would work as he had no intention of going anywhere else.

"No... no I can do that," said the now excited Manager. "Please give me twenty minutes and I'll get back to you."

"Okay, but before you go, I realise other people are staying in the hotel. Inconvenienced people who must fight their way in through this crowd and,... upset when they find out you can't serve their meals in the restaurant tonight. So here's what I propose. Please tell them you are hosting a major event and the owner of the Company sends his apologies. Then, ask them if they would like to step over the road to the Italian restaurant. Tell them I will foot the bill for all their meals and drinks. Will my proposal pacify them, do you think?"

"That is generous of you and I'm sure they will appreciate it. Thank you," said the Manager and left to attend to everything.

Dick walked around for a while checking everything he had

organised was running according to plan. He walked outside and counted eleven people who were still there, and inside, another thirteen, so he got them all into one group and had a chat to inform how things were progressing.

He listened to some as they told him where and what other car manufacturers they had worked for. Most of the companies they mentioned had either closed down or sold out to foreign countries. This left the employees dead in the water and having to live off benefits which, for most, was embarrassing. Unlike the bloody Government, Dick understood their situation and empathise with them.

By just after 8:00 p.m., they had seen everyone and were thankful the marathon session over.

"Is everyone still here?" Dick asked, and Lucy said, "Yes, as far as I'm aware."

"Okay... can we please make sure all of them are in the restaurant so I can chat with them."

While Lucy organised the interviewees, Dick sought after Julia. He found her in one of the meeting rooms with Gillian, Martha and the other four Managers.

"Well, I'm glad that's over with and good work all of you. I did not envisage we'd get through all in one day. Are there any figures available yet?"

"Julia and I are just about finished and we'll be able to give you those numbers once tabulated," said Gillian.

While he waited he chatted with the other Managers, including George, just to get some further insight into their overall characters and well-being.

"Mr Shepherd,..." said Julia.

Before she could continue, he said: "Please call me Dick."

"Thanks, Dick. We've got those figures now and they are: Factory personnel, which includes George and his three Foremen, plus maintenance crew, equals one hundred and thirty-five for all three shifts. The office staff, including my four plus one receptionist to start off with, and general office staff, is thirty-eight for now. At this stage, regarding cleaning staff, I suggest Gillian looks after that and we pay them a retainer. Also, regarding the lab personnel, well I'd like to speak to you about them as I was not eager to appoint anyone for those positions today. I thought it to be a sensitive issue and wasn't prepared to take a chance. Hope you don't mind? Therefore, the final figure for tonight, and that includes everyone, is one hundred and seventy-three."

"Brilliant," Dick said "This now leaves us enough room to play with, as the employee figure cannot exceed two hundred. Well done you guys, I'm more than happy with that. Also, regarding the lab tech people. Now when you meet Phil, I suggest the two of you recruit those people. Phil should know who he wants. Okay, it's time we ambled over to the restaurant."

As he walked out of the meeting room, he bumped straight into Phil.

"Hello,... by the look on your face I can see you've had a great day," Phil said with a wry smile.

"Well let's put it this way, I'm glad that part is over and done with."

"What part?"

"The interviewing. And now I'm about to take them for supper, so please hurry and come and join us."

"Okay" Phil replied not understanding how it was at all possible "I'll just shoot up to my room and I'll see you down there."

In the restaurant, once he had got them to simmer down, Dick congratulated all on achieving employment once again.

"For those of you with mobile phones, may I suggest you phone home and tell them you will be about another two hours. Please do it now and I'll give you five minutes."

As Phil approached the open restaurant's doors, he saw Dick inside and walked in to join him at his table.

"Ladies and gents, this is my nephew Phil, and he's in charge of the entire operation at the factory until Julia takes over, which shouldn't be too long,"

Phil had already met the girls from the employment agency, so he shook hands with Julia and the other four Managers.

Once they were all in and seated, Dick took a stand in about the middle of the room so they could all hear what he was about to say. He informed them, as the Management staff were in place, they were to report to the hotel by 9:00 a.m. the next morning. The Employment Agency had the details of all the rest and they would receive notifications in the post within the next three to four days.

Together with the notifications which would explain everything they needed to understand, there would be the employment papers. They were to please read and understand the full terms and conditions and the rules and regulations of their employment and sign where showed.

"Now you've heard all that, please eat and drink something before we call it a night. Thank you," Dick said, and they all stood up and clapped. Once seated again almost the constant noise associated with a room full of people talking, together with the sound of clinking glasses, coughing and laughter, started up.

He now found himself with Phil and Julia and noticed the Employment Agency girls weren't there. "Where is Martha and the other two?"

"Lucy and Gillian slipped out and have gone back to the agency to carry on with the paperwork. Martha's gone home, then she will join them later," Julia informed him.

"Oh, all right. I see you two are getting along okay. Is there space enough to make room for Julia in your office until they complete hers?" Dick asked Phil.

"Yes, if she doesn't mind the noise and the constant swearing."

"I've got three brothers and all of them swear like troopers, so it won't bother me, but it might bother him when I start," Julia said, and they giggled.

At 10:35 p.m. Dick got up to address them. After he got everyone to calm down and to be quiet, he said as he had a busy day ahead of him, he was retiring for the evening. He once again congratulated them one and all and said the bar was closing at 11:00 p.m. He bade them all good night.

Although he didn't notice it, they all stood up and clapped as he exited the restaurant. Just as he reached the reception desk, the hotel Manager greeted him. He looked rather flushed. Dick shook his hand and thanked him for his services and asked him to thank all the staff involved.

"I need another meeting room for tomorrow please and I hope I'm not too late in asking?" Dick asked the now exhausted looking Manager.

"How many will there be?"

"Oh, I'd say between fifteen and twenty-five."

"Consider it done."

He thanked the Manager once more and made his way up to his room where he showered before settling down with a whisky and water. "I must find out what the bloody Manager's name is," he said to himself.

At 7:00 a.m. the following morning, Dick and Phil had breakfast together as Phil was always at the site by 8:00 a.m. Once he had left, Dick sat there sipping at yet another cup of tea when he noticed three of the chaps, including George, had arrived. He beckoned them over to come and join him. "Morning boys, would anyone like breakfast?"

They accepted and there was just general chit-chat until all the others had arrived. When they did, they moved across to the meeting room which the Manager had laid on for them. It was there Dick briefed them as to the entire workings of the up-and-coming new business. He swore them all to secrecy and told them, in no uncertain terms, not to even speak to their husbands or wives about what's going on.

"This morning I will ask you to sign a secrecy clause. If it's proved beyond a shadow of a doubt you committed an offence by breaking any of the terms of this clause, you will be sacked, then a security guard will escort you off the property, understood?"

Dick asked, and they all acknowledged they did. He continued. "In fact, and I'm advising you now, it is a chargeable offence should you break any of the terms of that clause. Now,... this clause will stay active until such time as I cancel it."

Carrying on he said they were to report for duty at the factory grounds on the twenty-fourth of the month and also informed them of the available housing. They were to start, as and when they were ready, moving into their new homes after the twenty-fourth of the following month. When he had finished his briefing, he handed the show over to Julia and left the room to phone Phil.

"Hi, listen, Phil. Things are running along at a steady pace here, so is it all right if I bring this lot down there now to look around?"

"If you give me twenty minutes, it should be okay because by then another delivery truck would leave."

"Yeah, that's fine by me. Okay, I'll see you in a half-an-hour."

Back in the room he found a chair, away from Julia, and listened to what she was saying and how she was going about it.

"Excellent choice. Yes, even if I say so myself," he bragged to himself rather chuffed.

A little while later the door opened and in walked the receptionist who tip-toed over to Dick to say, in a quiet voice, the mini-bus had arrived. "Thanks," he whispered back to her.

Julia looked in his direction, so he stood up and walked over to her and addressed everyone in the room. "After hearing all that, you now understand why I chose Julia for the top job," he said giving her a broad smile.

"Okay folks, there is a mini-bus outside which will now take us to the factory, as I want to give you a tour. But please, be aware there are building works still in progress therefore don't expect to see a palatial building with the rolling gardens of Babylon surrounding it when we get there," he said. A shout of laughter greeted this.

Arriving at the factory, they spent as much time with a walk-around inside the building trying to cause as little upset to the work in progress as they could. Apologies here and there and they would move off to a different section and so on until they exited the building at the other end.

Once outside, he took them across to the electrical supply house. Moving on, he noticed a temporary security hut erected at the parking area and, the suppliers had delivered plenty more new cars.

"Shit," he exclaimed to himself "I hope we don't mess this up."

As they approached the hut, Gavin stepped outside and, upon seeing Dick, he stopped, straightened himself upright and saluted him as if he were saluting an army general.

"Oh for fuck sake Gavin, there's no need to go that far," he said to himself.

He walked up to Gavin and shook his hand. "This is the new Management staff who will run the Company, so get a good look at them as they will start here on the twenty-fourth. Let me introduce them to you."

Introductions over, and unable to resist it, he told the story about how Gavin had challenged him when he first got there. "And don't embarrass yourself by it," he said to Gavin "we should hire more conscientious staff like you."

From there they crossed over and walked towards the housing estate where they had changed the entire surroundings. It was looking ever so good even though there was still a lot of builder's rubble around the place.

"This is where you will live rent-free."

"What, the entire staff compliment?" Julia asked in surprise.

"Yes, all of you,... and you won't be paying for electricity either and you can use as much of it as you like. Because of that, I had all the gas supply lines removed from the houses as they will not be necessary and you, Miss Wilson, as you are the General Manager of this Company, you get first choice."

Turning to the others he said, "Sorry, but that's one perk when you're the boss." This followed a little laughter of approval.

"What you will need to do is to appoint a housing person to sort this out for you, but there's still plenty of time yet."

By the time they had finished, it was just after 1:00 p.m. and he suggested they all go for lunch.

While at lunch, he had a good long chat with Julia, after which he was confident enough to go back home the following day, so while still at the table, he booked his flight home. Just as he finished, Phil phoned to say Tom had one more movable, but even bigger, mobile office building and would he like him to deliver it there for them.

"How many desks can you get in there?"

"Tom said with ease it can seat six people plus filing cabinets for each desk."

"Bugger me, how big is this bloody thing?" he asked, and Phil said, "All Tom said is that it's big."

"Is he going to supply the furniture as well?" Dick asked, to which Phil said: "Yes, it comes all-inclusive if you like?"

"Yes, I like. And when can he do this?"

"He says it can still happen this afternoon."

"Righty-ho then. What the hell's he waiting for?" he said, laughing and ended the call.

"I've got office space for you, so if you like, you can start tomorrow, however, there's only space enough for six people. So may I suggest the five Managers? Then one Foreman whom I think should be George, but the decision is yours and not mine. It's your staff," he said. Julia thought for a moment and went the way of Dicks suggestion.

When they arrived back at the hotel, Dick handed the reins over to Julia and said the only person she should report to, apart from himself, was Phil, and once Phil had left the premises, it would only be himself.

"Okay, you've got my business card and you've got the Employment Agency's contact details."

"Yes," Julia affirmed.

"Good. Please don't allow them to rest on their laurels as I would like to get the employment signing stuff over and done with as soon as possible."

"I'll be onto them today."

"Wonderful, and don't forget you've got this lot standing around doing nothing so get them to work," Dick said with a smile which they returned.

"Has this all been surreal for you these past two days or what?" he asked them.

"Well for me it's a case of, please don't wake me up from this dream," replied George.

"You may not realise this but, if you had the qualifications to do the General Managers job, you'd now be in Julia's place," Dick said to George. "Julia," he now said to her "look after this one for me, please. This bloke doesn't know it but,... he's special."

George had a big grin on his face as he looked in Dick's direction.

"Don't you get cocky now," Dick said to him while sporting a big grin himself at which they all chuckled. He stood up to address all the others. "Please ask Julia questions no matter how big or small, or even if you think it's ludicrous and don't forget, until we are operational, Julia will need your full co-operation and support during this trial period which will not be too long either."

"Julia, I've checked with the Manager of the hotel and you guys can stay here for as long as you like and you can also include late night dinner, and the Company will take care of everything but, that's up to each individual. Right folks, if there's nothing else, I'd like to get back to Phil before I fly out tomorrow. It's been nice meeting you all and I'm looking forward to working with you."

They all stood up and shook his hand and thanked him for the opportunity. After saying goodbye, he drove back to the factory and straight to Phil.

"Okay, so you can show me now," Dick said struggling to hide his excitement.

"Show you what?"

"Your machine," he exclaimed, tensing his neck muscles.

"Oh that," Phil said to hide his inner feelings "Follow me then."

They arrived and stopped at one of the assembly desks "Oh bloody hell," Dick exclaimed yet again, but this time as he saw Phil's invention in motion.

"This is so god-damned amazing," Phil said "and I can't stop looking at it in action. It won't be long now before we say goodbye to the mains grid power supply and hello to our own."

"When is it you plan on installing it?" Dick asked, and Phil said, "It should be around the twentieth or the twenty-first, no later."

"Ruddy marvellous what," Dick replied in a somewhat silly voice "I can't wait."

"Are you going to be here when it happens?" Phil asked, and Dick said "If I can, then yes. But if not, I'll be here on the twenty-fourth. Any idea where Tom is?"

"Err,.... yes. He's organising that mobile office for you."

"Oh great, and that's today, you say? Okay, well I'll take another look round the housing area before I go."

"All right, I'll come with you."

"Okay, let's go."

They first walked back to Phil's office to put away a few small magnets Phil had been carrying around on his person before he led Dick around to the unseen side of the office building.

"Here, get in," Phil said pointing at a golf cart.

"That's a good idea."

"Yeah, Tom brought it over and said to use it as and when."

"So the bloke's not just a pretty face then?"

They spent the rest of the day together before going to the hotel for the rest of the night. Julia and staff were still there when they arrived at the restaurant, so they joined them. Phil informed Julia the additional mobile office would be ready in the morning for occupancy. When Dick had finished his drink, he wished them all the best and retired for the evening.

On entering his room, Joel greeted him. He was relaxing on the easy chair with his legs crossed and his long fingered hands interlocked and placed around his left knee. The sight gave Dick the impression the chair would, at any moment, swallow up the little fellow.

"Hello, Joel, and what brings you here?"

"We've admired your progress and decided to give you a present," Joel said, looking ever so uncomfortable in the chair.

"And what have I done to deserve a present?"

"It's for how you handled the entire project to date, and also for the speed at which you operated to get to the position you are in today. For example, look at what you accomplished today. I can assure you no one else on Earth could achieve everything you accomplished so far," said Joel. He held out his hand which contained a small box and gesturing to Dick he should take it.

Dick took the box from Joel, and upon lifting the lid saw it contained a gold ring which had a single word "Nuah" inscribed in the centre.

"What does Nuah mean?"

"That's a good question and I will give you the answer once you settle down in your new home in Argentina."

"Oh, thanks very much," said a deflated Dick.

"Don't upset yourself and be patient. Just wear it with pride and I will honour my word," Joel said, and if he could he'd smile.

"So when should I wear it?" Dick asked, knowing it was a ridiculous question but only realising when it was too late.

"Put it on now and never take it off."

"And when I die, what happens to it then?"

"It goes to the only obvious person, now doesn't it?"

"Yes it does," Dick replied rather foolish. "I realised that as soon as I asked the question."

"I'll be on my way now and as I say, wear it with pride," Joel said as he got up to leave.

"No, wait a moment, please. This ring,... it's not by any chance the one you, if it was you, gave to King Solomon to wear, is it?"

"No," Joel replied "and besides, his ring had the word God engraved on it. So, if you understand anything about that ring, you would realize it represented the authority from beyond your world and the wearer could compel anything or call on that source of Extra-Terrestrial power to do whatever he wished."

"Well yes," Dick replied "I am aware of that and that's why I asked the question."

"All right, fair enough. Now this ring is like that of Solomon's one, in a manner of speaking, but this one is not as powerful. However, wear it with pride and use it correctly and always in a positive light. The same will be for your daughter when her time comes, and so on and so on. Is that understood?"

"Oh yes. Understood."

"Right, I'm on my way but before I go,... wear it with honour and it will serve you well," said Joel. As he concluded his sentence, he disappeared in his usual fashion.

Dick sat down on the edge of the bed and admired the ring and its shape. It was a pentacle and had a pentagram engraved in a circle and in the middle was the name Nuah. On closer inspection, he noticed at the top was his first name. Then at the bottom his surname which followed the contours of the shape of the ring in a much smaller typeface. He concluded they designed his name in this way so as not to overpower the name... NUAH.

"Perhaps this is to be my new name instead of Noah" he thought to himself but wrote it off as being nonsense.

By 9:00 a.m. the following day he was at home and had the rest of the day off. Once he had completed organising the washing of his smalls and other various items, he set about getting the barbecue together which he and the rest of his, what seemed to be an ever-shrinking family, could enjoy when they got home from work.

Dick phoned Chloe to advise her he was home and was making a barbecue and would she please inform the others. Afterwards, he drove into the local village and bought items like pre-prepared coleslaw, potato salad and his favourite, beetroot salad. He did not forget the puddings for, in his book, that would be sacrilege.

They all arrived and by 8:30 p.m. were all filled to satisfaction with food and drink. Later, and to his absolute shock and surprise, Dick discovered his grandniece had done the washing-up of the dishes.

"Are you all right, mad child?" he enquired, and she replied "No. I think I've just suffered a rush of blood to the head."

"Well, how considerate of you, and thank you," he said, and pinched her right cheek, continuing to smile.

Chloe walked in and asked him if he were now relaxed as she had news for him. He said he was, so he sat down at the kitchen table and had a swig of his whisky and water.

"Fire away," he said.

She sat down opposite him but, before she said anything, she too had a swig of her drink. "Remember you asked us to keep you informed about Dominic's mother?"

"Yes, what's happening?"

"Well, she passed away yesterday around five in the afternoon."

"Oh, bugger," Dick exclaimed in response.

"I hope you don't mind, but I organised quite a large bouquet, and I included a card from all of us. Also, I asked the girls in the office to do the same," Chloe advised him "and I paid for that."

"Great, thanks for doing that. I take it Deon knows about this?"

"Yes he does for it was he who Dominic phoned to inform

everyone, and should you need any other information, you must ask him."

That news put a dampener on the rest of the evening even though he hadn't known Dominic's mother, but then he knew little of Dominic himself. Still, it wasn't nice news to receive, for he understood what it was like to lose one's mother through death.

Chapter Twenty-Three

The Art of Studying

FOR DICK, THE next day was all about the simulator. He wanted to start with the learning curve concerning the landing on the Argentine Area 51 runway and also needed to get to grips with the Airbus A400M. This was to find out what the flight envelope (the capabilities of the design in terms of load factor, maneuverability, airspeed, altitude, angle of attack) of the aircraft was before he tried experimenting with his new runway. Even although Joel said it wasn't necessary, he still told Deon no one should disturb him unless it was important.

Dick spent the next six days undisturbed until being informed his new office was ready for him to occupy. They built the structure in an elevated L-shaped configuration above the air-conditioning units. This included the computer control room area which would be the brains behind both simulators, and to round it off, a convenient flight of stairs lead up to the walkway.

This allowed a person to either access one of five different offices, or to access the simulator via a retractable bridge. Next to this, there was a vast open space for the VC10 simulator once it arrived.

While casting an eyeball around the area, he thought about having desks installed in all the offices. This would include telephones, computers, and a wall mounted monitor screen, including camera. It would allow them online meetings with all the relevant businesses around the country and the world if need be. His office would be number one.

As office number three was the biggest, he turned it into a meeting-room, of sorts, and this also was to have a wall-mounted monitor. Office number two would be for Chloe, with Cassie and Rachel sharing office number four. When Kerri and Ivan returned, they would use office number five and the final result of the overall layout, pleased him.

While occupying himself with this, Chloe, Cassie and Rachel were coping with their studies regarding radio, radar and general tower procedures. Considering they were into their early sixties, there was every likelihood they wouldn't put this training to any use, but it gave Dick satisfaction of knowing they were all doing something constructive and were learning something about the business.

The girls thought Dick was unaware about Erica being hard at work, not only studying the road code but also taking driving lessons through a professional driving school. He, however, would surprise them.

Later on in the afternoon, Deon popped in to see him. He said the funeral of Dominic's mother was to be the following day and wondered if he would like to go. "Yes I would and I'll travel with you if that's okay?"

"Sure, Dick. I'll want to leave here at around lunchtime, and as I've got a shed load on my desk that needs clearing, I don't want to stay for the tea and cake afterwards... hope you don't mind?"

"No, Deon, not at all. That will also suit me and besides, I'll be a stranger there to everyone except Dom, so in my case, it's more out of respect for him than for any other reason I should go, I suppose."

"Yes, the same goes for me. Okay, if I don't see you later I'll meet you in reception at one o'clock tomorrow."

Deon made as if to leave the office but, as he got to the door he stopped, turned around and eyed the office and the overall building. "Nice office block you've landed here. What I like the most about it is... there's no one around you."

"I'm not just a pretty face, am I?" Dick said, and they both grinned as Deon left.

As he settled back in his chair, his mobile phone laughed at him and it was Phil.

"Hey, guess what?" Phil asked sounding cheerful, and Dick said "That terrible Zimbabwean dictator has died?"

"No," Phil replied "Want another shot?"

"Mmmm... now let's see," Dick mused "All the illegal immigrants in the country have gone back to their various homelands of their own accord?"

"No," Phil said, now sounding irritated.

"Blast," Dick exclaimed laughing "No, I give up, so tell me."

"Well, you'll like this. I've installed the two generators that will supply electricity to both the factory and the housing estate and,... I'll test them tomorrow."

"I say, that's ruddy marvellous old chap," Dick replied in his best toffee-nosed accent. He now changed back to his normal speaking voice "But I take it you haven't connected them to the supply line yet?"

"No, not yet, but I've learnt a lot about this machine of mine, and I'm damned well-chuffed with myself."

"And so you bloody well should be. You're the only person on this planet who, instead of going down the complicated route when designing something, you went down the bleeding, bloody obvious one. And why? Because you understood it would lead to the answers you were looking for."

They chatted away for a while longer about the generators. Phil also said they now had over one hundred cars in the parking area while Tom had put up a far more substantial guard house for the security staff. This including monitors for the cameras which should be in operation within the next two days.

"Ah, that's fantastic," Dick replied. "Please tell Tom I appreciate it, and how are the offices coming along?"

"Well, as the reception area and all the inside offices are now complete, I've instructed Julia to move in, together with the other four Managers and George as we discussed and I'm leaving it to her to it arrange."

"Yes, and I agree with your decision," Dick said "She's getting paid to do the job so let's see if my choice was the correct one which I'm positive it is."

"Okay, I'll advise how the test run goes."

"All right, but take down this number. It's my new office one and if you can't get hold of me here, it has an answering machine installed. If it's anything urgent, you can call me on my mobile."

"If it's switched on," Phil said and they both chuckled.

Dick recited the number, but before he hung up, he asked Phil to instruct Julia to make sure she installs the same video conference call set-up he had. He gave Phil all those details, and she was to contact him when she was ready.

"Before you go. Have you sorted out the staff who will put your machine together?"

"I've spoken to Julia about it, in fact, and I've even shown her what it is and how it works, but in secret, so she knows the person I'm looking for and she'll advise once she has found any who fit the bill."

"Okay, stay in touch and we'll speak soon. Cheers," Dick said as they ended the call. "Mmmm... seems things going along at a great pace."

There was the familiar light and ever so slight sound Dick was, by now, getting used to, therefore recognising it.

"As I was in the area, I thought I'd pop in to see how you were getting on," said Joel.

"You... in the area? Now that's a bloody joke," Dick replied grinning.

"Well... you know what I mean, don't you?" Joel asked and Dick said "Yes I do, and you already know how I'm doing, so to what do I owe this pleasure?"

"I had nothing better to do, so I showed myself."

"Well that's kind of you to think of me. Question: I don't seem to see any difference now I'm wearing this ring? Are you sure it has the magical powers...? Wait a moment," Dick said in surprise "What was that you said? You've got nothing to do? Well, I don't believe it."

They looked at each other for a moment, then Joel said "If I had the ability to laugh the way you do, I'd join in, but I can't, and don't you go worrying about the ring. You will come to realize when and how it works."

"Oh... all right. I suppose I'll get used to it."

"Yes, you will. Now, the actual reason I'm here is to say we are, once again, pleased with the progress made and with the way you are handling everything."

"Thank you, Joel. You've said so more than once before and I appreciate it every time. It boosts my confidence no end but well, I've said this once today already and I will say it again,.... I'm not just a pretty face."

"Yes," Joel replied "and it's because we gave you more than just that new pretty face."

Dick burst out laughing as Joel had missed the joke.

"How's my child doing?" he asked once he'd got his laughter under control.

"Now don't you go worrying about them. They're doing great."

"That's good news, Joel."

"I'll let you and the girls, as you call them, get back to your studying. I'll see you when next I've got nothing to do," Joel said and in a flash he disappeared in his usual way.

"Thanks, Joel," Dick shouted out.

The door opened and in walked *the three must have beers,* and they sat down. "Yes, that's them" Dick exclaimed to himself "The Three Must Have Beers. That's an excellent nick-name for the girls".

"So where's the little man?" Chloe asked Dick who replied with a wicked grin "In his usual place. Why, have you forgotten?"

"No, I'm talking about Joel," Chloe said "We heard you talking to him."

"Oh, that little man."

"Yes, that little man. What else did you expect me to mean?" Chloe asked, and he looked at her with a naughty twinkle in his eyes.

"I can't take you any-bloody-where without you coming out with some or other sexual connotation."

"You've got to admit you enjoy them."

"Okay, once again, where's the little man? We heard you shouting to him," Chloe asked again, ignoring his comment.

"You've missed him."

"Darn, that's a pity. What did he want, anyway?" Chloe asked and Dick said "He came to say how pleased they were with the progress so far."

"That was nice of him."

"Yes it was, and I thanked him. So why are you all here?"

"We are taking a well-earned break," replied Cassie.

"Oh, okay. Well, now you are here, check these drawing, and if you don't like what I've come up with,... tough," he said pushing a plan of the offices in front of their faces for their perusal. "If there's anything else you think you may need for your office, place the order."

"Okay," Chloe replied "I'll check mine out."

The others followed, and he thought he'd join them. In Chloe's office, they all admired the similarity to what they had seen in his office.

"The same," he said, and he showed them the meeting-room and the other offices and they all seemed thrilled with everything.

As they stood on the walkway, Rachel asked if he could fly the simulator. He invited them to go inside where he would show them what it could do and asked: "Who's the better pilot out of the three of you?"

"Why?" asked Cassie, and Dick said, "Well, I have a vacant seat on my right and someone with a little knowledge about flying can sit there."

"In that case, we must wait for Kerri to come home," replied Rachel.

"Well, why don't you take it in turns, and as you, Chloe, are the closest, please pull up the co-pilots chair. You two can sit on those seats behind you," Dick instructed them. "Now nothing will mean anything much to you but I'll go through some motions, anyway. But, I won't be able to keep it simple because simple does not exist in a cockpit. Understood?"

"Yes," they replied.

"Right, you are learning the ropes of being an Air Traffic Controller, which is a good thing but remember, one of your main tasks is to stop aeroplanes from crashing into each other. If you do that, you've won, but if they do crash into each other, you've lost, and the only redeeming feature is, if it's a good enough crash, at the subsequent Board of Enquiry, you would be the only ones there," Dick said, and although confused, the girls seemed happy enough with this explanation.

He also informed them the reason there should be an Air Traffic Controller was a little unclear. The chances of two aeroplanes being at the same place, time, and height, was so mathematically remote, it wasn't worthwhile considering.

"All you do, as an Air Traffic Controller, is to force the planes down narrow corridors. This now increases the risk of a collision and therefore justifies the job of an Air Traffic Controller to keep them apart," he said straight faced. The confused looks on their faces had grown in intensity, so he burst out laughing.

"You little bastard," Cassie exclaimed and punched him on his arm.

"Now before we carry on, I want you to pretend you are all pilots. Not Captains. Don't get carried away,... just pilots. The lowest form of life on a flight deck. No, no, no,... disregard that last comment. I will be the Captain and not because I want to show off or anything like that, but your life is in my hands, and one perk with your job as a pilot, you get a good seat in the front but, one snag is, you are much closer to a crash than everyone else."

"What the hell are you talking about?" Chloe asked confused, to which Dick replied: "Listen and learn."

"But we're not pilots, so what's the point?" Chloe asked and Dick replied "Hey now, you were the ones who wanted to see what goes on in here, not so?"

"Yes, but I don't understand why you are going down this path," Chloe uttered.

"Can't you pretend and enjoy your education?" Dick asked as if he were addressing the village idiot.

"Oh okay, but don't confuse me," said Chloe, and he carried on explaining in such a manner to make it easier for them to understand.

"From what you have learnt so far, you already understand there are two types of airspace. They are important because, if you fly outside controlled airspace in the uncontrolled airspace, you fly VFR - Visual Flight Rules. It means you, as pilots, must focus your gaze out the window to make sure you don't crash into somebody coming the other way."

"Now an example is, if you wanted me to fly you tonight from here to, let's say Worcester, the answer is negative, and why? Well because it's dark. I don't fly in the dark. Birds don't fly in the dark either and I see no point in tempting fate so tomorrow, assuming it wasn't pissing down rain and is a nice day - and as you've probably noticed, birds don't fly in heavy rain either - we would fly VFR from here to Worcester." Dick explained to his now attentive pupils.

"Once in the air, we'd follow the A30 in a North East direction until we see the M4. We'd follow it until we reach the M5, following it until we reach our destination."

"Yes, but why are we looking for these roads?" asked Cassie.

"Because you have to see where you are going. If you don't, you'd probably end up going in the opposite direction and finish up maybe somewhere in France. Therefore, we would fly low-level so we could navigate by rivers, railway lines, roads, etc. and if need be,.... coastlines."

"But now please take careful note,... you cannot fly in cloud. From the ground, they might come across as being nice, white and fluffy but if you fly into cloud, it's like flying through The House of Horrors because it's dark. Yes, it can get dark inside a cloud, and because there could be other clowns coming down the motorway, you avoid cloud like the plague. Remember the rules, you must peer out of the window to make sure you don't hit somebody else," he reiterated. "Now these rules only apply to the small passenger carriers and not to the big airliners."

"So for instance, if you were to fly a big airliner from here to Charles de Gaulle Airport, you'd be a little upset if you went to Guernsey. From there to Jersey, linking up with the French A84. You now follow this road until you find the French A13 which, with luck, will take you to your destination, although all the while you expected to fly higher and faster above the clouds," Dick explained to the now puzzled and quiet faces gazing at him.

"You, therefore, fly IFR—Instrument Flight Rules—which is inside these corridors so you don't have to worry about the safety of the aircraft in that aspect. Now I'll give you a quick insight what I mean," he said, and turned himself around to face the instrument console.

"When we fly, there is only one method we use, and that's known as the quadrant method. Quadrant flying,... to dive, you push this side-stick controller forward. Right to turn right, left to turn left and, to climb, you pull it back towards you, okay. So that's the quadrant method of flying," he explained to the best of his teaching capabilities. He continued.

"Now there's only one other aircraft that's different and that's a helicopter. A helicopter has a single stick, but it's between your legs. The rule is you can do what you like with it but you mustn't hold it steady,... you just move it. You keep moving it all the time and you put on phenomenal amounts of power and it defies all known law and lifts off, whereas it should, of course, screw itself into the ground," he said making them all laugh.

Once the laughter had subsided, he gave an example when IFR was at its most valuable was during landing. "When it's foggy, you can't see the landing lights, so you use an instrument landing system to get you down. It has two needles. One point's left or right, when you come in, and you turn the aircraft left or right until it hangs straight, the other needle points high or low, to show whether you're too high or too low on approach. So you pull and push until you stay horizontal and until the two needles cross in the middle," he instructed his once again attentive pupils while pointing at the dials at the same time.

"Right, let's pretend you and I are flying the plane. I will fly the needles and you will call the heights as we fall towards the ground. Now we're in thick fog doing about two hundred and ninety kilometre per hour, and the wipers are going well but that's neither here nor there because you can't see anything, anyway. You will call out the heights calmly and clearly as we dive towards the ground while I keep the needles crossed." Dick continued talking to a somewhat stupefied faces.

"When we approach forty feet, you calmly and clearly call... FORTY FEET," Dick screamed which it made the girls jump.

"For fuck's sake, don't do that you bastard," Cassie cried out and once again punched him on his arm while he carried on laughing.

"So, there in front of us are the lights. If we can't see the lights at forty feet, full power on and we climb straight ahead. Go around and do it again which means we have overshot the runway. If we go around a second time and it doesn't work again, forget it. We go to another nearby airport where there's no fog, and we have diverted. It's as easy as that," he said.

"However, at the Argentine Area 51 runway we cannot do that, so we must get it right the first time around," he said looking at them and asked if there were questions.

"Why can't you go round at the Argentine airfield?" asked Rachel.

"Well, it's because there's this one almighty big mountain in front of you on your landing approach and, not forgetting the one that's on your immediate left. If you screw up, you'll end up flying straight into the bloody thing as the aircraft may not gain sufficient speed and height to avoid it. So, it's imperative to get it right the first time. That is one of two main reasons we used up as much ground as we could to construct the runway."

"And how long is that going to be?" Rachel asked again and Dick said "It should end up being about seven kilometres long."

"Bloody hell, that is long," Rachel exclaimed, and Cassie asked "How many miles is that?"

"Four and a half miles which is twice the average distance of the average airport runway, so I hope we encounter no problems. Right, theory lesson now over, who wants to fly the plane?"

"Now hang on a minute," Cassie interjected, "you said two main reasons. What's the other one?"

Dick turned his attention towards his sister. "Because the air on some occasions can become thin or less dense, this extra length of the runway will afford us a longer take-off run and, it will also allow for a higher landing speed, if we should so need it. Okay, now who wants to fly the plane?

All three of them answered together, like three people shouting for beers at the barman. As Cassie was by now in the co-pilots seat, Dick suggested she should go first. By the time they had finished learning as much as they could in the art of flying an aircraft, via a simulator, it was already dark outside.

The next morning he dressed in a dark suit and did this to save time, therefore there would be no need to come home again before he and Deon left for the funeral. He spent the morning contacting all the overseas suppliers for he needed to find out how the production and deliveries in each company were progressing before concentrating on the local suppliers. This, he wanted to put into good practice.

If the pressure's not kept on the suppliers and not kept on their toes, they had a nasty habit of wandering off. They would go off in a different direction putting the entire operation in jeopardy and, with all the different components he required, it would only take one to cause a complete system failure. He was not prepared to accept this at all as good money was being spent to avoid any such travesties from occurring.

At 1:00 p.m. Dick and Deon met in the reception area as arranged. Dick was always a stickler for not being late, so he made sure he was there first. They travelled together in Deon's company car and arrived at the Church in good time and saw Dominic in the distance. They walked over to him to pay their respects and a little while later they entered the Church. Dick couldn't help but reflect, yet again, on when and why he had last attended or gone to Church.

"Now let's see," Dick mused "weddings and funerals. That's right. Only weddings and funerals, out of respect for the individual, are the only times I attend Church."

Dick had no time for Bible punchers or people who acted all "holier-than-thou" and were, in fact, all a bunch of hypocrites. He despised them all. If they were not busy organising wars, they were bonking each other's neighbours' wives or husbands and, if they were not committing this adulteress act, they used illegal methods to relieve someone of their hard-earned money, or even worse still, the priests were violating little boys and girls. Sometimes, if the little girls were not being raped, in other so-called religions they were having their sexual organs mutilated while still in a state of consciousness and, when they turned eight or nine years old, they could be married off to men of forty-plus years old. If it so happened the little girl is raped to death on her so-called wedding night, the entire world turned a blind eye to it. All of this, and a lot more, done in the name of... God!

"What sort of sick perverted people carry on like that?" he would always ask himself.

These subjects, from time to time, were always one area which seemed to whirl around in his mind. Entering a church would always jog his memory and never ceased to make him uncomfortable.

"A bunch of damned A-holes they are, the whole bloody lot," he cogitated. "No wonder Joel and his clan are going to, once again, wipe out the vast majority of humanity."

He wondered if he would ever change his beliefs to how most of the world's populace operated? Yes, but only once Joel and his family had done what they were setting out to do. This time, when humanity had redeveloped itself, everyone could now live in peace and harmony and be free of any forms of religious practices.

Should this not happen, however, Joel had assured him they would, once and for all, eradicate the entire human race. In such a scenario it would seem Joel and his family had failed in creating a decent creature, a decent human being. Dick had agreed with him and asked if he could be there to witness the event should it ever happen.

After the funeral procession, Dick and Deon said their goodbyes to Dominic explaining they had to get back to work.

"Now you, young man, you take as much time off as you require, okay."

"Thanks Mr Shepherd, and thanks once again to both of you for coming along today. I appreciate it."

They drove away and travelled in silence for a small part of the journey back to the airport until Dick thought of something to say.

"I don't mean to offend you, Deon, but I hate, or rather detest, having to go to a Church. The entire meaning from centuries ago, in fact since Mary Magdalene herself started what we understand today as the Church, is no longer practised and the a-holes who run it these days are a bunch of bloody boneheads. Sorry if your perceptions are otherwise."

A little while later Deon plucked up the courage. "I have to admit

I'm from a religious family but,... I've always been on the fence with Jesus Christ and God and the whole nine yards in praying. You say Mary Magdalene started the Church?"

"Yes, the Church as you understand it today and,... she married Jesus and they also had children. Now you put that in your pipe and smoke it. So, if you would like more insight into Bible studies,... I'm your man."

"Where on earth do you get all this info from?" Deon asked, sounding surprised.

"Although I classify myself as being an extrovert, I'm not the type to have, what I call, verbal diarrhoea. I prefer to read, listen and focus and when I speak, I try not to spout a load of claptrap, like a typical career bullshitting politician but yes, I mean that on a serious note and not when I'm jacking around."

"If you want to learn a lot about religion, do yourself a favour and read the Old Testament, it's even got aliens and their flying saucers in there. I've advised many people about this but they're too bloody lazy or sceptic. Hell, they don't even bother to peek, let alone study. Leave the New Testament alone for that's another kettle of fish altogether—if you'll pardon the pun."

"What's the difference between the two?" asked Deon.

"I'll try my damnedest to explain it so you will understand. Right, now liken the Old Testament to that of a fruitcake. Now that fruitcake is for everyone and when it's handed to you, it so happens you don't like all the ingredients in it so you take from it only what you like. Now I'll carry on speaking hypothetically and say you only like the raisins in the fruitcake and nothing else. Okay?"

"Yes okay," replied Deon.

"All right, this is my view. If the original fruitcake is the Old Testament, what you have now removed from it in this hypothesis are the raisins and these raisins have now become the New Testament. Am I making sense?"

Deon thought about this for a while before he would commit himself to another question. "Okay, say this is true,... what has happened to the Old Testament, the original fruitcake before I got hold of it?"

"Well, nothing," Dick replied in all sincerity. "Nothing has happened to it because the powers that be forgot about it, or rather, they want *you* to forget about it. These controlling bodies will never in a million years tell you to buy a copy. They don't want you to study. They don't want you enlightened to the actual truth, and that's because it will cost them a bunch of money."

"Could you give me an example?"

"I can, but I can't explain everything now in one go about what happened hundreds, even thousands of years ago," Dick replied "so let's start with Jesus, one of the worlds first motivational speakers, and Mary Magdalene as examples. When they discovered Jesus had married her, they removed that reference from the Bible, however, they found recent evidence in an old manuscript in the British Library, item seventeen thousand two hundred and two, which proves it."

"Two letters dating back to 550 AD were attached to a book written by monks who came across these in the sixth century. The letters claimed the manuscript contained a dangerous encoded message about Our Lord, Our God, Who Became Flesh and Blood. This message they deliberately censored because it told the story of their marriage. Believe me, I'm not making this up. As I have said to so many others, be my guest and do research yourself," Dick advised him.

"Well now, that sounds like some serious stuff you've got there," Deon replied. "Mmmm... you say Jesus was one of the world's first motivational speakers, what do you mean by that?"

"Well, you may not be aware of this but at the time there were quite a few like *him* roaming around the place, so came the time when the people decided there could only be one,... they chose Jesus, the same like they did with the gods. Someone decided there were too many gods, so they dropped the 'S' in gods. Now they capitalised the 'G' and came up with a new one. One God! There you have it so yes, Jesus became *thee* number one motivational speaker. Like the motivational speakers you get today,... same approach but a different message, that's all."

"Fancy that. Would you by any chance have another example?" a

"All right, Deon try this one for size. You've always heard them talking about Joseph, right?"

"Right," Deon agreed.

"Well, would you believe strong evidence suggests Joseph is Jesus himself and that Aseneth was Mary Magdalene? and further evidence found suggests Jesus' father was Pantera, although I believe his father was an alien, but Pantera was probably an alien, anyway, perhaps even a human-alien hybrid, but be that as it may although not inconceivable."

"Now I've already said Jesus married Mary, and they had children but here's another thing. Jesus' followers depicted him as the sun and Mary as the moon, and now get a load of this—Mary was also co-founder of Christianity."

"What," Deon exclaimed. "If this is all true, why did they not include all this in the New Testament?"

"It's a case of don't do or believe the written word in the scriptures but do as I do and say and command of you, and if you reward my Church by putting money into the plate, I won't have grievous harm performed upon your person. Know what I mean? Oh, and who the hell in a so-called man's world wants' a woman at the helm? Makes you think, doesn't it?" Dick informed him and continued.

"Now for me, I liken the bible to that of Chinese whispers—and why? Well it's simple. We were taught that Jesus was born in

Nazareth, correct? Well if that's the case, why did Matthew and Luke say Jesus was born in Bethlehem and not Nazareth?" Dick asked and continued.

"It's because according to the prophecies about the Messiah and the Hebrew Bible, the Messiah is supposed to be born in the city of David, which is Bethlehem. Now don't forget, everything taught to you about Jesus comes from the gospels. These were written by Matthew, Luke, Mark and John nearly one hundred years *after* the crucifixion and,... they contain little or nothing about Jesus' life before he became a profit. Remember what I said—Chinese whispers," Dick said and, once again, continued.

"This is something else you may not be aware of but Jesus came from a large family. He was one of eleven brothers and sisters. The reason his siblings 'disappeared' is that of Jesus' mother giving birth to him while being a virgin. This story, remember, was only reported in two gospels, Matthew and Luke and nowhere else."

"Why, therefore, with this miraculous event was it not more widely reported? It's because she wasn't a virgin. It's as simple as that. This was all an attempt by Jesus' followers to justify their belief in him as the Hebrew Messiah and, there are a lot of other facts falsified to protect the Jesus followers fellowship."

"Over the years, the 'church' writes out Jesus' siblings because people don't like to think Mary might have given birth to anyone other than Jesus, so the 'church' explains them away as being

Joseph's offspring by other women. There are a few gospels that purposely left this out of the new testament because they were written by Jesus' one brother Thomas, known as The Infancy Gospel of Thomas."

"Now one thing mentioned in there about Jesus is that as a five-year-old boy playing with his young friends is that one of them purposely bumped into him, but what Jesus did, or rather said, is what will blow your mind. He said to that boy 'you'll go no further on your way' and the child falls down dead, but what is not said or explained is what actually killed the boy. So yet another example of the 'church' not wanting to give you the truth."

"Phew... you've left me dumbstruck," Deon said sounding confused.

"I'm not finished," Dick said and continued "Jesus was a mortal, no more, no less. Remember, like the bible itself, 'The Word of God', written in many languages, but it's up to mankind—yes, I'm saying mankind and not man-person as some absolute arsehole of a leader of one of the American countries said not all that long ago. Anyway, it's up to mankind to interpret them and not for the 'church' to tell the masses what they think it is. So, you've also heard so-called men of God denounce prostitution, adultery etcetera, but what they have omitted to tell you,... it's rife in the Bible."

"Oh yes, do yourself another favour Deon, and check out a bloke who called himself The Bishop of Egypt, but the one from centuries ago, I forget his actual name now. He'll give you a good insight into today's bullshit scriptures and how it was he who decided what should go into the New Testament and what should not and he edited it to his liking as well, for shit's sake. Remember, bullshit baffles brains, Deon, and there're a lot of brains out there full of bullshit... believe me."

"Now here's something else that should wake you up. It's about Moses and how he and his people escaped by God supposedly parting the Red Sea and dear old Pharaohs men got caught up in it when God drowned them out,... right?"

"Yes," replied Deon.

"Well now this is what happened," Dick continued. "Moses crossed on the marshy area known as the Reef Sea, east of the Nile Delta near the coast of the Mediterranean Sea. The Bible got it all wrong, or rather the bloke who read the story about this happening, well he spiced it up to his liking. It's his bullshit made-up version teachers taught the likes of you and I in Sunday school."

"Well, it had nothing to do with divine intervention at all, but by nature itself. Moses was in the right place at the right time. Now this caused it. A large volcanic eruption took place near Santorini, Crete, creating massive tsunamis. When the water rushed in to fill the void, it sucked the water in from all surrounding coastlines, which included the Nile Delta and this gave Moses twenty minutes to cross over with ease. When Pharaoh's men arrived, so did the tsunami which, would you believe, drowned ninety-nine percent. Amazing," Dick retorted "Hey, I nearly forgot. Have you heard of or about, the Borgias?"

"No," Deon replied "Who the hell are the Borgias?"

"Now this is another beauty of a Pope you should check and read about. This bloke, through absolute devious means, became the Pope and, whilst in power, he and his family became history's most notorious family through lust, corruption and murder. This, of course, was all done in the name of God. Oh yes, and the brother loved to bonk his sister—not that she wasn't in agreement you understand."

"The father, who was the Pope, well this 'Holy Man' bonked any woman who moved in front of him for shit's sake, and all this while his wife was in the next room," Dick exclaimed. He continued. "This Pope also stole as much money or wealth as he could from the people and,... should anyone get in his way, well that person met his or her demise. Now don't forget,... everything is carried out in the name of God,... right?"

"It wants to make me puke. It's because of all the double standards carried out by so-called Christians, or people of God, or God-fearing people, or whatever the hell they want to call themselves. All of this behaviour is, of course, still being played out today. Oh yes, check out the Medici Popes. Another wonderful bunch of conniving hypocritical bloodthirsty sods.

Now here's one last thing. Do yourself another favour and find out why they removed the Book of Enoch from the Bible in 400AD. It will blow your mind."

As Dick finished his history lesson, they entered the driveway of the airport. "So, are you enlightened?" he asked Deon.

"Errmmm... more confused than anything else."

"Well if confused, don't take my word for it but do as I've said to so many others and get a little studying under your belt. I'm sure your eyes will come out on stalks. The art of my studying found that many people researched the bible long before I started, so I picked up on this."

"These were educated people, discerning, or even astute if you like. They included Jewish Rabbi's and people of the cloth from all different races, creeds and colours, and being both men and women. I also learnt a tremendous amount from the archaeologist who've been digging up things buried many thousands of years ago, but that's another story. So, remember what I said—I'm not making this stuff up. It's all there in black and white for the entire world's population to check, read and study."

"But remember this," Dick said as Deon parked the car. "The reason nobody today, or even yesterday, has done anything about this is because of all the money that's involved. This greed is driven by hypocrites all over the world. Now everything I've told you be the mere tip of the iceberg. No, really it is, for it goes much deeper. Much, much deeper. In fact, I could speak to you for the next two days non-stop about it and not get anywhere near the end of it all. But in saying that, there's one thing that amazes me more than anything. It's the people... countless millions, who would prefer to eat a bucketful of bullshit before even contemplating drinking a teaspoon full of the truth."

As they got out of the car, he thanked Deon for the lift and said he was going home to change into something more comfortable. Deon laughed and advised him not to let the girls in the office see his comfortable attire.

Once Dick arrived back in his office, he noticed a light flashing on his new office telephone and wondered what it was. He realised that it was a message, so he pushed the relevant button and heard Phil's voice asking him to phone him as soon as he could. So he wasted no more time and dialled the number.

"Hello," said Phil, and Dick asked "You phoned and you've got good news?"

"Shit, good news you say. It's brilliant news," Phil replied, and Dick said "Okay, don't keep me in suspenders. What's the big deal?"

"Remember the test on the generators I said I would run? Well, it was indescribable," Phil exclaimed "It went a billion times better than I ever expected it to."

"Joel said you had a perfect design there, now didn't he?" Dick pointed out, and Phil replied sounding elated "Yes, but I didn't expect the results I got."

"Well if it's that good, you'd better check at governing the ones going into the cars, otherwise, when the drivers accelerate away at a high rate of speed, they may end up on the back seat," Dick said laughing.

"Yeah, I've thought about that so I will do some serious testing before we let the first car go," said Phil, and Dick asked "First car go? That sounds like something the French eat."

"What?" Phil replied confused.

"First car go... as in escargot... snails? Wakey-wakey."

"Oh, that. Sorry, my thoughts were otherwise occupied, I'm afraid."

"Never mind."

"Okay, got to go and I'll speak to you once I've done more testing," Phil said as they ended their call.

Chapter Twenty-Four

The Rewards of Gained Knowledge

AS IT WAS now approaching 4:00 p.m., Dick picked up the phone and dialled Felipe's number. After what seemed to be a long while, a young female voice answered the phone. In broken English, she advised him Felipe was at the construction site and please phone him on his cell phone. Within moments, Felipe answered and explained to him how far they were.

They had already completed the main feeder road (something which Dick could not get his head around). The digging up of the runway had already started, and they had advanced to such a degree the amount of soil already removed resembled a mini mountain and ran at ninety degrees to the main mountain itself. Felipe also advised Dick the alterations to the farmstead would take about another week before being habitable.

"Dick, you must come and see the progress for yourself."

"Yes I will, and I'll advise when I can make it. Tell me, are you two still getting your money transfers okay?"

"Yes Dick, there's no problem at all, thank you."

"How's Juan doing?"

"He's doing great. He's at the runway big dig at the moment."

"Good. Well, tell him I said hello and I'll see you in about two weeks' time, but I'll confirm with you first, okay?"

"Yes, thanks, Dick and I'll speak to you soon."

Once again Dick locked himself up in the simulator averaging sixteen hours per day. On the third day, Julia contacted him and spoke at length about how she and her team were doing. She said they were making the most of an uncomfortable situation because of the construction, but once completed, the business would settle down to being operated in the manner for which they had designed the building.

Julia also said she was more than half-way through hiring of what she now referred to as 'the delicate staff' for the assembly of Phil's machine. Dick said if she needed peace and quiet for the training, she was to hire a room at the hotel. All costs accrued would be for Phil's account.

"What I'd also like you to organise is a training session with the Nippon boys," Dick instructed Julia "together with the staff who will operate all the equipment they are installing. I would appreciate it if you do this before they go home once they've completed their task. Our boys need to gain as much knowledge as possible from them."

Julia agreed to this and said she would liaise with Phil regarding all the training sessions. She also said the new Company letterheads, business cards and general office stationary were due for delivery within the next few days.

"Have you found someone yet who will be in charge of the Housing Estate?"

"I've got three great candidates lined up and I have to decide who the best one is."

"Good," Dick replied. "You should hire him or her as soon as so he or she can become involved with the rest of Tom's work. That way, become familiar with the surroundings before the staff moves in, and please don't let, whoever that person is, forget they are to get in touch with the council regarding collection of the household rubbish and general waste."

"There might be a stumbling block there because of the estate being private property but, maybe not. Also, please make sure each home is at least fifty to seventy-five percent furnished, and with good stuff. Perhaps pay for the services of a professional designer, or whatever they call themselves, to give advice, but I'll leave that in your capable hands to hand over to the Housing or Property Manager or whatever preferred title you decide is more apt."

Julia had made a complete list of all his instructions and said she would get back to him as soon as she had answers.

"Now tell me, Julia, have you ordered one of those video conference call set-ups?"

"Well strange you should ask, Dick, because it's being installed as we speak, as is the one in the Boardroom. I'm sitting in the reception area at the moment because my office is in such a mess."

"Brilliant, I'm glad you're on the ball and it sounds like I've made the right positive choice in hiring you."

"Thanks for that. As you have used the 'p' word, may I say how much I admire your positive attitude in everything you say and do. Not one person I've met comes to mind who has it in the same way you do... perhaps you're unique."

("It has got to be the ring," he thought.)

"Thanks, Julia, but I look at it this way. Having a positive attitude may not solve all your problems but it sure will annoy enough people to make it worth the effort,.... if you get my drift?"

"Oh yes, one hundred percent. Would you mind if I use your statement in the training sessions?"

"If you feel it would be of benefit, then yes, by all means, please do." They chatted a while longer before ending the call and he spent the rest of the day back in training in the simulator.

The following day was quiet and nothing untoward happened,

but the girls had other ideas. They organised a barbecue as a surprise event for a special announcement. Dick, though, might have other ideas. After the mini feast, Erica approached her grandmother and asked if she may use the car to take Robert home.

"What?" Dick uttered. His voice rang out in clear shock and disbelief. "Did nothing sink into your brain the other day? Didn't I say you could not drive until you had your licence?"

In silence, she took out her purse and produced her Drivers' Licence. Much to Dick's pretended embarrassment, everyone erupted in laughter and clapping. Then, as if in unison, the girls chanted 'Got-cha', to yet more laughter. He stood up, walked over to Erica and gave her a big squeeze and congratulated her. As he made to walk away, he pinched her on her left cheek which resulted in a huge screech.

"You're still not using that car," he said to her.

"But uncle Dickie, you said..."

Before she finishes, he took her by the arm all the way to his larger-than-life heated quadruple garage. Opening one of the four big doors, he pointed to a covered article towards the back.

"What's that?" she asked.

"Have a look," Dick instructed her. As curiosity overwhelmed her, she walked over to the large article and stood next to it.

Dick said, "Well, remove the bloody cover, will you."

By now everyone was standing at the opened garage door looking in as they were just as curious as Erica and not having any idea what was going on. She pulled the cover until it revealed the hidden object. She looked at her granduncle, then looked at what was there before looking back at him once more.

"Is this mine?" she asked feeling overwhelmed.

"I believe it is... Got-cha back," Dick exclaimed and burst out laughing.

All of them looked at him in amazement as they did not understand how he had put the car in the garage and covered it up all in secrecy.

"And I hadn't a clue what this little madam was doing,... right? I've had this in mind all along and I've kept tabs on her progress and yes, even on her driving test and her Driving Licence she received yesterday."

"I told you it would be difficult to keep this from him," said Cassie.

"Well how on earth did you keep track?" asked Chloe.

"Vee haf vays und means, jah?" Dick replied in the worst German accent.

"Now listen here young lady. You can be the best driver on the planet but, believe you me, the rest of the world comprises millions of a-holes, all of whom are under the mistaken belief they too are the best. So please, reason not only of yourself when driving, but understand what's going on in their pee-wee brains. OKAY." Dick shouted the last instruction as he tossed the keys to her while looking at her with wide-open eyes.

"Yes, okay Uncle Dickie."

"Right, go on. Get out of here," Dick ordered. "I've taken care of the insurance, a printout of which is in the glove compartment." This he said over his shoulder as he turned around to walk back into the house.

Two days later he arose early to a bright cloudless day, and with great joy in his heart, for his beloved daughter would return around 9:00 a.m. that morning, therefore he wasted no time in getting over to his office long before then.

Just like an old mother-hen would, he checked his daughter's office was neat and tidy and nothing was missing from it. He even switched on the conferencing call unit to make sure it was working, but then it always was.

Dick faffed on over here, then faffed on over there until such a time there was nowhere else to faff. He now realised he was acting like a fool, so he decided to just settle down behind his desk and wait but waiting was not one of his strong points. As it was now only 7:30 a.m., he had to find something to do to take his mind off waiting for his daughter's arrival.

"Aaaarrrgh," he screamed out loud.

He rushed out to his car, drove back to the house and loaded his drum kit into it, and before anyone noticed what was going on, he drove back to the hangar. He laid out the rubberised non-slip mat in the part of the area reserved for the VC10 simulator and assembled his drum kit on it. Before connecting anything to the bass drum, he tuned the heads, starting with the snare drum as he always took good care of his kit.

What would be a half-day session dedicated to tuning the kit, now took him only a quick thirty minutes. He started by fitting the two tom-toms to the bass drum, then the double bass-drum pedals, before erecting the high-hat stand and the five other cymbals stands and cymbals. Once those were all in place, and for no rhyme or reason, he affixed the music stand to the front of the bass drum if only to perhaps fill up a little more time. He now erected the floor tom-tom in its place.

When he had completed the setup, he ran across all the drums with a pair of B5 drumsticks and, once satisfied the tuning was correct, he picked up the pace. The loudness levels grew in intensity and, because of the amount of sheer energy he put into it, in no time at all he broke out in a sweat.

Dick finished by doing a para-diddle on the snare drum and high-hat before switching to a single beat drum roll on the snare drum. He now picked up the pace until he reached his limit, then reversed this process and brought it back down to a slow enough speed until he stopped by ending with a rim-shot. He congratulated himself.

As he put the sticks down, he heard applause coming from behind him on the other side of the hangar and noticed he had attracted quite an audience. He looked at his newfound groupies and bowed in their general direction, picked up the sticks and offered them to anyone who might wish to have a go.

There were no takers, and glad he was too, for he liked no one to fool around with his drum kit. By now it was 9:15 a.m., so he made his way to the reception area to check up on the planes arrival.

"Was that you making that noise?" Chloe asked coming down the stairs.

"What noise?"

"Don't fool with me," she replied irked. "It was you."

"So why did you ask?" Dick admitted "Anyway, I wanted to get in some practice as I haven't played for quite a while."

"You mean killing time while you wait for your child to arrive."

"Mr Shepherd, your daughter's plane has just landed," he heard the receptionist say.

"Thank you."

"Oh yes, I was right," Chloe mocked.

As the plane came to a halt, he stood in line with the door and, as he waited there for it to open, he was grinning like a Cheshire cat and it seemed like an age before the door opened. The stairs uncurled their folded-up shape before dropping towards the ground ready for people to disembark placing their full weight upon them.

"Hello, Dick. Excited to see your daughter?" Helen called down from the top of the stairs beaming.

"Yes, I am. I hope you brought her back with you in one piece?"

As he finished asking, Kerri appeared, and before walking down the stairs, she gave Helen a hug. She walked to her father where they embraced and their hug took so long, Ivan had to make a comment.

"Is this going to take long?" he asked, and the two of them giggled and hugged more.

"Let's stand like this a wee while longer and see what happens," he whispered to her.

So they did until they heard a raucous row coming from the top of the stairs. John, Helen and Allan all shouted playful obscenities at them which prompted Ivan to join in. As they relinquished their embrace, there was a loud cheer accompanied by clapping. Dick decided it appropriate to flash a finger or two in their general direction, but this action caused even more glee.

When he had allowed Kerri and Ivan to go on their way, he climbed on board to say hello to the crew. He informed them he was going to Argentina for a few of days leaving on or about the twenty-eighth, should they be available and interested in taking him?

"Yes, we would love to take you," John replied "Do you want us to book the flight for you when we get back to base?"

"No, leave it as I haven't as yet made final arrangements for you see, I've got quite a lot on my plate at the moment. But by all means, mention it at the office and tell them I want you guys as the crew. Now I must tell you this, and it's going to make you jealous. I have mastered the art of flying the A400M and the landing at the new runway," he smiled as he bragged.

"You've already got a program for the runway?" Allan asked in surprise.

"Oh yes. Speedy Gonzales, they call me," Dick announced "Okay guys, I don't want to keep my child waiting so I'll see you in a few days' time," he said. John and Allan had the aircraft back in the air and were on their way to Biggin Hill Airport.

Meanwhile back at Kerri and Ivan's home things were a-buzz. Kerri tried to unpack while having to give all the sordid details to

The Three Must Have Beers (the nickname now entrenched in Dick's mind).

Ivan was ever so pleased when Dick arrived because it meant having a cup of coffee in the kitchen, away from the incessant chatter. While they sipped at their tea, Dick brought Ivan up to date what had transpired during their absence. He said both he and Kerri were to train on the simulator the following day.

"How long do you want us to train for?" Ivan asked him.

"Until you have mastered the art of landing on the new runway."

"Okay, but you said Kerri and I would fly the VC10?"

"That's true," Dick agreed "but, by the time you start on the VC10 simulator, you would already have had the full insight about landing on the runway for you see, it's not so much about flying an aeroplane as it is about negotiating the cutting. The cutting itself is what's important. Understand those parameters and,... well, you'll be able to fly any aircraft through it."

"Makes sense, I suppose" Ivan replied feeling enlightened.

When Dick discovered what the time was, he took it for granted none of them were going back to work,... or whatever it was the girls did.

Just after 3:00 p.m. his mobile rang. It was Phil informing him the electric motors were now ready for installation into the cars, so when Tom was ready to hand over the completed factory to them, production would start.

"That's absolute superb news, however, as much as I would love to be there, I can't. I've had a call from the chaps in Argentina and they want me to spend a few day's there. It seems they are now at a critical stage of digging holes. Well, that's how they put it. Would you like me to send any of the girls up to you?"

"Nah," Phil replied "They'll just drive me bloody bonkers. Besides, you can control them, I can't. So thanks for the offer, but you keep them there."

"Well thanks so bloody much for that," Dick said, and they both chuckled. "Okay, if I don't speak to you before I go, I'll see you when I get back."

As he put the phone down on the table he looked at Ivan and said he was to follow him. So Ivan followed Dick to his own bedroom where all the girls were and Dick asked them to please be quiet for a moment as he needed to tell them something.

"Felipe phoned me and asked me to please come over there for a few da......"

Before he finishes his sentence, all, including Ivan, responded "I'm going" which made him to conclude they had been practising talking in unison.

"Oh, for shit's sake," Dick mumbled to himself. "Who the hell's going to look after the fort then?"

"Deon," replied Chloe.

"I suppose I may as well phone Phil and ask him to come along as well?"

Cassie's face lit up "Yes, that would be nice because Julia is running the show up there."

"Oh great. You would agree, wouldn't you?" he said with an exaggerated sigh.

Afterwards, he drove home to go work out a schedule and later informed Chloe they were to depart on the twenty-eighth leaving Maitland Airport at 6:00 a.m., arriving at La Rioja by 3:00 p.m. the following afternoon. "So please organise the hotel there, and don't forget about the crew."

However, and because he had other ideas, he told her he would go to Blackpool first to spend a few days with Phil because deliveries were taking place.

Dick called Biggin Hill to organise the flight to Argentina and asked them to make sure there was an aircraft at Maitland Airport to take him up North to leave at 7:00 a.m. the following morning. Then he informed all of them about his finalised schedule, which included sending Deon an email of the details.

At 9:00 a.m. the following morning he arrived at the factory where he headed straight for Phil's office, knocked on the door and entered. "Just when I told you I would not come back, I arrive like a fart on the wind, or whatever the saying is," Dick said announcing himself.

"You've arrived just in time because I'm expecting the first lot of cars from Toby's this morning."

"Good, and I assume we still have enough parking?" he asked, and Phil said "Plenty."

"Good, and how's everything else going?"

"Like an absolute bloody dream. I can't understand why or how because nothing before in my life has ever gone so well."

"Well for goodness' sake, Phil, don't tempt fate. Let it go the way it is and,... how's our madam doing?"

"If you mean Julia, I have no qualms about her. She's doing a damn good job and I'm letting her run with it."

"That's music to my ears. Ah, yes,... music. I set up the kit in the hangar, so when you get there, you can have a bash."

Phil's eyes lit up like neon signs for he too was a drummer. "Great. I can't wait"

Phil's phone rang, and it was the security guard at the gate to inform him of the first shipment of cars from Toby's. "Shall we meet the new arrivals?"

"Yes, but aren't you going to inform Julia?"

"I don't have to as the guard has already informed her."

"Okay, let's go."

When Dick opened the door, there in the distance three truckloads headed towards the car park. When he and Phil got there, Julia, together with George and four other people, already watched the proceedings,

"Morning all."

"Mr Shepherd, so nice to see you again," George said with a huge smile and held out his hand which Dick shook.

"Good to see you too George and are you keeping everyone on their toes?"

"Oh yes, sir."

"Morning Dick," Julia said as she walked towards him. They too shook hands, and she introduced him to the other staff members he had not yet met.

The transport drivers offloaded the cars and as this took place, Dick noticed two security guards hovering around them. "What's all that about?" he asked Julia.

"Well, as the guards were going to just be sitting in their guard house most of the time, I trained them, so they now receive the cars as they are being delivered, day or night."

"Oh hell yes, that's a good idea," Dick acknowledged "and who parks them?"

"The guards do. Remember, there are no motors in the cars, so someone has to push them. It sort of makes them feel important. It gives them the sense of being more in touch with the team, as opposed to just being security guards," she replied. Dick nodded his head in approval as he watched the action.

"Now hang on a minute," Dick said puzzled "Tomorrow is the delivery date."

"Oh yeah, that's right. So it is," Phil replied. He looked at Dick, and making sure everyone heard him, he made a silly remark "Shall I ask them to take them back?"

This made them giggle.

Cindy Richards, the new Sales Manager, approached Dick and said: "Excuse me, Mr Shepherd, but may I ask a question please?"

"You may."

"I've noticed all the cars we have so far are only white. Are there by any chance any other colours our clients can choose from?"

"From Brimstone... no," Dick informed her. "They supply a variety of different colours but we changed that, so you will only get white cars. Phil and I decided it would help to keep the price down and production up. When the man in the street purchases them, which they will, they can have their car sprayed to whatever shade, colour or pattern they want, or keep it white."

They continued for a while longer talking about the cars and the parking area. Dick said to Julia he would like to meet with all of them in a few minute's time and said he had just decided he would pay a visit to Toby Manufacturing a little later on.

As the office block was still in a shambles, Julia called them all together and led them over to the reception area for the meeting.

Once there, Dick thanked them. He said because of how the infrastructure worked, in descending order the General Manager would be entitled to the top of the range 4×4 as a company vehicle. The second-in-charge, therefore, would get the next one down, and so on.

In exceptional cases, he also pointed out, others might qualify. Pleased with his demeanour from the outset, his attitude and overall outlook on life, George would be one. Therefore, on his instruction, Julia was to arrange for George to get a company car. He allowed the rest of the staff members to purchase whichever car they wanted at cost plus ten percent.

However, a rule of thumb would apply. The staff may buy only one car per household on that scheme and this included those who had a company car. However, if they so desired, they may purchase further cars but at the full retail price.

"Fair enough?" Dick asked, and they all agreed it was.

"Okay, make the most of the small amount of work you lot are doing at the moment. Come the twenty-fourth, it's full steam ahead," he said, and they gave him a round of applause.

"Julia, one moment please," he said beckoning her over. "I'm on my way to visit the Toby boys and I plan on dragging Phil along with me to get him away from here for a while. Should be back by about four o'clock and you and I can have a chat."

"Okay, Dick," she said with a shy smile. "Enjoy yourselves and we'll see you later."

They walked their separate ways and on their way back to Phil's office, Tom put in an appearance.

"Hi Tom, how's the building trade?" asked Dick.

"Blooming marvellous. I'm so sorry this contract will soon be at an end."

"But the housing project will still keep you on your toes for a while longer."

"True, but it won't be the same without the factory."

"Yeah, I suppose," said Dick.

"I wish I was as successful as you are."

"I'd rather be a person of value than become a person of success."

"Well, I'm of the opinion, Dick, you have achieved both and I congratulate you on that," Tom said and shook his hand.

As if Phil had read Dick's mind, he stood up and said they should be on their way, and as they walked out of the office, Dick cogitated and bounced the result off Phil. "Has Julia met the chaps at Toby's?"

"I cannot say, but I would say,... no she hasn't," Phil replied with a strange expression on his face.

"Well perhaps she should come with us,... or what do you say now?"

They sauntered over to the reception desk where he used the phone to contact her. She met them outside the front door and, as he was the Boss, elected Phil to be the driver of the day. As it would take them an hour to get there, he decided this to be a golden opportunity to fill them in on what the up-and-coming new venture would be.

"Once the cars are on the move and are being sold, I'll need you guys to look at truck manufacturers. That will be our next line of transportation to have the new motorized concept, and also not forgetting the manufacturers of farm equipment such as tractors and combined harvesters."

"What about trains?" asked Julia.

"Yes,... you may as well put them down on your list because we should follow that line."

"Any pun intended there?" asked Phil.

"Pun? What pun?"

"Yes, pun. You said we should follow that line."

"Oh hell no," he giggled. "No pun intended."

They arrived at Toby Manufacturing just on lunch time, so Dick insisted they all go to lunch. They sat and had a good chat so the Toby boys would get to know Julia as she would now be their contact. They spent the best part of two hours at the restaurant before going back to watch the production line in progress. The cars were on one long moving conveyor belt system which seemed to go on forever.

It was a non-stop situation as the cars led from one section to the other unaided, and as they approached another section, a new team of workers, or robots, would take over. They would do whatever their task was until the almost finished product reached the end of the conveyor belt line. It was a fascinating sight to witness. For Dick, time seemed to drag, but he didn't mind because he understood Julia would learn from the time spent with her supplier.

"What I suggest you also do is," Dick said to Julia "get the name and address of the supplier of the electrical motors and when you can afford the time, visit them."

"Yes, a good idea."

After much time spent at Toby's, he decided it was time to head back. Although he wasn't driving, he still didn't like rush hour traffic, so they said their farewells and hit the road.

The next two days he spent his entire time alternating between Phil, Julia and Tom and made sure he wasn't coming across as being the typical a-hole corporate boss who demanded more than his pound of flesh. He always sensed the corporate world looked upon their work-force as being convicts sentenced to hard labour, but without advertising the fact, and good at that they were.

"Never mind, those wankers days are so numbered," he mused and had a good chuckle to himself.

The day arrived when the work-force stopped working at the factory for it was now time for Tom to hand over the keys of the door to the Security. Tom had planned to have a red ribbon placed in front of the front entrance and also made sure he and his team were there early enough to stop any of the staff from entering the building before them.

For everyone there, they had to wait until 9:00 a.m. before Dick arrived. What he saw when he entered the driveway was the entire staff complement standing outside, for today was the first day of the new factory.

"What the hell's all this," Dick exclaimed out loud. "Don't tell me they've been waiting for me?"

As he got out of the car, the crowd clapped and he could not work out if it was a sarcastic one or not. Was it because he had arrived, or was it because it was now the official handing over of the factory? He put up his hands and apologised for being late.

"Sorry, but I met a nice young and attractive lady at breakfast at the hotel. She has invited me out on a date tonight," he informed them and they clapped even louder.

It was a lie, but he had to say something and as his eyes met Phil's, he appreciated that Phil understood. He shrugged his shoulders and smiled at him and Phil smiled back. Tom handed him a pair of scissors but, before he cut the ribbon, he had to make the unavoidable speech.

He thanked all those involved and also to welcome the new staff members. Afterwards, he asked Phil and Julia to join him at the ribbon, and before cutting it, and while holding the scissors with both hands, he asked the two to hold his hands.

"What a handsome trio we make," he said, and they giggled like naughty school children as they cut the ribbon. Tumultuous applause greeted the falling of the severed ribbon to the ground. "Oh how nice," he mused, then asked "Why was I not told about this?"

"But I assumed someone had informed you," Phil said in response.

"So did I," said Julia.

"Oh dear. Something's gone awry or lost in translation, or whatever it is they say. But never mind, nothing of importance lost, I suppose."

As they walked into the reception area, once the entire staff had found their way through the entrance, Phil grabbed hold of Dick and they stopped. "How do you like the electricity that's flowing through the building?"

"Oh, is this from our new generators?"

"Yes, but only from the one as the other is for the housing estate."

"What do you reckon the lifespan will be of each one?" Dick asked, and Phil said "two years non-stop running, even one hundred years non-stop running. The thing is, I can't say yet as I haven't had enough time in which to do conclusive tests. The bloody thing may even run forever although that's not possible."

"Yes I understand, therefore, we should build another building next to it housing another two generators as a back-up. Or what do you say?"

"Bloody good idea is what I say and I'm going to hunt down Tom right away."

For the rest of the day, and for the next three days, Dick made his presence felt as he wanted no slacking in any shape or form. He was, therefore, pleased at seeing how George was rallying his troops and was now sure he had hired a good man in George.

As they had mounted the first new motor into the engine bay of its recipient, they halted production to carry out a quick test-run before continuing the line. It astounded all those who witnessed the event at the wonder they saw unfurl before them.

With no prompting from Dick, and as George absorbed the success before his eyes, he got his staff back into the factory to get the production line back underway.

"Yes, I hired the right person there," Dick said to himself.

On the day before leaving for Argentina, Dick met with Phil and the entire Managerial staff. He asked them to advertise by inviting the press and the advertising agencies to the factory.

This would be Dick's way of getting the message across to the people of the country what the answer was to the fuel crisis. This would include how the electricity supply to the Nation would take over from the National Grid but only once they installed the new generators and motors. So, the sooner, the better.

Dick also said he did not want to be part of any interviews and was leaving it all to Julia because, she would be the one representing the company. He also instructed Josie Holland, the Financial Manager, to open a new bank account and any purchaser who needed credit, they would have to do it through a bank and not the company itself.

Come late afternoon, both Dick and Phil left the factory grounds. They drove to the hotel to have an early night as they had to be at the airport by 4:45 a.m. the following morning. So after a few snorts and wishing Phil goodnight, Dick bedded down. As he drifted off into the land of nod, he dreamt about their own Utopia, or was it perhaps about the new faraway home they would one day move to?

End of Book 1

# OUR NEW HOME

Epilogue


To the survival

of the Human Race


The Human Race.....; the only extant member of the Hominina Tribe, characterised by erect posture with bipedal locomotion and manual dexterity with increased tool use compared to other animals.

# OUR NEW HOME

Fragment from Book Two

Dick looked at Joel and apologised again before carrying on laughing. He now realized the nervous energy had dissipated from his person and was at total ease with his mind and body. This gave him the confidence in sorting out the problem with the creators of the death threat letters.

There were twenty seven, both male and female and all of different shapes, sizes, and age. They were also from all walks of life, with different religions and believes and came from far and wide from around the world, but they all had one common denominator, the crude oil business linked to the cartel.

Together they huddled, some scared, others apprehensive, however in this type of situation there's always the one who *drinks* eau de cologne for breakfast each morning. This person believes by doing so, it takes the shit smell out of his body from within, including his bowel movement. How little these a-holes know, and it's this person who likes to take control of a situation, and why? because he is the man of the moment, the type of person Dick detests.

Dick let them stew for a while longer for he still busied himself with final preparations before entering, thanks to Joel's help.

They were in an area of the mountain which gave them the impression there were no walls. The brilliant white light, which was ever so soft on the eyes, seemed to give them the impression there was no ceiling either. There were no doors, and in fact from what they made out, they were the only things in the area.

There wasn't a single curtain, or chair to sit on or toilet for them to use. Not even a water dispenser for them to drink from, should they so desire, to help quell their anxiety. Although a vast area, they dare not venture away from where they stood as the fear within stopped them. They also could not work out why they were surrounded by,... nothing.

One of them spotted a lone figure in the distance but could not work out what it was as it only resembled a black shadowy silhouette. As it walked towards them, it seemed to change shape and size and also gave them the appearance as if it were walking through a thin layer of mist.

As it got closer, it got bigger, and they stood in silence trying to work out what it was or who it might be. They worked it out to be of human form, a man in fact, and this man only wore a loin-cloth, a subligaculum, the type the Roman gladiator all those years ago wore to hide his modesty.

When he got even closer, they noticed his physique and it was of herculean type properties. The muscle definition true and perfect, and by his height and size, they appreciated he possessed tremendous strength. What they also found amazing was the ease with which he moves his torso with such grace and elegance, his entire body in fact, but also to move in complete silence.

He had a slight overall tan and his skin gave off an attractive sheen in the light while his hair, long. It too had a slight sheen about it. Its length reached just over one foot below the nape of his neck and kept neat and tidy. However, there was one thing about his person who when they found out, it scared the living daylights out them and those were his eyes. They were light brown in hue but also eyes that penetrated the inner soul of a person when making eye contact.

The figure stopped, turned ninety degrees to face them and when he did, they looked straight at Dick. Without a word he looked at each one and sized them up while looking inside their brains. He wanted to gather the information he needed to carry out what it was he wanted to do. One of them tried to make conversation with him so he stopped, turned around and faced the person. Then without so much as flinching a muscle, he stood there and glared at him.

No more words came out of the bloke's mouth for he realised discretion is by far the better part of valour, so he shut up. However, the eau de toilette idiot decided otherwise and demanded of Dick what was going on and where they were. A fatal error on his part.

Dick grabbed him under his left armpit, and with effortless ease, moved the idiot to the front of the group. Dick stood him there so he faced them, then stroked his left index finger across the idiots mouth. To their absolute amazement, but more so horror, the upper lip fused with the bottom one. This now became the cue for them to only speak when spoken to.

Dick carried on moving around the group, still studying their pea-brains, when he came across a likely candidate. She was a middle aged woman of slight build and never looked after herself for she sported love handles in the appropriate region although it didn't make her unattractive by any means.

He grabbed hold of her hand and moved her forward to the front of the group. Leaving her there, he grabbed hold of the idiot and moved him back into the group. Dick now placed them in a wide semi-circle, with all facing inward, and placed the woman in the middle of the semicircle. When he had completed this, he spoke to them for the first time, and although his voice had taken up a different tone, sound and quality, they were none the wiser.

"Your facial expressions say none of you recognise me. Now to make sure, I will ask one simple question and each one of you will answer it as and when I say. That will be the only time you open your mouth to address me, and for your own sake, you'd do well to remember that. The question is, do... you... know... who... I... am?" Dick asked by enunciating each word so they understood him.

He started at the first person on his left. "No," he replied nervous.

He looked at the second person and he too replied, "No." This went on until he came to the last person who also just so answered in the negative and the idiot had to move his head from side-to-side.

"Before me stand twenty-seven people, sorry... twenty-six people and so far, one idiot, and each of you say you don't recognise me."

Dick paced around, all the while glancing at each one.

"You've no idea who I am," he now hissed at them. "Mmmm... what if I told you all of you do and that you know me well? What would you say to that?" he asked, and as he got towards the end of the question, his voice gained in power.

He again looked at them one at a time, searching for an answer, but they had none to offer. "What would you give me if I proved to you right here that I am familiar to you... hey?" he asked while his stern approach created the correct facial expressions.

"Would each of you, for example, reward me with a million American dollars? Or perhaps two or more million dollars apiece? Or would you rather just give me your life?"

He looked into a younger woman's eyes and repeated the question, only this time he blurted it out in her face so much so she bowed her head and cried from absolute fear.

"Look at me when I speak to you," he billowed.

To this she somehow found the nerve to lift her head and, with a quiver in her voice, said she could not say. "What about your life? Would you offer me your life if I proved to you beyond a shadow of a doubt you know me?" he now barked at her.

There was no response from her other than her crying, so he looked at another person, then another. He again searched for an answer, but none of them had one to give, and if because they had no knowledge, or just from a genuine fear, he didn't care in the least.

"Right you miserable fucking lot, and especially you, you fucking bitch. Watch what I am about to show you," he ordered them but bellowed to the woman he placed in the front as he turned her around by one hundred and eighty degrees.

He now moved his right arm in a slow but methodical motion. There before them appeared a screening, of sorts, and they did not understand how he played it because there was no screen or projector. They also did not understand from where the sound came because there were no speakers either. But as their fear was greater than their thirst for knowledge, they stood there and viewed what Dick showed. It was the speech he gave to the scourge on the day of the announcement.

"Right... now I'll ask you one more time... who am I?"

This time he once again enunciated the words and as he looked each one in the eye. They now realized who he was, and they said so.

"Yes, you fucking wankers, you're right. That was me you viewed and now the next question will be all about why you are here. So,... why are you here?" he asked, and once again they did not answer.

"You are supposed to be... not only cleverrrrr... but also well-to-do people, and not only in your own societies, but around the world," Dick said in a loud sarcastic manner. "You are also supposed to be influential types and this is the part I do not understand."

"You are supposed to be highly intelligent people," he shouted. "If you were not, you would not be doing your contracted jobs. But here you are and you don't know a fucking thing about something that directly involves all of you, and that's both in the singular and collective format," Dick said as he billowed his statement while towering over them. "Before I tell you why you are here, I need you to view this next interesting footage as it will affect you."

Dick now screamed at the top of his voice to the woman he put in the front of the group. "And especially you, you fucking bitch."

They viewed a truck being driven by two guys, best described as *shit that walks about on legs* for when born, their mothers must have given birth to them via their anuses. They were unshaven, their clothes had not seen the inside of a washing machine in years and, they gave one the impression their body stench must be a rotting nature. Although they had teeth in their mouths, they didn't have all while the remaining ones had years of nicotine stains on them. And as for the truck? Well it suited their personalities to a tee.

They drove at a slow pace down a road in an affluent suburban area and a young girl dressed in her school uniform walked home from school minding her own business. As she turned her head towards the noisy truck, the woman in the front let out a blood curdling scream. She had just realised it was her own daughter who they viewed.

The driver stopped the truck, and before the girl realized what was happening, the passenger jumped out, grabbed hold of her and bundled her into the truck between the driver and himself. They sped off inconspicuous.

This is when Dick stopped the screening and addressed them "Now,... things are going to get interesting and will, as I said, affect you, so this is what's going to happen. You will be unable to close your eyes or move any part of your body. The reason I'm doing this is I want you to view everything that happens to the little girl. Yes you, you fucking bitch. It's your own fucking daughter," he said to her in a loud voice as he waved his arm to start the screening again.

They watched as the two filthy stinking hermits drove for twelve kilometres where the truck proceeded to a desolate building unoccupied for many a year. The only residents to adorn the place were the dreaded vermin, in all shapes and forms, and there were plenty of them. The place may well have been a certain town or city somewhere in an Asian country, perhaps, where they in all probability worship the disease carrying disgusting rats as gods.

The two guy's man-handled the girl out of the truck and found, what they believed to be, a good place where they set upon her. There was nothing in their approach in undressing her for they just simply ripped the clothes from her tiny frame. They took it in turns to observe each other as they violated her to within an inch of her virgin life. Once both had had their fill, they left her there.

"You can find your own fucking way home, bitch."

At this point Dick stopped the show and turned his attention to the girl's mother. "Now you look me in the eye and you tell me if you enjoyed that?" he asked in a quiet but strong voice.

With a waterfall of tears cascading down her cheeks, and through howls of crying, she screamed out "No" in reply.

"Fantastic, and I'm sure no one else did either" Dick replied in a sarcastic voice before continuing. "Now let me see… whose turn is it now?" he deliberated out loud while he, once again, glided in and out between them.

"Ah yes you… scumbag… check this out," Dick said loud as he again moved his arm in a waving motion and the screening continued.

They now viewed a paedophile, who had abducted a nine-year-old boy and was also unceremonious in his approach when he raped the boy in a wood near to where the little boy lived. This time, however, when the sick bastard had finished his act he took out a knife and slid it up on the inside of the little boys rib cage until the knife point pierced the heart thus causing his death. All the while the paedophile held a tight cupped hand over the little boys mouth to suppress the screams. Should someone have witnessed this act, they may well have noticed the paedophile wearing a white dog collar.

When the screening stopped, Dick approached the father. "Well… did you enjoy the rape and death of your son?" he screamed.

Although the father was in absolute turmoil, he too blurted out "No" in reply. "No,… for God's sake why are you doing this?" he pleaded while trying to shout the question at Dick through all the crying.

www.ingramcontent.com/pod-product-compliance
Lightning Source LLC
Chambersburg PA
CBHW020454020726
47493CB00001B/23